Praise for Julia Amante's Novels

L*et Us Begin*

"Julia's best work as she writes the oh so familiar drama of immigration with a special twist. She shows her mettle as a storyteller with her heart in her hands and poignant memories that serve to reinforce the challenges and drama immigrants face even today."

—Nora de Hoyos Comstock, Ph.D. Las Comadres Para Las Americas

"A moving and thought-provoking book called Let Us Begin describes the difficulties that immigrants face while trying to build a better life for themselves. It explores themes of sacrifice, resiliency, and the unfulfilled promises of the American dream while capturing the essence of the immigrant experience. Readers are compelled to consider the complexities of individual ambition and the true cost of success through Salvador's journey."

—TheLatinoAuthor.com

"Julia Amante's Let Us Begin is a bittersweet exploration of one man's pursuit of the American dream. Love, loyalty and loss are Salvador's companions on his journey from his family home Argentina, as a lonely immigrant in New York, and finally to California where he settles into an imperfect life of his own making. Let Us Begin is a compelling novel that is written with honesty and compassion."

—Margo Candela, Author of The Neapolitan Sisters

"In the pages of this book, you can feel the ups and downs in the life of a man who is in search of opportunity, is willing to take chances, and in the process runs into the hard realities of living away from home."

—Delila Alvarez Vasquez, Producer and Co-Host of Cafecito Con Podcast

EVENINGS AT THE ARGENTINE Club

"A story of family, culture, class, success, and love."

—Booklist

"A big, beautiful novel of love, family, and the close-knit community they inhabit. By turns touching, funny, tragic, and triumphant, it's the story of an endearing group of people in search of their own American dream."

—Susan Wiggs, New York Times bestselling author

"Julia Amante understands the ties that bind all families regardless of culture and nationality—the struggle for identity, the importance of dream, and above all, love. I truly enjoyed Evenings at the Argentine Club."

—Jill Marie Landis, New York Times bestselling author

SAY YOU'LL BE MINE

"A gorgeous romance . . . A compelling search for one woman's search for her identity and of what it means to fall in love just as you're discovering who you are."

—Michelle Buonfiglio, Romance B(u)y the Book

"[Amante's] characters are sweetly written and complex...[she] writes them with insight..and explores the moderating line where each individual lives, neither good nor bad, but only human."

—RT Book Reviews

This Is Now

"A compelling and emotional journey about three women dealing with life, love, and loss."

—Caridad Pineiro, Author of The Family She Never Met

Let Us Begin
JULIA AMANTE

WISE WRITER PUBLISHING
Rapid City

Books By Julia Amante

EVENINGS AT THE ARGENTINE Club
Say You'll Be Mine
That Was Then
This Is Now
Sign up for the JA Newsletter to be the first to learn about upcoming books![1]
www.juliaamante.com[2]
Follow Julia on social media.

[3] [4] [5]

Are you a writer? Julia Amante shares writing advice on Youtube[6].

---

1.   https://julia-9d457.subscribemenow.com

2.   http://www.juliaamante.com

3.   https://www.facebook.com/writerjulia

4.   https://www.linkedin.com/in/julia-amante/

5.   https://twitter.com/juliaamante

6.   https://www.youtube.com/channel/UC8m22bHSpqfquD7W5e2WX2Q

Let Us Begin

Published by WISE WRITER PUBLISHING

Copyright © 2023 by Liliana Monteil-Doucette

Cover design by The Killion Group Inc.

Edited by: Latoya Smith

Amante, Julia, 1967-

Let Us Begin / Julia Amante. – 1st ed. p. cm.

ISBN-13: 978-1-931627054

1. Immigration—Fiction.

2. American Dream/Struggle–Fiction.

3. Marriage/Family - Fiction

4 New York–Fiction.

Title: LET US BEGIN.

10 9 8 7 6 5 4 3 2 1

1st edition, August 2023

Printed in the United States of America

Dedicated to the memory of my father.
And in gratitude to my mother for her starring role in all our lives, for her wisdom and her love.

Acknowledgements

The only grandparent I really knew was my father's mother. She was a strong woman who loved her husband, children, and grandchildren fiercely. I thank her for the love and sacrifices she made for her family.

I thank my grandfather, whom I only knew through his letters. He was a passionate man with an amazing vocabulary. He was a writer, a thinker, a loving father, and I wish I'd known him better. Thank you for saving those precious letters, Grandpa.

I thank my mother for all the stories she told me, for giving me the okay to write this story, for being my friend, and for her never-ending love. I love you, Mom!

And lastly, I thank my husband and children, who have for so many years, endured the hours I spend alone in my office dreaming of my next story, writing, editing, and pursuing my American Dream.

Dear Reader:

What is the immigration experience like? Many books have been written about and by immigrants, sharing the joys and challenges of immigrating to America. It is, in many ways, the story of the United States as wave after wave of settlers came to this land to look for a better life or what has become known as the American Dream.

What we don't often think about is how immigration affects not only the people who left their home country but their children and future generations. The second generation often does not know where they belong or how they fit in as they try to "be American" and understand their roots.

Part of understanding my roots was to try to understand my father and his dream of moving to the United States; to empathize with my mother and why she followed a man to a foreign country to begin her young life away from everyone she knew and the people who loved her.

My grandmother gave me a binder full of letters that my father and grandfather wrote to each other. I read about my father's early days in New York City, about his experiences, first jobs, joys and disappointments, and I learned about the man he'd been before I knew him.

This was a great gift.

The story that you will read is not my father's story though many of the character's feelings, experiences, and historical events did happen as they do in this fictional novel.

What is true, is that each immigrant who arrives to this country brings with him or her three things: dreams of a better future, aspirations of fitting-in and being accepted, and memories of whom they used to be. They are often pulled back by the tether of their past and pushed forward by the promise of the American Dream.

Is the American Dream achievable and something we should strive for? Even after writing this book, I don't have that answer. I do know that life gives each of us opportunities, immigrants or not. But we must recognize and take advantage of the gifts we are given. If we do, I believe we can have a happy and beautiful life.

*So **let us begin** anew—remembering on both sides that civility is not a sign of weakness, and sincerity is always subject to proof. – John. F. Kennedy*

American Adventure

"If we were meant to stay in one place, we'd have roots instead of feet." –
Rachel Wolchin

CHAPTER ONE

The year was 1964 and life was good in Argentina. The 1950s, said to be the golden decade of abundance and overall well-being, bled into the early '60s, and it was especially good for my family. My parents owned a pizzeria bar frequented by neighbors. Every night started slowly and became a festive celebration by evening as music from Palito Ortega, Leo Dan, and of course, The Beatles played in the background, and beer and wine flowed. The salon had about twenty tables which were rarely open for long.

All through high school, my brother Theodoro and I helped by busing the tables and taking food orders. You never knew who would stop by, so most of the time, work felt more like hanging out with friends and family.

That year, I was about to make a decision that would change all our lives and my future forever, and I made it because I believed in the promise of a man I had never met. An American President who challenged the world to dream in his inaugural address in 1961. I was only 19 years old when I listened to his words about what we could all do worldwide to fight for the "freedom of man" and liberty. Every word he said was magic to my ears. The challenge he said, was for our generation, *my generation*. I had been enchanted.

It wasn't until three years later, as I bussed the table of some friends of my parents—friends who had just returned from a trip to the United States—that I considered accepting that challenge.

"What's it like?" I asked the couple and took a seat beside my parents to hear about the grand country to the north.

"Everything you imagine and more," Mr. Martinez said. "It's a place where you envision what you want, and it appears before you." He slapped his hands together and spread out his fingers.

We all laughed.

But Kennedy's words came back to me, "Together let us explore the stars, conquer the deserts, eradicate disease, tap the ocean depths and encourage the arts and commerce." *Of course*, all was possible in America. The word "limits" didn't exist in their vocabulary.

"For a young man like you, there's nothing you can't achieve. There's work everywhere. Don't waste your life here. Go there and become someone great."

I listened with rapt attention and nodded. My mother told me to stop asking questions and take care of the other customers, so I stood and moved away, but I kept coming back, wanting to know more. I went to sleep that night excited and filled with the dreams only a twenty-two-year-old can have.

IN MY HALF-ASLEEP, half-awake state, I saw a light blue sky full of clouds that formed various shapes before dissolving into nothing, then reforming into something new. Was I asleep or was I dreaming? I didn't know.

But dreams are like clouds, aren't they? You see them, almost feel like you can touch them, that they're real. But as the wind begins to blow, they fade away, change, transform into something ill-defined and vague. You realize at that moment that the pictures were never real at all. That dreams are just illusions that fool you into trusting and believing in them, leaving you feeling absurd.

I frowned, rubbing my eyes with the heels of my palms, and stretched, forcing myself to wake up.

I had dreams all right, and I was going to make them all come true. I was as sure of that as I was of the breath in my lungs. I didn't have any doubts. My whole life was stretched out ahead of me, and I was ready for it all.

"Salvador, Salvador, get up," my mother's voice pushed my thoughts away. I opened my eyes and reached for my glasses on the nightstand. My mother was on the other side of the closed door of my tiny room that barely had enough space for my Mahogany bedroom set that included, the nightstand and an armoire. The room had no windows.

"*Si, Mamá*, I'm awake," I called out.

"You're going to be late for classes."

"No, no, I'm up." I kicked my legs out of my twin bed and stood, scratching the back of my head. Quickly, I flipped on the lights and pulled a pair of pants out of the armoire and a button-up shirt. I went to the bathroom down the hall to wash my face, brush my teeth, and comb my hair. I grabbed my wallet and keys and strolled out of the apartment we owned behind our pizzeria bar.

Mamá worked tirelessly from morning to night, ensuring the restaurant ran like clockwork. Up before dawn, she prepared the pizza dough, cut and sliced the ingredients for the pizza, and placed them in their refrigerated slots. She kept everything in the kitchen spotless, from the appliances to the tables to the floor. I teased her that she could run a military regiment with her discipline and sense of organization.

Papá hired the employees which he hadn't needed to do lately. He ordered the ingredients, handled the finances, and took care of the back end of the business. He'd been diagnosed with diabetes and often wasn't well. We all relied on *Mamá* too much, but she never complained.

Together, they made a good team.

"Ah, finally, the king gets up," *Papá* said as I entered the restaurant, grabbed a quick cup of coffee, and drank it while standing.

I grinned, kissed my father good morning on both cheeks, downed the last gulp of coffee, and hurried past my *viejo*, who stood at the counter. "I'm late," I told him

"You don't say."

"I had a late night." I'd gone out after things slowed down at the restaurant, too excited with thoughts of my future swirling around in my head.

"An irresponsible man is never rewarded, Salvador. I expect you to help tonight. Remember that."

"I will."

"We can't afford to hire more help."

"I know, I know." I didn't have to be told that they were struggling. I knew that. Before *Papá* got sick, he'd been a journalist and then worked for an insurance agency making good money. My parents had saved enough to buy the restaurant and were doing well, but now they had to rely only on the profits from the pizzeria to pay for everything, and things were tight. "You can count on me. *Chau, Viejo.*" I was almost at the front door, ready to escape before *Papá* could remind me that usually, they couldn't count on me, but I ran back in and kissed my mother. "*Chau, Vieja. Te quiero mucho.*"

She beamed and patted my cheek. "*Mi hijo querido,*" she said. "*Te quiero mucho, tambien.*"

I ran out, jumped on the motorbike that my father bought me last year, and sped off, honking at the cars on my way out. Damn cars will run you over if you don't warn them. Stop signs were only suggestions to most Argentine drivers.

I hurried to downtown Rosario, not to the school of engineering where my class had started fifteen minutes ago. I had no interest in taking classes. Yes, I was doing well, and sure, the classes were interesting, but the world didn't need another chemical engineer. And I didn't need to become one more overworked engineer making a big company rich. Instead, I'd asked Luisa to meet me by the river, and as I pulled my motorbike into the parking lot, I saw my elegant, thin, always perfectly dressed girlfriend sitting on a bench, waiting for me.

I jumped off the bike, pulled out my cigarettes, shook one loose and lit it. I strolled toward her, happy and excited to share the biggest decision of my life. When I reached the bench, I placed a foot on the seat beside her, rested my elbow on my knee, and leaned close to her. "Hey, beautiful," I said. "Mind if I join you?"

"Salvador." She smiled. "I thought you forgot that you told me to meet you here. Or that I had the wrong day. What are we doing here anyway?"

I took another drag of the cigarette and put it out, blowing smoke away from her, then reached for her hand. "Let's walk."

The first time I'd seen Luisa, I had been only fifteen. On New Year's Eve, she came to the restaurant to dance, literally walking into my life. My parents closed the restaurant after ten, and we partied all night. I thought she was cute in her bright red dress with no defined waistline and crazy high-heeled shoes, but she didn't pay any attention to me. She danced with older boys or stayed shyly beside her sisters. But, she continued to show up every New Year's Eve with her sisters, whom I came to learn were related to my neighbor. Each year, she looked sexier, her dresses got shorter and shapelier. Her short brown hair grew a little longer until it finally touched her shoulders and curled around her ears. Finally, when I turned eighteen, I asked her to dance. She'd said yes, and we'd been going out ever since.

She took my hand, and we walked along the paved path beside the Paraná River that crossed the city of Rosario where I'd spent many happy summers with friends. No breeze blew today, and the dark chocolate river water moved almost lazily.

"So, I have something important to tell you, to ask you."

"Okay," she said, sounding unsure.

"I'm going to move to America, to the United States," I blurted out and wished I'd said it differently, but I couldn't keep it inside anymore.

She looked momentarily shocked but recovered with a couple of blinks of her caramel eyes. She continued to walk beside me but pulled her thin hand out of mine and brushed some of her shoulder-length hair back. "Really? When?"

"Soon, I don't know."

"What about your school, getting your degree? Your parents —"

"The hell with the degree. What's that going to get me? My *viejos* are struggling at the restaurant. They're supporting my brother until he gets his law degree. They're supporting me, and I don't want them to do that anymore. I'm twenty-two. I'm a man and still living with my parents." Not that living with my parents was so out of the ordinary. Everyone usually lived in their family home until they got married, but that wasn't what I wanted anymore.

"Listen." I stopped walking and took both her hands. "I can go there for a few years. Make money. Then I can come back, and we can get married and have a great life together."

Luisa nodded, still looking like she didn't believe me, like she was sure that if I left, she'd never see me again. "Married?" she asked.

I grinned with a cocky smile because I was kind of sure of her answer. "Yes, you want to marry me someday, don't you?"

"I don't know. You never asked."

"I'm asking, Luisita. I don't have a ring right now, but I want you to marry me. What do you say?"

A smile grew on her lips. "Okay," she said.

"Okay? How about yes? Yes, yes I want to marry you because I love you."

She laughed. "Yes, yes, yes, I want to marry you."

I pulled her tight against my body, hugging her and not wanting to let her go. Leaving her would be the only bad part about moving to the U.S. With heels, Luisa was the same height as me. At five-foot-seven, I was not a tall man. But today, she wore simple sandals, so her head rested on my shoulder. I picked her up and twirled her around. When I stopped, we both laughed, and I kissed her.

"I do love you," she said.

"We're going to have a wonderful life," I promised because why wouldn't we? We were young and in love, and I planned to create a great life for us. "Remember President Kennedy's inauguration speech?"

She shook her head, a confused frown creating a wrinkle between her eyebrows.

"He said it was up to our generation to build the future. That whether we are an American citizen or a citizen of the world, we can all work together to create a better world." I retook her hand and walked away from the river. "Before the bastards killed him last year, he had a vision and goals that were good, Luisita. And I do too. I want to live in the greatest country in the world. I want to be part of Kennedy's vision and know I can be."

I looked across the park where the National Monument to the Argentine flag stood proudly. The majestic monument, shaped like a giant ship about to enter the river, seemed to question my words defiantly. The gorgeous monument filled me with pride. I loved my country, of course. Argentina *was* a great and proud country, but only a baby compared to America. There was no comparison. "And when I come back, I want to work to better our country, too," I said, almost as an apology to my own nation. But I wouldn't feel guilty about following my heart.

"Aren't you scared to go to a foreign place? You don't speak the language and don't know what it's like."

"I can speak some English. My parents' friends were visiting the restaurant last night, and they have family members living in New York. They said that it's ridiculously easy to get a job. Everyone is hiring, and they pay a lot. I can make a couple hundred dollars a week. Do you know how amazing that is? My parents won't have to support me anymore."

"Have you told them?"

"Not yet." I didn't know how they would take it. "I think I have enough saved from working at the pizzeria to get my airline ticket." My parents didn't actually pay me. They just told me to get what I needed from the register. I put a little away each week, whatever I didn't spend on Luisa or cigarettes.

The lids of her eyes lowered, and the corners of her lips dipped for a moment before she flashed a soft smile. "I'm excited for you."

"For us. Be excited for us. I'll write you every day."

She shook her head, knowing me better than that.

"Okay, every week. And when I come back, we'll start our life together."

CHAPTER TWO

October 17, 1964

My Dearest Parents,

I write this first letter on Lan Chile stationary to share that the trip to New York has been a success. They sat me in a seat where I could see the takeoff and landing perfectly. We dined using excellent silverware. We had two stops in Chile and Panama before we landed in Miami. Miami appears to be a pleasant city though I can't tell you much because I was only there a couple of hours—two hours and forty minutes to be exact—before I caught a Greyhound to New York. A Greyhound is a large bus. We passed through Washington D.C. Washington has an Obelisk just like the one in Buenos Aires which makes sense since they are both two grand capitals. I saw the White House also! The road that the bus took gave us a perfect view.

I will share nothing about New York for now. It's too impressive for words, but I will share more in future letters.

I'd like to tell you that Pepa's sister and her husband welcomed me into their home as if I were their son. When I arrived, they made me feel very comfortable.

Well, I believe my pen has run out of ink. I blame the pen for ending this letter so quickly. My hope is that you feel the love I send through these words, and I await your response, filled no doubt, with your love back.

Your Son,

Salvador

FINDING A JOB IN NEW York wasn't difficult. Pedro Llonch, the friend of my parents who agreed to let me stay with them, had connections. One of his friends, Raul worked at a fabulous steak-house and seafood restaurant in downtown Manhattan. They needed a cook, and I had two hands, a brain, and had watched my mother cook all my life. That made me qualified both in Pedro's and my opinion. I dressed in the one suit I had brought with me, slicked my hair back, put on a little cologne, shined my dress shoes, and went for the interview.

The tables were already half full at six in the evening, and people waited to be seated.

"For how many?" the man at the door asked.

"Excuse me?" I asked. I had been practicing my English, but honestly, it was going to take me a while to learn to speak well and to understand.

"How many in your party?" he asked again.

"I interview," I said. And when the host frowned, I added, "I new cook."

"Oh," he said, looking at my clothes as if still confused. "Sure. The kitchen's that way. Stay to your left and go down the first hallway. The office is the second door on the right."

"Thank you," I said, not quite sure what he'd said, but he pointed, and I headed in that direction.

When I got to the back, I looked into an office where a pretty blonde sat at a desk. She smiled. "Sir, are you looking for the bathroom?"

"I new cook," I repeated. "Speak to Raul? Interview, please."

"Interview?" She stood. "Just a minute." She disappeared for a few seconds and returned with an older man who introduced himself as Carlos.

Carlos dressed in a nice suit like mine and eyed me curiously as he held out his hand. I shook it and tried to explain again why I was there. I stated that Raul, one of his waiters, had mentioned they needed a new cook.

"Yes, yes, you're Raul's friend?" Thankfully, he spoke Spanish, and as soon as he started talking and I heard his accent, I realized he was a Spaniard.

"Not exactly. Raul is a friend of a friend, but I want to say that my parents own a restaurant in Argentina," I explained in Spanish. "It's a pizzeria, of course, nothing fancy like this, but I helped out all the time. I know a lot about running a restaurant. And I'm quick to learn."

He patted my shoulder. "Young man. I need a cook. You can leave the running of the restaurant to me. I can pair you up with the chef if you're willing to learn, and if you will show up to work on time every night, you've got the job."

"Absolutely. You can count on me."

"Then you're hired. Get out of those clothes, grab an apron, and go to the kitchen."

I looked down at my suit. "This is all I have with me today."

He motioned for me to follow him. In the back, he threw a pair of jeans and a T-shirt at me. "Change. Meet me in the kitchen."

And that was how it started.

The kitchen was a busy place, and I was introduced to a Gallego who was the main chef. He looked me over like he wasn't impressed, frowning at my baggy jeans and dress shoes. I didn't blame him; I felt foolish.

"Stand here," he said, pointing to a corner of an extraordinary island with burners on both ends and a food preparation area in the center. Behind us was more room to prepare food and a sink.

He handed me a crate of vegetables. "Wash these."

I nodded and took them to the sink to scrub carrots, potatoes, celery, and other vegetables. He showed me how to cut and steam the carrots. Some potatoes were set aside for baking while others were roasted with chicken, and others for mashed potatoes.

I spent the first week learning my way around the kitchen, being no more than an errand boy and jumping every time the chef needed something. When I asked his name, he said I could call him Chef.

By the second week, he started teaching me how to make a few dishes. I came in before the evening diners arrived, and I worked with him and another cook, a Puerto Rican named Javier, who had been there a month longer than I had. The Spaniard Chef was strict but an amazing cook. Over the next weeks, I learned to make Paella Valenciana, *tortillas de papa* which were potato omelets similar to the ones my mom made in Argentina. I also learned the perfect way to cook lobster, how to grill steaks to perfection, and to make various delicious tapas.

The atmosphere and constant activity challenged me, but it was fun. I learned that this upscale restaurant in Manhattan had a good reputation where people with money dined before and after going to Broadway plays.

Being in New York, in the buzz and thrill of the city, energized me so much that I didn't sleep for hours when I got home.

Of course, the hot work in the kitchen could get exhausting; I hadn't worked this hard my entire life, but the Spanish owner, Carlos paid well. He came to stand beside me when I escaped outside, smoking a cigarette one night. I thought he was going to yell at me, but he said, "You're a good worker, Salvador. And you're smart. Chef Hugo is impressed with you, and he's not easily impressed."

Ah, so his name was Hugo. I nodded my appreciation. "Thank you, sir."

"Do you like the job?"

Did I? I did. Time went by fast. I made good money. "I appreciate the opportunity," I said.

"But do you like cooking?"

"Sure."

"Maybe you should consider going to culinary school. You're talented. I could see you becoming a great chef someday."

I laughed. "I don't think so."

"Think about it, Salvador. Think big. I don't know what you're doing in this country, but you're well educated, polite, clean, and you can go far if you use your intelligence well." The Spaniard disappeared back inside, and I put my cigarette out. The freezing night air penetrated my clothes so that I couldn't stand outside for too long.

I intended to go far, but I wasn't going to become a chef and work at a restaurant for the rest of my life. I saw how hard my parents worked, how they were slaves to a restaurant, and never had a night off. They worked, worked, worked.

No, thank you. I'd stay here for a while, but I had bigger plans. I wasn't sure what yet, but someday soon, it would come to me. I felt it in my bones, those that weren't frozen.

When I got home that night at almost 2AM to the little room the Llonch couple offered me, I lay back in bed and pulled out the photo of Luisa and me, dressed up for her sister's wedding. We looked perfect together. My heart picked up speed when I thought of Luisa. I didn't want to live without her for the next year or longer.

I could see now that it would take some time to earn enough money to return home to Argentina. I wanted to have a few thousand dollars saved, enough to buy a home and to do something important. But I didn't consider that I wouldn't be able to save everything I made. I'd have to live and spend some of my money. I stood and looked out of the window. I could see the glow of the city lights from this small apartment. I also knew that I didn't want to leave right away. The electrifying city, one I'd never see again once I returned to Argentina, had everything a man needed to succeed. My future lay out there, somewhere, waiting for me to catch up with it. And to do that, I needed more time.

What if ... what if I didn't wait to marry Luisa until I returned to Argentina? What if I brought her here, and we moved toward our future together? Would she come? My heart picked up speed like when I drank one too many Coca-Colas. Why wouldn't she? What did she have in Argentina? A lousy job? Her family, of course, but I was her future, not her sisters. She had no parents; they'd both died when she was a young girl, so no one could tell her she couldn't come.

I immediately sat down at a small desk and pulled out a sheet of paper to write her a letter. I proposed all over again, but this was a different kind of proposal. I poured my heart out, my words of love and adoration, my desire to build a future together, the promises of adventure and excitement. I told her how much I needed her, that I couldn't survive in this big city alone. Man is not meant to be alone. Someone important said that. God, of course, though I don't believe in God. The author of the bible, then. Either way, it was true. I was lonely. And living in someone else's home, how was this different than living with my parents?

I needed to get my own place. A place for Luisa and me. I needed to be the one in charge of my destiny. I finished the letter, signed it, and placed it in an envelope.

Dropping into bed with my hands behind my head, I stared at the ceiling, excited, imagining that she'd say yes, believing that she would because we loved each other and were meant to live our lives together.

CHAPTER THREE

October 29, 1964
    Dear Salvador,

Yesterday, we received your letter dated October 17th. We had a postal strike that delayed your correspondence from arriving to us quicker.

I will begin this letter by saying that the details of your trip were intriguing; however, I must tell you that it is essential that you write clearer. Between the penmanship and grammatical errors, some of what you said was hard to understand.

I also read the letter you wrote to Luisita. She was quite excited to share news about you with us. Her letter also contained a spelling error. Aren't you ashamed? When one doubts how to spell correctly, one consults a dictionary. Understood?

From the story of your trip, I see that it was magnificent. I am glad. It will be something to record in the memories of your youth as you embark on your life that just now begins to take shape. I hope that this trip eases the restlessness you carry inside. I also hope, of course, that your dreams are realized and that you find success. Everyone here, your mother, your brother, your family and friends, and even those who only know that you are our son are all hoping you will succeed.

I wrote to the Llonch family to thank them for the hospitality that they have offered you. How kind they have been to us, right? You see, my son, we can always find an Argentine with a kind heart to help. Of course, we would have done the same for a son of theirs. Life is like that. We extend ourselves, help others who are in need. No matter where we are in the world, we can find good and generous people.

Okay, young man. I wanted the first letter you received to be from us, your parents who love you. Your mother and I send you a hug as wide and deep as your heart. Good luck and until next time.

Your Parents

I ONLY HAD ONE DAY off from work, Mondays. And I had to get my laundry done, write my father, and try to see a little of the city.

I also started to scout out apartments for Luisa and me. She hadn't replied to my letter yet, and I anxiously awaited her response, but I wanted a place to bring her once she agreed. Jose, the Puerto Rican dishwasher at the Spanish restaurant, introduced me to a couple of Argentine guys he played soccer with on the weekends.

We met in Central Park one day to kick around a soccer ball and get some exercise. They recommended a place in Jackson Heights. The older building wasn't fancy, and they warned that it could get rough, but the apartments were reasonably priced.

I mentioned my idea of moving to Jackson Heights the next morning with Mr. and Mrs. Llonch while sharing a cup of coffee for breakfast.

"But Salvador, you don't have to move out yet. You're welcome to stay longer."

I'd been with them for a month. "I appreciate your hospitality, don't think that I don't. But I wrote my fiancé and asked her to join me soon. When she does, we'll get married, and we'll have to get our own place, you understand."

They looked at each other, and Mr. Llonch cleared his throat, "Salvador, you might want to take some time to get established, save some money before getting married. Does your father know you plan to get married so soon?"

I'd told my parents after I proposed by the river in Rosario. Not right away, but I did tell them. They were a little surprised, but not as much as I expected them to be. They knew I was crazy about Luisa and wanted to spend all my free time with her.

My dad had even lectured me about being honorable and "not wasting her time" a year into our dating. He asked if I was serious about Luisa, and I'd told him I thought I was. And it was then that he told me I was too young.

"Love is love," I'd told him. "It doesn't have an age."

"You can be a man at 19 or 29, it depends on the man, I agree. But someone who is serious thinks of the future, not just about tomorrow."

So, when three years later, I told him and my mother that I'd proposed, he didn't look surprised. He looked proud. To him, it probably meant that I would settle down, get serious about my studies, and prepare for my future.

When I returned to them a couple of weeks later with my decision to go live in New York City, they were floored. My mother sat down and didn't speak. My father was already sitting, but his brow furrowed.

"I thought you planned to marry Luisa and make a life with her."

"I will, but first, I want to live in New York, see the most amazing country in the world, earn money and get ready to start my life with her."

"Son," my father said, sighing deeply. "I see in your eyes that you've made up your mind about this. That it's something you've thought about."

"Jorge," my mother said, but he held up a hand to keep her from speaking.

"If you need to do this, you have our support." He looked at my mother. "Right?" But she had tears in her eyes, and she looked away.

My father turned to me, gazing thoughtfully into my eyes. "You're a man now, and men have to fulfill their dreams and find their own way. If you feel you need to go far away from your home to find yourself and your destiny, then we won't stop you."

I nodded, a lump in my throat. "Thank you."

"Where will he live? How will he survive?" my mother added, desperation in her voice, speaking to my father as if he were the one making the final decision. She didn't realize I'd already decided.

My father placed a hand over hers and one on mine. We sat at the square wooden restaurant table, surrounded by over a dozen empty tables. The restaurant wouldn't open for another two hours. For that moment, the three of us were connected, knowing our lives would change forever.

"I have friends who have relatives in New York; maybe they can help the boy for a little while," my father said. He turned to me. "We'll pay for your airline ticket."

"*Papi*, you don't have to pay for my ticket. I have money."

"You take your money with you. We'll pay for your ticket. Then when you get established. When you're settled and comfortable, you can repay us. But I don't want you to look at it as a debt. You don't owe us anything. In the future, if you're able, you can repay the ticket if you want."

I reached for my father and pulled him close. He patted my back, then gripped me tightly against his chest before pushing me away.

"*Mamá*," I knelt by her side and took her hands. "It will only be for a little while. A year. Maybe two. Then I'll be back. Luisa and I will make you a grandmother, what do you say?"

Her tear-filled eyes were joined by a smile. "*Loco*," she said. "I'm too young to be a grandmother."

I had laughed and knew they would support my dreams, as Luisa had.

Nodding at Mr. Llonch, who was now sitting at another table in New York, I said, "My parents know how much I love Luisa and that I want to build a life with her. I just don't want to wait a year or two to start that life."

"Well, Jackson Heights is not a good place to bring a young bride," Mrs. Llonch said. "You might want to find a different place."

I agreed. Mr. Llonch said he would go with me to find a respectable place, and I was grateful and excited.

"Also, young man, since you're planning to make your stay here somewhat permanent, you need a permanent visa. You realize that, don't you?"

I didn't really know a lot about visas, but I knew I had a temporary one. I shrugged. "Does it matter?"

"It matters quite a bit to the government. You don't want to overstay your visa. We'll also apply for a permanent visa when we look for an apartment. Do things the right way, and you'll always succeed, huh?"

"Sure," I said, though I didn't care much for rules and restrictions. But I did know that governments were not entities to anger or defy, even a government as wonderful as this one. "Of course."

THE TRUTH? RENTING an apartment of my own was complicated. I'd only been working two months. I barely understood the language. I was twenty-two years old with no family. In the end, Mr. Llonch co-signed for me to be able to rent an apartment.

"I promise I'll pay my rent on time."

He didn't seem to doubt my sincerity, though he worried whether I'd make enough money, and he said so.

"I'm making twice what they want for the monthly payment already and if I need to, I'll get a second job."

We left with a rental contract for the next six months. The apartment had one bedroom, a decent kitchen, a spacious living room, and a bathroom. I didn't think the neighborhood was the best, but it would be fine. When Luisa arrived, if she didn't like it, we could find a better place.

I spent the next two weeks, every spare moment I had, preparing the apartment. I cleaned and painted the living room and bedroom because the walls looked dirty and moldy. Cleaning with bleach and the fresh coat of paint made the apartment look brighter. Then I worked to furnish the place. The great thing about America was that you could buy things and pay a little at a time on credit. I bought a bed, a living room set, and a dining room table and chairs. The delivery truck arrived, and the workers carried and brought the furniture up to the eighth floor, and all I had to do was point and tell them where to place it. I felt like a king.

"Looks nice," one of the workers said. He pointed to the paint cans in the corner of the living room. "You're a painter?"

"No, but I painted this apartment."

He nodded as he looked at the walls. "You did a good job. My brother is looking for a painter for his business." He searched in his wallet and pulled out a business card. "If you need a job, give him a call."

I took the card and thanked him. What a great country. Money might not grow on trees like some people in Argentina said about the U.S., but jobs apparently did fall in your lap. "I'm working at a restaurant now, but I'll keep this in mind," I told him.

Then I adjusted my new sofa so that it faced my only window. I eased down on the cushions and spread my arms out on the backrest. I put my feet on the beautiful redwood coffee table, then took my feet down, not wanting to ruin the finish. But I sat tall and proud in my first apartment that I got on my own. Well, almost on my own, with a bit of help from Mr. Llonch. I relished the moment for a few seconds, recording this feeling. I didn't ever want to forget these important firsts of my life.

All my clothes and personal items were still at the Llonch's apartment, so I went back to their home to pack and say goodbye.

Mrs. Llonch offered me dinner. She'd made a warm stew that I ate with a chunk of bread. They had already eaten, but they both sat with me as I shared the story of my exciting day.

"Are you planning to go back there tonight?" Mrs. Llonch asked.

"Yes, I came to pack."

"Do you have sheets for your bed? Dishes and pots and pans to cook with?"

"Well, no," I said. "I didn't think of sheets and blankets." I smiled. "Maybe I'd better buy some tomorrow and sleep here one more night."

She smiled as well. "That sounds like a smart idea." She stood. "You got a letter from your girlfriend." She handed me the envelope with Luisa's writing on the front.

I was so excited that I wanted to rip it open and read it immediately. But I took it and waited to read it in private. I finished the stew and asked if it was okay to retire to my room. I'm sure they sensed my eagerness to read Luisa's letter, so they kindly told me to go. Mrs. Llonch cleared the table and Mr. Llonch sat to watch television.

Once alone, I ripped the corner of the envelope and read Luisa's reply. She seemed surprised by my offer and request that she join me. *If your marriage proposal is genuine, and you truly want us to begin our married life in New York, I will leave everything, my job, my sisters, my friends, and fly out to be with you. I honestly thought I'd never see you again, that you'd fall in love with America and another woman and forget all about me. But I hoped I would be wrong, and I'm glad I was. So, how do we do this? What do I do first?*

My heart felt like it had been beating out of control since I stepped foot in this country or since I left Argentina. Everything was exciting, even the most mundane tasks were amazing because they were stepping stones toward my future life.

But today, this second, my heart beat a new rhythm. I didn't know her next steps. I hadn't thought that far ahead, but Luisa needed to get a Visa. I knew that much. We needed to make arrangements for her travel, so I had to buy her a ticket to fly to New York. And I needed my father to help me, to help Luisa on that end.

I sat to write my father his weekly letter, this time with the news that my girlfriend had agreed to join me in New York and become my future wife and their new daughter. First, I shared my excitement about getting my apartment in Queens, emphasizing how close I lived to Manhattan. With the efficient subway system, I'd be minutes from my job, I told him.

I shared how grateful I was to Mr. Llonch, not only because he cosigned for the apartment, but he also signed my permanent visa, saying in effect that he would be responsible for me and my behavior. My father would be as grateful as I to this man who was only an acquaintance yet had been so kind and generous.

I then told my father that the money I hoped to send them would be delayed and that I hoped he would understand. I explained that I had proposed to my fiancé again, but this time I wasn't saying that we'd marry someday, but I intended to marry her as soon as she arrived. As a matter of fact, her sisters were not pleased that she, as a single woman, intended to live with "the boyfriend" as they called me, but Luisa made it clear that if she traveled to the U.S. it would be to become my wife.

I asked my father to look after Luisa and help her with her travel paperwork.

Then I wrote to Luisa to tell her that she'd made me the happiest man alive. In a few months, we would be married and begin our search for the American Dream together.

CHAPTER FOUR

The next day, I got up early and went shopping to buy a few things I needed for my apartment. As Mrs. Llonch suggested, I bought bedding items and a few dishes, glasses, and pots and pans. I didn't want to buy too much because I figured Luisa would like to choose the items she wanted and decorate as she saw fit.

I couldn't wait until the day I'd be able to walk into the apartment and find her here waiting for me, queen of the apartment. I could picture it now, opening the front door to delicious smells of homecooked meals made by my bride, looking beautiful as always in her short dresses that molded to her thin body and high-heeled shoes she liked to dance in. Well, maybe she wouldn't wear those shoes to cook, but a man could enjoy his own daydream, couldn't he?

I rushed to the apartment to drop off the items before I had to go to work and found that the door had been pushed in, the lock broken.

"Damn it," I said and hurried inside. Nothing was missing, but then again, I didn't have much. I placed the items I bought on the kitchen table and did a quick check of the bedroom. No one was inside, but it didn't mean that they wouldn't be back.

Checking my watch, I hurried out of the apartment and found a hardware store a couple of blocks away. I bought a strong lock and an additional bolt. I installed it as quickly as I could. It didn't take long. Tomorrow, I'd have to tell the landlord that I changed the lock and give her a key. Hopefully, it would be okay.

I would be a few minutes late to work, but at least I'd secured the door.

When I got to work, the pretty office manager told me I was late.

"I know, I'm sorry," I said.

She stood and ran her manicured fingers through the hair on the side of my head. "Salvador, you're so polite, you know that. You're not like the other cooks we've had working here."

She smelled delicious, and her smile made me smile back, but she made me a little nervous too. "I try to be polite," I said. "I'd better get to work."

"Your English is getting better too."

"Thank you."

"If you'd like to practice a little more, we can have some coffee. Talk. Get to know each other better. What do you say?"

Normally, I'd say absolutely, but I stepped back. I didn't want to get myself in trouble. "I say no."

She laughed. "Really? Don't you think I look pretty? You don't want to get to know me better?"

I looked behind me. I really needed to get to the kitchen. "I'm going to get married. Soon. But you are very pretty." I looked over my shoulder again. "I have to work, sorry."

I turned to the kitchen. To safety. Yes, I loved America and her beautiful women who were very friendly.

I GOT BACK TO MY APARTMENT at two in the morning, tired, but it had been a good night at the restaurant. We all worked smoothly now, and Chef Hugo seemed to trust me more even though he continued to hover over me and yell out orders. Still, I learned and prepared more and more fancy dishes every week.

I was about to change and shower when I heard someone messing with my door and new locks. I yanked it open.

"What the fuck," one of the guys said. There were two of them.

"What do you want?" I asked.

"What you mean, what do I want? What are you doing in my pad?"

"This is my apartment."

"Not tonight," he said, pushing his way inside.

"Hey," I tried to push the door closed, but between the two of them, I didn't have the strength to stop them. So, I let the door swing open and punched one of them in the face.

"Mother fucker." He and his friend pushed me down to the floor, and one of them jumped on top of me. My glasses flew off my face, and he got in a punch that made my nose bleed and my left eye ache. I struggled to push him off me, turning my body to reach for my glasses. As soon as I rolled on my side, he reached for my wallet in my back pocket.

Then a third guy came in with a baseball bat. "Get the hell out," he shouted and nudged the guy straddling me completely off. I patted my back pocket to ensure I had my wallet and scrambled to my feet. The other guy was going through my suitcase, so I kicked him in the butt and shoved him out of the door. "I'm calling the police."

They both ran out, and the guy with the bat looked at me as I tried to catch my breath. I guessed that he wasn't with them.

"You're my new neighbor, I suppose," he said, lowering the bat and swiping his light brown, straight hair away from his eyes.

I rubbed a hand through my hair and touched my sore eye, realizing I had blood all over my face. "I just moved in. Thank you for helping." I walked to the bathroom and pulled enough toilet paper off the roll to wipe the blood away.

"They're probably looking for some quick cash for drugs. They shouldn't be back," he called out to me.

Returning to the living room, I eyed this guy closely. Just because he'd helped me didn't mean I could trust him any more than the other two.

"I'm Mateo," he said. "I live two apartments down."

I shook his hand. "Salvador."

"You're Argentine," he said, switching to Spanish.

I recognized his accent, and an overwhelming feeling of home made me want to cry. "So are you. Where do you come from?"

"Rosario."

The guy looked young, probably about my age. "No kidding? Me too."

He told me the barrio where he'd grown up, and I figured we probably ran with the same groups back home. "Maybe we've been to the same Newell's Old Boys *futbol* games."

"Oh man," he said. "I knew there was something wrong with you. Only a Newell's fan would get his ass kicked by a couple of bums."

I laughed. "And I didn't travel all the way to the greatest country in the world to live next to a *canalla*." A *canalla* meant scoundrel as the Central Soccer League had been nicknamed in the 1930s when the team refused to play a fundraiser for leprosy patients.

"Well, it looks like you did. Anyways, be careful. I've been here two years and this kind of stuff happens all the time. You need to be aware of your surroundings."

"The nerve of those guys to come into my apartment, though. They're crazy."

"Crazy, drugged out, and just plain bold. I'm going to go back to bed. Welcome to the building."

I locked the door behind him. Then I went to look at my eye which had started to swell. Son of a bitch, that's all I needed, a black eye.

After that incident, I realized the importance of caution. Yes, America was wonderful and amazing in so many ways, but New York

City attracted all kinds of people from all over the world. Large cities simply had more crime. New York wasn't like Rosario where life was laid back, and the few petty thieves were basically harmless.

The following month, I worked and saved money. I didn't have time to do much else. Thankfully, I didn't have any more visits from the thieves. I did, however, have visits from the Llonch couple who worried that I wasn't eating well and wanted to ensure I had all I needed.

To show them how capable I was, I invited them for dinner one night and cooked steaks with a lettuce, tomato and onion salad. They seemed grateful and proud of my cooking skills. They treated me like the son they never had. They didn't have children at all in fact, no son or daughter.

Aside from that, the only other interesting thing I did outside work was find an Argentine store. Mateo, my neighbor and new friend, told me about it, so I went with him and his girlfriend one weekend to check it out. I bought Yerba Mate to drink in the mornings and other things to remind me of home. The owners dressed like gauchos which made me laugh. It was nice to be among other Argentines, but it did make me feel a little homesick.

Mateo often invited me over to his apartment to listen to tangos he played on his record player. "Nice," I said. "I need to get one of those and some records."

"Come over anytime and listen to them with me. I also have folklorico."

These little pieces of Argentina were gifts I appreciated. I started to feel more comfortable in the United States, but of course, I missed home.

I got Thanksgiving Day off from work. I didn't understand the significance of the holiday, but an amazing parade took place in Manhattan, and it seemed like the entire city came out to see it. People dressed in crazy costumes and decorated floats traveled down the streets. The celebration was phenomenal, and I wished I had a camera to take pictures to send to my father and Luisa.

That evening Mr. and Mrs. Llonch invited me to their apartment to eat turkey. I'd never eaten that bird before, but it tasted good, gamier than chicken. "Everyone eats the same thing on this day?" I asked.

"It's tradition," Mrs. Llonch explained. "Along with the mashed potatoes, yams, and cranberry sauce."

I didn't care for the cranberry sauce, but I didn't say anything to her. I rubbed my full stomach, now full of delicious food, grateful for the nice day of celebration.

"You haven't had any more run-ins with those bums on the street, have you?" Mr. Llonch asked. He had been horrified when he'd seen my black eye on one of his visits to my apartment.

"No, I never saw them again. Did I tell you that the landlord got mad at me for changing the locks? Instead of thanking me, she yelled at me."

"You were probably supposed to tell her and let them change the locks."

"Sure, and let the criminals come back and steal my things. No, thank you."

"You have to follow the rules, Salvador. Learn their ways here and do things on the up and up, not how you think things should be done."

When I left, they gave me a big hug and kiss, and again I felt lucky to have found such warm-hearted people to make my transition to this country an easy one.

Christmas was a lonely time, the only bad part about living alone in a foreign country. I bought Christmas cards and sent them to my parents, Luisa, and my brother. I strolled the cold streets on my way to work and wished I had someone from back home to share the season with.

Another thing, New York was freezing at this time of year. I kept licking my lips and they got so chapped they cracked and ached. The very friendly office manager pulled me into her office and took out a tube of chocolate-flavored Chapstick and rubbed it on my lips. "This will help you," she said, standing close to me. I thought for a second, she was going to kiss my wax-slathered lips. But she stuck the Chapstick in my pocket, said I could keep it, and stepped back.

I learned not to lick my lips anymore, and I also bought a heavier jacket to survive the frosty winter. The one I brought from Argentina was too light. Armed with Chapstick and a heavy coat, I walked the streets more instead of taking the subway since the bright city had been transformed overnight into an amazing Christmas snow globe. Strings of Christmas lights wrapped around trees and beautiful ribbons and bows hung everywhere. Living in this fantastic city felt magical.

I spent Christmas Eve with some of my new friends, guys from work and their friends, all from Latin American countries: Puerto Rico, Argentina, Cuba, Colombia. We played music, shared stories, and played cards. Most of the guys had their girlfriends with them or their wives. Being with these happy couples made me miss Luisa even more. Still, it was fun to be with other people my age. I had a few beers and champagne. We celebrated each time midnight struck in one of our home countries. I finally switched to coffee before heading home.

In the new year, I sat down to look at my bank statements, and I knew that if I had any hope of paying my parents back for my airline ticket and buying one for Luisa, I needed to make more money. Out of my wallet, I pulled out the business card of the man who needed a painter and went to see him.

I told him I needed to work around the restaurant's schedule, and he agreed. I ended up painting for a couple of hours midmornings, then going home to shower and scrub paint off my fingers and underer my nails before going to work at the restaurant.

At the end of the month, when I was supposed to get my first paycheck, the guy, my boss said he hadn't been paid for the jobs we'd done, and he didn't have the money yet which irritated me. But I kept showing up for work, trusting that he was telling me the truth.

However, the following week, he still didn't have my money. And a week later, he gave me some cash, about one-fourth of the money he owed me for the first month.

"Look, I can't keep working if you're not going to pay me," I explained to him.

"Don't be a smart ass. This is the way this business works. Sometimes we don't get paid for jobs right away. You'll just have to be patient."

I didn't like it, but I kept working. At least, I'd stick with it for a few more weeks. If he didn't pay me what he owed me soon, I'd look for another job. As soon as Luisa had her paperwork ready for travel, I planned to have the money to buy her a ticket so I didn't have time to waste.

CHAPTER FIVE

January 17, 1965
        Dear Salvador,
    We received your last letter and were happy to hear from you. Spending the holidays without you was difficult since it was the first time you were missing from our dinner table. We had friends and family over, and they all wanted to know about you and how you're doing. We toasted that all your dreams would come true. With the beauty of the human imagination, we pretended that you were here with us.

A couple of young men, friends of yours, visited this week, stating they hope to travel to the United States too. If that's true, I will give them the chemistry book you asked your brother to send you, and I'll send you a record also, so you'll have some music from your country. But be careful with these young men. I don't know them well. They seem like nice boys, but we wouldn't want them to make you look bad, especially with the Llonch family.

Speaking of books, you borrowed a book to learn English from a young lady who stopped by to pick it up. I imagine you took it with you. If you cannot mail it back to her, I believe the reasonable and just thing to do is reimburse her for the cost of the book so she can buy another. I'm sure you agree with me.

I spoke with your mother about your jobs and shared with her what you to told me in your last letter about not getting paid for the painting job. That disturbed both of us. We want you to know that if life there is ever not what you imagined, you can always return home, Son. The pizzeria can be turned over to you, and you can run it as you see fit. We intend to keep it for a couple more years before we retire, but if you want it, it's yours. Or if you need a few dollars, please let us know, and we will do what we can to help from here. We wouldn't want, under any circumstances, for the Llonch family to have to pay for any of your expenses.

That said, life is about struggle. Right now, you are struggling to pay for Luisa's airline ticket. Later you will struggle to establish your household, someday you will struggle for your children. That is the law of life. In between the struggle, we try to find the beauty.

In the meantime, it's good to hear that you keep listening to music. The soul needs music since it makes life better. The rhythm, the beat, and the lyrics help to lift the human spirit and help us interpret the meaning of life.

We continue to work on Luisa's paperwork. Your brother is taking care of it for her, but it is taking a while because she is applying for permanent residency, unlike your tourist visa. Hopefully, we will have good news for you soon.

Since you shouldn't enter into marriage lightly, be sure you are financially ready to assume this enormous responsibility and use this time to prepare for her arrival. I'm sure you've thought it through, so I'm not going to say more about that.

Your loving father,

Jorge

I ENDED UP QUITTING the painting job. The guy was a crook. I threatened to beat the shit out of him when he said that he had already paid me for the whole first month. "You paid me a quarter of what you owed me," I told him.

"Look Pal, I paid you. If you're not happy, you can go."

I took a step toward him, ready to pound him into the ground, but two other guys who worked for him were there too, and I didn't want to take on three of them. My temper still got the better of me, and I kicked a can of paint across the room, sending white trim paint all over the unprotected carpet and the freshly painted tan walls. I rushed out of there as they yelled and called me all kinds of offensive names. I'd learned how to cuss in English already; they were angry. Let them buy their customer new carpet with my money since they refused to pay me.

I would find other work.

The next three months passed by quickly. I got to know New York better, not that I went to many places, but I did learn the subway system well. I ate in all the different boroughs. One week I went to Little Italy and had a bowl of ravioli with a bottle of wine. They were okay, but nothing like the ravioli they make in Argentina; the sauce didn't even come close to my mother's masterpieces.

Another week, I went to the Lower East side to a Jewish delicatessen and had a giant, thick pastrami sandwich with mustard and sauerkraut. Oh, my stomach hurt when I left there, but I had to eat every bite. I even went to Chinatown and had Chinese food for the first time in my life. I have no idea what I ordered; it had beef and noodles and was a little spicy. I don't know how I feel about that meal.

I also consulted a lawyer to ensure I was handling Luisa's immigration paperwork well, and he promised to help the procedure go smoothly.

Then finally, the happiest day of my life to that point happened. After taking a simple test at the immigration office, as Mr. Llonch had suggested, I put my own immigration status out of my mind to focus on Luisa. But the immigration office called me and asked me to report for an interview.

I dressed in the suit I hadn't worn since I went for my job interview at the Spanish restaurant. I made sure I looked sharp. During the brief interview, a gentleman asked me about my plans and how long I intended to stay in the United States. I wasn't sure what the right answer was, but I told the older man, who was probably in his fifties, that I came because I had been excited by Kennedy's speech and that I wanted to do great things for this country. I had only planned to stay for a year or two, but I was really loving it here, and if they'd let me become a permanent resident, I'd be proud to stay longer.

He nodded, a serious, apathetic expression on his face. "What kind of great things do you intend to do?"

I thought about it. I wished I knew. "Well, I was going to make a lot of money, but it's harder than I expected."

He chuckled, and it made me a bit nervous. Still, I continued. "I'm still very young, and I didn't finish college like my mother wanted me to, but I'm intelligent and a hard worker, so whatever I decide to do, I will be a huge success. I promise."

He smiled. "Well, young man, I wish you luck." He signed his name on the form and sent me off. A week later, I received my permanent United States residency. I stared at it when I opened the envelope, a lump in my throat. Like many before me, I would now become part of the fabric of this nation.

Bursting with excitement, I had to tell someone, but only my father would understand what this momentous accomplishment meant to me. So, I sat at my kitchen table and wrote to my old man to share my joy and tell him how proud I was to have been accepted and welcomed to America. I would be able to get better jobs now and maybe have my own business someday.

⸺ ⁑ ⸺

THE DAY FINALLY CAME to pick Luisita up at the airport. My child-like excitement that had me changing my clothes three times and applying probably too much cologne dimmed when Mr. and Mrs. Llonch insisted that she should stay with them until we were officially married.

"I appreciate that you want to offer her a place to stay, but you don't have to do that."

"We do. We promised your parents to look after you and that young lady. How would it look if she moved in with you without being married?" Mr. Llonch asked.

Part of me wanted to tell both of them to mind their own business and that they weren't my parents. I was frustrated with their interference and that they were inserting themselves into my moment with my future bride. Still, the more reasonable side of me understood their logic and insistence. There was a proper way of doing things and an improper way, and appearances mattered. My father always said so.

So, we picked her up at the airport, and I couldn't stop hugging her when she walked through the gate where we stood impatiently waiting. She looked beautiful, even more so than I remembered, and she would soon be my wife. I introduced her to Mr. and Mrs. Llonch; then, we went to the baggage area to collect her suitcase.

We took a taxi back to the Llonch's apartment and spent a couple of hours talking about her flight and how things were back home with my parents, her sisters, and Mrs. Llonch's sister, who still lived in Rosario. Mrs. Llonch made delicious milanesas with mashed potatoes and a salad. Mr. Llonch opened a bottle of wine which we all shared while eating. My smile felt permanently etched on my face. To me, the day felt like another holiday as we celebrated Luisa's arrival.

I didn't want to leave their home, especially without Luisa, but I held her hand, kissed her, and promised I'd be back the next morning before I had to be at work. She was tired and seemed just fine with the idea that I leave her alone with a couple she didn't know.

"They are wonderful people. You'll be fine," I promised her.

"I know. I've heard nothing be great things about them. You go back to your apartment and get some rest. Don't worry about me."

"I just want to be with you. I've missed you."

"I've missed you too. I'm so excited to be here."

But she looked more tired than excited. So, I kissed her good-night and left, but it was damned hard.

The following day, I woke up early and took Luisa to breakfast at a café close to my apartment. I admit that I chose this café so we could go to my place next because I couldn't wait to show her what it looked like.

I held her hands as we sat across from each other at a small square table. "I still can't believe you're sitting in front of me."

"I can't believe I'm sitting in a café in New York City. Do you walk around in wonder every day?"

"I do. It's amazing. It's magical. It's . . . more than I imagined."

"Mrs. Llonch, Maria, she told me to call her Maria, is so nice. She was so worried about me going out with you alone in this big city."

I tried not to be offended by that. "Well, you'll be fine. I've been here almost seven months now and know how to navigate the city. I don't even know why they insist you stay with them."

"Because we're not married."

I let go of one of her hands and touched her cheek. "We will be. Come on, we've been dating for four years now. Doesn't it seem ridiculous to have to stay with them?"

"Absolutely not. What would your parents say if we lived together before being married? Or my sisters?"

"Who cares? They're not here. How would they even know?"

"The Llonches would tell them. Besides, I want to start our life together the right way. Don't you?"

I leaned back in my seat and took a sip of coffee. "Of course." But it didn't matter to me how quickly we got married. I wanted her to be my wife, no doubt about that, but I preferred not to rush. If this was what she wanted though, we'd get married immediately. "Well, then, let's go to the courthouse and get married right away. This week."

"You don't want a church wedding?"

No, I didn't. "If that's what you want, we can do that too." I laughed, thrilled with my life and the future we would build together. "I just want us to be together."

She reached into her purse. "Your father insisted on buying our rings, their wedding gift to us."

"I know, he told me."

She handed me the two boxes that held our rings. I pulled out her engagement ring and put it on her finger, then brought her hand to my lips and kissed above her knuckles. "I promise that we are going to be happy forever."

"I'm already the happiest woman being here with you." She leaned across the table, her nose touching mine. We stayed like that for a moment.

"Come on," I said and stood. "Let me show you where you're going to live."

I paid my check, and we walked to the apartment, enjoying the cool air and the sound of honking horns, hissing busses, and people chattering as they walked past us, all sounds of a busy city.

Proud and being a bit of a showoff, I had her sit on the couch when we got to the apartment so she could see how comfortable it was. I explained that I hadn't decorated much, or at all, because I wanted her to do it. I showed her where I cooked and slept and dreamt of her. She laughed and seemed happy.

"Luisita, this is it. The beginning of our life together. What do you think?"

She wrapped her arms around my shoulders. "I should be frightened and nervous, but I'm not. Everyone told me I was crazy to fly out here to be with you."

I stared into her light brown eyes that sometimes looked sleepy and always looked sexy. "I guess you are. It's a risk being here, and I don't know what will happen. It's not as easy as I originally thought to make and save money, but we can do this, right? You and I, especially now that we're together."

"All we can do is try."

I angled my head and kissed her, loving the feel of her lips and holding her in my arms. I pulled her close and held her, grateful that the best part of Argentina was with me. "Let's try. Let's build the future of our dreams."

"And when we return, we'll take all these memories with us."

I wasn't thinking of going back. Not yet. I had too many things to accomplish first. I gave Luisa another peck on the lips and pulled away. "Let me change, and I'll take you back to the Llonch's apartment."

"Why do you need to change?"

"I work in a hot kitchen. I usually wear a T-shirt under my apron."

"Maria said that she would get me a job as a seamstress. That way, I can help pay for expenses."

I changed out of my nice clothes while she spoke. "I know you like to work, but you don't have to." Although the extra money would definitely help. "We'll talk about it after we get married."

"Of course," she said.

WHEN I GOT TO WORK, I asked to speak with my boss. "Yes, what is it, *muchacho*?" he asked, getting ready for the night.

"I have to ask you for a night off, and —"

"What night?"

"Friday because —"

"Impossible. You know how busy we are on Friday night. I can't be short a cook."

I ran a hand through my hair and balanced back on my heels. "I know. That's why I haven't missed a day. I've been here faithfully since you hired me. Always giving my best. I'm the last one to leave. You know that. I leave the kitchen spotless."

He stopped fidgeting on his desk. "Salvador, what the hell is so important on Friday that you're standing here bothering me instead of standing in the kitchen preparing for the dinner crowd?"

"I'm getting married, sir. I'd like to spend the evening with my new wife."

He stared at me without emotion for a moment, then he smiled. "Married, huh? Big step."

"I know. She flew all the way from Argentina to be my wife. It's just the two of us here now. No family. But I couldn't be happier."

"I'll give you Friday night off, but not Saturday, understand?"

I offered him my biggest smile and reached for his hand to shake it. He took my hand and slapped my upper arm. "Congratulations. After your wedding, why don't you come here for a fancy dinner? My gift to you. Unless you have another place to go celebrate?"

I shook my head. I didn't have anywhere in mind to take her. "That's very kind. Thank you."

He nodded. "You have been a good employee, Salvador. I hope you're going to be happy with this life you're starting."

That night, full of nervous energy, I worked as if music played in my head the whole night. I practically danced in the kitchen as the other kitchen staff frowned and looked at me like I'd lost my mind. Maybe I had. True happiness I realized, came from being in love, and maybe that did make a man a little crazy.

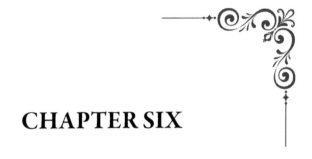

CHAPTER SIX

Thursday morning, Luisa and I went to the courthouse to get the paperwork to file for a marriage certificate. We were like two little kids, laughing and teasing each other about how this piece of paper would change our whole lives.

"You will belong to me after you sign that paper."

"This isn't Argentina," Luisa said. "The woman doesn't belong to the man."

In Argentina, the old tradition was to add "de" before the last name. In her case, Luisa would become Luisa Susana Alvarez de Moreau. The "de" indicated that she belonged to me. It was old-fashioned; my mother used it in her signature, but modern women didn't use it anymore even in Argentina. In this country, she'd lose her maiden name and simply be Luisa Susana Moreau which had a beautiful ring to me.

We told the clerk behind the counter that we were all alone in this country and wanted to get married so we could live together and hoped to get an appointment for the next day. The woman broke out into a huge smile. "Well, this young woman can't be in this city all alone."

"She's not exactly; she's staying with family friends." "Hold on," the clerk said and left to speak with a supervisor. When she returned, she said we could stand before a judge that day, and they'd marry us right then.

Luisa and I looked at each other and smiled. We didn't have the rings with us, but we'd have them at the church. I nodded. We filled out all the paperwork and were married within an hour. As we left holding hands, I couldn't believe it. "We're married. It's legal."

We stopped outside of the courthouse steps and kissed. "I love you," I said.

"I love you too."

It didn't go quite as well at the church that the Llonches recommended. Our Lady of Guadalupe was a Spanish-speaking Catholic parish that served working-class Hispanics, mostly Spaniards, since the area was called little Spain.

The priest shook his head, "I can't marry you this Friday. Where is your proof of baptism? You haven't gone to confession."

We hadn't done anything that we were supposed to do. But Luisa spoke to him in that sweet voice of hers, asking him to please perform the marriage ceremony.

"Please, please, Padre," she begged and gazed at him with those mesmerizing eyes. "I flew all the way to America to marry Salvador, and I'm all alone without a soul who knows and loves me. No family, Salvador is my only family now. We're officially *legally* married as of a few hours ago, but in my heart, it doesn't count until I'm married by the church."

After deep consideration, sighing and thinking and sighing again, he nodded. "Tomorrow at 2pm, I will marry you."

"Thank you so much, Padre," Luisa said, reaching for his hands and squeezing them warmly.

"Thank you," I echoed, grateful, knowing how important this was for Luisa.

FRIDAY MORNING, ON July 30, 1965, I got up early and went to get a shave and haircut. I already had my nice suit that I took to get pressed Thursday after I dropped Luisa off and before I went to work. Friday morning, I picked it up.

Then I went to a flower shop and bought as many flowers as I could afford. I filled the bedroom with red roses. I placed pink and white carnations in the living room and kitchen. I even bought a few candles so that I could turn the lights down low tonight and create a romantic atmosphere. Then I showered, put on cologne, and looked at myself in the mirror. "Not bad," I said.

The Llonch couple said I should meet them at the church, so I did. They were our only two attendants, our witnesses, our friends and family. When I arrived at Our Lady of Guadalupe Church on 14th Street in an area of Manhattan called Chelsea, I stopped outside and admired the Spanish baroque façade. Engineering still fascinated me, chemical, mechanical, architectural, all of it. What I wasn't attracted to was going to college.

Then I saw Luisa, and my heart felt like it would burst right out of my chest. She wore a beautiful white dress that molded to her thin frame. I wanted to touch her, talk to her, and to kiss her, but instead I smiled, and we walked into the church, the four of us.

"You're beautiful," I whispered.

We stood before the priest, and he offered his words of wisdom. He read from the bible, and I'd lie if I said I heard any of it. All I could do was stare at my wife, the girl I'd met when I was only fifteen. I knew from the first moment I saw her that I wanted her to be mine. And now here she was, holding my hands and saying 'I do.'

Here *we were*, in this foreign land, away from everything that was home, together, promising to love each other forever. I placed the ring on her finger, she put one on mine. We kissed when the priest told us to, and I knew that I had met the first part of my destiny.

When we walked out of the church, Mrs. Llonch showered us with rice; we laughed and hugged them.

"You kids have a wonderful day in the city," she said.

"Luisita, you can come to pick up your things anytime." Mrs. Llonch handed her the overnight bag she'd packed.

"I don't know how to thank you for everything you've done for me, for us," I said to the husband-and-wife couple.

"No thanks necessary," Mr. Llonch said. "We're happy to help a young Argentine couple who is starting out."

We said our goodbyes as we climbed into a taxi, feeling like celebrities.

"Where are we going?" Luisa asked.

"Well," I said, placing my hand on her knee. "I'm going to take you to the top of the world."

"I think I'm already there."

I asked the taxi to take us to the Empire State Building. We stopped on the 86th and 102nd floor and took pictures. I finally broke down and bought a camera. She posed for me like a model and took as many pictures as the roll of film allowed.

I wrapped my arms around her waist, and we looked down at the city. "Mrs. Moreau, thank you for becoming my wife."

She rested her head on my shoulder, and I held her.

In the gift shop, she bought New York skyline post cards for my parents and for her sisters. And I bought her a large box of mixed chocolates.

From there, we went to the Spanish restaurant. "This is where I work."

"Wow, it's gorgeous," she said. "We don't have to eat here, Salvador. It must be expensive."

"Don't worry about anything."

The host greeted us. "We have the best seat for you tonight, Mr. Moreau," he said.

The server brought a basket of bread, two glasses of wine and a bottle of champagne to chill in a bucket of ice as we ate. I ordered an antipasto and paella Valenciano for the main dish. We pretended we were very important people. Luisa laughed when I deepened my voice and said that this was one of the many restaurants I owned in this city.

"You're always so silly and kind of crazy." She reached across and tapped my nose.

"It's what you love most about me, admit it."

"I admit it. Your unpredictable nature is definitely an attraction."

We ended the night with dessert and coffee. My boss stopped at our table to congratulate us. "Salvador is becoming a great cook. Our chef is impressed with him."

"He's good at anything he puts his mind to," Luisa said.

By the time we left, I was full, tired, and ready to be alone with my wife in our apartment. We strolled through the city hand in hand for a while, then caught a taxi back to Queens. When we got to the apartment, she clapped with excitement to see the display of flowers in every room.

"Wine?" I asked.

"Oh no, I can't eat or drink another thing. Except maybe one of these chocolates we bought today.

So, we sat on the couch and ate a piece of chocolate each. "Mm, good," I said. "Let's make a deal, and let's not leave this apartment until we finish this box."

She laughed. "I think there's probably a couple of pounds of chocolate."

I kissed her neck and her jaw. "Then I guess we'll be spending a lot of time inside."

It had been a magical day, and I never wanted it to end. As we made our way to the bedroom, I counted my blessings. I was a lucky man. I probably didn't deserve all the good fortune I'd been born with and continued to receive, but I'd accept it all gratefully.

As I took her in my arms, hummed softly, and danced with her in our living room—the traditional dance of a newlywed couple—I was determined that this would be the first of many happy moments I would share with my wife.

CHAPTER SEVEN

August 2, 1965
Dear Salvador,

It's been a week since we said goodbye to Luisita. When we traveled to the airport in Buenos Aires, her head was in the clouds. She was so excited. We had a slight hiccup when they weighed her bags and found that they were too heavy, but thanks to the intelligence of your mother, we solved the problem.

I kissed Luisa and then hurried off to the viewing terrace. Your mother, your brother and his girlfriend, as well as your uncle Enrique and his wife, who came to see Luisa off, all stayed until Luisa boarded the plane. Then they hurried up to the terrace also. We watched that giant monster lift up into the sky like we did when you left. It felt like a scene from a movie. Some people cried and others laughed. Goodbyes always touch the heart, don't they?

We spent the night and a couple of days in Buenos Aires at your uncle's house and drove the long way home the next day in bad weather. When we got there, we found your telegram saying that Luisa had arrived well and that you would be married in a few of days.

So, on Friday, your wedding day, your mother prepared homemade pasta, a beef stew, bought pastries that she serves with fruit, and opened two bottles of Reserva wine and a Fillippini champagne. She closed the pizzeria and invited your brother and girlfriend, of course. Ricardo and Rosita, Henry and Rosana, Santiago and Nely, your aunt Aurora and your cousin Dolly and her husband were all invited, and by coincidence, Mrs. Llonch's sister stopped by and was surprised that we were celebrating your wedding. We had a wonderful little party in your honor.

You are now a Mister, as they say in America. You are a married man. Marriage gives you benefits but also obligations. The most important and the one that I strongly advise you to keep is to make Luisita happy. She deserves it since it was your dream, your adventure that you embarked on, and she has followed, uniting her soul to yours forever.

I had better stop writing. I'm an old man and sometimes get wistful and sentimental. Only your saint of a mother puts up with me and my thoughts. She'll probably tell me that I'm trying to ruin your honeymoon. But I'm only trying to give you helpful advice, man to man.

By the way, Luisa sent your mother a beautiful card right after the wedding. Your mother cried as she read her words. I admit that I too got emotional knowing that you were both so happy. I hope it will be that way until the end.

Well, my boy, your dream has come true, but always remember that dream was born here in this grand country of Argentina. God willing that in your new nation that has welcomed you with open arms like a favorite son, you will find the happiness and good health you had here. We wish the same for your partner, our new daughter. We hold her now, like you, in our hearts.

Your father,

Jorge

MARRIED LIFE IN A NEW country had its challenges. Luisa wanted to explore the city and be independent immediately. The grocery store was the first place I thought she needed to explore for both our benefits.

"It's only five blocks away," I showed her as we walked down 148th Street. "You turn right when you leave the building, walk three blocks and turn right again. Remember. You don't want to get lost."

"How am I going to get lost? It's five blocks."

I nodded. "It's a big city. And it can be dangerous."

"I think I can manage five blocks."

She loved the grocery store when we got there. "It's so bright and full."

Argentine grocery stores were full also, but people tended not to buy everything in one grocery store. They went to the bakery for the bread, the meat market for their beef, the vegetable stand for their lettuce and tomatoes, and so on. I pushed the cart around and explained how to read the prices and let her find the things she liked and compare them to the products sold in Argentina.

"They don't have fresh bread. It's all sold in a bag?"

"There is a bakery close by, but the bread differs from what we're used to. I'll take you to the Argentine grocery store next weekend, but you have to take the subway to get to Manhattan, so I don't go often."

When she'd chosen everything she wanted, I showed her how to check out, and we headed back home.

Luisa's first month in America, I wanted her to get orientated and to feel comfortable. She got to know the neighborhood. She learned to take the subway and speak a few words in English.

She made the perfect Argentine breakfasts which consisted of coffee and toast, and delicious dinners before I went to work. I think she practiced her full repertoire of meals since in a month, I never had the same meal twice. Seeing how much she loved flowers, I brought her a bouquet of mixed wildflowers for our one-month anniversary. We spent all morning together in bed, living in marital bliss.

But after the first month, as I was putting on my cleats to play soccer with the guys in the park, she surprised me.

"I should find a job," she said, sitting on the arm of the sofa and running her fingers through my hair.

"You don't need one yet. I'm taking care of things. Is there anything you want that you don't have?"

"It's not that, Salvador. I don't have anything to do. I'm not used to sitting in an apartment twenty-four hours a day."

"If you're sitting in an apartment all day, it's because you're stupid." I finished tying my shoes and stood, pointing out the window. "There's a whole city out there. Go explore. Go feed pigeons in central park."

"Did you just call me stupid? You want me to feed pigeons? What am I, five years old?"

"Maybe I should buy you a TV. Would you like a TV?"

"A TV? I need to do something productive. In Argentina, I had a job. I never sat inside all day. I worked. I went out with friends."

I thought about it for a second, seeing that she had a point. "You want friends? Good idea. Come here." I grabbed her hand and pulled her toward Mateo's apartment.

"What are you doing?" she asked, planting her feet and resisting.

"Trust me." I knocked on his door, and Mateo opened it, yawning.

"Is Camila home?" I asked.

"Yeah, I think she's sewing something."

"This is my wife, Luisa. I thought we could introduce them."

Luisa pulled on my arm. "What are you doing?" she hissed. "I'm not a puppy. Let's go home."

But Mateo nodded and shrugged. "Come in. Nice to meet you," he said to Luisa.

She didn't answer. I pulled her inside their apartment.

"Hey Camila, come here," Mateo said.

She sat in a corner working on a sewing machine, tossing us a disinterested glance, then stood. "*Hola* Salvador," she said.

I leaned across and kissed her on the cheek. "Hi Beautiful. I want you to meet my wife, Luisa."

She eyed Luisa, then reached out her hand. "Nice to meet you."

Luisa shook her hand though she seemed confused. A handshake is not a greeting typically used by friends in Argentina. Friends and even acquaintances gave each other kisses on the cheek when they met.

"I thought you would like to get to know each other. Luisa is bored, and you both are home all day, so you could do things together, what do you think?"

Mateo playfully slapped Camila's butt. "You'd love that, wouldn't you *Amor*?"

She didn't respond to Mateo, but she looked at me, "I'm home all day because I work in the evenings. You do know that, don't you?"

"No, I didn't." I turned to Mateo. "What are you doing, *Viejo*? You want to kick the soccer ball around so they can get to know each other and talk."

"I'm tired," Mateo said. "I was sleeping."

"You're always sleeping."

"He's tired, and she's busy. Let's just go home," Luisa said.

"Come on, *Canalla*. What are you afraid of? Let's go."

He sighed and gave a longing glance at his comfortable apartment, but he jerked his head toward his bedroom. "Let me change."

When he returned, he kissed Camila goodbye, and I did the same with Luisa.

"Where are we going?" Mateo asked, yawning again.

"Central Park. I meet friends from work there on Saturdays. You should join us. The girls can have some girl time, and we can get some exercise."

"I'm not interested in getting exercise."

I slapped his shoulder. "Come on, *Flaco*, you need some muscle on those bones. Some energy."

In the park, I introduced him to the guys. We all had a good time kicking the ball around for a couple of hours. After a vigorous game, we sat on the grass, cooling off and shooting the shit about nothing in particular. "How's married life?" they teased me.

"Wonderful, amazing. But Luisa wants to work. I'm a little worried, you know. She doesn't speak the language, and I also want her to wait until she has her residency. She's not supposed to work yet."

"Maybe there's something she can do," Mateo said. "Babysit, or you know, little things like that."

I shrugged.

"Are you still painting?" Jose asked

"No, that jerk wasn't paying me."

"I have a friend who owns a really nice hotel. He needs a painter. I can introduce you. You paint and maybe they'll find a job for your wife too."

"Like what?"

"Who knows? Sewing curtains, doing laundry, whatever. I'll get you his number."

"Okay," I said. I'd think about it.

When we got back to Mateo's place, Camila said that Luisa had returned to our apartment, so I thanked them both and went home.

Luisa was sitting on the couch. I leaned down to kiss her, but she pushed me away. "Don't you ever leave me alone with that woman again."

"Why? What happened?"

"She sat there sewing for an hour and a half and didn't say a word. She even ignored her poor baby, who was an angel playing in her playpen all by herself."

Camila tended to be quiet, but I figured it was just with me since we had nothing in common. "So, you didn't hit it off, huh?"

"Are you dense or something? She didn't. Say. A. Word."

"Okay, okay, don't be mad at me. I tried."

She stood and placed her palm on my cheek. "Salvador, you can't just throw two women together and tell them to be friends. *Mi Amor*, I'm going to talk to Maria Llonch and see if she can help me find a job."

"I may have found *us* a job, something we can both do together."

This got her attention. "Really? What?"

"One of the guys knows someone who owns a hotel, and they need help. I'll find out exactly what and let you know, okay? Just give me a few days."

She jumped into my arms and kissed me. "Thank you. Salvador."

I smiled. "Don't thank me yet. But I'll see what I can do."

"Okay. Now, will you do something else for me?"

"What?"

"Take a shower."

I laughed, kissed her and headed to the bathroom. "Alright, then we're going out to lunch. You need to see the Statue of Liberty."

Marital bliss was salvaged, at least for now.

ON A BEAUTIFUL NEW York morning the following week, Luisa and I took the subway into Manhattan and met with the hotel's owner. This man owned a boutique luxury hotel on 42nd Street that he was restoring and upgrading. We sat with him and the head of maintenance. He asked me about my experience. I told him about the work I did painting apartments and that Jose had recommended me. He asked me about my life in Argentina and my major at the university.

"I studied chemistry, intending to become a chemical engineer."

"Are you planning to finish your degree here?"

"I don't think so," I said.

He gazed at me, then shrugged. "Well, we're looking to paint all of our 120 rooms this year. If you can paint five a week, you should be able to finish by the end of the year."

Five rooms a week was a lot. "I can work part-time. Right now, I'm a cook at a Spanish restaurant and . . ."

I stopped speaking because he started shaking his head. "I need a full-time guy. Once every room is painted, you'll stay on to do touch up and eventually start again with the first room, repaint at a slower rate." He told me what he'd pay, and it was almost double what I made at the restaurant, but of course, it sounded like twice as much work too.

Was I ready to leave the restaurant? I hadn't planned to stay there forever, so now was as good a time as ever to leave.

"Is this your wife?"

I nodded, then remembered that my father always told me to speak up. "Yes, sir."

"Is she looking for work too?"

Reluctantly I told him she was. She didn't need to work if I'd be making that much more money, but she wanted to.

The maintenance manager said he could offer her a position cleaning and straightening up rooms after guests left. I translated and asked her if she was interested, reminding her that she didn't need to accept, but she nodded.

"Okay," I said. "We can work."

"Perfect." He clapped his hands together. "Antonio can show you around, give you your schedule, and you can start when he says. Welcome aboard."

We got a tour of the impressive hotel with marble floors in the entry and red brick walls. The rooms were different sizes. Some were small, so it made me feel better about the expectation of painting five rooms a week.

"Is there another painter?" I asked.

"We have two guys already, so you'll have help."

"Good. It takes time to tape and prepare the rooms."

"Yeah, yeah," he said. "If you don't finish all five rooms each week, it will be fine. That's the target, you know?"

I nodded, then took Luisa's hand. "The rooms are simple," I said to her in Spanish. A bed, a couple of nightstands, and lamps. The cleaning wouldn't be too crazy.

"The hotel is beautiful," she said in awe.

When we left, we strolled through the streets. "We won't always be doing these kinds of jobs, you know?"

She held on to my arm as we walked, hooking her arm around mine and leaning her cheek against my shoulder. "What are you talking about? We're so lucky! It's what we want to do, work and make money. A job is a job. And look where we get to work." She meant the city not just the hotel. All the grandeur and newness of New York impressed her as much as it had me.

I nodded. But that night as she slept, I sat in the living room, looking out of the window at the wall of another building. Below us was a filthy alley. For the first time, I felt a hint of dissatisfaction. I didn't like the idea of my wife cleaning up other people's messes.

I'd be approaching a year here soon, and I had nothing saved, no plan to create a future for the two of us. In fact, I had bills that were difficult to pay, rent and furniture payments. This new job would help. I'd make more money and become successful faster. But I wasn't fooling myself; I would still only make enough to survive.

I lit a cigarette and sat in the dark. The hotel owner asked if I was going to finish college, and the look of judgment in his eyes pissed me off. I didn't need to finish college. I needed to do what he was doing and make my fortune, build my own empire. Then I'd take that money and go back to Argentina and enjoy my life, help my parents, be happy. I just wasn't sure how to do it yet.

I turned on a small lamp and took out a sheet of paper and a pen.

AUGUST 29, 1965

Dear *Papi*,

Your description of Luisa's departure was touching. The truth is that for the person who is leaving, it's a busy moment that also leaves one flattered by the attention. And yes, for those who are left behind, I'm sure there's always someone who gets teary-eyed. Luisa arrived full of emotion herself. She kept saying, "You have magnificent parents." She mentioned that the whole family was amazing.

For now, we're living in a small apartment, and every day, Luisa seems more radiant and happier. Her only complaint has been that I leave the dresser drawers open when I pull out my clothes. So, I have a minor fault to work on.

I will be mailing you a picture or two of the wedding. We took photos in front of the church, and Mrs. Llonch took a few inside as we said our vows. I was going to buy Luisa a beautiful white wedding dress. We even went to a huge store to shop, but when she saw the prices, she said it wasn't worth it. She wanted to wear one of her own dresses. She looked gorgeous just the same, you'll see. I'll warn you that I look a little fat because I eat well.

And with Luisa here, as the queen of the apartment, I'm probably not going to lose any weight. The other day, she made a delicious roasted chicken with potatoes, onions, and red peppers. I almost ate the whole thing by myself. The only thing left were the bones.

I appreciate all your advice. You didn't ruin my honeymoon. We are still enjoying it. I appreciate also, the records that you sent and the newspaper cutouts with news of Newell's Old Boys. Hopefully, they will make it to the finals.

I look forward to hearing from you soon. I wanted to share with you what it's like to live in paradise, and now I have. Until the next time, my desire for you and *Mamá* is happiness and excellent health, *Papi*.

Chau,

Salvador

I signed my name, stared at my happy words, and thought about how misleading written communication could be.

CHAPTER EIGHT

I've never had a hard time delivering bad news. I feel like people spend too much time preparing others to hear something they won't like. It's kinder and more honest to just say what has to be said.

My boss at the restaurant was disappointed when I told him I was quitting. "Where is painting hotels going to get you?"

"Where is chopping onions going to get me?" I shot back.

He shook his head. "It's the training ground. You young kids think life is supposed to be easy. It's work, and you move up slowly. You don't snap your fingers and make money rain down on you."

"I know that. That's what I'm trying to do. Work hard and make more money. I have a wife now. I'm barely getting by. I'm sorry, but this is the best thing for us right now."

I finished out the week, giving the restaurant and my boss my best during those final days. Then I started work at the hotel. They scheduled Luisa during the day and me at night, which pissed me off. She ended up having to take the subway alone every morning while I slept fitfully, worried about her walking the streets in semi-darkness. She assured me she'd be fine and was excited to begin work.

We ate dinner together in the evening at least, then I kissed her goodbye and went off to work. By the end of the third month, we got into a routine that worked well.

As we were eating dinner one night, Camila knocked on the door, and I let her inside. She held her one-year-old in her arms. The little girl was not Mateo's. Camila's boyfriend left her when the kid was born, a real jerk, but Mateo fell in love with both of them.

"I'm wondering if your wife can watch Niki for a few hours. I got called into work."

"Come in," I said.

"His wife has a name," Luisa said. "And you can ask me directly."

She smiled at Luisa. "Can you do me this favor, please? She's really a good baby."

"I know. She sat alone and played in the playpen for hours while you ignored both of us when I was a guest in your home."

Luisa had refused to go back or do anything with Mateo and Camila since that awkward introduction.

"What do you say? Will you watch her?"

Luisa looked at me, and I shrugged. It was up to her.

"I'll go to your house and watch her there. I have nothing for babies here. Is that okay?"

Camila gave her a wider smile. "That's perfect. Thank you, Luisa. And I'm sorry about last time. I was mad at Mateo. It had nothing to do with you."

Once Camila left with little Niki, Luisa and I finished our dinner quickly. I dressed for work, and we both walked out of our apartment. She headed down the hall toward Mateo and Camila's house.

"Hey," I said.

"What?"

"You're a kind, wonderful person, you know that?"

"What am I supposed to do? She has a baby."

I winked at her and ran down the stairs, which was faster than taking the slow elevator that was broken half the time anyway.

LUISA AND CAMILA BECAME good friends after that, and I was glad. At least Luisa had someone other than me to talk to. They went shopping together often or sat around in one of the apartments chatting. Camila was sort of bossy, the opposite of Luisa. She also bossed Mateo around; I don't know why he put up with her. But since my friend and wife liked her, I shut my mouth.

For our sixth-month anniversary, I brought Luisa red roses instead of carnations like I'd done every month since we got married. She put them aside without a thank you.

"You don't like them?"

"I do. But you don't have to spend money on flowers every month, you know."

"I know I don't have to, but I thought you liked them."

"I'm worried that we're not saving any money."

"We're doing fine. I even took my driving test so that we can buy a car soon. That way, I can drive you to work in the mornings. We'll save on subway costs."

Her mouth opened, but she didn't say anything. She turned toward the kitchen and started putting the dishes in the strainer back into the cupboards.

"What's wrong with you?"

"Nothing."

I didn't need this shit. "Fine, you don't want flowers anymore?" I took the flowers and tossed them in the trash. "There. They're gone."

"Oh, that's really mature."

There was a knock on the door. I yanked the door open, and of course, it was Camila. "No, she can't watch your daughter, she can't go shopping, and you can't sit here all night talking."

"Go to hell, Salvador. Who do you think you are to tell her what she can do?"

"Her fucking husband." I slammed the door and stomped to the bedroom, dropping down on the mattress, irritated and hungry.

Luisa must have opened the door because I heard them whispering, then the door closed again.

Luisa came into the bedroom. "Are you finished acting like a five-year-old?"

I glared at her from my spot on the bed. She sat beside me and placed a hand on my arm. "Do you want to know what she wanted?"

"No, I don't give a shit."

"Mmm, well, I'll tell you anyway. I'm not making dinner tonight. Mateo and Camila are going to take us out."

"I don't have time to go out to dinner. I have to be at work in a couple of hours."

"I know. We're going down to the little Cuban restaurant around the corner to celebrate."

My head hurt. I sat and started to push off the bed. "So, you're telling me you didn't prepare any food?"

She shook her head. "I went to the doctor today with Camila."

I frowned. First of all, why did Luisa go with Camila and not me? And what was wrong? She seemed kind of tired lately, but I figured it was because she was working so much. "Are you okay?"

"I will be in about seven months. I'm two months pregnant."

I stared at her, not sure I heard correctly. I felt like someone socked me in the stomach, and then this mixture of fear and joy began to fill my chest. "We're going to have a baby?"

"We are."

"Oh shit. Wow. Sit down," I said and pushed her onto the bed. I ran both hands through my hair. Then I knelt and looked into her eyes. "A baby?"

She smiled. "Are you happy?"

"I'm . . . shocked." Part of me was happy, but another part was sorry I wouldn't get Luisa to myself a little longer. A baby would change everything.

"Well, it was bound to happen eventually."

I smiled. "Yeah, but can you see me being a father?"

She gave me a teasing smile. "Not when you yell at our neighbor and throw my flowers in the trash."

"Shit, I'm sorry." I leaned in and kissed her. "We're going to be a family." The idea started to grow on me, and I couldn't wait to write my parents and tell them.

I stood. "Come on, I'd better apologize to Camila and see if they'll still take us out to eat. Even though I'd rather celebrate with just you."

"She was so excited this afternoon and so kind to go with me. You were a real jerk."

We got dressed and went to knock on Mateo and Camila's door. She called me an asshole, but then we all laughed and went downstairs, a couple of blocks away, and had a great meal of black beans, white rice, and flavorful shredded pork, talking about how our kids would grow up together, being the best of friends.

The crappy evening turned out to be a good one. I left the three of them at the restaurant and hurried off to work, promising Luisa that we'd celebrate more when I got home in the morning.

MY STRENGTHS HAD ALWAYS been that I learned quickly and worked hard. I managed to paint a room per night like the owner wanted. The hotel owner and the maintenance department manager were both happy with my work. They liked that I was clean, precise, fast, and reliable. But painting was backbreaking work. Being on my feet for so many hours, rolling paint on walls put incredible strain on my back, upper arms, neck, and shoulders. I was physically exhausted when I got home every morning.

When I met the guys to play soccer on Saturday, even the back of my legs killed me.

"Well, *Viejo*, you need to have an accident," Jose said.

"I *need* to have an accident?" I used my T-shirt to wipe the sweat off my forehead, then took my glasses off and wiped them with my shirt as well.

"Sure," he said. "Nicolas had a car accident and made enough money to buy his own apartment. And this other guy I know is a construction worker, and he fell three flights and made so much money he went back to Argentina and is living like a king in Buenos Aires."

I laughed. "What are you talking about?"

"You buy insurance. Then you have an 'accident,' and the insurance company pays you."

I stood up off the grass and pulled up on my socks until they almost touched my knees. "If I have to fall three flights to get an insurance pay off, I think I'll just keep working."

He stood and socked my arm. "You fake it, *Pelotudo*. You don't have a real accident. You're a painter. You know how easy it would be for you to get hurt and sue?"

I shook my head and chuckled, getting ready to go home. I wasn't sure if he was serious, but he seemed to be, which meant he was crazy.

"You think you're going to work your way into wealth in this country? Guys like us don't get wealthy unless we're smart. You think the rich in this country got that way working hard?"

"My dad says that a man who works hard will never want for anything."

"Is that what you want? To barely get by?"

I planned to do more than that, especially with a baby on the way. But I wasn't going to cheat my way into success. I ignored him and headed home.

I took a shower, and Luisa and I went to enjoy the city. She dragged me into Macy's to look at baby things, and then we took the ferry to see the Statue of Liberty. I held her close as the ferry crossed the water, enjoying the salty air blowing on our faces, her hair whipping back and exposing her neck that I loved to kiss. After many months living in New York City, I still hadn't gone to see the Statue of Liberty up close. Of course, I saw it from the island and took Luisa to Liberty State Park in lower Manhattan to gaze at it across the water. But this was the first time we would be on Ellis Island and climb to the statue's crown.

Watching it now as we approached took my breath away and left a lump in my throat. She welcomed immigrants like us to this land, offering freedom. No other country promised opportunities to those who wanted to work for them. I thought of what those guys said, disappointed that they'd suggest there was no way to succeed legitimately in America. I thought of what my father would say. He'd tell me to stop hanging out with them. But they were the only friends I had, and no one was perfect. Besides, they were probably joking around. Guys always exaggerate or say dumb things.

I held onto Luisa's hand as we disembarked, taking care that she didn't slip and fall. We walked along the park and then climbed to the top of the statue, admiring the Manhattan skyline.

"Sometimes, I still can't believe we're here," I said, feeling this need to conquer the city, to make my mark, as they say. Jose's comment about *just getting by* bothered me. I didn't want to just get by. So many in this city came with less than I did, and they became rich and powerful. Why couldn't I? Not that I needed or wanted that, but at the very least, I wanted to return to Argentina with a nice nest egg so my family would never need to worry about money.

"I feel that way every day about being here." Luisa pulled my attention back to her. She seemed a little tired as she smiled lazily. "I feel so lucky."

"You know, before we return to Argentina, I want to fly my parents here and let them see all this. What do you think?"

She turned to me with a big smile and a look in her eyes that made me feel proud for suggesting the idea.

"I think that would be wonderful. Maybe next year? That way, they can meet the baby," she said.

I kissed her chin and her cheek and her lips. "That's a great idea. After the baby is born."

"We should catch the next ferry."

"Yeah," I said. "It's getting late."

We made it back to the apartment when it was dark, and Luisa seemed really tired by then. She hadn't had morning sickness or anything like that, but she'd come home from work drained every day. Today's outing took a lot out of her, and I wondered if she ate enough.

I made dinner for the two of us while she rested on the couch. She kept telling me that she felt guilty sitting down while I worked, so I teased her about how she could make it up to me later in bed. I made a simple pan-fried steak and a tomato and onion salad.

After dinner, she fell asleep, and I sat down to write my father a letter to tell him about my new job and the upcoming baby. I didn't tell him about my friends or the doubt they planted in my head.

CHAPTER NINE

October 8, 1965
    Dear Salvadorito and Luisita,

With great joy, I read your letter and sit down now to respond and let you know that we are doing well, except for the minor issues that come with age.

I'm sure you are both enjoying the euphoria of life. You see the beauty in everything and the good. That is the way it should be. Of course, there will be some days when dark little clouds appear. They come on their own without you having to go looking for them, you know? But tolerance, forgiveness, and love chase those clouds away, along with the misunderstandings of life. You must always have faith and trust.

Thank Luisa for the photos she sent; you both look like movie stars, especially Luisa. I haven't forgotten that you asked us for pictures also, but we called the photographer, and there's always a reason why he can't make it. It's been cloudy and rainy lately, so that has been his latest excuse. I think he's afraid of your dog, Toby.

I hope Luisa is learning English. You should both go to school to learn together. Read newspapers or magazines in English. The more you read, the more you will learn.

I won't share anything about Newell's Old Boys because they're doing terrible, and it's better not to talk about it. Maybe I'll have better news in the next letter.

For now, I will end this letter. I send you and our new daughter a hug and kiss and our unalterable love like always.

Your father,

Jorge

THE PHONE RANG AND rang. I pulled myself out of a deep sleep, consciousness not coming easy as my brain refused to leave behind the dream of sitting in the pizzeria with my friends, drinking beer while discussing deep issues of life, like which soccer team had the best chance to win the championship this year.

The phone rarely rang, so as I awoke, I grew alarmed and stumbled out of bed and into the living room, groggily answering it.

It was from the hotel. "Your wife is in the hospital," the female voice said.

"What? Which hospital? What happened?" I searched the wall for the clock, but I'd left my glasses on the nightstand.

"I was just told to call you. I'm not sure what happened." But she gave me the name of the hospital and the phone number. They took her to New York Medical Center in Queens, which wasn't too far from our apartment. I dressed hurriedly, got my wallet and keys, and left the apartment. Damn it, I wish I had a car, but I jumped in a taxi and got there in a few minutes.

When I arrived and gave the front desk attendant Luisa's name, she directed me to the right floor. Luisa waited in a lobby. She wasn't in a room. When she saw me, she stood, and I pulled her into my arms. She had tears in her eyes.

"What happened?" I asked. "Are you okay?"

"I lost the baby," she said, her voice cracking and her thin body trembling against mine.

My heart sank. I tightened my arms around her and caressed the back of her head.

"I started bleeding, and it wouldn't stop. One of my coworkers drove me to the hospital, but it was too late."

I nodded and pulled back, keeping an arm around her back. "Are you waiting for a room, or are you okay to go?"

"We can go. The doctor already evaluated me, and there's nothing he can do. I didn't even need a D&C, but we need to pay the hospital bill."

I spoke to the front desk again and arranged to make payments since I didn't have insurance to cover the cost. When we got outside, I hailed a taxi. Luisa rested against me, listless, her head on my shoulder.

"I'm sorry," I said, not sure what to say. My emotions had jumped from fear to worry, to now a feeling of emptiness and grief.

"The nurse said it's common for a first pregnancy, but I was so excited about the baby."

I kissed the top of her head. "We'll try again. When you're able."

When we reached the apartment, I carried her into the lobby, but she was afraid I'd drop her, and she reassured me that she could walk. Still, I kept an arm around her waist and told her to lean on me as the jerky elevator slowly climbed to the eighth floor. Once inside the apartment, she went to bed, and I sat beside her, brushing her hair away from her face.

"I need to call work and tell them I need a day off. The doctor said I could go back to work in a couple of days," she muttered.

"No, you're done. I'll tell them you're not coming back."

"But why? We need the money."

"We really don't. This wouldn't have happened if you hadn't been working so hard."

"You don't know that. And besides, what does it matter now?"

"Stay home. Rest. Get strong. And we'll try again, but I don't want you working. I'll make enough, don't worry."

She didn't look happy. Instead, she slid down into the bed under the covers and turned away. I knew she was sad, and so was I. But I changed my clothes to get ready for work and went into the kitchen to cook some food. I opened a can of sardines, got some crackers, some cheese, and a bottle of coke. That would be enough for the night, then during break maybe I'd buy a sandwich or a slice of pizza. I wasn't that hungry.

I STOPPED IN TO SEE the hotel owner, who sometimes was there in the early evening and sometimes was not. He invited me into his office and offered me a seat in front of his desk. I told him about Luisa's condition, and he listened sympathetically.

"I'm sorry, Salvador," he said.

"She's not going to come back. She's too weak, and I want her to get strong so we can try to have a baby again soon."

He nodded and seemed to understand.

"I can work extra if you have more work."

"I don't think you're suggesting you'll clean the rooms."

"No, but other maintenance?"

"I'll keep you in mind for other jobs, but right now, just focus on painting. You're doing a great job." He dismissed me, not unkindly, but I could tell he was ready for me to leave. I nodded, thanked him, and left. I'd think of something else to replace her income. She wasn't making that much anyway.

I tried to cheer her up when I got home the following day. I brought her home a box of chocolates.

"Thank you, but Salvador, I'm fine. I'm sad, but I'll be okay. I even think I can go back to work."

I shook my head. "No, just relax for now, okay?"

She agreed and slipped out of bed to make me breakfast of eggs with toast and orange juice. We ate together. Then she returned to bed to wait for me.

I couldn't share any of what happened with the baby with my father though he knew Luisa was expecting. Why worry him? What was done was done now, anyway. But I sat at the table to write a few lines before going to sleep.

October 18, 1965

Dear *Papi*,

I'll take advantage of the few moments I have to write you while Luisa sleeps. I think you're correct that at our age everything looks bright and positive, and that fills us with happiness.

The truth is that life, daily routines, etc. are things that tire people out, or maybe better said, it is what creates boredom. But when you have someone beside you to talk honestly with, the challenges of life (as unpleasant as they may be) seem better, not as dark, and sometimes even optimistic. In my case, I often wonder if it would have been better if Luisa and I had united much earlier than we did.

Luisa is an angel. Like always, she's delicate yet strong, sensitive, understanding, enterprising; she has a hundred wonderful virtues that, in all honesty, I feel happy to be by her side. And because of that, we haven't encountered those little dark clouds that you refer to.

The truth is, we never have run into those clouds, not as boyfriend and girlfriend and not as a married couple. Maybe this is why I love her as much as I do.

I asked for a picture of you and *Mamá* because I longed to see you. It doesn't have to be anything fancy. Send one when you have the time. Please kiss *Mamá*. And now, I will end this letter and join my wife in bed.

Your son,

Salvador

Before going to bed, I sat alone at the kitchen table for a few moments longer and allowed the tears I'd been holding in to fall. I hadn't been convinced that I wanted to be a father or that I was prepared and could be even half the father that mine was to me, but the idea had started to grow inside me like a magical seed, especially when I saw the happiness on Luisa's face.

We'd try again soon. I'd give her the baby she wanted because I desperately wanted this first dark cloud to blow away before it created a prolonged darkness over our lives.

CHAPTER TEN

A month later, I received a letter from my father that knocked me off my feet. He started with all these pleasantries about Toby, my dog and how he greeted his favorite guests at the restaurant, and news about my favorite soccer team, then he tossed in the bad news in two paragraphs:

I've had complications from my diabetes. The numbness of my feet and leg had worsened, and standing had become impossible. Your mother forced me to see my doctor, and they scheduled me for surgery. Unfortunately, they could not save my leg and were forced to amputate. Blood flow to the lower extremities of my leg had stopped, and the tissue died. I'd developed gangrene, and in all honesty, I started to suspect that because my leg was turning purple.

I spent a week in the hospital after the surgery and another excruciatingly painful week in bed at home. I'm healing well. I will be fitted with a prothesis soon, and maybe things will improve for me. This isn't good news, of course, but I am looking forward to walking again. The way my leg was before, it wasn't serving me anyway, and I spent most of my days sitting in a wheelchair. We must look at the positive at every opportunity, no?

I dropped the letter on the coffee table and covered my face with my hands as bitter tears clouded my vision and finally fell through my fingers. My father was a hard man, a proud man who found a lesson in whatever shit life threw at him. I pictured him with a missing limb, and my heart clenched.

Luisa came out of the bathroom where she was taking a shower. "I think I want to change the shampoo and find something else. The perfume they use is so strong that — what's wrong?"

She came to sit beside me, but I couldn't speak. She picked up the letter and read it. "Oh no, Salvador. I'm so sorry."

"What should I do?"

"What can you do? Send him a telegram so that he gets your message faster than through the post office?"

"I mean, should we go back? My mother was already struggling with the restaurant doing almost everything herself."

"If you think that would be best."

I shook my head. "I don't know what's best. Going back, I'd help run the restaurant, but we'd all have to live off the same income, you know? We're not going to increase the number of customers. Then when we have kids, it'll be more mouths to feed."

She sighed and leaned back. "I'll support whatever you decide, but it sounds like you're not ready to return."

"It's not that I'm not ready." Though I wasn't, I hadn't saved money or achieved anything yet. I'd be going back with nothing. "I think if I keep doing what I'm doing, working hard, I can make more money here...be of more help to them."

"You're probably right."

I wiped my eyes and leaned across and kissed her. "I love you, do you know that?"

"Yes."

I smiled even though my soul felt heavy and reached to slip the letter out of her hands. "The poor old man."

She caressed my arm but said nothing.

"I'll write him and ask him what I can do or if he needs anything. Money. Something. I'm going to have to tell him you lost the baby. I couldn't bring myself to tell him the last time I wrote. My parents were so excited. It's going to break his heart. Dammit." I stood. "This piece of shit month."

When she didn't say anything or move, I turned to look at her. She sat with her legs crossed, looking too thin and tired. I had to do better. I had to make money and succeed. Going back a failure wasn't an option. If I returned home now, I'd be nothing but a burden to my parents. "Get some sleep," I told her.

THE NEXT COUPLE OF months were mostly happy. Luisa made delicious dinners and visited with the Llonch family. They were going to retire and move to the suburbs, but they really loved Luisa and said they would come and pick her up anytime she wanted to visit.

Mrs. Llonch convinced Luisa to get a job at a sewing factory which I wasn't happy about, but she'd be sitting most of the time, so I figured it would be an improvement to cleaning rooms. Her enthusiasm as she shared the news made me keep my disapproval to myself. Instead, I forced a smile and hugged her as I told her how I was happy for her.

"I'm going to make twice what I did at the hotel," she said. "Isn't that great?"

"It's fantastic."

"We can start saving for your parents to visit."

I wrote to my father and told him how devastated we were to hear about his leg, not to worry about the trip to visit us. And I got the balls to tell him about the miscarriage since I didn't want him to think we still had a baby coming. But he insisted he would still travel to New York to visit his kids.

I nodded at Luisa. "That's a good idea, but I was thinking of buying a truck with some of our savings."

"For what?"

"The guys said that truck drivers make a killing. I can make three times what I'm making at the hotel. Maybe we should get my parents' ticket after I get enough money for the down payment on the truck? That way, he has more time to recover." At least this time, my friends had suggested something honest. And the more I looked into the idea, the more I liked it. I enjoyed driving, and it seemed like an easy enough job.

"No, Salvador, they really miss you. And your father needs to have something to look forward to."

"I know," I said. Maybe I'd be able to do both. "Well, we'll see. For now, it will be nice to save your income."

LUISA TACKLED THIS project with focus and dedication. She put money away and kept reminding me about having my parents visit. On a bright yellow piece of paper taped to the kitchen wall, she would write in the money we had saved from her weekly paychecks: $75, $100, $150, $100. "We almost have enough for one ticket," she said after a couple of months.

I saved money from my paycheck too, though not as much because I paid all the bills. But I did miss my parents. Maybe in about six months, we'd have the money. My father needed to heal anyhow, and it took time to get travel visas.

Their visit would fill Luisa's need for connection and love from back home. I sensed that planning for my parents' visit distracted her from the miscarriage. As sad as we were still about losing the baby, we didn't talk about it. We went on with life, not trying to get pregnant, but also not using any birth control. Though we still felt the void of what should have been. Disappointed, she packed up all the baby clothes she'd purchased and put them in the closet. "For later," she'd said.

I wrote my father, and we made plans for them to visit when he felt well enough to travel.

I STILL WANTED TO BUY a truck because I felt it was my first step to owning something important. Maybe it would grow into a business, who knew? Before work, I went with Mateo to a truck lot out in Brooklyn. "You just need a small down payment," the salesman said. "Then you'll make more than enough for the monthly payments."

The beautiful, shiny trucks and the slick sales pitch definitely tempted me. But I wasn't ready to sign a contract. Not with my parents coming to visit. I'd have to get a different license and start applying for work first. Still, it was fun to look. We went to a few auto lots after to admire the new cars. I wasn't ready for a truck, but a car was a different story,

"We should buy one together," Mateo said. "You buy it in your name, and I'll make half the payment."

"Yeah, sure, then we'll fight about who gets the car each weekend."

Mateo shrugged. "We'd work it out."

I shook my head and strolled toward a red, gorgeous Buick Skylark.

"You like that?" a salesman asked, appearing out of nowhere.

"I do."

"Would you like to test drive it?"

I glanced at Mateo, and he shrugged and smiled.

"Why not?" I grinned.

The salesman went inside the showroom to get the keys and told me to get behind the wheel. Mateo sat in the long back seat, extending his arm out and smiling. I pulled out of the lot, loving the feel of my fingers wrapped around the wheel and how my body fit comfortably into the vinyl seat.

"Feel that power? It has a strong V6 engine."

"Yes, it feels good," I said. I imagined driving my parents around in the car and how much easier it would be than making them take the subway or a taxi. My father said he walked well using his prosthesis, but I didn't like the idea of him being shoved by careless people whose only concern would be getting into and out of the subway.

We drove around for about ten minutes, then he directed me back to the lot.

"It takes very little to get you into this baby," the salesman said.

"How much?" Not that I could afford it, and my heart sank when he told me it would be two months salary.

"Let's go," Mateo said, tapping my shoulder.

I considered his idea of buying the car together, but that wouldn't work out.

"I'll think about it," I said.

"Wait, if that's too much. We can work something out."

Before I knew it, we were sitting inside a small room, and I was talking with the finance manager, trying to figure out how to "get me into the car."

I thought of the places I could take my parents and Luisa to visit and of eventually having a car for when we have a baby, and before I knew it, I was signing the contract, and Mateo and I were driving back to Queens in my brand new first car!

I drove home with a grin that wouldn't go away, charged with so many emotions.

"Luisa is going to kill you, *Loco*," Mateo said. "Did you actually use your parents' airline ticket money?"

"Yeah, but I'll get paid again before I have to buy the tickets. I'll figure it out. Maybe I can pick up extra work."

"Where?"

"I don't know."

He shook his head, but I saw the admiration in his eyes.

When I got home, I told Mateo to get Camila and meet me back here. I almost ran up eight flights of stairs instead of taking the elevator because I was bursting with excitement. Luisa was in the kitchen making dinner, and I told her to stop and put everything away. We were going out.

"What? Why? What's going on?"

"Come on, come on. Get dressed."

She put on a dress and started messing with her hair.

"Leave it. You look great. Come on." I took her hand, and we hurried outside where I'd parked the car. I pulled out the keys. "Get in."

"In where?"

"The car. Where do you think?"

She frowned. "Salvador, don't tell me you bought a car."

"Isn't she a beauty?"

"Are you crazy? What did this cost?"

"Don't worry about that."

"How are we going to afford a car?"

"I said, don't worry about that. Do you like it or not?"

She stared at me with her mouth open.

"Never mind, get in. We're going out to dinner." I saw Mateo coming with Camila, who didn't look happy to be dragged outside either.

"Shit, you're crazier than Mateo is. What's this?"

"My new ride. Let's go."

They got in the back seat, and Luisa sat beside me. "Doesn't it feel amazing?" I asked, then leaned across and kissed her cheek. "Smile."

She shook her head and offered a small smile. "You *are* crazy."

"Life is crazy, and I'm taking it for a ride in my new car."

We drove around Manhattan for about an hour until we found a nice steakhouse to have dinner.

Mateo ordered a bottle of champagne. "To my crazy new friend who can barely drive but has a new car."

"Go to hell. I can drive just fine." I placed my arm around the back of Luisa's chair. She wasn't saying much, and I could tell she wasn't thrilled. "Now I can drive my wife to work."

"I was doing fine on the subway."

"Well, it's a beauty," Mateo said. "Congratulations, *Loco*."

"Let's eat and drink and enjoy this spontaneous night. I left the baby with the old grandma down the hall, and I'm afraid she'll fall asleep and forget Niki is there."

Luisa looked worried. "You don't think she will, right?"

Camila laughed. "She's really taken a liking to Niki lately, and she's watched her twice already, and each time, I had to convince her to let me take my daughter home."

Mateo leaned over and nuzzled Camila's neck. "Enjoy the night, and don't worry about Niki. In fact . . ." He stood and then knelt in front of Camila's chair. "I've been wondering when the best time to do this was, and maybe tonight's the night, here with our friends."

Luisa screamed and then covered her mouth when she saw Mateo go down on one knee and stare adoringly at Camila. Camila just stared at Mateo, looking completely confused.

I nearly choked on the bread I'd just bit into. I wanted to grab Mateo by the back of the neck and pull him to his feet.

"We've been together a year and a half, and it's been enough to know I want it to be the rest of my life, Camila. I want to adopt Niki, and I want to marry you if you'll do me the honor."

Camila continued to gape at Mateo, and I thought he'd gone crazy. Camila seemed nice enough, but she came with baggage—another man's baby, an attitude, and she was Cuban. Maybe it was just me, but I'm glad I have an Argentine wife who understands my culture and shares my love of tangos and, well . . . my vision of the world.

"What do you say, *mi amor*?" Mateo asked.

Camila glanced at Luisa and me. Luisa nodded as if encouraging her to say yes, but seemed fearful that she'd say no.

Finally, Camila smiled. "I don't know if this is the most romantic proposal, but yes, I'd love to marry you."

He stood and wrapped his arms around Camila's waist, lifting her out of the chair and kissing her. Camila was slightly taller than Mateo. Her arms wrapped around Mateo's neck. Luisa clapped, and I whistled. People at other tables looked at us. Camila turned around to address them. "We're getting married!"

The patrons clapped and called out their congratulations.

Mateo had the biggest grin on his face when he sat back down. He looked at me and lifted an eyebrow. He'd surprised us all. What could I say? I held my champagne glass in the air. "To your future."

"To us," he said.

We all touched our glasses together. "To us."

CHAPTER ELEVEN

On a glorious day in July of 1966, after nine months of planning, we drove to the airport to pick up *Mamá y Papá*, and it was one of the best days of my life. Seeing my *viejos* again, the smiles on their faces, made my heart swell with pride. My mother held onto me for what seemed like an hour, and my father hugged me tight and slapped my back hard. He got along well on his rubber leg. I was glad I had the car to drive him around, though. He would have struggled to get on a subway, just like I'd imagined.

They hugged and kissed Luisa too, telling her she looked beautiful, and of course, she did.

As we left Kennedy Airport in style in my impressive Buick Skylark, my father couldn't stop talking about it. "Salvador, look at this car. *Dios mio*, it's a car for a king."

I laughed. "It's priced for kings too, but we needed a car."

My parents beamed as they sat in the back seat and took in the city lights.

"Look at these roads!" my father said. "Our roads in Argentina are like horse trails compared to these highways."

I tried not to puff my chest out too far as I drove and rested my elbow out of the window, but my father was so proud, and it made me feel good to please him. I hadn't done anything special to deserve his praise. I was just surviving and working like a slave at that, but to him, we'd made it. We were living the good life.

When we got to the apartment, they continued to admire our furniture and how Luisa decorated it with modern trinkets. Truthfully, she hadn't done much. She was a minimalist, but she did choose a few nice vases and pictures for the walls.

"This is the bedroom," Luisa said, pulling their suitcases into the room. "You make yourselves comfortable."

"But this is your room."

"No, *Mamá*," I said. "We borrowed a mattress from friends, and we're going to sleep in the living room. Don't worry. You and *Papi* enjoy the bed."

We chatted about Rosario for a while and about my brother's life.

"He's excelling in law school," my father said. "He's always had a spectacular mind."

"I'm glad one of your sons does," I said, teasing him.

"Both of my boys have sharp minds, but the younger one is a bit of a rebel and has a wilder spirit. Never compare yourself to your brother, *Hijo*."

"Naw, I don't. Believe me, I'm glad he's the one who went to law school."

They shared other family news too, and I listened enthusiastically. Then, tired from the trip, they went to bed.

Luisa and I dragged the mattress from the bedroom and lay it on the floor. Once we turned out the lights and it got quiet, she rested her head on my shoulder. "They're so happy," she said. "You did good, Salvador."

I kissed her. "Yeah, thanks for pushing me to bring them. I told them at work that I needed a couple of weeks off so that we can take them around."

She gave me a sleepy smile. "It's going to be great having them here. It will make me miss Argentina a little less."

I gazed down at her. "Do you miss home?"

"Yes. I love it here. But I do miss my sisters, and you know, just being home and speaking to people who are like me and having them understand me."

"You need to learn some English."

"I know."

"I'm serious. Maybe you should take some classes. You can't rely on other people to translate for you forever."

"I can say thank you, and please, and steak and wine."

I chuckled, kissed her one more time, and turned over to sleep. I'd worked late last night and couldn't keep my eyes open. She rubbed my back as I fell fast asleep.

LUISA INSISTED ON MAKING breakfast the next day even though I wanted to take my parents to an American breakfast.

"Eggs and bacon?" my mother said, wrinkling her nose. "No, Luisa is right. Just some coffee and toast is fine."

"The bed was very comfortable," my father said. "Are you sure you slept well out here?"

"Yes, we slept perfectly," Luisa said. "Except for your son's snoring. Sit down, please," she told my father.

"We heard him through the closed door." He laughed. "It's good to see you two doing so well. It sets my mind at ease."

"Of course, we're doing well." I sat across from my father at my small square table. "Have faith in your son."

"I have faith, Salvadorito. Don't be too smug. A man has to stay humble. And I don't mind telling you that your mother and I spent many sleepless nights wondering how you were really doing here in this great country."

"You can sleep well. We're fine."

"I brought the flag you asked for and some records." He stood and grabbed a bag out that he'd set on the couch.

"Hey, look Luisa! Our flag. We can hang it on the wall in the living room so we can see it every day."

She smiled.

He handed me two tango record albums. "Oh, thank you! We can practice our dancing, Luisa." I kissed both of my parents.

"And Luisa, we brought you a little something, and your sisters sent a couple of gifts."

"You didn't have to bring me anything."

"Well," my father said. "We did, and it's because we love you."

They handed her a wrapped present, and she opened it to find a delicate gold watch. "Oh my God," she said. "This is too much!"

"Nonsense."

Her sisters sent her some handkerchiefs and a scarf. Luisa looked both happy and sad, and I thought about how she'd said she missed her family.

"Well, I have a surprise for all of you. You too, Salvador."

I frowned. She had a surprise for me?

"You know we lost the baby a few months ago."

My father reached across and covered her hand with his wrinkled, darker one. "We were brokenhearted to hear that, *Querida*."

She turned her hand around and gripped his. "We were sad as well. But I'm happy to tell you that I went to the doctor the other day, and I'm two months pregnant."

I stared at her as both my parents got up from their seats to hug her, then they turned to embrace and congratulate me. I was still in a bit of shock. Why hadn't she told me?

"Wow! That's a surprise all right."

She nodded.

"Okay then," I said. "Let's go enjoy the day and celebrate."

I took them to the Empire State Building, Rockefeller Center, and the United Nations building. Over the next two weeks, we visited Coney Island and walked along the boardwalk. We ate Nathan's hotdogs which my father really loved. My mother thought they were just okay and wanted to know why Americans put everything between slices of bread.

They enjoyed walking barefoot on the sand. My father, of course, only had one leg, but he made the best of it.

As we sat on the sand and I expressed my regret for the pain he had to endure, he said, "I'm getting along fine, Son. Life is always a challenge, Salvador. This body is on loan to us anyway. If I had to give up a piece of it to survive . . . well, I gladly did it."

I looked out at the waves as my arms rested on my knees. "I don't think I'd be so accepting. I'd find it difficult not to be bitter and angry."

"What would that get you?"

I shrugged.

He shoved my shoulder. "Tell me. What would anger get you?"

I angled my head to look at him.

"Bitterness destroys your soul. It steals the joy you still have to extract from life."

"I suppose."

"You're young. You can't imagine losing a leg or an eye, or any part of yourself. I understand. But as you grow older, you appreciate what you have left. I'm grateful, not bitter."

I glanced over at my wife, who was pregnant again, talking with my mother. I had a lot to be grateful for, but if I were in his shoes, I'd probably drown in a pool of self-pity.

On a different day, we made the long drive to see Niagara Falls, got a hotel, and spent a couple of days enjoying the impressive group of falls and the grandeur of nature. *Mamá* seemed to like this tourist site best of all. Back in Manhattan, we ate exquisite meals, and Luisa insisted on taking my parents to see a Broadway play which they enjoyed.

When it was time for them to return to Argentina, I didn't want them to go. I felt like a little boy again, clinging to the security of my *viejos*. Something inside me told me I wouldn't see them again for a long while.

My mother cried even though she was usually a stoic woman.

"We'll come to see you when the baby is born. I promise," I told her. Maybe I'd be able to swing that.

She held my face with both hands as if trying to memorize it. "Be good and remember that your home is in Argentina, and it's always there for you to return."

"I know. That's the plan. But not yet, *Mamá*."

"Don't take too long. Don't get lost in this country. It's beautiful, but it's not where your roots are."

I kissed her cheek. "I understand."

America was becoming part of me, though. The longer I stayed, the more the United States dug itself into my soul. I thought of a mite that burrows under one's skin undetected and wreaks havoc. But if I was honest, I'd been infected long before I'd stepped foot on this soil, and it didn't feel like I had a parasite inside me. No, it felt like my destiny.

CHAPTER TWELVE

The day after my parents left, I got to work early to prepare my brushes and lay out my paint. I whistled tango "El Choclo" as I worked, wishing I could dance like Luisa and I last night. Luisa always says *I think* I can dance, as if it's not true, but I'm pretty good and I have fun. We played my favorite records as we ate our last dinner together in our apartment, and this morning the melody stuck in my head.

"Hey, the hotel owner wants to see you," one of the other workers said.

I nodded, put the brushes and rollers down, and headed to his office, continuing to whistle.

"WHAT DO YOU MEAN I'M fired?"

"You take two weeks off and want to stroll back here and get your job back?"

"I've been a loyal employee. Never missed a day. I don't deserve some time off?"

"You know what you deserve? To be fired when you don't show up to work."

"But I told you—"

"You don't *tell* me anything. I give the orders here. We replaced you. We need a painter who comes to work."

"You know what? Fine." I held my hands up in surrender. "If you don't value me enough to give me a couple of weeks off, then I don't need to be here." Even though he was calling me back, I stormed out of his office. Fuck him. I'd find something else.

ON SATURDAY, TO RELEASE some of my frustration after spending a week searching for work and finding none, I played an intense, brutal game of soccer with my friends. They kept telling me to take it easy. This was supposed to be for fun, and no one would offer me a contract to play for a professional team if I scored more points than anyone else.

When I got home, Luisa stood at the door arguing with a couple of guys.

"Hey, what's going on."

"Do you live here, sir?"

"Yeah, what do you want?"

He handed me a piece of paper. "We're here to repossess your furniture for nonpayment."

"No, I'm going to pay soon, but I lost my job." Truth was, I hadn't paid them last month either because I needed the money to buy my parents' airline tickets. I figured I'd make it up this month.

"I'm sorry, sir, but you missed last month's payment, and the contract you signed clearly stated that if you miss a payment, we can repossess."

Luisa spoke a mile a minute in Spanish, asking me to explain.

"Look, we're just doing our job. We don't want any trouble, but if we have to call the police, we will."

"No, no," I said. "Is there anything we can do?"

"You can pay what you owe right now."

"I can't do that."

He shrugged.

I nodded. "Okay, come in." I placed my hands on Luisa's shoulders and explained that we had no option. We had to let them take the furniture.

"But where are we going to sleep? And sit? They're taking the couch and kitchen table."

"I know. I'll replace it all when I get a new job."

"I have some money."

"We need that for food right now. Just hold onto it."

Mateo and Camila came out of their apartment. "Shit, what's going on," Mateo said.

I shook my head. "I need a new job, that's what's going on. Or they're going to kick us out of the apartment next."

"There are some secondhand stores we can go to, Luisa," Camila said. "You can replace the furniture cheaply."

We thanked them and went back inside.

"I'm sorry," I said.

"I can't believe they don't have a grace period."

We should have had some money set aside, but I used it all to entertain my parents and to pay for the car. I always seemed to be living month to month.

"I'm glad this didn't happen when they were here. What an embarrassment."

I nodded and scratched the back of my head as I looked around at everything missing. Shit. I needed to get a new job and soon. I didn't want Luisa working for too much longer. The baby in her belly was getting bigger, and I wanted her to rest the last few months of her pregnancy.

"I'm going to go find a job."

"Where?"

"Anywhere." I left and found myself driving to the truck lot Mateo and I visited a few months ago. The salesman came out with a smile. "How can I help you?"

"I'm looking for a truck."

He laughed, making a grand gesture with his arms. "You're in the right place."

I negotiated the best I could and lied, saying I still worked at the hotel. With Luisa's income, I qualified by the skin of my teeth. Now, I'd have to find a job quickly to make the payments.

"Can I leave my car here overnight, and I'll come back to get it tomorrow?"

"Well, okay, I'll give you one day. But you have to come back, or we'll consider it abandoned."

"I'll be back in the morning."

I climbed into the truck and drove it to a trucking company my friend had told me about. I parked it on their lot and went to the hiring office. "I'm here to apply for a job."

The secretary handed me an application that asked about my background and previous experience. I didn't have any experience driving a truck. I looked at her.

"Do you have a question?" she asked.

"I'm just . . . what if I don't have any experience?"

"We need people with experience and the right license, of course."

I'd forgotten about the license. "I meant . . . in this country. What if my experience is from Argentina."

"Write it down," she said.

I sighed and invented my driving experience in Argentina, adding businesses I'd remembered seeing. It wasn't like they could check. My license was something else entirely. I'd have to get that. "I just bought the truck, so I'm going to DMV to get my license in the morning."

"Thank you, Mr. Moreau. We'll call you."

"Can you call me soon? I really need to work."

"Get your license. If or when we call, you must have it."

I flashed her my most confident grin. "I will."

In the morning, since Mateo was working, I asked my friend Javier to drive me to get my car. "I don't know what the hell I'm going to do about this car. They're going to end up repossessing this too. I can't afford to make the payment."

"You'll have to pay the difference of what they resell it for."

"*Mierda!* Can't they just take the car back? They have my down payment, all the payments I made, plus they'll have the car."

"Doesn't work that way. If they can't sell it for what you owe, they will come after you for the difference. I've got an idea, but you're not going to like it with your squeaky-clean attitude."

I stared at him as he drove. "What's your idea?"

"You have insurance, right?"

"Yeah, I had to buy it. I can't afford that either now that I'll have to pay for the truck."

"Well, what if your car got stolen? They'd pay it off."

"I don't understand."

"Look, if you're interested, meet me tomorrow with the car, and I'll take care of the rest. We'll both make some money."

I wasn't sure. This didn't feel right. Who was I kidding? It wasn't right. But neither was taking my shit the second I couldn't pay for it. "Okay."

We agreed to meet in the morning.

I rescued the car from the truck dealer and drove it home, feeling sad that I would need to give it up. But the truck was more valuable to me right now. I'd buy a new car someday soon. I parked the car in front of my apartment and ran a couple of blocks to get my truck. I drove the truck to the Bureau of Motor Vehicles and told them I wanted to apply for my commercial driver's license. I took the written test and passed. "Can I take the road test?"

She handed me a booklet. "Make sure you can perform these skills on the road. I recommend a driving school if you don't have experience."

"I have experience."

"Then make an appointment for next week."

Dammit. "Okay." Well, I'd better practice anyway. I paged through the checklists and diagrams in the booklet. Thankfully, Mateo had the time to go with me to an empty lot, where I practiced making turns and driving strategically.

We set up cones and rocks, and I practiced going around, backing up, and parking. Mateo motioned when I got too close to the cones or when I ran them over completely. After a week of practicing, I felt confident about passing the driving portion of the test.

AFTER I DROPPED LUISA off at work, I drove to Queens, to Cunningham Park. I parked and waited for Javier to show up, which he did with two other Puerto Ricans.

"Nice car," one of them said.

"Yeah, it's a real beauty. I hate to lose it."

They laughed. "Well, lose it, you will." He held out his hand. "Keys?"

I glanced at my friend, who nodded. Reluctantly, I handed over the keys to my car. He pulled out his wallet and gave us each $300. "Good doing business with you guys."

He got into my car and drove off. "So, now what? I still have to make payments on a car I don't own. I just sold it to that guy."

Javier shook his head. "Let's go play a soccer game. Then we're going to call the police and report your car stolen. You didn't sell anything."

"And they arrest that guy?"

"Your car will be in pieces and on its way to Mexico by tonight. Your troubles are over. Call your insurance company and mail them the police report. They'll pay off your loan, and you're off the hook."

"Are you sure it's that easy?"

"Trust me."

Anxiety ate me up inside. What the hell had I just agreed to do? I tried not to think of my father or what he would say about this. Was I going to lie to a police officer? Shit. My hands trembled, and I felt lightheaded.

But a few of Javier's friends showed up to play soccer with us. He tapped my shoulder and pushed me toward the grass. I played soccer like an elementary school kid, couldn't concentrate or focus.

"Come on, Salvador!" Javier yelled at me.

"Why are we playing this game? Why aren't we calling the police now?" I whispered.

"He needs time to get away." He slapped my shoulder. "Plus, this is fun!" He ran off, and I drew a breath, trying to get my head in the game. After a couple of hours, we finished, said goodbye to his other friends, and Javier and I walked back to where I'd given my car away.

"Didn't you park here?" he asked loudly. "Shit, where's your car?"

I sighed and rolled my eyes.

"Someone stole your car!" he shouted.

I scratched the back of my head and watched his acting job. "Yeah."

"Let's see if we can make a phone call in that little grocery store over there."

We walked across 210th Street, a long, guilty, miserable walk. The grocer at the register was ringing up a customer, and Javier said, "Hey, excuse me. Someone stole my friend's car over there at the park. Can you call the cops for us?"

"Stole your car? Yeah, hold on a sec." He finished with his customer and shook his head. "Every day, the neighborhood gets worse."

"Yeah, tell me about it," Javier said.

About twenty minutes later, the police arrived and took the report. What were we doing? Did we see anyone suspicious? Did I leave anything in the car? I had to answer all kinds of questions. I thought I was going to be sick.

"You okay?" the officer asked.

"No, I don't feel too good," I admitted.

"I get it. We'll do our best to find it. Sometimes young kids take cars for joyrides and then abandon them. You never know."

I nodded, and he promised to contact me if they heard anything.

Javier gave me a ride home, and when I got there, I took a hot shower to try to wash off the sweat and filth that came from more than running on a field. I wrapped a towel around my waist and looked at my empty apartment. And now I had a missing car. I felt like I was sinking down a dark well and slowly being submerged in the water. I leaned on my wall and sat down.

I'd better pass that road test and get the truck driving job. I planned to spend the rest of the week practicing on that lot.

I decided to get dressed and meet Luisa. She expected me to pick her up in the car. She didn't know about the truck yet. I didn't tell her. Once I got the job, I'd let her know.

I took the subway to the factory where she worked and waited outside.

When she walked out, I called out to her.

"Hey." She smiled. "What are you doing out here?" I usually waited in the car around the corner where there was parking.

"We're going to take the subway home."

"What? Why?"

I drew in a breath. "Ah, because someone stole the car."

She stopped walking. Her mouth opened wide. "Were you in it? Are you hurt?" she asked finally, checking my face. "What happened?"

I felt terrible lying to her, but I had no choice. "I'm fine. I was in Queens, and someone stole the car while I was playing soccer."

"Playing soccer? I thought you were looking for a job? Why were you playing soccer in Queens? Don't you usually play in Central Park?"

"Look, that's just where I was, okay? I had a shitty day and don't need an interrogation from you."

Her eyes widened. "Okay."

We walked toward the subway. "What are we going to do now? Did you report it?"

"I called the police. Filed a report. Tomorrow, I'll call the insurance agency and talk to the dealership."

"This is terrible. How does something like this happen?"

"People steal things all the time."

We descended into the subway tunnel. I held onto her hand. I didn't want her to get bumped or hurt. "As soon as I start working, you should quit this job."

"I don't think you should worry about that now."

"I'm not worried. But you don't want to lose another baby."

She made dinner while I sat on the floor and brooded all night. We ate on the floor like a couple of bums. Life was not supposed to be like this in the wealthiest country in the world.

She took our dirty dishes back to the kitchen, and when she returned, she handed me some money. "Here, for the rent."

"I have the money for the rent," I said. I shook a cigarette out of the pack and lit it.

"You do?"

"Yeah, I did a job for Javier. He gave me some money."

"Oh, okay."

"Or did you think all I did was play soccer all day?"

"I didn't say that. I don't know what you did."

"I'm taking care of things."

"Fine. I know you're upset about the car, but you don't have to take out your bad mood on me."

I wasn't taking anything out on her. I stood, took another drag of the cigarette, and put it out. "I'm tired. I'm going to go to sleep." I entered the bedroom where we'd placed the mattress on the floor. I took off all my clothes, curled up on my side, and fell into an uneasy sleep, worried that someone would find out what I'd done and I'd go to jail. Wasn't that what happened to all criminals . . . and now I'd become one.

CHAPTER THIRTEEN

August 21, 1966

Dear Salvador and Luisa,

I regret that it's taken me some time to write to you. I'm sure you are waiting impatiently to learn how we've arrived home. We hit a few air pockets on the way to Brazil, which shook the plane quite a bit. When we landed in Brazil, they redirected us to a military base instead of the airport. Then Aerolineas Argentina put us on a bus to travel the rest of the way. They said it was because of bad weather and it wasn't safe to fly. But when we arrived in Buenos Aires, we learned that there had been subversive movements in Brazil.

Anyhow, we arrived in Ezeiza much later than we expected, and the Bustamante family, who was going to pick us up and allow us to spend the night with them, were not there since they expected us hours earlier. We finally got in touch with them, and everything worked out.

When we got home, Toby celebrated for an hour, jumping, crying, and begging for attention. Various family members came to see us to hear about our trip of a lifetime. They all send their love.

Your brother said he's going to write you about the nationality of my future grandson or granddaughter. He's sure your child can be Argentine even if born in the United States. All you have to do is go to the Argentine Embassy and tell them about your desire to renounce the American citizenship and instead register your child as an Argentine. See, there will be no problem.

I am tired and will now end this letter. Write me when you have time. I send you kisses, love, and a hug bigger than New York's Central Park.

Your father,

Jorge

I PRACTICED DRIVING the truck every day until my DMV appointment date. On the day of, I showed up early, excited, and ready to take the road test. I shook the stern-looking man's hand when he showed up with his clipboard. I guessed that I wasn't supposed to do that since he sort of awkwardly accepted my hand and then began to ask me to point out various parts of the truck, which I did confidently since I'd studied well.

I hooked up to the trailer as he directed. When we got inside the truck, I followed his instructions, maneuvering through the streets and route he selected. I made my turns well, as far as I could tell. He didn't say much, just took notes on his clipboard. When we got back, I had to back up and unhook the trailer. None of it was all that difficult, but I wasn't sure how I'd done because the DMV official didn't speak.

He gave me a piece of paper and told me to return it inside.

"Did I pass?"

"You passed. Congratulations," he said, with little emotion.

I drew in a deep breath and let out the nervous energy, my chest filling instead with anticipation. I received a temporary permit which I immediately took to the trucking company. "Congratulations, we'll call you in a couple of weeks. You should have your permanent license by then."

A couple of weeks? Dammit, I needed money, but at least I was closer to getting work, and I'd have my own trucking business.

When I got home, I took a shower and waited for Luisa to get home to share my news. I also found a pay phone and called the insurance company to tell them about my stolen car. They told me they would mail me some forms to fill out and that I should return them with the police report. As I hung up, I was glad to almost put that behind me.

I bought a pack of cigarettes and stood out on the sidewalk, watching men in suits walk past, busy with their own lives. Cars, taxis, and busses hurried on their way, impatient, often getting stuck behind a line of vehicles. This was a city full of people in a rush to get nowhere, to succeed. I blew out the smoke. I wondered if they, like me, were all on the edge of disaster. One bad deal, one lost job, and all their dreams could come tumbling down.

THE NEXT FEW MONTHS went by quickly. After being hired by the trucking company, I worked all day picking up and delivering loads, coming home exhausted, only to get up and do it again. Luisa slowly grew a bigger belly. Though she seemed healthy, I worried about her working.

As we sat to eat dinner together and she looked as tired as I felt, I reached across and caressed her chin. "I think you should quit, Luisa. Stay home for the next few months. You're not going to work when the baby is born anyway."

"I don't know," she said, cutting into her baked chicken.

I leaned back in the chair. Camila and Luisa went to the second-hand store and bought a kitchen table and a couch so we had places to sit again. "In fact, I've been thinking that you should go back to Argentina to have the baby."

She frowned. "Why would I do that?"

"I don't want my son to be born in America. I want him to be Argentine. Look at all the crazy stuff that's going on with the Vietnam War. It's never going to end. I don't want my son being drafted to fight in a foreign war that has nothing to do with the Americas. I know my brother said I could go to the embassy and fill out a bunch of paperwork, but it's so much easier if you just fly there to have the baby."

"The baby's not even born yet, and you're worried about him going to war? Plus, how do you know it will be a boy?"

"Of course, I'm going to have a boy."

She shook her head, her eyelids drooping. "It's an expense we don't need."

"Wouldn't you like to be with your sisters when you have the baby? And my parents can help you."

"Don't you want to see the baby when it's born?"

"Sure, but I'll see him when you come back."

"Are you serious about this?"

Was I? I'd just thought about it, but yes, it would be best for her to be among family. "I am. I'm working long hours anyway, and we don't see each other much. Give your two weeks' notice, and I'll get you the airline ticket to leave after that. I'll write my father and tell him you're coming."

"I'll stay with my sisters, though, not with your parents."

"Stay wherever you want."

LUISA LEFT THREE WEEKS later, a couple of months before the baby was due. Though I hated to see her go, I told myself it would be for the best. I could work long hours without worrying about her because she'd be well cared for by family.

Driving was physically taxing but mentally unchallenging. I figured I'd do it for a while to save money, but it wasn't something I wanted to do forever.

Mateo talked about moving to California. As I unloaded a truck in 10-degree weather, moving to sunny California, where movie stars dined in all the local restaurants, sounded nice. Maybe when Luisa returned with the baby, we'd talk about it too.

During the weekend, Javier asked me to help him carry a load with my truck. We delivered it together, but I had no idea what I was moving. We took the trailer to the harbor, and he paid me for helping him. So, I didn't ask questions. It was his business. Occasionally, he had side jobs, and he asked me for help. He always gave me cash, but mostly I did these favors for him because he helped me while I waited to get called by the trucking company. And he'd been correct about reporting the car stolen to the insurance company. They paid off my bank loan, and I never had to make another car payment.

He gave me a couple of hundred, and I pocked it. "Thanks, it'll help me pay the rent. Without Luisa's income, things will be a little tighter."

"Forget next month's rent. Why don't you move in with me while your wife is gone? Why pay rent just for you?"

"You think?"

"Sure, I have a big apartment. You'll probably need a bigger place once the baby arrives anyway."

So, he helped me pack our things. He was right. Why spend my money on rent when Luisa was gone and I was barely home? He lived with three other guys, but we'd make it work for a few months.

Camila rolled her daughter out of her apartment in the stroller and saw us carrying my mattress. "What in the world are you doing? Are you moving?"

"Very perceptive." I leaned on the mattress to catch my breath.

"Luisa didn't say anything about moving. Why are you moving while she's gone?"

"Let me ask you something, Camila. Why is it any of your business?"

She looked baffled because she butted her nose into everyone's business, and no one said anything to her. "Maybe I'm just wondering where my friends are going. I'm speaking of Luisa, of course, not you."

I grinned. "Just trying to save some money. Plus, I'm tired of living in this dump, aren't you? I'm going to be a father. I should live in a better apartment. You guys should consider moving too if you don't go to California."

"Where?"

"I don't know. I'll think about it. I'll stop by and see Mateo soon. Or let him be a man and come to play soccer with us."

"I don't decide where he goes."

"Right."

"Let me take the baby down the elevator before you take that mattress down."

"It's not working. You have to take the stairs."

"Dammit, again?"

I nodded, then watched her pick up the stroller with Niki inside. I grabbed the stroller from her. "I'll carry the baby. You go first." So, I followed her to the first floor and placed the stroller in the lobby.

"Thanks. And let us know where you land, okay?"

"Will do."

"Let me know when Luisa gives birth and when she returns."

Camila wasn't one of my favorite people, but she was a good friend to Luisa. "I'm sure you'll be the first person she calls."

CHAPTER
FOURTEEN

November 2, 1966
Dear Salvador,

I will write a few short lines to let you know that we received your certified letter announcing when Luisa would arrive. Your brother went to Buenos Aires to wait for Aerolineas Argentina to land. They had dinner with Pedro and Maria Llonch, who are visiting Argentina and considering returning permanently. They then caught a plane to Rosario, where Luisa's sisters waited anxiously to greet them. Luisa is tired but doing well.

I've spoken with Dr. Fernandez, and he will add Luisa to his patient list. Your mother and Luisa will see him tomorrow for an initial checkup. We are covering the costs of your baby's birth, so don't worry about that.

In my previous letter, I mentioned that if you plan to return to Argentina, I have spoken to some of my contacts here about possible work. One friend said he might be able to get you a job at the U.S. Embassy in Buenos Aires. They also know of a couple of American businesses looking for employees who speak English and are familiar with the American system. They would be happy to have you. You'll just have to decide if you'd like to come back home or continue to stay in the U.S.

We send you our love and wish you well.

Your father,

Jorge

I SAT AT MATEO'S KITCHEN table, reading my dad's letter. I had to remember to send my father my new address. I was lucky I received his letter because I went back to the apartment to borrow a record from Mateo and decided to check my mailbox.

"Hey, *Flaco*, thank you. You should come and hang out with us this weekend. We're going to have a little barbeque, listen to some tangos and milongas."

"Nah, Camila doesn't like that Argentine scene much."

"Argentine? There are guys from all over, and there might even be Cubans. Plus, did she forget she's dating an Argentine? You are still Argentine, right?"

"She has to get a sitter, and it's not easy."

Camila sat in the living room sewing and could probably hear them. "I never could figure out why you want to tie yourself down to a woman with a baby?" I whispered.

"Come on. I love Niki."

"Well, if you change your mind, come. Camila will have fun."

During the week, I had little time to do anything but work. The loads I delivered were mostly local around Manhattan, Brooklyn, Queens, and Newark, but I also went as far as Trenton, which was on the border of New Jersey and Pennsylvania. Driving wasn't difficult, and it was great when I dropped a load and picked up a new one or an empty container because I got paid to go both ways. The only part I didn't like was when I had to help unload because it was exhausting..

My new roommates had different work schedules. Some stayed up late, inviting friends over and making it hard for me to sleep. But I still appreciated having company. I would have been lonely in the apartment without Luisa.

Mateo didn't come to our weekend party that night but showed up for a picnic at the park the following week and brought Camila and Niki.

We played soccer and ate empanadas and sandwiches. Drank beer and wine.

"How is your wife?" Camila asked.

"Last I heard, she's doing fine. Shit, I need to send my father my new address. Thanks for reminding me."

She rolled her eyes.

"So, you still thinking of moving to California?" I asked Mateo. Here we were, the weekend before Thanksgiving, and the temperature was still warmer than average. The cold hadn't hit yet, allowing us to enjoy this weekend in the park, but soon it would be miserably cold. I imagined it would be nice to live somewhere with mild weather.

"We've been talking about it."

"Maybe we'll go with you. For now, I'm thinking of getting a place out in West Village when Luisa comes back. You guys should move too. That way the girls can babysit for each other, and the babies can play together."

Camila laughed. "Your baby won't be ready to play for a while."

I shrugged. "Whatever."

I played soccer and drank a little too much. That night, I wrote Luisa a letter to tell her I'd moved. Told her I missed and loved her and that I couldn't wait to see her and the baby.

In the morning, I had to leave at 4 a.m. so I asked Francisco, one of the guys living with me, if he'd drop the letter off at the post office since he worked at a grocery store next to it.

"Sure, no problem."

At work, my boss called me into his office before I picked up a work slip for the day.

"Yeah?" I walked toward his desk. "You wanted to see me."

"Don't sit down. You need to get trailers back on time if you want to keep working here."

I didn't know what he was talking about.

"I got a complaint that you brought a container back late two weeks ago."

"You're upset about something that happened two weeks ago?"

He stared at me, and veins were bulging from his neck. "That's what you have to say about what I just told you?"

"I mean, I don't know what happened two weeks ago." Though I did know. That was the day the guys asked me to take their load to the harbor. I dropped the tailer, took their load, and it was too late to return my empty container, so I did it in the morning.

"I do! You didn't return the trailer until the following morning, which meant they couldn't reload it until morning, and it set them behind."

"So, what do I do about that now? I was late. I'm sorry."

He stood and ripped my work ticket out of my hand. "What you can do now is leave."

"Wait, come on. I've been a good driver. I was tired that night. I won't do it again."

"No, you won't. You can find another place to work."

Damnit. I turned and left. Great. How many times was I going to get fired?

CHAPTER FIFTEEN

January 19, 1967

Dear Salvador,

Yesterday, we received the letter you sent your brother. We opened it and read it because we were worried about you. It appears that the postal service here or there is losing a lot of letters. We wrote to you prior to the holidays on December 12th to let you know that if you wanted to join us for the Christmas holiday or New Year's, we would gladly pay for your ticket home, that way you wouldn't have to spend these special days alone. Your brother was married on January 9th, so you could have also been here for his wedding.

Sadly, we didn't hear back from you, but you were in all our thoughts, and we toasted to your health and that you have much success with your work. Your wife is due to deliver the baby at the end of January. I'll make you the same offer. We will pay for your round-trip ticket as well as Luisa's ticket back to New York if you would like, so that you can be here for the birth of your child. If you are too busy with work, we understand.

Again, I implore you to think about the work opportunities one of my acquaintances has for you. He's very interested in you and states that you can stay in the United States but represent the Republic of Argentina. Understand?

Tell me, how are things? How is your health? How is your work? Write as soon as you can.

Your father,

Jorge

JANUARY 28, 1967

Dear Salvador,

We received your letter dated the 18th of January. First, let me tell you that we don't know where to write you. We mailed the early letters to your first address, then sent letters to your new apartment to the address you sent Luisa, and you didn't seem to be receiving them. Not even your wife knows a reliable address to send letters. We sent you a telegram yesterday to announce the birth of your daughter. Her name is Julia.

We know you are busy, and your job doesn't allow you to have much free time, but you should get in the habit of writing a few lines every couple of weeks. It's good to exercise your hand and fingers.

We hope you are well and wish to hear from you soon.

We love you, son.

Your Parents

FEBRUARY 2, 1967

Dear Salvador,

On the 28th of last month, I wrote you. Who knows if you are receiving my letters? I write you again with hopes that you will receive this one.

We celebrated the holidays together but were though worried about you each time we got together. I repeat that your brother got married on the 9th of last month.

Your wife gave birth to a little girl. I am the grandfather of a little girl who looks exactly like you. Her name is Julia. She is lucky to have two mothers right now since both Luisa and your mother are doting on her. She's tiny. I still haven't held her in my arms because I'm afraid to hurt such a fragile creature. She's had many visits and presents. When she gets nervous, she screams and moves her little arms and legs. Toby is curious about her and maybe a little jealous. The other day, Luisa said he bit her diaper when the baby cried. He doesn't want her to cry. He won't leave her side.

I also mentioned in my previous letters that if you want to come visit Rosario, your mother and I are happy to pay for your ticket. If you are unable, we can leave this for another time, we understand. But as I always say, what can be accomplished today, we should never leave for tomorrow. If you're able to travel, you have an open invitation. Luisa will not be able to travel with the child until she's three or four months old. It's the airline's rule, but you can come and see her.

It's time for me to end this letter that I hope you receive in good health. We all send our love.

Your father,

Jorge

I READ THROUGH THE letters that were delivered to the wrong addresses and returned to the post office, and that they thankfully kept. Since they were international, they were not returned to sender immediately. I stopped by to ask when I hadn't heard back from my family and the postal clerk handed me the stack of letters.

I sat back in a chair in the living room, the letters scattered on my lap, tears marring my vision. I had a little girl. And here I was, living with a bunch of guys that worked long enough to pay the rent and buy cigarettes and alcohol. The place stunk.

We had a good time, but I wasn't making progress toward any goals. I was wasting my life away here. Somehow, I'd started to lose my vision, my desire to become something spectacular. Maybe, I'd started to lose faith.

I picked up my father's letter with the name of the guy who wanted to offer me a job. It wasn't clear what type of job it was, but it sounded good to work for an embassy. I dialed the number my father wrote in his letter for the Argentine Embassy.

"Hello," I said when a woman answered. "I'm calling to speak with Claudio Garay."

"Who's calling?"

"My name is Salvador. My father Jorge Moreau is a friend of his and he suggested I call him."

"Just a minute."

"Hello," a male voice came "Salvador?"

"Yes, sir. You're a friend of my father, Jorge Moreau."

"I am. Your father is a good man. I knew him back when he was a journalist."

"He's said many good things about you, and he suggested I call you about a position you might be able to offer me."

"Yes, yes. But this was the end of last year, Salvador. I was interested because you can speak both English and Spanish and I figured you were a trustworthy man given your father is such an upstanding gentleman. But unfortunately, I've filled the position since you never called—"

"I apologize. There was a mix up with the letters. I moved and . . . well, this was why I didn't call immediately."

"Listen Salvador. I'll keep you in mind for future positions, okay?"

"Sure, sure. Thank you."

I hung up and sighed. Just my luck. Shit. I'd gotten Dad's letter last November. I should have done something about it then, but I was so excited about the truck driving job.

After being fired, I lucked out since it was the holiday season and businesses needed drivers. I approached Common Market and spoke with the office manager. "I have my own truck and can work any hours you need."

She checked a large ledger book. "I can use you during the holidays to deliver meat for Swift Fresh Meat, but work might slow down after that. Is that okay?"

If it kept me working, I was fine with that. "Thank you so much!" I filled out the paperwork she gave me, and she told me to come back in the morning.

So, I worked like crazy through December. After the new year they stopped offering me work because everything slowed down, but maybe things were picking back up. I hoped so because now I had a truck to pay for and no job.

I grabbed my wallet and headed for the subway station to see if Common Market had more work.

When I got to their offices, the dispatcher fielded multiple phone calls, so I waited, smoking a cigarette and watching her work efficiently.

Finally, she looked up at me. "Sallll, ah, Salvador, right?

"Sal is fine." My friends had started calling me that. They said it was easier for Americans to say. "I'm wondering if you have any work for this week or next?"

"No, our own drivers have it covered for now, Sal. I'm sorry."

"Me too. I have a truck payment to make."

She angled her head. "Interested in selling it?"

"Selling my truck? Then how will I work?"

"The company is expanding. We're actually going to merge with Swift and buy them out. We're going to buy a few more trucks for our fleet."

"I don't know. I'm thinking of hitting up a few other trucking companies."

"Okay, well, it's an idea if you get stuck with truck payments and no work. We'd give you a little money for it and buy out your contract."

"I'll think about it. Thank you."

That night Mateo and Camila came over to have dinner with us. Another Argentine guy bought sandwiches and beer, and we sat around chatting about soccer. Camila looked bored, but I told her Luisa and the baby were thriving, surrounded by our family, who constantly spoiled them both.

"Ah, a girl! You were so sure it was going to be a boy."

"The next," I said and smiled. "Hopefully, Luisa will be back in a couple of months."

"When are you going to get out of this shithole?" Camila asked. "Seriously, this is a pigsty."

I shrugged. "It's cheap. But, as soon as I get more work for the truck, I'll start looking for a new place."

"They need a painter at the building where I'm washing windows," Mateo said.

"Painting again? Naw, I can make so much more driving."

"When you work," Camila said. "Think about your wife and baby."

"Look, you don't have to tell me to think about my family, alright?" I was tired of listening to her mouth.

"Somebody does."

Mateo placed a hand on her leg. "*Mami*, let him figure it out. *Mirá, Loco*, if you want the job, come on by. Maybe you work for a few months, then go back to driving. At least then you can make your truck payments and get your apartment, huh?"

I nodded. Maybe Mateo was right. If I sold the truck, Common Market would pay off my loan, and it would help build my credit. Then when business improved, I could buy another truck and create my own trucking company.

February 10, 1967

Querido *Papá*,

With much enthusiasm, I read in a cut-out of *El Clarín* newspaper that my brother sent me that our boys beat *los Canallas*. Reading the article about the game in Spanish and the commentaries was truly gratifying. I also collected a group of your letters from the post office dating back to last January. You might have written some in December that I never received. My old landlord might have thrown them out, or maybe the post office returned them to you.

In each letter, you underscored the depth of your paternal love, and the more I read those words you wrote to me, the more shame I felt for my ungrateful behavior and attitude. I must admit that my situation the last few months has not been ideal, and I've been lost in the overwhelm of life, but I have not reached a point where I am desperate and ready to give up on my dreams. After you visited us, I left my painting job and decided to dedicate myself to this new trucking venture. But I'm coming to realize that my efforts have been in vain.

It appears that I have the opportunity to return to painting which is a more secure type of employment. I will have to begin from scratch and at the bottom again, but thanks to a friend, I will start work next week. Luisa can fly back anytime she's ready and when the airlines allow the baby to fly.

Thank you for all that you've done for us. I don't know how to repay your kindness. I fear that I will never be able to do so appropriately.

You son,

Salvador

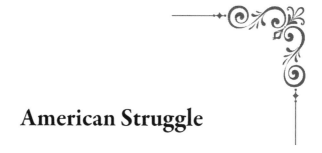

American Struggle

Inside each of us, there is the seed of both good and evil. It's a constant struggle as to which one will win. And one cannot exist without the other. — Eric Burdon

CHAPTER SIXTEEN

Holding your child for the first time is an overwhelming glorious joy that I wasn't sure I would be fortunate to feel. Since I wasn't really all that curious about my baby girl, I had started to think something was wrong with me as a man. I enjoyed reading letters from my father telling me how grateful he'd been to be there for Julia's birth and how blessed he felt watching her grow and develop the first few months of her life. He described in minute details her daily changes as if he lamented that I was missing it all. He made braggadocios claims of her being the cutest baby in all of South America. This brought a smile to my face. Still, I wasn't eager to meet my baby. I felt happy that my father was pleased and that he got to spend these moments with his first grandchild, but that was the extent of my emotions.

Maybe a part of me was unsure about being a father. I'm nothing like my own father. I feel that in many ways, I'm still growing up. What do I have to offer a child?

But after picking Luisa and Julia up at the airport and taking a taxi to our new apartment, one I found in Greenwich Village, not far from Jackson Square, Luisa sat on the couch to feed little Julia. I watched them both, and a feeling of tenderness filled my heart. The baby enjoyed drinking her bottle and stared at her mother with such focus and love.

My father was right, she did look a little like me. When Julia finished the bottle, Luisa burped her, then sat her on her lap. "Come here," she said.

I sat beside them, and Luisa placed Julia on my lap.

"Just be careful with her head and neck."

I smiled and held her. "Well, look at you," I said. "Don't you know you were supposed to be a boy?"

Luisa slapped my shoulder. "Don't say that."

I laughed. "What am I going to do with a girl, huh?"

Julia watched me and moved her arms. I brought her closer to my face, and her little hands touched my chin without purpose, just randomly, and it looked like she smiled. She made little gurgling sounds. At four months old, she still seemed tiny.

"I guess your dad will have to teach you to play soccer like a boy," I said.

She cooed and made her lips tremble, widening her eyes as if trying to figure out who I was and what I was saying. I laughed and handed her back to Luisa. "I bought her a little crib like you asked for in your letter. I put it in the bedroom next to our bed."

"She slept a lot on the flight. I'll just hold her for a little while."

"I also bought this. Well, actually Camila suggested it and said she didn't have hers anymore, but that you'd want one." I went to the bedroom and came back with the contraption. "It's a little portable seat or rocker or something. The baby can sit there and be safe while you do what you need to do around the house."

"Wonderful!" Luisa said and placed Julia into the little seat that cupped the baby. "It's a little infant bouncer. Yes, I'll need that. I brought a baby carriage. I hope it didn't break on the journey."

I was shocked at all the stuff she had for the baby. She left with one suitcase and returned with three of them and a giant crate which must be the baby carriage. "You could have left those things and bought them here."

"No, your parents insisted I bring them, especially the carriage. They bought it for me."

I looked at the baby; she seemed content in the bouncer, reaching for plastic rings and kicking her legs. "Well, okay. I guess we're ready for round two." I took one of Luisa's hands and pulled her up against me. I wrapped my arms around her waist.

"What's round two?"

"Life as parents. Maybe we'd better start thinking of a permanent home, huh?" I nuzzled her neck. I'd missed holding her.

"Eventually. Or returning to Argentina. We still have the land we bought. If we save, we can build a nice home there."

I released her and sighed. "We're not ready for that yet."

"We can be. Your parents miss you, and your mom cried when we left. Before Julia was born, I stayed with my sisters, but after, they insisted we stay with them. They both were amazing with Julia, and she should grow up with family, with her grandparents."

I stepped back, drawing a breath and feeling the tension returning in my neck and back that had been there all day. "And she will. But not yet. If you wanted to stay there, you could have, you know. You didn't have to come back."

Luisa's eyes widened. "Where is that coming from? Of course, I wanted to come back."

"Well, it doesn't fucking sound like it. Julia should grow up with her father, not her grandparents."

Luisa nodded, looking tired all of a sudden. "I'd like her to grow up with both." She stood and placed a hand on my cheek. "I love New York, don't get me wrong. I'm starting to feel torn. Part of me loved being back home where people know me and I'm loved."

"You're loved here."

"Let me finish. And the other part loves being here where we're building a future together, even though it's an unsure future full of obstacles and we're all alone. It's still exciting and full of promise."

I ran a hand through my hair and eased back. I pulled a cigarette from a pack of Marlboros on the coffee table, grabbed the lighter, and cupped my hand to light it. I inhaled a couple of times, letting the tobacco have its calming effect as I watched my wife. Then I went to the refrigerator to get some Swiss cheese, prosciutto ham, butter and bread. "I'm going to make a sandwich, you want one?" I called out to Luisa. When she didn't respond, I peeked out of the kitchen doorway.

She nodded.

"I don't know where Julia is going to have a better life," I admitted, blowing out smoke. "But I think . . . I hope, I'm making the right choice for now by staying here. I need you to stand by me, though."

"Haven't I always?"

I stared at her, she in the living room beside the baby, me at the kitchen door jamb. Life was hard in America. Harder than I ever thought it would be, and I'd have to become harder too if I was going to survive and succeed. I hoped she was ready for this newer version of me.

MY NEW JOB AFTER SELLING my truck was painting office buildings where Mateo washed windows. He put in a good word for me, and they hired me immediately. Working at the same location allowed us to travel to work together. Sometimes, I'd see him 50 stories or more off the ground. It was crazy, and something I couldn't do. Although, painting again made my back ache, at least I wasn't risking my life.

They kept us going at top speed. Unlike the hotel owner where I'd worked before, the corporation that owned the office buildings didn't care about quality. These were offices, so if the rooms were clean and freshly painted, the maintenance manager was happy. We worked one building at a time without a guarantee of continued work, but for now, I had a job.

When I got home, Luisa had dozens of stories about everything the baby had done. I found out how often Julia ate or pooped and how many hours she slept. Luisa was a great mom and loved her new role.

On Friday, Camila and her daughter were visiting. Just the person I wanted to see when I got home from work. "Where's Mateo?" I asked her. I didn't see him when I left work.

"He's going to stop by later. He said he's going to take a shower and have a nap."

"And you couldn't wait for your man, huh?"

She narrowed her eyes. "Your wife and I are catching up. I'm telling her about all the fun we had visiting your bachelor pad while she was giving birth to your child."

Camila was a real bitch, and if I didn't like Mateo as much as I did, I'd kick her ass out and tell her never to come back. I ignored the comment that was intended to rile me up. I picked up little Julia and held her up over my head.

Both women jumped up.

"Her head, *bruto*!" Camila yelled.

But Julia smiled. She was strong and had no problem holding her head up, but I gently lowered her to my chest. "You like that, don't you?" She was a good baby, hardly ever cried unless she was hungry. I kissed the top of her head and put her back in her seat. "I'm going to go shower."

When Mateo got there, we had dinner. Luisa made delicious spinach cannelloni in white sauce. Then we sat at the table to play canasta. Both babies slept. Niki entertained Julia with rattles for a while, then she lay on the couch with a bottle and fell asleep.

"I'm looking into getting a place in this building too," Mateo said.

"You should," I replied. "I like this area." The West Village had a better vibe than anywhere we'd lived before. I felt comfortable and more at home here.

"I took the baby for a stroll yesterday and liked it too," Luisa said. "There seem to be some interesting cafes and bars."

Mateo leaned closer and kissed Camila. "Let's move next month if we can get an apartment in the building. What do you say?"

"If you want to pack all our stuff and move again, I'll move. But be careful this time. I don't want my things broken."

"The rents are better here too," I said. "Well, now that *that's* been decided, I'm going to kick you guys out of our apartment. I'm exhausted." Luisa seemed tired too. The baby was good about sleeping most of the night but still woke us up at least once.

"Yeah, I'm tired too," Mateo said. After hugs and kisses, they were gone.

As we were getting ready for bed, Luisa handed me a photo.

"I forgot to show you her baptism picture."

I looked down at my tiny daughter getting baptized, Luisa's sister holding her as a priest held his hand over my baby's head, probably dropping holy water on her forehead, and a sudden rage bubbled up inside me. The muscles in my arms tightened, and I clenched my fingers around the 8½ by 11 size picture and tore it in half.

"What are you doing?" Luisa yelled, grabbing the two halves of the picture.

"Why didn't you *ask* me before baptizing her?"

"Ask you? You were here, and I was in Argentina. Your parents and my sister were all there. Why wouldn't I baptize her?"

"You know how I feel about religion and the Catholic church."

She stared at me with her mouth open. "We got married at a Catholic church. What are you talking about?"

"Because it's what *you* wanted!" I shouted. "I didn't want that. Those hypocritical priests judging us, that idiot making us beg him to marry us. Shit." They use a man's love for his wife to force him into that farce. Who needs them?

"I can't believe you tore her picture," Luisa cried. "Our baby."

"I didn't tear up the baby. She's sleeping right over there. Stop this idiotic crying."

She glared at me, grabbed her pillow, and headed to the living room.

"Where are you going?"

"To get away from you."

"Well, that's great." I plopped into bed, cussing out religion, the saints, and the entire church, too angry to sleep. I turned on my side and closed my eyes, trying to rest. Then the baby started crying. "Ugh, she's crying!"

Luisa ignored me. I put the pillow over my ears. In a few minutes, the crying stopped, and I heard Luisa talking to the baby in the living room. I sighed and, after a while, calmed down enough to fall asleep.

IN THE MORNING WHEN I woke up, Luisa slept on the couch with the baby nestled beside her, looking like a little angel. I reached across and caressed the top of her little head. I then toasted a piece of bread and heated coffee on the stove. I ate alone at the kitchen table.

Maybe I shouldn't have torn the picture. I overreacted, but I couldn't control myself. Julia was my baby too. They should have asked me. As I was getting ready to leave, Luisa woke up. She placed the baby in the bouncer and didn't say good morning.

"Hey," I said. "I forgive you, okay? You do what you want with this baby. If you want her raised a Catholic, so be it. But the next baby is mine. No baptism. No church. Understand?"

"Next baby? You're a bastard," she said and disappeared into the bathroom.

I shook my head, grabbing my wallet, my cigarettes, and my sunglasses. She needed time to cool down, and I had to get to work.

Three days later, she still wasn't talking to me.

CHAPTER SEVENTEEN

August 3, 1967
    Querido Salvador,

As I write this letter, I ask you to forgive me for taking so long to get in touch. I've felt terrible lately. I haven't felt like going out, working, writing, or doing anything physical or intellectual. I'm sure Luisa noticed while she was here that I've become worthless. But that is life when one ages.

Even your dog is showing signs of aging. He's ten years old now. Like us, he wasn't happy that Luisa and Julia left. He searched for the baby everywhere and walked into every room in the restaurant, searching and sniffing her bed. Finally, he lay beside me with a sigh. And there we sat, two old men with nothing to do but sit with our memories.

Moving on to happier matters, now that you have a daughter, if you'd like to return and start your own business here of any kind, I remind you that you have people here that can help you. Being isolated, separated from one's roots for too long, can damage a man's psyche. I mentioned it to Luisa, and she didn't seem excited about the idea of returning, but maybe she didn't want to agree to anything without speaking to you first.

I know you, Salvadorito, and you can be too proud or pigheaded to return home and ask for help. No one is expecting you to return as William the Conqueror. In other words, stay to achieve your goals if they are important to you, but don't stay to prove something to us. Your friends and family don't care if you return a wealthy or poor man, only that you return as the man we love.

That's all I'm going to say about that.

Take good care of our granddaughter, you hear me?

Your father,

Jorge

MATEO AND I TOOK A lunch break in the lobby of the building where we worked, eating a sandwich Mateo picked up from an Argentine market.

"The market owner's name is Lorenzo. He was from Buenos Aires, but he's been in New York about ten years," Mateo said. "I told him about you, and he invited us to his house after work. You want to go?"

"To do what?"

"Meet him. Get to know another Argentine. Apparently, he has made good money with his business. Could be a good connection, right?"

I shrugged. "Well, he makes good sandwiches." I put the last bite in my mouth and stood. "I want to go home and shower and change first."

"What about the girls?" Mateo picked up all his trash and took mine as well.

They really enjoyed living in Greenwich Village. The electric vibe of streets filled with young people always protesting or celebrating something, carrying signs, blasting music from their car speakers, or walking the streets in colorful outfits made living there exciting. While San Francisco was having their summer of love, here in the Westside, we had our own milder version, even if it wasn't quite the same. Regardless, Julia was almost nine months old now, and Luisa took her everywhere in her baby carriage. "I don't think Luisa will want to go."

"I mean, will she be upset if you come home and leave again right away?"

"No, why would she care? She usually waits to eat dinner with me, but I'm not hungry after that sandwich. I'll tell her to go ahead and eat and not wait for me."

SINCE HE OPENED IT in the late 1950s, Lorenzo's business thrived, but he worked long hours. His apartment was on the Westside too, but it was nice, not full of trash like where we lived. As always, when I met guys like this and like Carlos, who owns the Spanish restaurant I worked at when I got here, my mind began to spin. How did they do it? And if they did it, I can too.

"Nice to meet you," he said and shook my hand. "Mateo tells me you're a painter."

"No, I'm not a painter. I have a job as a painter."

Lorenzo laughed. "Same thing, no?"

I shook my head. "Of course not. I don't define myself by my job. But I'm doing it while I wait for something better to come along." We sat in his nice-sized living room covered with hardwood floors, a dark blue area rug, and luxurious furniture made of soft leather and mahogany wood.

"You can't wait, Salvador. You have to hustle in this country, or you'll get left behind."

I pulled out my pack of Marlboros and offered him one. He shook his head but motioned for me to go ahead. Mateo declined too. "I always work hard," I said, lighting my cigarette.

"Sometimes it's not about working hard. A group of us Argentines meet at a parrilla in town once a month. It's a good place to network. You both should come."

"Sure."

"My brother takes care of the import/export part of my business, and I don't have to worry about that much. It took him a while to learn, but now he's doing well. We get regular products from Argentina." A lady brought us some wine and a cheese platter. "This is my wife, Marla."

We stood and thanked her, greeting her Argentine style, a kiss on both cheeks.

"Anyhow, Mateo tells me it's been a struggle for you. He's doing okay as a window washer, but you haven't found your thing yet, so I thought it might benefit you to meet other Argentine families at our gatherings."

"I appreciate that. We'll definitely go."

"And maybe you'd be willing to paint my store? Just the outside. It needs an update."

Ah, the reason for this visit. But was he offering me work, or did he think a plate of cheese and wine meant I'd work for free? I shrugged and put my cigarette out on an ashtray. "Of course. Get the paint you want, and I'll stop by one weekend and get it done for you."

We chatted a while longer about Argentina and soccer and enjoyed the wine and cheese. Lorenzo shook my hand and patted my upper arm as we said our goodbyes. "Stop by the store, and I'll show you what I need painted and give you the address of the parrilla where we meet."

OVER THE NEXT FEW MONTHS, Luisa and I met people from the Argentine community, and it felt like I was home among other Argentines. We met an Argentine dentist, pediatrician, accountant, all professional, well-spoken men with status who reminded me of my father. Luisa socialized and responded politely, she was even friendly while at the restaurant, but at home, she told me she didn't care to keep going. "Those people are fake," she said.

I wasn't exactly sure what she meant.

"They all want something from you."

"From me? I have nothing to give anyone. It's called networking. It's good to be among important people." Though that wasn't exactly true. I ended up working all weekend painting the outside of Lorenzo's store in light blue and white like the Argentine flag, and he sent me home with a tray of sandwiches and a case of wine, hardly enough pay for my time. But to be fair, he gave me a bag of groceries every time he saw me, claiming he'd ordered extra that week.

Luisa caressed my back. "What makes them important? That they have money or a profession? You're just as important, Salvador. Those people don't impress me."

I pushed her hand away. She didn't understand. I didn't care about their money. Luisa lacked the sophistication to see the importance of connecting with people of influence. Sometimes, I went to the *parrilla* without her and explained that my wife had to stay home with the baby.

I met one of Lorenzo's workers, Edmundo, who was a sharp, friendly guy. We started to hang out. I liked him, but he did tell me he sometimes "borrowed" some of Lorenzo's products and sold them on the side. He offered me a half dozen tubs of dulce de leche one time.

"Awe, come on man, Lorenzo is a good guy," I said. "Don't steal from him."

"Of course he is, but it's fine. His brother wouldn't mind. He's honestly a bit of an idiot and doesn't know what he's doing. I have to help him all the time; otherwise, Lorenzo wouldn't profit at all. Taking some product is a way to pay me back for correcting his brother's mistakes. Lorenzo keeps him around because that's what you do for your brother. These are losses that Lorenzo writes off, so it doesn't hurt him at all. Here, take the dulce de leches."

I took one jar and felt guilty. "This is enough. I'm telling you, I don't want to take anything from Lorenzo."

"Suit yourself."

But aside from this quirk of Edmundo's that made me uncomfortable, I had a blast with him. Mateo and I hung out with him when we weren't working. He got us into professional soccer and baseball games. We ate for free at many restaurants because he knew the owners. Every weekend was a party with Edmundo.

We were on our way to a jazz club in Harlem one night, and I brought Luisa since I thought she'd enjoy it. Camila watched Julia for us. Since I ran out of cigarettes, I jumped out in a sketchy part of town, but I figured I'd run into the small market and run back out.

But when I walked in, I realized a couple of black guys with guns were robbing the place.

"Hey, I'll just leave."

"Naw, you stay." They pushed me up against a wall, the back of my head bouncing against it. "Take out your wallet."

I was momentarily dazed, but I shook my head. "I don't want any trouble." I glanced at the market owner behind the cash register, where the other guy held a gun to his head, yelling at him to empty the register.

"Your wallet," the one with his hand on my shoulder shouted at me.

I don't know what came over me, maybe I just don't like people shouting in my face, but I kicked the guy in the balls. The other one swung his arm around and pointed the gun at me. I lifted my hands in surrender, immediately thinking that I'd fucked up. The guy I kicked recovered and reached for my neck, squeezing the life out of me. Futilely, I pulled on his arms and gasped for breath.

Over his shoulder, I saw Edmundo walk in. Like a football player, he ran forward and with his shoulder, he pushed and knocked over a display case. It fell on the guy with the gun. Then he grabbed a broom and used the stick like a baseball bat at the guy strangling me, connecting with his skull, making him release my neck as he fell to the floor.

"Come on," he said, and we ran out. A part of me worried about the store owner, but if he was smart, he'd run out too or call the police.

We ran as fast as we could and jumped into Edmundo's car.

"What happened?" Luisa asked when we got back, panting, completely out of breath, and unable to talk. "You were taking so long that Edmundo and I got worried."

"There were two *hijos de putas* robbing the place," I said.

"They had your husband up against a wall choking him," Edmundo shared as he started the car and screeched away from the curb.

"Oh my God, are you okay?" She looked at my neck, touching my cheeks and chin.

I nodded, but the adrenaline in my body still made my heart race.

"There is so much crime and craziness going on—protests and trash everywhere. I like the stores and music and some of the people in the village, but it's dangerous too, Salvador. One of our neighbors, a Puerto Rican lady, yelled at me for walking the baby on the wrong side of the street. She told me I was on the black side and had to stay on the Puerto Rican side. What kind of nonsense is that? No one was bothering me."

"I don't know," I said, still a little shaken. We didn't have these racial problems in Argentina. "Let's just go have a good time, huh?"

We picked up Edmundo's girlfriend and drove to the club. We ended up having a great time, and as we retold the story, it started to seem funny. "Edmundo was crazy. You should have seen him! Pushing the shelves, swinging that stick. Pow! Bam! Those guys didn't know what hit them."

But I thought that maybe Luisa was right, and the West side had gotten a bit too rough for us to raise a baby. Luckily the gun hadn't gone off as the guy went down under the shelf full of cans and boxes of food. Maybe we should move again before there was a next time when I wasn't so lucky, or it was Luisa who got robbed or attacked.

I DIDN'T HAVE TIME to look for a new apartment. And besides, I had almost finished painting the office building, and the company said it would be the last one for a while. They were going to lay me off for a few months, so I didn't want to make a move until I found a new job.

Edmundo came over one Saturday. We were going to watch TV and eat snacks and relax as Luisa made pasta for dinner. I told him about the job situation. "I think I'm going to go back to trucking. The business seems to be getting better. Less product is going by rail, and more is being moved by trucks.

"You know Lorenzo works with companies that import international products. I can help you get a job. In fact, I'll talk to his brother. You won't even need your own truck. You'll use their company truck."

"The import companies?"

"Right. And we can arrange for some of the trailers to get 'lost' sometimes or broken into to make a little cash on the side."

"We can?"

"Sure. The insurance covers the loss of product. We'll sell it and —"

"What are you proposing to my husband?" Having walked into the room unnoticed, Luisa stood at the edge of the couch with a frown on her face.

He stood, glanced at me, and nervously smiled. "Luisa, it's just business."

"It's crooked business, and you're not going to get my husband involved in that kind of thing."

"Luisa," I warned.

"No, you have a child. How can you even think of doing something like that?"

"I haven't thought about it. I haven't done anything. Calm down."

"I'd like you to leave, Edmundo."

"Come on, Luisa," I said.

"No, it's okay," he said. "I'm sorry. I didn't mean to offend you," he said to Luisa. "I'll talk to you later."

I turned to her, enraged. "Who the hell do you think you are to kick my friend out of *my* house?"

"Who do I think I am? Your wife! And you'd better start remembering it. I don't like these friends you've made and hang out with all the time."

"You don't like anyone!"

"Look, Salvador. I'm not going to be married to someone dishonest."

"It's how business is done, the way people get ahead in this country. What do you think happened to our car a few years ago?"

She looked baffled. "You said it was stolen."

"Javier and I made it look like it was stolen, so the insurance would pay it off. We would have been screwed if I hadn't done that. The bank would have made us pay for a car they repossessed and didn't even own. It was the only way, and my friends, the ones you don't like, saved my ass."

"I can't believe this." She placed a hand on her forehead and paced. "I don't want to hear it." Then she stopped and stood centimeters from my face. "Promise me that you'll never do anything like that again."

"Luisa, I —"

"Promise!"

I stared at her.

"This isn't who you are. Is this the person you came here to become?"

I swallowed a lump in my throat and felt like I'd been socked in the stomach. Then I shook my head.

"Good." She sighed. "Stop hanging around those men. Just stop. They're no good, Salvador. You're not like them."

"Okay," I said. She was right. There had to be better ways to succeed. Nothing was working, but there had to be an honest way.

OCTOBER 8, 1967

Dear *Papá*,

I have to admit that in my haste and excitement to meet my daughter and hold her in my arms, I didn't even consider the pain that losing her might have caused you and *Mamá*. I'm sure it lifted your spirits to have both Luisa and Julia living with you for a few months. She told me how you insisted she move in instead of returning to her sister's house after Julia was born. She was glad she did because it made you and *Mamá* so happy.

I'll share, however, that I'm completely in love with the little girl. She was quiet and so well-behaved when she first arrived. But she has gotten used to her new living quarters and can now stand in her crib and run around in her walker. She talks to herself in a language that only babies understand. When I get home from work, she demands that I pick her up, and if I don't, she starts to cry. So, I think she's in love too. She definitely has my nervous personality and character. When Luisa tries to feed her and she's full, she hits her hand away, tossing food all over the place and complains. Honestly, it makes me laugh.

I hope you are feeling better. It saddens me to hear that you about your lack of interest in going out or doing anything, especially since you were always so active. But it's understandable; you've been through a lot in the past few years.

As far as starting a business in Argentina, it's not something that will happen soon. Luisa didn't tell me that you'd discussed it, but she did suggest that we might think of moving back. It will happen, but the time is not right yet. I hope that you understand.

Take care of yourself and give my love to *Mamá*.

Your son,
Salvador

CHAPTER EIGHTEEN

April 15, 1968
Dear Salvador,

I hope this letter finds you well and that our little princess is happy and healthy. We see from the last pictures you sent that she gets more beautiful each day.

The other day we received letters from you written in January, February and March. We got four letters all at once. Our postal service must be deteriorating along with the rest of the country.

I'll share with you that from November of last year to March of this year, our business has suffered a considerable upheaval, and there's been a lot of commotion from the changes happening in society. This month we've experienced a complete stand-still caused by strikes which will most likely last the rest of the year. Workers, employees, and small businesses like ours are affected by deteriorating economic conditions. Even getting goods like Coca-Cola or condiments to serve customers has become increasingly difficult.

On top of that, the government has dissolved previous tenant/landlord law, and we had to either close the business or sign a new agreement that only benefits the landlord. We will find it challenging to meet the terms of the contract, but we hope that things will turn around and we will be able to maintain the business and keep it open.

Watching the news from over there, I see that you all are having your own protests and problems. What is going on with the racial tensions and riots? I hope that you are safe and not affected by the violence.

To give you some good news, your brother's wife is pregnant and will soon give us our second grandchild. We will let you know if it will be a boy or a girl. We think of and miss little Julia every day and lament that she is growing up without us. The pictures you and Luisa send help us to feel a little closer to her.

We send you our love and hope that you are doing well.

Your father

Jorge

AS SHE WATCHED THE news, Luisa picked up teething toys and rattles from the carpet, where Julia tossed them when she was no longer interested in playing with them. Luisa started watching more TV to try to learn English. Her favorite show was the soap opera *Dark Shadows*. But today, she watched ABC news. I sat at a small desk I'd placed in the living room, trying to think of what to write my father.

Then Luisa screamed and dropped all the toys in her hands. Julia seemed just as startled as I was and stared wide-eyed at her mother.

"What's the matter?" I asked and walked over, glancing at the TV to see what had captured her attention.

"They just shot Kennedy."

"Kennedy?" I turned the knob for the volume and watched the mass of people calmly making their way out of the Ambassador Hotel lobby, then the image of Howard K. Smith, the newscaster announced that Senator Robert Kennedy had been shot and that they weren't sure how serious his injuries were.

I sat on the edge of the couch and listened to the reporter go over what had happened. There was a lot of confusion, and the media weren't exactly clear why Kennedy had been targeted, but those in attendance had apprehended a suspect.

Luisa and I watched the news for about two hours, listening to more and more reports, needing to learn every minute detail, as if understanding what happened would help us comprehend this senseless, violent act. The reporters interviewed people in the room with the senator and in the lobby, and each person shared what they'd seen or heard. The witnesses talked about the blood on Kennedy's face, and for a while, no one knew if he was alive or dead. Even after hours of reporting, they were unsure if Kennedy would survive the attack, but he was still alive. He had been taken to the hospital and was in surgery.

I turned the TV off and paced in front of the TV for a moment. "They tried to kill another Kennedy."

"It's terrible," Luisa said, shaking her head.

I remembered my shock when President John F. Kennedy was killed. All the hope wrapped up in that presidency had been shattered in an instant. My excitement at hearing his inauguration speech turned into grief. The reason I was in New York at all had so much to do with President Kennedy's vision of the world, a vision that touched me deep inside and called out to me. Now, I dropped back down on the couch and rubbed my face. Since that time, the vision of America seemed to have vanished. The war in Vietnam grew worse every year. Riots and racial tension in the streets, and war protests were common. I was hoping to vote for Robert Kennedy for President to see if he could fix the craziness of the last few years. Would I get that opportunity?

We went to bed sad that night, probably like many Americans. This time, I wasn't an Argentine boy, a world away. Four years later, I was here, an American, part of this country, so different from the young man I used to be in many ways. But also the same inside. I still had my dreams and goals, and though it wasn't as easy as I had expected, I still hoped to find that elusive key to success. It was here, in this country, I felt it in my soul. I just had to locate it.

When we got up the following day, we turned on the news and learned that Senator Robert Kennedy had died early that morning in California. Tears filled my eyes. I grabbed my truck keys and wallet and looked at my typewriter, where I had never finished writing my father. I tore the paper out, crumpled it, and threw it in the trash. All the happy, positive crap I had written seemed like nonsense. We lived in a cruel, violent society. I felt that America was no longer a nation filled with innocent optimism and might never return to what it had once been.

I kissed Luisa and looked at Julia, who sat strapped in her highchair, ready to eat her cereal. What kind of world would she inherit, and did it matter which country I raised her in? When a giant went down, those in the shadows were also crushed.

ALTHOUGH LUISA DIDN'T want me to remain friends with Edmundo, and I honored my promise to distance myself from him, I still enjoyed attending the Argentine gatherings. As I sat at a round table discussing the state of the world and financial opportunities, one of the men there said he planned to sell his gas station, and if any of us were interested, he'd give us a break on the cost of the business.

This caught my attention. The opportunity to have my own business rather than relying on someone else appealed strongly to my entrepreneurial spirit.

"It's small," the business owner said. "It only has four gas pumps, a service garage, and a small store. But for someone willing to work hard, it's got great possibilities."

"Why are you selling it?" I asked.

Some of the other men, all older than I was, looked at me, and one patted my back. "This might be great for you, Sal. You're young and smart."

The gas station owner said, "I'm just getting older and don't want to work so hard. In this type of business, an owner needs to keep the place up, and it can get exhausting. If you were to buy it, you'd have to hire workers to be there when you can't and to work in the store ordering supplies, stocking, and selling items to customers. You might want to hire a mechanic for the shop. You'll be busy dealing with suppliers. I buy my products and gas from American Oil Company."

All of that didn't sound like work; it sounded like an opportunity to have my own business, something that was mine. "Where is it?"

"It's in Copiague, Long Island."

"Can I go see it?"

"Of course, stop by anytime this week."

The other men congratulated me even though I hadn't decided yet. They all said this could be a wise investment and encouraged me to take a chance. "You're young. What do you have to lose?" they asked. Good question. I didn't know.

Later that week, when I had a break from work, I drove to Long Island to see about this gas station. The small building looked sort of run down.

"I haven't had the time to keep it up," he admitted. "I'm getting older, and I'm tired," he repeated. "But a young man like you can get it all shiny and perfect again."

"Yeah, maybe," I agreed.

"Sure, and you've got a built-in customer base and money rolling in. You just have to do some physical work and bring your ideas and effort."

"How much will I need to put down?"

"It won't be much. As long as you can get credit from the bank, you'll be fine."

Though excited, I decided to talk to Luisa to get her opinion. When I bought the car and truck, she resented that I'd decided on my own.

"Would you have to use all our savings to start this business?"

"Yes and sign some contracts with American Oil and the banks."

"It's risky."

"Well, we came here to take some risks, right?"

She looked worried, and glanced at the baby playing with plastic keys on the carpet. Then she smiled. "Do what you think is best."

I rushed to her and hugged her, picking her up off the ground. She laughed, and I kissed her. "I'm so excited about this."

"I can tell. Now, I made some *milanesas* with mashed potatoes. Are you hungry?"

"Starving!"

We ate and discussed the possible success of the business and how we would finally be able to reach our dreams of making real money for the future.

July 29, 1968

Dear *Papá*,

I hope that things have gotten better in Argentina. I can get news from Argentina easier now since an Argentine market sells the *El Clarín* newspaper. The paper is about a week old, but it's recent enough. It appears that the political situation is stabilizing—as much as it can, I suppose. I understand your desire to keep the restaurant open, but maybe it's time to consider closing it and retiring so that *Mamá* doesn't have to work so hard.

I have some good news! I am now the proud owner of a gasoline station. I was presented with an opportunity to buy my own station, and Luisa and I decided it was a shot we had to take.

But let me tell you that all good news has a flip side. I've been working like an animal for the last four months. The seller promised I'd take over an established business, but it wasn't true. I had to invest practically all my money to get the station up and running. As far as customers, I didn't have any since the previous owner kept the station closed most of the time.

So, I've gotten the station running to start bringing money in while I fix it up, but I gradually went more and more in debt the first two months. But finally, in the last month and a half, things are looking up. I've started getting regular customers and making some money.

Inspectors from American Oil Company came to see the station last week and were so impressed that I'd gotten the station in working condition so quickly that they offered me a second station. It is bigger and has six pumps instead of four. Considering that money has done nothing but fly out of my pockets with this station, I don't know if I should believe the pretty picture they're painting about a larger gas station. I think it might be best to stick with this one for now. I'm tired of getting burned by others; I'm learning it's the American way to take advantage of other people. I don't want to be the type of person who doesn't trust or have faith in others, but when it comes to business, no one is honest.

Your granddaughter is big and chubby. She's over a year and a half now, can walk and dance, and has taken control of the house. She loves all her toys, especially a little blue and white tugboat that she takes into the bathtub. She's the happiest little girl in the world, and I'm the luckiest father.

I send you a fierce hug and kiss for both you and *Mamá*.

Your son,

Salvador

CHAPTER
NINETEEN

October 2, 1968
     Dear Son,

We received your last three letters. Forgive me for not writing sooner. Lately, I feel like one of those toy tops that goes round and round aimlessly but gets nowhere, and it's difficult for me to write. I was supposed to travel to Buenos Aires to see a friend off to Europe. His first stop is Germany. But I couldn't go because of the repeated blisters I've gotten on my skin, all issues related to my diabetes, as always.

Congratulations on your new business. I pray that God helps and guides you with this new opportunity. I've been thinking that it might benefit you to trade your current gasoline station for a larger one, but it's something you have to debate in your mind. You might also want to consider side services that you can offer, like a tow truck for cars that have problems on the road. All these extra services can bring in money while you are growing the business.

You might also consider hiring a lawyer to handle all the paperwork. You mention that it's the American way to take advantage of others, but I'll argue that it's the human way. There are opportunists there, here, everywhere, and it's in your best interest to protect yourself.

The thing to remember Salvadorito is that good decisions bring us joy, while bad ones or mistakes, as you know, depress us and attack our mental state, lower our morale. These negative emotional states are worse than losing material things because we start to lose faith in our own abilities to make choices. But always remember that there is a solution for every problem, so think carefully before you act, and you will always have more joy.

Lastly, I'll remind you that you always have our support. If despite all your efforts, you find that things are not going as you wish, you can always come to live and work in Argentina. You might not live as well as you do there, but you will survive and be with those who love you. Understood?

Your brother may have written you with the good news that he had a little boy. I now have a grandson as well as a granddaughter. What a blessing I've been given.

Kisses and hugs for all three of you. Your mother and I wish you luck.

Your father,

Jorge

I READ THE LETTER IN bed at one in the morning, then reached across and dropped it on my nightstand. Luisa and Julia slept. I was exhausted but couldn't fall asleep. I'd been working at the station eighteen, sometimes twenty hours a day, barely breaking even. Some weeks, I still lost money.

The problem was that I didn't have enough savings to wait for the station to make money. I tossed and turned and finally, I got out of bed at 4 a.m., got a cup of coffee and piece of toast, then left.

I drove back to the station to open it in time for the early risers. It wasn't easy to stay awake without sleep, but I kept busy. I took delivery of a couple of cases of Coca-Cola and a few snacks, potato chips, and candy. I didn't carry as much food in my tiny store as I could because I didn't want to lose more money. Sales of those items were few and didn't have a high margin.

During the afternoon, I closed and went to meet with the Argentine group. The man who sold me the gas station retired and moved to the suburbs. Bastard. Coward.

One of my friends, Juan Paredes and I sat drinking coffee.

"You really look terrible," he said.

"I don't know how I'm going to pay next month's rent on the gas station. I'm just not clearing enough, and I don't have more of my own savings to sink into it."

"I can lend you a few dollars, and you can pay me back when you start making money."

"I appreciate that, but . . ." I brushed my hair back and slumped in my chair. "I wasn't telling you this to get money out of you. Who knows when I will be in a position to return your money."

"What if I didn't ask you to return it?"

"What do you mean?"

"Would you like a partner?"

"Weren't you listening?" I laughed. "This place is a dump that's doing nothing but sucking me dry. You want it to do the same to you?"

Juan shrugged. "You've done a lot of work. It looks great. When I stopped at the station last week, it was clean, organized, and attractive. I think you just have to be patient. Give it time. Your problem is that you don't have time. I do."

"You have time? You mean money?"

"Both. I'll pay the next three months' rent, and let's see what happens."

"What do you get?"

"Fifty percent ownership."

I whistled. But what options did I have? If I didn't pay the rent, I'd lose the business and everything I put into it anyway. "Okay," I said.

"You run it as you have been, do whatever you need to do to make it successful, and I'll pay all the costs for the next three months. Then we'll reevaluate."

We shook hands, and he said he'd draw up a contract that he'd bring by the station later.

"Bring it tomorrow. I haven't slept in over 36 hours. I'm going home to get some sleep."

MY ROUTINE OF GETTING up in the dark, driving to the station, opening it, and working all day alone continued. By the time I got home, Julia was curled in her crib asleep. I adjusted the blankets she'd kicked off and brushed her wispy hair off her cheek and forehead. I felt like I'd barely seen her in the last few months. The same with Luisa. She came with me on Saturday a couple of times. She helped me by pumping gas for customers or selling a candy bar or two, but working while keeping an eye on a toddler made her too nervous, so she preferred to stay home.

I stocked the small store with motor oil and other supplies customers might need. I also bought more varieties of snacks since Jose was paying. But our profits were negligible. In fact, I think I drank half our stock of Coke.

As we neared the three-month trial, I didn't think we should continue this venture. I met Juan in downtown Manhattan to share a deli sandwich and chat. "Maybe we should sell it and get out of it what we put in," I said.

"I'm not ready to give up yet, Sal. Let's give it another six months."

I shook my head. "I'm tired of never seeing my wife and daughter. And I'm not making any money. I can't live without a salary. You still have your job. For me this *is* my job."

"Are you taking some money from the profits?"

I laughed. "What profits? Aren't you listening? We're just losing money. Everything we make I use to buy more gas, and more supplies. Yes, I'm taking $20 here and there to buy groceries for my wife, but I can't keep working like this for free."

"It's your business."

"Let's sell it," I insisted.

He shook his head. "I'll tell you what. Walk away if you want. I'll take over. Just sign the business over to me."

I looked at him and thought about what my father had said. Everyone is an opportunist. "No, you buy me out."

He considered this. "How much?"

"I put in a lot of money."

"So have I."

"And I put in all the work. I paid for the paint, the repairs and practically lived there the last six months."

"I'll give you a couple of thousand. It's all I can do."

I thought about it and decided that was fair enough. I could walk away from this disaster and get some of my money back. So, I agreed.

When I got home that night after closing the gas station early, I kissed Luisa and sat at the kitchen table to have dinner with her for a change. Usually, she left food on the stove. Sometimes she got up at midnight or 1 a.m. and watched me eat. Other times, she was fast asleep.

"What do you say we get out of New York?" I asked Luisa.

"For the weekend?"

"No, for good. Go West and see what opportunities are available."

"What about the gas station?"

"It's done. I sold it to my partner. It's his nightmare now."

"But why?"

"Because all it does is cost me money. We've been broke since I bought it."

"Where do you want to go? California? You and Mateo talked about moving there."

"Maybe. Let's go on an adventure and see where fate leads us. We can have California as our ultimate destination, but maybe we'll find something we like better along the way."

She looked unsure. "I like New York."

"We'll come back. One day."

WE WENT TO THE CAR lot the next day to look at new cars. I had the $2000 burning a hole in my pocket. As we looked around with the salesman, Luisa shook her head.

"Let's go," she said.

"You don't like them?" I asked.

"They're too expensive."

"But I have most of the cash. I'll only have to finance a little bit, and I'll pay it as soon as I get a job."

"We haven't had income in six months. We need some of what you have to live, especially if you want to travel."

"Look Mrs." the salesman said. "Why don't you sit inside and have a cup of coffee? Take care of your little girl, and let us men work out a good deal. Okay?"

Luisa frowned. "No, it's not okay. We're finished. I want to leave."

She was right, but she was making me look like a fool, so I got angry. "I'll decide when we're finished. Go inside like he said."

Luisa didn't move. I leaned in and whispered in her ear. "I can do this. Trust me."

"I won't forgive you if you spend all our money to buy this car. Let's get a used one. We don't need a new car."

I gazed into her pleading eyes. I knew I should listen to her, but my ego was getting the better of me.

"Are you going to let your woman make the decision for you, buddy?"

I turned to him and saw the manipulation in his eyes, the greed, and the fear that I'd walk away. "No," I said. "*I'm* making this decision." I placed my hand on Luisa's lower back and walked out of the lot. He kept calling me back, but I ignored him.

We went to a used car lot next, and I bought a 1960 Chevrolet Impala for $900. We drove home, and that weekend, we packed as much as we could fit into the car. We sold our furniture. Luisa gave some things to Camila. Mateo and Camila told us to keep them posted on where we decide to stay and live.

Mateo wanted to leave with us, but he said he would meet with us later. After an accidental fall, the stupid son of a bitch ended up in the hospital with some cracked ribs, a fractured hip, and his leg broken in three places. Luckily, he didn't break his back.

He was waiting to collect the insurance settlement as he healed. I asked him if he did it on purpose, and he swore that he didn't, but I didn't believe him. Luisa was right about these guys. They created one get rich quick scam after another. But I liked Mateo. He was my buddy. And Luisa liked Camila. The four of us were a team, so I wasn't going to end that friendship. Luisa didn't know anything about Mateo's insurance settlement, or maybe she did if Camila said anything, but we didn't talk about it.

We drove out of the city, leaving our friends and the big buildings behind, and a little part of me was sorry and disappointed to leave with my tail between my legs, but a bigger part couldn't wait to see what awaited us.

NOVEMBER 29, 1968

Dear *Papá*,

In these first few words, I want to express my desire that you and *Mamá* are both healthy. We are doing well. Julia is big and happy, and Luisa is beautiful and as energetic as always. And I, well, I continue to be like a truck that runs over everything with my nervous energy. In other words, I'm simply me. No change.

I will also share that in the last couple of weeks, we've been driving through many states as we have left New York in search of a more comfortable life where we could live at a slower pace without the pressure of having to work 24 hours a day just to survive.

We stopped in Council Bluffs, Iowa, for no reason other than tired of driving. We checked into a hotel, and the next day I got a humble job working for Pontiac, a General Motors company. I will work Monday through Friday, having the weekends free to spend with my wife and daughter, whom I've almost forgotten the last few months because I had to work so hard at the gas station.

What a great country where one can get a job from one day to the next, don't you think?

Yesterday, we rented an apartment next to the hotel where we were staying when we stopped here. It is fully furnished and looks nice. Council Bluffs is not a large city like New York, but it's nice. I'm ten minutes away from work. The people are super friendly. Immediately, our neighbor invited us to spend Thanksgiving with their family. Can you imagine? They don't even know us. And another neighbor invited us to dinner at their home next Sunday.

As far as the country, it's in crisis, and it has been for quite a while because of the Vietnam war. To pay for this ridiculous war, they tax those who can least pay. For example, when you work, before you get your check, the government takes 10% of your wages. And that's not the only tax on the poor. If you want a cup of coffee, you pay a tax. Here in Iowa, it's 2%. In New York, it was 5%. You pay tax on everything. And by everything, I mean everything: milk, bread, clothes, air, everything. In Iowa, they seem to have placed all their hope on Nixon. The people here have voted for him as if the world's future depends on how this election turns out.

All I know is that each bomb the United States drops on the poor Vietnamese can pay for a ton of bread and clothes for the poor. Instead of funding a war, they could be allocating the money toward a program to reduce poverty. Of course, the hope is that every "made in the USA" bomb ensures that the free world maintains a balance. It's a slap in the face to China, of course. They resent America more and more every day. The hope is that Nixon can turn this around, that China and the rest of the world will look at the USA as friends again.

I don't know. All I know is that this is a different country than the one I thought I was immigrating to. Somebody needs to get it back on track, back to Kennedy's vision.

I didn't mean to go on and on about this, *Papá*. I wanted to let you know about our new adventure. We'll see where it leads. I send you and Mamá a big kiss and a warm hug from your son, who appreciates you more than you know.

Salvador

CHAPTER TWENTY

I didn't go into details in the letter to my father, but the reason we were in Iowa was a little more involved. We had no problems driving through Pennsylvania. We got on Interstate 80 and crossed Ohio, Indiana, Illinois, and almost all of Iowa. We were eleven miles from Nebraska when the engine in the car died outside of Council Bluffs. I pulled into a service station, and the mechanic told me the car had no hope. I'd have to replace the engine or have it rebuilt, and it would cost more than I had. We had very little money left.

"I'm sorry," the mechanic said.

I sat on a stool and looked at my wife and two-year-old baby. "What the hell am I going to do?"

"Where are you headed?"

"California," I said.

He whistled. "You have a long way to go."

"Is there somewhere I can sleep tonight? I'm going to have to stay longer than a night if I don't have a car," I muttered to myself.

"There are hotels in Council Bluff. I can give you a ride."

I nodded. What choice did I have? I leaned into the car to talk to Luisa. "He can't fix it. We need a new engine. It's going to mean a new car. We're going to stay here in Iowa for a while."

She looked around this place so different from New York and sighed.

And thankfully, I did find a job with Pontiac washing the new cars on the lot. With some luck, if I worked for a few months, I might be able to buy a new car and keep going. Or we could stay in Iowa if things worked out. I was open to anything.

The following week, I went back to the mechanic to talk about the car and see if I had any hope of salvaging it. "If you keep it on your lot for a while, I'll see about replacing the engine."

"I'll hold it, but it's not worth changing the engine. Your money will be better spent on another car."

"That might be true. Also, you wouldn't know of an apartment to rent, would you? We can't stay in a hotel for long."

"A friend of mine is renting his house in Omaha month to month. It's just across the river. I can call him if you want to stay in the area."

Twenty minutes later, a guy named Matthew showed up. I explained my situation, and he agreed to rent us his house for $80 a month. I didn't have much money left, but I paid him for the first and last month's rent.

The mechanic agreed to tow my car for free to the house until I decided what to do with it.

I was grateful that these people were so kind.

We emptied our used car, still packed with all our things. We hadn't bothered to unload it while we were in the hotel. We got settled in the home. I carried our stuff into the house, and Luisa busied herself with Julia, making her some cereal and mashing up a banana. We had a couple of bags of non-perishable food, things that were easy to eat in a hotel room without a kitchen.

I placed my arms around her waist from behind and kissed the side of her head. "Well, welcome to our new home."

She leaned her head back. "You think we'll stay here for good?"

"I guess we'll see. It's as good a place as any, right?"

"I'm not sure about that," she said. "Compared to New York, I feel like we're in the middle of nowhere."

I smiled. "Not a fair comparison, though I know what you mean. Even compared to Rosario, this feels quiet and remote." But we got settled into the house and neighborhood, and I started work at Pontiac.

Luisa couldn't stand the snow and weather and the isolation she felt in Omaha, but she didn't complain. She found the local grocery store and discovered she could walk there, pushing Julia in a stroller. The weather was different and more severe here than in Manhattan, where it never got so bad that you were snowed in. And in a big city the roads stayed clean.

One day, the dealership closed, and all employees were sent home in the early afternoon because of a tornado warning. I got off the bus close to home and hurried through the wind. I saw Luisa and Julia walking home from the grocery store, Luisa pushing the stroller while carrying a couple of bags of food, the wind tossing her hair all over the place. I ran up beside her. "What the hell are you doing? Didn't you hear the tornado warning sirens?"

"I heard sirens," she said. "But didn't know what they meant."

"Give me those bags." I took the groceries. "Let's get inside quickly."

She told Julia to sit back in the stroller, and we practically ran with the groceries and stroller to get into the house.

"Ugh, I hate this place," she said. "It's so hard to get around. And now we have to deal with tornados?"

"If it gets bad, we're supposed to go into the basement. Let's wait and see."

We waited it out, had dinner, and listened to the news to see if it got worse. But it moved past us, and we were fine.

IF LUISA DIDN'T LIKE Omaha, the feeling was mutual; this place didn't like me much either. After two months, Pontiac let me go. They were cutting back after the holidays, and I was the last one hired, and heck, the salesmen could wash the cars if they wanted the sale.

When I got home, I sat at the kitchen table and held my head in my hands.

Luisa's hands rested on my shoulders. "Are you okay?"

I looked over my shoulder at her. "What am I doing wrong? It feels like everything I try to do goes to hell. I lost my job."

She sat beside me at the table, looking as depressed as I felt. "Right about now, it would be nice to be walking along the Parana River, enjoying the warm sun, wouldn't it?"

I met her eyes. "Then going to eat an *asado* with friends in the afternoon. Drinking a few bottles of wine. Taking a nap."

"Life seems so much easier in Argentina."

I placed a hand over hers. "We were single and didn't work."

"Speak for yourself. I had a job."

I wanted to chuckle and let her lighten the mood, but my depleted spirit couldn't make room for joy. "If we lived there now, we'd have to work as hard as we do here."

"Maybe, but it would be different. We wouldn't be so alone."

I pulled back and ran a hand through my hair, feeling my face and body heat. "If we went back now, all of this would have been for nothing. We'd have to start at zero."

"No one is judging you."

"I am," I shouted. "I'm not ready to give up. Are you?"

She shrugged. "I guess I don't consider it giving up."

"Because it's not *your* dream." I slammed my hand on the table. "I'm the one struggling. I'm the one working to make this happen."

"You think this isn't my dream too? You, Julia, our family is all that matters to me. But where we live isn't important. Except . . . I don't think I want to stay in Nebraska. It's too quiet, remote, and cold."

"I agree. I say we keep going to California."

"But we don't have a car or money to buy one."

I stood. "I know. I've been thinking about what to do, and I have an idea. I'm going to find a phone booth and call my old trucking company in New York. Maybe they can connect me with a place out here. That way, I'll get enough money to continue to California."

I reached down and took a curtain chord out of Julia's hand. I tried to pick her up, but she wiggled and screamed, "no."

"Don't put things in your mouth then." I let her go, and she ran to the other side of the room with pretty good balance.

"Okay. Maybe I can look for work here too," Luisa argued.

"You can't. You've got to look after Julia. I'll start looking for work tomorrow. But just in case, I'm going to call New York to see if there's driving work available in this state."

She picked Julia up. "I think you're hungry. Wave bye to *Papi*."

"*Chau Papito*," she said, warming my heart before I stepped outside into the cold.

I walked a few blocks looking for a payphone but didn't find one. I stopped at a small market to ask.

"I'm not sure. But you're welcome to use my phone."

"I've got to make a long-distance call to New York."

"Oh, I think the Woolworth downtown might have a pay phone. It's about a mile away."

I thanked him and kept walking. Thankfully, when I got there, I found the payphone. I called and spoke to the office manager at Swift. She remembered me, and we chatted for a while. "I was on my way to California, but my car broke down. Can you believe it? I'm hoping you might have a connection in Nebraska or Iowa, a company that needs drivers."

"We don't, Sal, but you can come back, you know. We still need drivers."

"Well, I'm no longer living in New York. Plus, I'm stuck in Nebraska without a car right now."

"Take a train and head back."

"Yeah, I'll think about it," I said. "Let me give you my address in case you hear of anything."

When I got back to the house half frozen, Julia was toddling around, exploring, and Luisa searched the kitchen, looking for something to make for dinner. "What did they say?"

"She offered me my job back if I want it."

"Let's hope you don't. Look for work here first."

"What are we eating?"

"Canned sardines with potatoes and canned corn."

"Wonderful." I couldn't even afford to buy decent food. Great provider, I was.

She laughed. "You can have all of the sardines for yourself."

I SPENT A WEEK LOOKING for work and didn't find anything. Then I got a telegram from Swift telling me they had a load going from Lincoln, Nebraska to New York. If I could bring it, they'd pay me well.

"Look at this!" I read the message to Luisa.

"Well, that's a short-term job. Then what? You have to spend money to come back."

"No, I'll take the load. Work for a month or two there to save money, then come back, and we'll continue to California. This is perfect!" Seemed like an answer at least. I could leave Luisa and Julia here where they were safe and settled. It was cheaper here too. I could sleep on Mateo's living room floor for nothing. I'd save enough money to keep traveling in no time.

"You want us to stay here and wait for you?"

"Sure, you'll be fine. I'll pay the next month's rent with my last check from General Motors and give you the rest for food. Then I'll send you more money."

"I don't know."

"It will be fine, don't worry."

AS I SAT DOWN TO WRITE my father, I wasn't sure what to tell him. I never wanted to worry my parents, so telling them about this minor setback didn't seem worthwhile or wise.

Omaha, January 28, 1969

My Dearest Parents,

Let me begin by sharing my desires for health and happiness for you both. We are all doing well, though the monotony of life in Omaha is indescribable. It snowed yesterday, and it snowed today, and the news said it would snow tomorrow. It's cold all the time. This kind of weather traps you inside, and it's enough to make anyone unhappy. Luisa and I were saying that we still don't know what the sidewalks are made of because we have yet to see the ground under the snow.

Although this is nothing compared to what people further north face in states like Minnesota, where the temperature was negative 47 degrees Fahrenheit. Can you imagine? Montana wasn't quite as bad; they were only at 23 below zero. I guess I shouldn't complain since it's 19 degrees here. It's quite a spectacle to see the river completely frozen. The lakes too. The city has a truck that clears the snow from the lake to allow the kids to skate. I'm sure I'm boring you by talking about the weather, but it's fascinating to a boy from Rosario who has never seen anything like this.

Moving on to news that might interest you more, your granddaughter turned two yesterday, and we had a little party for her. We invited the neighbors, had some cake, and took pictures that Luisa will send you soon. What makes me happy is that she speaks Spanish quite well. She can ask for what she wants and have conversations with us. Now, don't misunderstand me. We haven't had deep, philosophical discussions yet, but she can tell you what she's seen on TV and speak like an adult. Thank you for the dress you sent her for her birthday. She wore it on her birthday, along with little shoes that Luisa found at the store. She looked like a doll.

Give my brother my love. This son sends you a fierce hug and kisses.

Chau,
Salvador

CHAPTER TWENTY-ONE

It took a couple of days to pack my bag and get on the road, but the freight needed to be moved, and they wouldn't wait for me forever. I kissed Luisa goodbye and got a ride to Lincoln from the mechanic who had towed my car to our house weeks earlier. "When I get back, I'll put a new engine in. We'll order one," I told him.

"I don't know if it'll be worth it, but I'll put it in if you want to buy one."

I gave him some money for gas and thanked him for the ride.

Then I picked up the paperwork, got the truck keys, got into the company truck, and made my way back to New York. This opportunity turned out to be a gift. I made good time on the road and delivered the load as promised. Then I returned the truck to the lot.

"I guess I'm back," I said when I went to see the dispatcher.

"Sorry your move to California didn't work out, but we're glad to have you back, Sal. Work has really picked up, and we need drivers."

That night, I went to see Mateo and Camila.

"What in the world are you doing back?" Camila asked. "Where are Luisa and the baby?"

I told them the whole story. "Maybe I can sleep on your couch for a few weeks?"

"Sure," Mateo said. At the same time, Camila said, "One week."

"Come on, *Amorcito*. Where is he going to go?"

"One week is fine. I'll stay with Javier. It will only be a month or two. How are you feeling, Mateo?"

"My leg is almost completely healed. But my hip and ribs are going to take a while."

"Then what? You're not going back to window washing, are you?"

"Probably not."

"Then you should drive back to Omaha with me, and we can all head to California." Maybe this pitstop in Omaha had been a blessing after all, allowing us to wait for our friends to join us.

But Mateo shook his head. "We're going to wait for California. Camila wants to stay here a little longer."

Our California dream was starting to fade. I left and went for a walk, strolling the streets of New York, feeling like I'd returned home. What the hell was I going to do in California anyway. I dropped in on Javier, who slapped my back and welcomed me into his apartment, seemingly happy to see me after over a year of not talking.

"Wondering if I could stay with you a few weeks."

"Anytime, brother."

I felt as if I'd never left.

WORKING FOR SWIFT WAS much better than it had been when they were Common Market. They had a lot of work, and the trips were all long-haul, so I regularly drove into Pennsylvania and Connecticut.

Javier's apartment never changed; only his roommates did. Since both bedrooms were occupied, I slept on the couch. I paid a little rent but not much. I bought groceries and tried to contribute, but since I traveled for work daily, most of the time, I bought a sandwich or hamburger at a cafe. The only drawback to sleeping on the couch was that sometimes I came home from work, and everyone was sitting around the living room, watching TV, drinking, playing cards, or just chatting, so I couldn't sleep. Not having any other option, I sat with them, watched TV, ate, and drank.

I drank too much actually, but what was a guy living with other guys supposed to do? And I had to admit that I enjoyed being with my friends again, like before Luisa moved to New York, and definitely before I became a father. We always had a reason to party. For St. Patrick's Day, an Irish holiday, Javier invited his girlfriend and her friends, and we ate corned beef sandwiches with sauerkraut, drank beer until I thought I'd throw up, and danced and had a blast.

Mateo and Camila decided to move to New Jersey, so I helped them move on my day off since Mateo could not carry anything heavy.

"It's a lot cheaper to live in Jersey," Mateo said as I carried a chair up three flights of stairs.

"Yeah, it's not too far from New York, so why not? And now you have a car."

He grinned. "I'm finally ready to get married! Camila has been patient. Actually, she never brings it up. I'm the one that keeps telling her we're going to do it soon."

"You can still change your mind if she's not pushing you to do it." I put a heavy chair down and caught my breath.

"I want to be married and settle down. Aren't you glad to be married?" he asked.

"Of course. But my wife is nice. Camila is . . . well, she has a big mouth."

Mateo laughed. "I like her mouth and everything else about her. Come on, let's finish."

I carried the chair into the apartment and placed it exactly where Camila wanted. Then I brought up a heavy record player unit with another friend of Mateo's that nearly killed us. And Mateo carried lots of boxes of dishes and kitchen appliances.

"Hey, be careful," Camila said as I took a box from Mateo's hands and placed it on her counter.

I rolled my eyes and went down to get their kitchen chairs. I poked Mateo as we headed down the stairs. "See what I mean?"

He pushed me back, almost knocking me off my feet, then cringed and held his ribs. We kept climbing down a little easier until we got to the lobby, then I couldn't resist, and I poked him back, and we both laughed. "So, I need a best man. Are you going to California or not because you can't attend the wedding if you're not here?"

"That's the idea. Luisa is waiting for me to return."

"What if you didn't go to California yet? What if you went back to get *la flaca* and stayed in New York a while longer?"

I sat on the bottom stairs. "You think?"

"*Claro.*" He sat beside me. "There's no place like New York, and you're doing fine now driving trucks again. Get an apartment here, next to us."

I placed an arm around his shoulders. "I guess I'd miss you if I moved to the other side of the country and you didn't."

"I'd miss you too."

"So, I'm the best man?"

"You're my best friend. Who else would I choose?"

I patted his back and stood. "Well, then maybe I'd better go get my wife and stay in New York a little longer."

MY OTHER FRIENDS THOUGHT I was crazy to leave New York too. We were back to playing soccer on Saturdays, or I was back to playing with them. They'd never stopped.

"Are you really going back to Nebraska, *Loco*?" Francisco kicked the ball my way.

I ran and headed toward the goal. "I have to go get my wife and kid."

"You don't have to," he said, trying to steal the ball.

I ran harder and darted away from him. "Pass it, pass it," the other guys yelled. But I had this. I ran toward the goal. "Of course, I have to."

He pushed me to try to get the ball. But I did a little fancy footwork and kept moving forward.

"Why do you want to be tied down at your age? Didn't you have a good time with Javier's lady friends on St. Patrick's Day? Get a divorce, be free of that woman who doesn't let you have any fun."

"Fuck you. You're talking about my wife." I was instantly sorry about giving Mateo a hard time about Camila; it didn't feel good to have Francisco do it to me.

He pushed me again and rushed the ball, but seeing the goal in sight, I kicked the soccer ball, shooting toward the net. It flew straight and was about to go in, but the goalie hit the ball with the tip of his fingers, and it flew over the goal.

I fell on my back. Francisco looked down. "Missed," he said and ran off.

"Story of my life." I stood and slowly walked back to the group.

AFTER FOUR MONTHS OF working all day and hanging out with my friends at night, I was ready to head back to Omaha.

It took me a little longer than I expected, but I finally made enough to buy another used car, a Pontiac Catalina 1968, so it wasn't too old. I had it checked out by mechanics who swore to its excellent condition. The mechanic in Iowa was right that it was dumb to buy an engine for an old car that broke down.

I put down a deposit and paid the first month's rent for an apartment in Jersey, so Luisa and Julia would have a place to return to.

I drove back to Nebraska, excited to see my girls. When I walked into the house, I couldn't believe how big Julia had gotten. She gazed at me as if she didn't remember me. "Hey Beautiful. Do you have a kiss for *papi*?"

"*Papito*?" She walked over and handed me a little doll she had. I picked her and the doll up and kissed her, inhaling the sweet baby smell. "I missed you," I said.

Then I put her down and leaned across to kiss Luisa, who turned away from me.

"What?" I asked.

"Do you know how long you've been gone?"

"Yes."

"Four months! And do you know how much money you sent us?"

"What are you talking about? I sent you money as soon as I got my first check."

"Salvador, is there something wrong with your brain? We're behind on the rent here. I'm lucky that the landlord didn't throw me out. She didn't because of the baby. And the kind neighbors, my God, they brought me a basket of food and suggested I petition the state for assistance. One of them opened my refrigerator and saw that it was empty, that we were down to nothing. Do you know how humiliating that was?"

I felt guilty, but . . . "I did the best I could. I was trying to save money. But I'm here now. We'll leave tomorrow if you can pack today."

"I babysat a little boy to get grocery money. It was the only work I could do."

"There you go. You figured it out. So why are you giving me a hard time?"

She turned away from me with a look of disgust. "How many days to California?"

"We're going back to New York, well New Jersey. I got a place in Union City, a safer place. You're going to like it."

"We're going back to New York?"

"The work is good. I'm driving out of state now. They're paying well."

She turned away without a word.

I sighed, annoyed that she wasn't happier to see me and angry that she wasn't more grateful for how hard I'd worked the last few months to get back to her and get us an apartment in New Jersey. I sat in front of the TV, feeling unappreciated.

After sitting alone for a half hour, I glanced at her playing with Julia, and my heart swelled with love. I got up and opened the fridge, and she was right; she had a bottle of milk, some bread, and a little fruit. I thought of all the food and alcohol at Javier's apartment and how much I'd honestly enjoyed living with them and partying, and all the money I'd wasted eating out, and I felt a twinge of shame. Maybe I'd wanted to forget the obligations of being a married man and a father, just for a little while.

I closed the refrigerator. "Let's go out to dinner," I said.

She gazed at me. "Is that really all you have to say?"

"I'm sorry," I said because I knew it was what she wanted to hear. And I was sorry that I made her suffer. But I wasn't sorry about this failed move. She loved New York, and she knew it. Even if she pretended to be upset, I knew deep down returning to the city where she had her best friend and the ability to get around on her own would be a great relief. But to be honest, right now, I didn't care what she thought. I wanted to return to Jersey and my job and forget this detour in our lives had ever happened.

CHAPTER TWENTY-TWO

It was 1970, the first quarter of a new decade and I was determined to make this my decade. I worked hard and the long-haul trips paid well. We lived in a nice big apartment for a change. As we dressed to attend Mateo and Camila's wedding, I looked in the mirror and decided I looked good. Most of the time, I dressed in a hippy style I thought looked fashionable, but some might feel I looked like a slob. Since I didn't have to be a prince to drive a truck, I wanted to be comfortable. But it felt good to wear a suit and dress like I used to when I moved to this country.

Mateo and Camila waited two years to actually get married after his grand proposal. But now that his injuries had healed, he had money in the bank, and he was settled in the apartment in Union City, they were ready to make it official.

Camila had a sister and father living in Florida that I didn't know about, not that I knew much about her. It's strange how you don't think of friends as having their own families. They sort of belong to you in this bubble of a world you inhabit together. Mateo's family was all in Argentina, but he flew his mother to New York and invited our New York friends. They had less than 50 people attend the ceremony.

Luisa and Julia looked beautiful sitting in church watching the ceremony. I focused on Mateo and Camila, who stared at each other as the priest spoke. Mateo was crazy about her. Everything from the way he spoke to her, to the adoring way he watched her, to how he let her boss him around proved there was no other woman for him. The man never even looked at another woman. And he loved Niki too, whom he planned to adopt. Since he'd raised her since the kid was an infant, he was already her father, so he should.

Afterward, as they walked out of the church, I stood beside Luisa. "Hearing them take their vows reminded me of ours," I whispered.

She didn't say anything.

I kissed her cheek. "You're more beautiful today than you were then."

"Shh," she said.

We quietly walked out of the church, where everyone threw rice and congratulated the happy couple. Then we took a taxi to a Spanish restaurant where they would have a small reception. Mateo invited Lorenzo, the owner of the Argentine market. I still kept in contact with him even though I no longer attended the Argentine get-togethers. I introduced him to Luisa.

"Nice to meet you," he said. "Salvador, you stopped coming around. *Porque?*"

Why? *Because your employees are crooks, my wife doesn't want me to associate with them.* Could I say that? Plus, the gas station venture didn't exactly go well, so taking advice from other friends of Lorenzo no longer appealed to me. I offered a smile and shrugged. "I work long hours. You know how it is."

"Your husband is a good man," he said.

Luisa held Julia. "Mm," she said and glanced at me. "He has a lot of his father in him."

"Then your father-in-law must be a good man too."

"A great man."

We ate and then when Julia fell asleep, we placed her in the baby carriage and danced to the music of the Carpenters, The Jackson 5, and of course, our favorite tangos. I enjoyed the wine and champagne and continued to socialize and have fun. But after a couple of hours, Luisa sat with the baby.

"Come on." I took her hand and pulled her to the dance floor.

"It's getting late, and you're drunk," she said. "Let's go."

"It's early still. Everyone's having fun."

"I'm not."

"You don't know how to have fun," I said, sick of her attitude. She acted like she was 40 years old.

"And you're loud and making a fool of yourself. Let's just go."

Mateo and Camila stepped up beside me. Mateo put an arm around my shoulder. "Hey, you two. Let's take a picture together."

Luisa smiled at Camila and stood. We'd danced quite a few songs together early in the night, the four of us. I put my arm around Mateo too. "I wish you lots of luck, *Flaco*. You deserve to be happy."

"I am," he said.

I placed my other arm around Camila. She flinched as if my arm was too heavy, but I pulled them both close. "I love you guys, you know that? You're going to grow old together and have babies, and maybe one day we'll all go back to Argentina and retire as old people, remembering these days."

Mateo laughed and called Luisa over. "Let's get the picture."

Luisa stood on the other side of Mateo, and he placed an arm around her waist. "Looking good, *Flaca*," he said. And he signaled the photographer to take the picture.

A bulb flashed a couple of times. The four of us, friends forever, were now memorialized in the photo.

FOR SOME REASON, NEW Jersey became the steadiest place we'd lived. Maybe because I stuck with truck driving, we weren't hurting for money.

Julia grew bigger and more adorable every day. We couldn't get her to stop talking.

She learned about Santa Claus right before her fourth birthday. She got a spaceship, a car that ran on batteries and crashed into things, then rotated and kept going. She spent a lot of time watching it and repositioning it. She got a new doll and some dishes and silverware, so she was constantly "cooking" food for me and serving it on her plates. But her favorite gift was a purple and white Radio Flyer tricycle with little streamers coming out of the handlebars. When she rode it, no one could do anything but watch her. Forget watching TV or listening to records because she crashed into everything, probably imitating the toy car; then she screamed and drove us crazy.

"*Papi,*" she said the week after Christmas. "Is Santa coming back?"

"Yes, next year."

"But I want him to come back again this Sunday."

I laughed and placed her on my lap. "You think Santa is going to come back every weekend? No, he comes once a year."

"How long is that?"

"It's a long time."

"But I want more presents."

"Didn't you get enough?"

She shook her head full of long curls.

"If you don't appreciate the gifts you got, Santa will not bring you more."

"I do appreciate them."

"Good."

"Can I ride my tricycle?"

"No."

"Please."

I sighed and got her tricycle out of the hall closet. I opened our front door and took the bike out into the hall. Then I knocked on

Mateo's door to see if Niki could come out and play with Julia. The girls loved each other. "Ride your tricycle here, and no screaming. The neighbors will get upset. Okay?"

"Okay."

I went back into the apartment and turned on the TV. Luisa was sewing or doing something in the bedroom. Every so often, I glanced out and saw Julia zooming past the door, Niki chasing after her on foot, and another little girl who must have heard them playing rode past with her tricycle.

Thankfully, the holidays were almost over. I worked overtime doing deliveries for Christmas and was ready to have a regular work schedule again.

Luisa walked out of the bedroom. "Where's Julia?"

Almost on cue, Julia let out a blood-curdling scream. We ran out to the hall where Julia was flat on her back on the tile floor with Niki crying over her, "She's dying, she's dying."

And for a second, that's what I thought too. Blood was literally squirting out of Julia's mouth like a fountain. I looked down to where the girls had parked two tricycles and were apparently running around the bikes. Julia tripped and fell face first, catching her lower lip on a spoke sticking out of the back tire of her friend's tricycle.

I yelled for Luisa to get me a towel, and placed the towel on Julia's lip to stop the bleeding. Mateo shook his car keys in front of my face. "I'll drive you to the hospital. It's not going to stop bleeding."

We all ran down the stairs, barely remembering to close and lock our doors. Mateo made it to the closest hospital in ten minutes, and when we walked in with a child full of blood on her face and a soaked towel, they immediately admitted us to emergency.

Julia had stopped screaming and lay limp in my arms. Luisa had alternated between crying and trying to calm Julia down.

The doctor who examined her quickly administered a local analgesic and sewed Julia's lip, sealing the small hole. I had to hold her down along with the nurses who pinned her to the table, and it broke my heart because she was so scared and cried so hard.

"Done," the doctor said. "Keep her still. I'll have a nurse wash her face. She'll need to get some sleep. Her lip will be tender, but she'll be fine once her body replaces the blood she lost."

Luisa sat beside her and held her little hand. The nurse washed her face with a moist towel, making her look less scary.

I sat on a chair in the corner and held my head. Shit! I never should have left her alone out there. I walked out to the lobby where Mateo, Camila, and Niki waited. "She's fine," I said.

"She's not going to die?" Niki asked.

I shook my head, drained of energy. "She'll be ready to play again in a couple of days. But not out in the hallway."

"They play out there a lot," Camila said.

"I shouldn't have let her take the tricycle out there alone."

"Hey," she said, "This wasn't your fault. It was just a freak accident." Her voice sounded kind and compassionate for once. "They're kids, and kids get hurt. She'll be good as new soon, right?"

"Yeah. We're going to be here a little longer. We can catch a taxi back if you want to go home."

"No," Mateo said. "Of course, we'll wait for you."

They were good friends. I went back into the hospital room, and Julia was already better. They had given her a little stuffed bear, and her mother was telling her a story.

I smiled at her. "You got a new toy after all, huh *Gordita*?"

"I'm happy, but it hurts to smile. I'm smiling in my heart."

I caressed the top of her head. "I'm smiling in my heart too."

CHAPTER TWENTY-THREE

February 18, 1971

Dear *Papá*,

My deepest desire is that you and *Mamá* are well and staying healthy. I know it is getting more and more difficult for you to write, so I don't want you to worry about that. We appreciate the letters that *Mamá* has sent with news about you both.

Julia news is that she is now four years old and a terror. She has yours and my temperament. She wants what she wants, and if she doesn't get it, she throws a temper tantrum. She reminds me of you, *Papá*. But she has a heart of gold, for example, she cries when her mother or I are hurt. The other day, Luisa had a stomach ache, and I found Julia crying in her room. When I asked her why she said that her *mami* had a belly ache. Aside from being empathetic, she now realizes that clothing matters and fashion is important. She chooses her own clothes, and if Luisa tries to dress her in a dress that is getting old, she refuses and makes Luisa pull out a new one.

Honestly, we have to be a little strict with her; otherwise, she will walk all over us. Luisa is a bit of a push-over. Julia does not give her a moment of peace, and when I tell her to leave her mother alone and go to her room, she cries. But I think Luisa suffers more because I won't let her comfort our spoiled child. Oh, and we had to officially give away her tricycle. She refuses to ride it. Even though we explained to her that she tripped and fell, and that it had nothing to do with riding her tricycle, she blames her tricycle for the "blood that almost killed her." Yes, she is dramatic, but I think she says that because her little friend kept saying that she was going to die. Anyhow, that is life with your granddaughter.

Luisa and I are doing well. I continue to work driving trucks, and we are slowly, finally putting away some money into savings. We haven't spoken about returning to Argentina or moving from here into the suburbs because it's been so nice not to move for over a year.

Since I know you are not well, I think about returning to be with you and to help, and I feel guilty that I'm so far away when you might need me.

Please know that you are always in our hearts. Luisa, Julia, and I send our love to you and *Mamá*.

Your son,
Salvador

LUISA RETURNED FROM work, hung her coat in the hall closet, and placed her purse on the coffee table beside the couch without saying much to me or Julia, which wasn't normal. Julia excitedly pulled on Luisa's hand to drag her into her bedroom.

"I made a doll show. Come see," she said.

"I have to make dinner." Luisa disentangled her fingers. "I'll see it later."

"Now," she whined.

"Julia, your mother said later," I scolded her. "Go play by yourself."

"I don't like playing by myself. My friend has a sister, and I don't have one. So *Mami* has to play with me."

I frowned at her, folded my newspaper, and leaned forward on the couch. "Go to your room like your mother told you, or you're going to be in trouble."

"I don't like trouble." She pouted and stomped away.

I fought not to smile until she left, then I placed the newspaper on the coffee table and joined Luisa in the kitchen. "What's wrong?" I asked, noticing her long face as she pulled a package of chicken out of the refrigerator.

She'd gotten a job in a factory sewing fancy dresses like the ones Broadway stars wore when they went out to dinner and got their pictures in magazines. She'd been thrilled to have something to do aside from being home with Julia. Between Camila and I, we watched Julia for a few hours. Usually, Luisa came home happy and rejuvenated.

"I'm not going to have a job anymore."

"Why?"

"My boss is closing the factory and moving to Miami."

That surprised me. "I'm sorry. What bad luck."

"I know. I worked for three months, and now I'm out of work again."

"You'll find something else if that is what you want. Of course, you don't have to work."

"But I want to. You know that."

I held my hands up. "I know. I know." We'd had a big fight when she said she had been offered a job. I told her no way was she going to work and leave Julia with strangers.

"You can watch her when you're home," she'd said. "And Camila said she'd help out."

"Forget about it."

"I'm not going to forget about it, and I'm going to take the job."

"The hell you are," I screamed and had a fit that mimicked my daughter's. Julia cried because I scared her. My blood pressure went through the roof, but Luisa stayed calm. She picked Julia up and took her to her bedroom to comfort her.

When they came back out of the bedroom, Luisa started serving dinner. "So, I will start on Monday," she said.

"Son of a bitch," I said, left the kitchen table, and stormed out of the house. But I knew I'd lost that battle.

After seeing how happy she'd been to work a few hours a day, I was glad I'd lost. Now, I walked up to her and placed a hand on her shoulder as she pan-fried the chicken in garlic and onions, which made my mouth water. "New York is a big place with lots of jobs, and I bet you'll find a new one next week."

She gazed at me and smiled. "Maybe."

"Tomorrow, I'm headed to Connecticut, dropping a load and picking up a new one the following morning. Why don't you and Julia come with me? We'll get a hotel and have a nice dinner out, what do you say?"

"I don't know. The truck isn't very comfortable, and she doesn't sit still for long."

"Julia," I called.

She came running out of her room.

"*Si, Papi?*"

I picked her up. "Ugh," I said. "You're getting big and fat, do you know that?"

She nodded. "Because I'm four. I'm not a baby anymore."

I kissed her chubby cheek. "That's true. Would you like to go in Papi's big truck?"

"Salvador," Luisa said. "I'm not sure that's a good idea."

"It will be good for you to get out, and you'll keep me company on the road. And Julia will love it, won't you?"

"Yes," she agreed and wrapped her arms around my neck, dropping kisses on my cheek and making my heart swell.

"See?" I said to Luisa. "And she'll be good, won't you?"

"I'll be good, *Mami*. Can we go?"

Luisa laughed then wagged her finger at me. "You're a manipulator, you know that?"

I put Julia down and wrapped my arms around Luisa's waist. "I don't want you to be sad, and I want my family with me. Is that such a bad thing?"

She hugged me. "I hope we don't both regret it," she said as we glanced down at our daughter, watching us with an angelic look on her face.

"I think she's the manipulator." I waved my arm at her and added her to the hug.

WE GOT UP EARLY THE next morning. Luisa packed an overnight bag for all three of us. I picked Julia up from bed and carried her sleeping body on my shoulder like a sack of flour. We were on the road by 4 a.m.

I placed Julia on Luisa's lap, and she continued to sleep for the first two of the four hours. When she woke up, Luisa made her eat a banana which she didn't want but promised to eat it if Luisa told her stories. Luisa told her the story of the tortoise and the hare. Then when Julia demanded more, she made up these ridiculous tales, and Julia loved them all. She never tired of hearing the same thing again and again.

"Tell me another one," she said.

"I don't know any more stories."

"Tell me the one about the rabbit again."

"I already told you that one twice," Luisa tried to reason.

"But I want to hear it again. And tell me why the rabbit decides to take a nap during a race. It doesn't make sense. I wouldn't take a nap if I was running a race."

"Just because that's the story," Luisa said.

"But why?" she pressed.

"Julia," I interrupted. "He does that because he's sure he's going to win the race."

"But why?"

"Because he's fast, and the tortoise is slow. The tortoise has no hope of winning."

"So why didn't the rabbit keep running and win and then take a nap?"

"Because he's arrogant and proud. Do you know what that means?"

"No."

"He was too sure of himself. He believed that the tortoise was so slow that he could take a nap, then get up and still win the race. But the rabbit slept too long, while the tortoise never stopped. He kept going, slow and steady until he won the race. The story shows you never to give up and to never brag about how good you are."

"But —"

"No more buts and no more whys," I said. She just wasn't going to get it and would keep asking questions forever.

"I'm glad the tortoise won," she said.

"Me too."

"The rabbit was mean. You shouldn't tease other animals."

"No, you shouldn't. The story is called an allegory, and it's supposed to teach you that it doesn't matter if you're fast. It only matters if you keep going. Do you understand?"

"Sure," she nodded.

I wasn't sure that she did, but she was satisfied. And that got us a few moments of peace before I pulled into my stop on the outskirts of Hartford.

I BACKED UP TO DROP the trailer and unhitch it from the truck. I gave my paperwork to the dispatcher and waited for a few moments to get the okay to leave. Diane, who handled all the paperwork, brought it to me on a clipboard.

"How are you today, Sal? Haven't seen you in about a month."

"I've been driving all over. How have you been?"

"Not bad. Last weekend I painted my bathroom using the tips you gave me."

"That's great!"

She rubbed her lower back seductively. "I'm sore, but it saved me a lot of money doing it myself. Thank you."

"Oh, you're welcome." I winked at her. "I would have done it for you, but I'm always so busy and short on time."

"I understand. It wasn't hard, just time-consuming. Are you staying overnight? Do you want to go have a drink?" She brushed some of my hair off my forehead. "I should do something to thank you for being so sweet."

I laughed and took a step back. "Not this time." I pointed to my truck. "My wife and daughter are here with me, and we're going to enjoy the day together before we head home tomorrow."

"Okay," she angled her head. "Maybe next time."

I handed her the clipboard with a smile. "Of course. Am I good to go?"

"I think you are. Have a nice day with your family."

I nodded and strolled back to the truck.

"All right," I said when I climbed back inside. "Time for lunch. Are you hungry?"

Luisa nodded. "A little bit. Who was that? She sure was friendly."

I started the truck. "Diane? She handles the paperwork. And yes, she's nice. Ready?"

Luisa gave me a searching look but didn't say anything else, and for that, I was glad.

CHAPTER TWENTY-FOUR

I parked the car on 19th Street and checked my watch as I walked to pick up Julia, who just started pre-kindergarten daycare. Since she was a few months short of her fifth birthday, the school wouldn't allow her to attend regular kindergarten this year, which was a shame. But she liked her daycare, and it gave Luisa a chance to work a little.

Luisa found a part-time job sewing again and happily worked, proud to contribute to our expenses and savings. She had plans to put money away for a little trip we promised my parents we'd take to Argentina. It would be a short vacation so my parents could spend time with their granddaughter.

When I got to the school, her teacher sat on the steps outside with Julia.

"I'm so sorry," I said because I had arrived a few minutes late.

"*Papito*," Julia said and ran to hug my leg.

"No problem," the teacher said without much warmth. She stood and walked back into the school.

I unclasped Julia's arms away from my leg. "You act like you missed me."

"I did miss you," she said with a slight frown as if I'd said something stupid.

"Did you have a good time in school today?" I took her hand, and we walked to the car. Well, I walked, and she skipped.

"Aha, *si.*"

When we dropped her off the first time, she didn't like it. She cried and cried, and Luisa watched her from a small window with tears in her own eyes. I had to pull her away and promise her Julia would be okay. And she was. After a week, all Julia talked about was the new songs she'd learned, the stories the teacher told her, and the snacks she'd eaten. She was learning more words in English too.

"I think we need to get a dog. One like Lassie. They protect people and love children," she announced as if this had been a major issue she'd decided.

"I told you, we can't right now. Your mother says no dogs in the apartment. You have a cat."

"He's only there to kill rats. *Mami* said not to kiss him. And plus, he tries to scratch me."

"Because you grab him and try to kiss him."

"I want a dog."

"Someday." I opened the door for her, and she hopped into the backseat. Her short legs still stuck straight out on the long bench seat. She was going to be short like me. "You want to go get *Mami*," I asked when I got behind the wheel.

"Okay."

We drove to Luisa's job, and a big smile appeared on Luisa's face when she saw us waiting for her outside of the factory doors. "Hey, this is a surprise. I was going to rush to the daycare and pick you up," she said to Julia, hugging her. She looked at me. "I thought you said you couldn't do it."

When she called, I was annoyed because I'd gotten home from work late last night and didn't want to get up early. I shrugged, "You woke me up, so I thought I might as well get her. I'm hungry. Let's go home."

"Me too." Julia bounced up and down. As we walked back to the car, Luisa held Julia's hand and glanced at me as if she wanted to say something but looked unsure. Maybe she thought I was still angry that she woke me up.

"What?"

"I went to the doctor because I missed a couple of periods."

I raised my eyebrows. "And?"

"I'm pregnant."

I reached for her and gave her a huge hug right there on the sidewalk on John F. Kennedy Blvd. A few people walking past glanced at us with mild interest. Cars zoomed by on the busy street. But I ignored them all, caring only about how my family would soon expand. We'd wanted another baby and thought it had happened a few months earlier, but it had been a false alarm. "I'm so happy," I said. "Are you sure?

"Don't get too excited, and don't say anything to your parents yet. I want to make sure nothing happens, but yes, I'm sure."

"Nothing is going to happen."

Julia looked at us with a confused frown. "Why are you happy?"

Luisa looked at me, and I nodded. "You're going to have a little sister or brother soon."

"Really? I want a sister."

"We don't get to pick."

"Why not? Don't I get to choose anything? No dog? No sister?"

"Julia," I warned.

She shrugged. "Okay."

And that was that.

SINCE WE WERE FINANCIALLY stable and I had paid down our debt, I invested in purchasing my own truck again. I bought a used truck, but it was only a year old. Being an independent contractor meant I could choose the companies I worked with and that I got to keep more of the money I made. Of course, it also meant that I had all the expenses of owning a truck, but I still came out ahead.

I started delivering fruits and vegetables locally around the longer hauls to other cities and states, which meant I spent a lot of time working. I didn't mind the work. Those times between jobs were when I began to question my life and purpose and doubt all my decisions. But when I kept busy and productive, I was happy.

One day when I went into the office to get my long-haul trip plan for the week, I found out they were sending me to Canada. I'd never had to drive out of the country. Excited, I called Luisa and told her.

"How long will you be gone?"

"I don't know, probably about a week. I have multiple stops. So, make whatever adjustments you need to make at work to pick Julia up from school."

Luisa never complained about me being gone. Between her work and Julia, she probably didn't have time to miss me.

With my trailer loaded, I headed to Montreal. I drove straight through without many stops, except for a break at a coffee shop in Northern New York where I ate a sandwich with French fries and had a cup of coffee.

I sipped coffee and looked out of the window at the changing color of leaves and Lake Champlain. What a gorgeous country. Seeing such beautiful sites mesmerized me, and I knew being on the road where I could drive through all of this was a major reason I enjoyed traveling long distances. What other job would give me the opportunity to see so much of North America?

Argentina was beautiful too, but sadly, I hadn't explored any of it. The only exceptions were my family's trips to Cordoba when I was a young boy. Cordoba had rolling mountains, and we got to hike and ride horses. Typically, my brother and I ran ahead of our parents and tossed marble-sized rocks from the top to see how far we could throw them.

When our parents reached the top, we'd sit to drink *mate* and eat pastries that my mother had carried in a bag all the way up. We'd enjoy the fresh dry air, the sounds of cardinals, finches, and *doraditos* calling and singing to each other as we sipped the bitter green tea. We'd also listen to my father tell historical stories about the explorers and heroes of Argentina.

"I'm going to be an explorer one day," I'd said once.

"You're not going to be an explorer," my brother had scoffed. "That era is gone."

"Theodoro, your brother can be anything he wants to be. If he puts his mind and heart into it, there's nothing he can't achieve."

But Theo shook his head. "You always have your head in the clouds," he'd mumbled.

I sighed; he'd probably been right. Those were good times before we got older and my father got sick.

My parents still want Luisa, Julia, and me to visit, but I'm going to have to postpone the trip. With a new baby on the way, we will probably have to move to a bigger place. I finished my coffee, paid the bill, and got back into my truck. The trip to Montreal was only a seven-hour drive, but I needed to drop off the load before the warehouse closed.

When I got there, they had a new load for me to take to Quebec City by morning. I found a place on the side of the road to park and went to sleep. When I awoke early in the morning, I lit a cigarette, started the truck, and kept going. By lunchtime, I'd delivered that load, and they gave me a new one to take to Saint John in South New Brunswick. Before getting back on the road, I ate an omelet with toast at a little Bistro. I was charmed by the French spoken in this part of Canada. The little French I'd learned in high school in Argentina didn't help much. I didn't understand a thing, but I still liked listening to the musicality of the language.

From Saint John, I drove to Maine, then New Hampshire, Massachusetts, Connecticut, and finally back home to New York.

I actually made the trip in four days. When I got home exhausted, I peeled off all my clothes, took a quick shower, and dropped into bed with just my underwear. I didn't hear Luisa or Julia get home that afternoon. I slept through the night and finally woke up the next day as Luisa prepared Julia for school.

I slipped a T-shirt on and joined them for breakfast.

Julia sat on my lap and wanted to feed me some Fruit Loops. I ate one, then I told her I'd had enough, and placed her in her seat.

"We got a letter from your brother and a bill for the truck payment." Luisa handed them to me.

I opened the bill first because I already knew what that would say. My $640 payment was due. Even though I'd put a hefty down payment down and drained our bank account, the payment was still ridiculously high. But I worked a lot, so I didn't expect to have a problem.

Apprehension made my fingers shake as I opened my brother's letter because he didn't write often, and I feared what it might say. As I read his words, my eyes filled with tears because, as I expected, *Papá* was not doing well. Theo's letter confirmed my fears. *Papá* had been admitted to the hospital, where he was fighting for his life.

My brother recommended that I not worry my parents and that I behave as if all was normal when I write them. "Tell him about your life in America, about Julia, but don't speak about your fears of losing our father," he wrote. It would upset my mother, who hoped against all hope that my father would pull through.

I handed the letter to Luisa, and she read it. "Your mother isn't dumb. She knows better than anyone your father's condition."

"Of course. But my brother is right." He was always right.

When Luisa left to take Julia to school and to go to work, I wrote my father a short letter telling him about my travels. I shared that

I was proud of our soccer team and that I knew they were doing well because I'd read about the last games in the sports section of *El Clarín*. I told him stories of Julia, especially how much she loved school. And I shared that Luisa was pregnant and that soon he would have a new grandchild. Maybe that would help him to fight and stay alive a little longer.

As I finished the letter, I folded it, sealed it, and put a stamp on the envelope to take it to the post office immediately. I got up to get dressed, but as I put my pants on, I sat on my mattress and started crying. As much as I'd resigned myself to eventually getting this type of news and the one that would surely follow if *Papá* didn't improve, there was always that hope, that agonizing hope that these letters would never arrive and that I would never have to face the terrible reality of his eventual death.

And the other reality was even more depressing. Knowing and admitting to myself that live or die, I would never see my father again.

CHAPTER TWENTY-FIVE

October 24, 1971

Dear Mamá,

With happiness, I received your last letter with news that *Papá* is improving. Lately, I've felt like my own spirit was fighting between life and well, the other side. My soul has felt like an evaporating reservoir slowly drying under a cloudless sky. But now, I'm left feeling that the sky is filling with clouds and it is beginning to rain. Each drop, one by one, gives me hope. It gets stronger and stronger and fills me with happiness to know that all is not lost. What I'm saying is that I feel a renewed hope that I never really lost and will never lose.

These hopeful words that you have written were what my heart needed to hear. As your devoted son, I will continue to send my wishes that *Papá* makes a full recovery and that his life continues to illuminate the path he has taught me to follow.

I know you only share things with *Papá* that will not harm him, so I say this to you alone. If I am not there with him, it is not because I don't want to be. I will be frank with you that I've thought of flying home, but I have expenses that if I were to stop working, I would be unable to pay. I don't have enough savings to cover the trip.

It is perhaps our destiny to be apart, and whatever happens next will not change whether I'm beside him or not. Please know that though I am not there in person, I am with you in spirit. *Papá* occupies a part of my heart that will always be there.

We continue this journey, all of us together.

Your son,

Salvador

LUISA ASKED AS I GOT dressed to drive to Chicago if I was sure I didn't want to fly to Argentina to be with my parents. We hadn't heard from them in two weeks, and we were both worried.

I called my mother, and she said that she had to be honest and that my father had good and bad days, but mostly bad ones where he suffered agonizing pain. His body continuously fought infections, and his kidneys were failing.

"Just go see him," Luisa said. "We'll be fine."

"Go for what? To watch him die? No."

I left in a bad mood, but I was always in a bad mood lately. When parents reached the end of their lives, there was little that a child could do. I didn't want to see my father suffer. I didn't want to see him weak and be only a hint of the man he'd always been. Maybe this made me a coward, but not a bad son.

My father wouldn't want me to lose my business to fly back and see him in that condition. Yes, it would give him a momentary joy to see me one more time, but at what cost to my family? As my mother told me over the phone, a man takes care of his family first. That's what my father would say to me also.

So, I left for Chicago. I delivered the load. I listened to music and tried to put the inevitable out of my mind.

When I stopped for dinner, I called Luisa.

"We got a telegram from your mother," she said, and my heart sank.

A telegram. Not many people sent those anymore. Why not a phone call? "Read it to me."

She read it, her voice cracking. It was over. My father was gone the day after I'd spoken to *Mamá* on the phone. She'd probably known that it was almost over, and that was why she discouraged me from flying home. He would have been gone before I'd made it back.

"Okay," I said. "I'm on my way home. I'll see you soon."

"I'm sorry, Salv—" But I hung up.

I flipped the radio on, and George Harrison's voice singing "My Sweet Lord" filled the cabin. *I really want to see you; Really want to be with you.* Harrison's soft voice and music guitar chords filled my cabin.

A dark cloud-filled sky opened up as soon as I hit the highway and began pouring sheets of rain. My eyes filled with tears, and I didn't know if the water on the windshield or the tears in my eyes were blurring my vision.

I wiped my eyes with the back of my hands, and when I looked at the wet road again, I saw my father's face. I shook my head and blinked my eyes, but he wouldn't go away. I reached out and tried to caress his face, feeling only the cold windshield. Feeling foolish, I slowed down and pulled over to the side of the road. Then the image of my father disappeared, and I saw instead a tree that I was about to hit. I slammed on the brakes and tried to avoid it, but there was no use. I hit the tree and came to an abrupt stop. The truck cracked the tree trunk, and it came down, its fall cushioned by neighboring trees. I was driving empty with no trailer, or the tree wouldn't have stopped me. Instead, I'd damaged the tree and the truck. I sat there for a moment and lowered my head on my arms that rested across the steering wheel, sobbing like a little boy.

Papi, how can I continue without your words of wisdom? The last few months, your silence has already felt like I've been missing a part of myself.

I'm not sure how long I sat there crying, but a knock on the door and a flashlight made me lift my head. I tried to block the light with my forearm.

"Lower your window," a police officer said.

I did as he asked.

"You hit a tree. License, please."

No kidding, I hit a tree. I handed him my license. He asked me a few questions that I had to ask him to repeat.

"Have you been drinking, sir?"

"No, I haven't been drinking. What kind of stupid question is that?"

"I beg your pardon? Get out of your truck."

I jumped down. He shined the light in my eyes.

"Your eyes are red. Have you been crying? Are you hurt?"

"No," I sighed. "I'm . . . fine."

He wrote me a ticket and asked if I'd need a tow.

"I don't think so. Can I go?"

"Why didn't you see the tree?"

Because the image of my dead father blocked it? He'd really think I was crazy or drunk. "The rain," I said. "I guess I was distracted. I just found out my father died," I admitted.

He gazed sternly at me, probably trying to decide if I was lying. "I'm sorry."

"Me too. He was my moral and spiritual compass. You know what I mean?"

"Yes, sir," he said. "I'm sorry, but you have a broken headlight, and you'll want to get the truck checked before I can allow you to get back on the road. However, I'll allow you to follow me to a service station about a mile off the highway. Once the truck is safe and re-paired, you can continue."

I didn't have any fight in me, so I nodded. "Okay, I'll follow you."

The truck started like a champ, and I followed the officer to the service station, which was closed because it was late.

"You can park here and ask them to see you in the morning. I know the owner. He's a good man, and he will help you out."

"Okay."

"Can I give you a ride to a hotel?"

"I'll sleep in the cab."

"Can I trust you not to get back on the road?"

"Yes."

He probably saw my crestfallen face and body, so he nodded and left me there feeling completely empty. I climbed into the truck, curled up in a fetal position under a blanket, and closed my eyes, waiting for sleep to come.

DEATH, BIRTH . . . both were part of life, and both brought waves of joy and sadness.

I dove into a dark depression, but it wasn't apparent to others. I continued to work long hours. Around the longer drives, I accepted the local loads to deliver fruits and vegetables. They paid well for the short trips. And I often brought home boxes of damaged produce. The fruits and vegetables weren't really damaged, but the workers set aside anything bruised or what they deemed unsellable and allowed the drivers to take them. Was this right? I didn't know, and I didn't care anymore. Corruption was part of business, and there was no escaping it.

Luisa loved the healthy produce. Her belly grew big and round, and thankfully, she felt great. The baby was growing well and was still due to be born any day. Unlike with Julia, I couldn't wait to meet and hold the new baby, but my passion for life had faded.

Luisa and I cried together, embracing each other and sharing the pain of loss when I got home the day after my father died.

"What's wrong?" Julia had asked.

I didn't want to fill her little heart with sadness, but she was old enough to understand death, so I took her little hands and explained that the next time we traveled to Argentina, she would not see her grandfather. "You know he was very sick, and his body was tired of living. Your *abuelito* died, Julia."

"But," she said, her lips trembling.

I knew the why questions she loved so much were coming. And maybe a deeper explanation of what dying meant would be required.

She nodded. "That's why you're so sad."

"Yes. He was my *papí,* and I'm going to miss reading his letters. I'll miss not seeing him when we go to Argentina."

She hugged me. "Me too." She looked up at Luisa. "Are you sad too, *Mamí*?"

"Yes," she said. "I loved him very much."

Julia let me go and hugged her mother.

The whole exchange broke me up, and tears streamed down my face. My father would not see her grow up and would never meet my next child. I covered my face and sobbed. Luisa took Julia's hand and left the room, leaving me to grieve alone. It was for the best, I suppose.

Over the next month, I looked forward to the longer drives, just to get away from everyone and be alone. On one of my trips to Chicago, when I got to a truck stop, I sat to write my mother, who had written me twice since my father's passing, and I had yet to respond.

NOVEMBER 14, 1971

Querida *Mamá,*

This is a different letter from the last one I wrote. I received your last two letters, and I'm sorry that it's taken me some time to respond. I have not been mentally well. *Papá* was always my inspiration and an example for me to follow. How to treat my family, how to treat myself, he demonstrated those things to me. He took me and my brother by the hand and led us down the path of manhood. What can I say? He was the best friend I've ever had.

In your letter, you shared that even on his deathbed, his last words were advice for his boys. I should stop smoking. I shouldn't drink so much. I should think of the effect these things will have on my family. It shows the kind of man he was—a father until the end.

I also want to tell you how proud I am of you, *Mamá*. *Papá* couldn't have been in better and more loving hands than yours. The years of love and dedication you poured into your marriage until the very last moments can only be evidence of the amazing heart you have in your chest.

I spend hours alone driving, thinking of you, *Mamá*. I picture you always as the standard of dignity and love. I see you as you are, one of the strongest women I know physically and morally. But I worry and ask myself, what will my mother do now? I wonder if you feel alone. I wonder what your plans are for the restaurant. You have sacrificed for years simply to survive, and I want to tell you that there is a future for you. I hope that you do see that, and if not now, soon you will go through an enlightened period, and it will become clear to you what you should do next.

From this day forward, I will hold and save what I think and what I feel in regard to *Papá* as if those thoughts and feelings were a precious treasure. I will not bother you with them again. But I will continue to write you about my life. I will await your thoughts and responses to my questions about your future.

Your son,
Salvador

CHAPTER TWENTY-SIX

We welcomed 1972, just us and Mateo's little family. We played tangos and other music. Danced passionately in the living room as we had back in Rosario when we were first dating. The girls danced together, imitating us and making us laugh.

Luisa made homemade *tallarines*, noodles with tomato sauce. Camila made traditional Cuban pork with black beans. Mateo and I went to the Argentine bakery in town and brought back a box full of delicious, sweet *masas*: bite-size pastries with honey and dulce de leche and merengue. I bought wine and a couple of bottles of champagne.

I imagined my father smiling and telling me proudly that life goes on and is meant to be lived. I didn't believe in heaven or that he was looking down on me or any of that nonsense. My father was alive and now he wasn't. But he left behind the memories of who he'd been, and I knew he wouldn't want me moping around because he had died. I missed him, but I was determined to make the best of my life.

As we entered the new year and I kissed Luisa, I reminded myself that this was my decade, and so far, despite the loss of my father, it was turning out just as I wanted.

BY MARCH, LUISA WAS huge. I kissed her goodbye to head out on my trip to Chicago and then Philadelphia. "Don't have the baby until I get back," I joked. The doctors did say we could expect the baby to make his or her appearance this month, but it was only the fifth, and I would be back in a couple of days.

She pushed the blankets off her to get up to serve me a cup of coffee, but I told her to stay put in bed. The varicose veins in her swollen legs were really bothering her lately. Thankfully, she'd given up her job in the new year. She needed the rest.

I headed out, stopped at a gas station, and filled up the tank in the truck, enjoying a cigarette while I waited. Then I picked up the trailer and the paperwork from the New Jersey office. From there, I drove almost non-stop because I wanted to get home as soon as possible. My one quick stop was at The White House restaurant, which sounds impressive, but it was just a 24-hour coffee shop where I ordered a burger.

I arrived in Chicago before the warehouse opened, so I parked in a shopping center to get a few hours sleep. When I awoke, I went to a liquor store to get a pack of cigarettes and a coke. I thought about my father's last piece of advice that he delivered through my mother to stop smoking and take better care of myself. Since I wasn't getting any younger, I should consider that advice a little more seriously. As I was walking out of the store, contemplating my poor willpower, a couple of guys with a gun grabbed me and pulled me to the side of the liquor store.

"Shit," I said, not feeling the fear that perhaps I should have while looking down the barrel of a gun. With all the crime in New York, I think I had become desensitized. "What the hell do you want?"

"Wallet," one of them said as he looked around nervously, waving his stupid gun in my face.

"Fine, fine, no problem. I'll get it, okay? Just get that gun out of my face." I reached for my wallet in my back pocket.

"Careful," he said.

"Put the fucking gun away, man. Here." I handed him my wallet. "My wife is about to have a baby. I don't want to leave her to raise two kids alone. Okay? Just take my wallet and leave me alone."

In his eyes, I saw a little bit of humanity. We were both victims trying to survive. He took out all my money and tossed my wallet at my feet. Then he and his friend ran away. I thought maybe they were going to hit me or hurt me, but they didn't. I sighed. "Son of a bitch." I picked up my wallet and climbed into my truck, leaving a string of curses behind.

I delivered my load, and then at the Chicago office, I handed the office manager my paperwork to get the trailer I would take to Philadelphia "Hey, do you think I could get an advance for this load?" I asked. "I was just robbed, and I don't have any money to get home."

The dispatcher's eyes widened. "Holy shit, are you okay?"

"Yeah, just angry. The crooks took all my money but took pity on me at least and let me keep my wallet and driver's license."

"Probably bums looking for quick cash for drugs. I'll see what I can do about paying you for the load you just delivered and the one to Philly. Sit tight."

I got a cup of coffee and took a seat, running a hand through my hair. Just my luck. But I was lucky they didn't kill me. Now, after it was over, I started to think about that gun he pointed at my head. As nervous as he was, he could have lost control and pulled the trigger. The thought of never holding Julia again or meeting my second child made me involuntarily shiver.

The dispatcher came back into the room, so I stood. "Sal, they can issue a check tomorrow. We'll give your Philadelphia load to another driver and have you take a different one tomorrow morning. Okay?"

It wasn't okay. I didn't want to wait around for a whole day, but what could I do? I thanked him and went back to my truck to rest and read *Bless Me Ultima*, a new book released by New Mexican author Rudolfo Anaya. One of my Mexican friends gave it to me and said I'd really like it. I'm not sure if I do yet, but it's keeping my interest because, as a little boy, I probably would have been just as interested in a *bruja* like Ultima. Kids easily believe in the supernatural and spiritual. I quickly saw through the deceptions of the Catholic Church, though when as a young boy, whenever I asked questions, the nuns told me to shut up. And when I grew older, I realized the whole system was corrupt and only interested in money and power.

As I drifted off to sleep, my last thought was to remind Luisa that she was not going to baptize my second child.

The following morning, I picked up my check and immediately cashed it. With my truck gassed and loaded, I headed to Philadelphia. But I had to stop at the Ohio office on the state border between Ohio and Pennsylvania.

I presented my log and other paperwork. The office manager took the paperwork and handed me a message. I opened the New Jersey office note saying that Luisa had given birth to a baby boy and that both were healthy.

"Oh, damn it," I said too loud apparently because the office manager looked up startled. "Sorry," I said, then smiled. "My wife gave birth to my son this morning, and I missed it."

She grinned. "Congratulations."

"Thank you, thank you. I have to go."

I drove as quickly as possible, bypassing my Philadelphia stop, and headed directly to the New Jersey office to let them know I'd get the load delivered in the morning. When I walked in, everyone started to clap and congratulate me. "Thank you. Can I borrow the phone to call the hospital?"

"Sure, Sal."

I spoke to the maternity unit, and they told me I had ten minutes before visiting hours were over.

"But I'm the father."

"Then you'd better hurry."

I hung up the phone. "How am I going to get there in ten minutes," I said. "Visiting hours are almost over."

"Come on," a guy who worked in the office said. "I'll take you in my car."

We rushed to the hospital, maneuvering around other cars and pedestrians. When I got there, Camila stood in the waiting room. "You finally made it," she said.

I ignored her and said, "Where is she?"

She pointed out the room where Luisa lay, looking remarkably alert and happy. I sat beside the bed and held her hand. "How are you?"

"Good. Did you see the baby?"

"Not yet."

"He's so cute. The doctor held him upside down from one foot and said, 'You have a redhead.'"

"Red?"

"Can you believe it?"

"Are you sure he's mine?"

She slapped my hand. "He screamed like you."

I laughed. "So now we have a boy and a girl. Perfect."

"You look tired."

"I've been driving all day since 4 a.m. I stink. I need to go home and take a shower."

"Go, we're fine. Julia probably needs to see one of us. Camila drove me here in a hurry, and Mateo stayed with the girls."

"In a little while." The nurses allowed me to stay past visiting hours, but at 8:30 p.m., one of them came to tell me I had to leave.

She said it nicely, though. "Let me take you to see your son on your way out."

I had to look at him through a window. He had his little name tag on his crib, Alexander, named after my father, Jorge Alejandro. He slept like an angel, and Luisa was right; he was light-skinned and sort of blondish. Go figure. Julia took after my side of the family, but it looked like this little guy would look more like his mother.

Camila came up behind me. "Ready to go home?"

I was glad she'd waited for me. "Yeah. Thank you for bringing her."

She raised an eyebrow. "What else could I do when you weren't around?"

"Can you keep Julia overnight and tomorrow? I'm exhausted, and I have to go deliver my loaded trailer in the morning."

"You're leaving again?"

"I have to. I rushed here and missed my last drop. It's just to Philly. I'll be back as soon as I can."

"Then, of course, she can stay with us."

"Thank you."

"Anything for Luisa."

And not for me. I got it.

I took a shower and dropped into bed, emotionally and physically drained. I didn't wake up until ten in the morning, then took a cab to the office to get my loaded truck and hurried to get on the road to Philadelphia. I returned to Jersey empty with no trailer hooked to my truck and went directly to the hospital almost at the end of visiting hours again.

"Is my wife ready to go home?"

"She and the baby need to stay one more night. I'm sorry."

I was disappointed, but rules were rules. I stopped to look at the baby again through the window wishing I could hold him. I sighed, still exhausted as if I hadn't slept the night before.

When I returned to the apartment, I first stopped by Mateo and Camila's apartment to pick Julia up. "*Papito*," she said when she saw me and came running and jumped into my arms. I kissed her, thanked my friends, and carried Julia back to our apartment.

"Did you bring *Mami* and the baby home?"

"The hospital said we have to wait another day, so tomorrow morning, we'll go get them together, okay?"

"Okay."

"Did you eat dinner?"

"Yes, Aunt Camila made us grilled cheese sandwiches."

Disgusting. We entered our apartment, and I put her down. "Well then, it's time to brush your teeth, get into your pajamas, and go to sleep.

"I'm not tired."

I looked in the refrigerator and pulled out a couple of eggs. From the vegetable drawer, I got an onion and garlic bulb. "Well, *Papi* is very tired, so do me a little favor and go to bed early tonight, so we can see *Mami* in the morning and both look rested and good."

"Okay, *Papi*." She skipped away.

I fried the eggs, tossed in some chopped garlic and onions and then sat down to eat them with a piece of toast.

Julia came back with her pajamas and sat beside me. "Is it good?" she asked.

"Delicious."

"Tia Camila said that the baby is cute."

"He is."

She placed her elbows on the table and rested her chin on her hands. "Did you hold him?"

"No, because they have the babies behind a glass window. Only the *mammies* get to hold them when they feed them."

"I want to hold him."

"Me too. We'll get to do that tomorrow, I hope."

I finished my food and leaned over to kiss her forehead. "Are you going to be a good big sister?"

"Of course," she said, making me smile.

"I believe you. You've got a heart of gold."

"What does that mean?"

I groaned. "I'll explain later. Did you brush your teeth?"

She pulled her lips back in an exaggerated smile to let me see. She still hadn't lost any of her baby teeth. "Excellent," I said. "Now, bedtime."

"Are you going to tell me a story?"

"Once upon a time, there was a little girl who just got a new baby brother. Her daddy was very tired, so they all went to sleep, they snored really loud, and in the morning, daddy bought the little girl a lollipop."

Her eyes widened. "Really?"

"You like that story?"

She nodded. "Yes!"

"Okay, off to bed, and we'll see if the story comes true."

I tucked her into bed, then took a shower and went to sleep immediately.

AT THE HOSPITAL, I had paperwork to fill out, and a bill to pay.

"What are you doing?" Julia asked.

"Paying for your brother."

"You have to pay for him?"

"Yes, we have to buy him from the hospital."

The woman at the counter laughed. "Don't tell her that. No, honey, your father is paying the hospital bill to pay for the doctor who took care of your mommy."

"Oh," she said.

I smiled at the woman and winked. "Thank you."

They wheeled Luisa out, holding the baby in her arms. Julia ran to see her, jumping up and down. "I want to see him. I want to see him."

"Okay, calm down, baby," Luisa said, uncovering the blanket to expose little Alejandro's face.

"I'm not a baby, silly," Julia said. "He is."

"Oh, that's right."

We admired the little boy for a few minutes, then Luisa stood, and we all walked out of the hospital.

At home, they got settled. "Can you go to the store and buy this formula and diapers?" Luisa asked, handing me a sheet of paper with a list of items she wanted.

I didn't really want to go back out, but I nodded. "Come on, Julia. I owe you a lollipop."

"But I want to stay with *Mami* and the baby."

"We'll be right back," I ignored her. Luisa needed to rest and not deal with an inquisitive child.

We shopped together and returned with the items Luisa wanted and a few extra things.

When I got home, the phone rang, and it was my work asking me if I could take a load. If I said no, it would be two days before I had another opportunity, so I agreed. Luisa said the baby would sleep for a long time, so if I returned in time, I could give him his first bottle.

I hoped the trip wouldn't take me too long, but I didn't get home until after ten at night, and the baby had already eaten and was sleeping. I stood by his crib and touched his face with my fingertip. I placed my finger by his tiny hand and looked at the little white fingers wrapped around my dark, dirty one. I pulled it away, not wanting to contaminate him with my filth.

"Hey, little man," I whispered. "You're going to have a great life. I promise you that." I stared at him a little longer, showered, changed, and went to sleep.

But a couple of hours later, we were all awakened by his loud cries. Luisa got up and tried to comfort him, but he kept crying.

"What's wrong with him?" Julia said, walking into our bedroom, and rubbing her eyes.

"Come here," I said. I tucked her in beside me. "Go back to sleep. He's not used to his bed and the house. Maybe he's hungry."

He cried off and on throughout the night. I had forgotten what it was like to have a baby in the house. We all had bloodshot eyes the next day. Luisa took naps throughout the day, and the next night, we had a little party to introduce our boy to our friends.

"You act so proud, like you did something special. It was all Luisa," Mateo teased me.

"You're right there. She did all the hard work."

But I got to hold Alex in my arms for the first time and feed him his bottle while listening to his little cooing, satisfied sounds. His eyebrows moved up and down as he greedily swallowed the milk until it sank and disappeared from the bottle. Then he released the suction on the nipple, and his head tilted to the side, falling asleep. I *was* proud to have helped create this tiny little human. My family was growing, and we were living the American Dream.

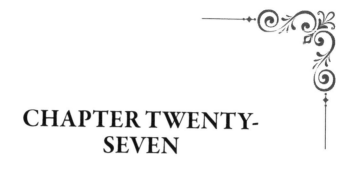

CHAPTER TWENTY-SEVEN

I wrote to my mother often because I worried about her. My brother said she continued to handle the business well. Still, he worried about *Mamá's* health and ability to care for a business alone without Papa's emotional support.

I think it's time you thought about returning home if that's still your plan, he wrote me.

It is. But it isn't that easy, I told Theo. After all, I had two kids now and a life that was working well even if I didn't have huge savings yet.

Well, if there's ever a time to return, now might be it.

I closed his letter and sat back in my living room chair, lighting a cigarette and wondering what I should do. Did I want the kids growing up in this city forever? Julia finished kindergarten and was in first grade already. In the winter, Luisa trudged through the snow to take her to school, and Julia came home all bundled up, looking so cute. We were in September of 1973, and little Alejandro had celebrated his first birthday almost six months earlier. We were about to go into another winter in New York. We had a life and routine here.

But maybe the time to return to Argentina had arrived. I could run the pizzeria, as my brother said. It would not give us a windfall, but we'd make enough to survive. We'd be okay. And the kids would grow up in my country with their cousins, where life was simpler.

Luisa had taken Julia to school and took Alejandro with her. I glanced at the clock, noticing I had to leave for work, so I put out my cigarette and grabbed my truck keys, filing away the idea of returning to Argentina. I would think more about this as I drove to Chicago and back. I did my best thinking while driving. But the only thing I came up with as the miles ticked off on the odometer was to talk the idea over with Luisa.

When I got home, I parked the truck in a lot close to home like always and walked two blocks to my apartment.

As I approached my street, people were standing on the sidewalk, looking up, all talking and gasping. When I followed their gaze to see what the commotion was all about, my heart nearly stopped. Alejandro's red head hung out of the open window of our third-floor apartment.

I started screaming for Luisa. "That's my son," I said, grabbing my head. "Luisa! Luisa!"

Those on the street encouraged me to run up there. "Go get him before he decides to hang out any further and falls out.

"No, no. Can someone please go for me? Apartment 312. Please, I need to stay down here to catch him if he falls." I pulled my keys out of my pocket and held them out to a woman. She nodded and took the keys. She and two other ladies ran into the apartment building.

Alejandro leaned out the window further; half his body hung outside. All it would take for him to fall would be for the balance to shift. I thought I was going to throw up.

I kept screaming for Luisa, praying that she would hear me. What if he fell and I had to catch him? Could I? Or would I lose my son before he reached his second birthday?

It seemed like forever, but finally, Luisa came to the window and pulled the baby inside. Everyone who had gathered in the street started clapping, but I dropped down to my knees and held my head. "Thank you, thank you," I said. Holy shit. I was going to kill Luisa.

An older man patted my back and helped me to my feet. "The boy is fine. It's all over."

I nodded, wiping the sweat off my forehead.

The lady who had my keys handed them back to me. Without thinking, I hugged her. "Thank you." Then I practically ran up the three flights of stairs.

"Where the hell were you?" I shouted when I pushed through the front door.

"I was—"

"He could have fallen to his death. Do you realize that?"

"Yes, I—"

"You have the window open, and you're not watching the kids? What the hell is wrong with you?"

"Stop yelling at me!"

"Luisa, for God's sake!"

"I was in the kitchen making dinner. He climbed out of the crib. Last I knew, he was sleeping. This scared me too."

I ran a hand through my hair. "Shit, I'm going to have a heart attack. It's still beating out of control." I entered the room where Julia and Alex played on the carpet as if nothing had happened. I picked him up and hugged him against my chest so hard that he started to kick me and scream.

"Julia, didn't you see your brother climbing out the window?" I snapped at her.

"No, *Papi*."

"He could have fallen and died. Do you understand what that means?"

She nodded.

"I asked you a question, Goddammit! Died means he's gone forever." I slapped my hands together, and she jumped. "Splat, a bloody mess. You keep an eye on your brother and tell your mother if he's doing anything dangerous. Understand?"

She frowned. "Okay."

We stared at each other for a second, then I turned around and left.

Exhausted and finally calming down, I walked into the bathroom to shower and stood under the water for at least ten minutes. When I got out, I no longer remembered what I wanted to talk to Luisa about. We ate in silence. Only Alex mumbled and asked for more or less food, innocently unaware of the tension. After dinner, I went to bed.

I WISH I COULD SAY that was the only time Alex scared me half to death. Not two weeks later, Julia came running out to the living room where I sat watching TV, telling me that Alex was turning red because he was eating a shoestring. I ran into the bedroom and found Alex choking, his face indeed red.

I quickly put him over my knee and hit his back while at the same time pulling on the string. Julia cried and talked the whole time. I didn't even know what she was saying; I frantically pulled the shoestring out of him. I held him upside down, hitting his back harder until finally I dislodged the string. He gagged, coughed, and drew multiple breaths before he let out the loudest, angriest scream I'd ever heard. He cried and cried, kicking and punching me. I put him on the carpeted floor and let him have his fit.

"Where did he get this shoestring?"

Julia wiped her own tears. "I guess he took it off of my shoes."

I let out a string of curses. So much for yelling at Luisa for not watching him. Now, I was in charge at home while she did the grocery shopping, and the kid managed to get into another mess.

"Did he almost die again?"

I huffed. "Yes." Then I thought better. "Wait, no, no. Don't tell your mother he almost died."

"Why?"

"Because he's fine, and she'll just get worried." I reached for her and put her on my lap. "You did good, Julia. Thank you for telling me. If you hadn't been watching him . . ." I shuttered, and tears filled my eyes. I hugged her close. She hugged me back.

Alex finished his tantrum, so I knelt on the floor beside him and picked him up, wiping his face. "Are you okay, *Loco?*"

He complained and moved away from me.

Julia told her mother anyway, and I had to explain what had happened. Luisa was nice enough not to ask sarcastically if I had been watching him. She just said she would move all the shoes with shoestrings up on the shelf in the closet where Alex couldn't reach them. Even though the truth was that the world was a dangerous place for children, and as much as we wished we could, we would never be able to protect them from everything.

I also realized that my wife was a better person than I was. She looked for solutions while I looked for someone to blame.

WHEN ALEX TURNED TWO the following year, he could speak, run, and climb on everything, finding new ways to get into trouble. One day, I came home to Julia in tears while Luisa tried to soothe her. Alex had stacked multiple chairs and boxes to climb high enough to knock all her dolls and toys off her shelves.

This time I laughed. Maybe my son would become a mountain climber, a fireman, or climb those telephone or electrical poles.

"It's not funny," Julia said.

"It's kind of funny. At least he didn't almost die this time."

Luisa smiled at me, turning away from Julia. "Well, it was close when Julia saw what he'd done. She screamed at him while he slapped her to make her stop yelling, making her yell louder and cry. It wasn't pretty."

"*Mami* will help you put it all back the way it was," I promised her.

That night over dinner, I asked Luisa what she thought about returning to Argentina, finally bringing up the topic since my brother had written me again the last few months to see if I'd made a decision. It had been over six months since he'd first asked. I'd told him I had to think about it, and he wanted to know how long it would take me to think.

Julia helped Alex with his food. He cooperated and ate instead of fussing and tossing his food all over the place like he usually did. He'd do anything his sister asked him to do.

"Move back permanently?"

I nodded.

"Is that what you want?"

"I wanted so much. I've been here almost ten years, and things are okay. We have what we need, but I thought I'd be wealthier by now, that I'd be going back with so much money that I wouldn't even have to work. That we could build our own home and . . . well, you know."

"I know. So, do you want to keep trying to make that happen or not?"

"We have some money saved. Not enough to build our dream home, but probably enough to buy a condo in a nice neighborhood. What if you go back with the kids, get settled in with *Mamá*, see if we can take over the restaurant, buy a condo, and then I'll wrap things up here and meet you there?"

"Go without you?"

"For a few months."

Her eyes narrowed. "I don't want another Nebraska."

I offered her a soft smile. "You'll be home where you have family and can navigate on your own. Not exactly the same thing. I've apologized for that a million times."

"If you want to return, if that's what you *really* want, then I'm ready."

An ache settled in the pit of my stomach. Too much of my adult life—practically all of it—I'd been in this country. Returning to Argentina was starting to feel like a dream that would never happen. Part of me was overjoyed, excited, and a nostalgic sadness made me wish I could be that boy who left almost ten years ago. Another part of me, the American part, rebelled at the thought of leaving this world I knew well. The excitement of a large city, the hustle, the possibilities of making it big—I still believed in it even if this country hadn't offered riches on a silver platter like I'd expected.

"When should we leave?"

"I guess whenever you're ready, there's no big hurry. I'll send *Mamá* a letter to see what she thinks. She might want to visit us here first."

She nodded. "Give me a couple of months. I'm going to miss Mateo and Camila. They're not family, but they're our best friends."

"Maybe they'll follow us. You know they always do."

"And if they don't, we'll have someone to visit here," Luisa said, but we both knew that once we moved back to Argentina, we wouldn't be returning to the U.S. Airline tickets were too expensive, and we wouldn't want to be reminded of the life we'd once had. It would be goodbye to our American Dream.

CHAPTER TWENTY-EIGHT

April 12, 1974
   Querida *Mamá*,

I hope you find yourself well as I write this letter. In your last letter, you shared that you were seeing a doctor to deal with your nervous tension. I can certainly understand after all the stress of the previous few years. I'm glad that you are seeing a doctor and feeling better.

We are doing well. Your grandson has gotten big and strong and brings us hours of joy. Your granddaughter loves her school and speaks English fluently now. I spend many hours on the road driving my truck, but when I'm home, I enjoy playing with them. I used to spend a lot of time with friends, but now I'm comfortable just being with my family. Though I do still play soccer on some Saturdays, and sometimes I play pool with my friend Mateo.

Mamá, we would love to have you visit us for a few months. What do you say? Would you like to spend some time with your grandkids? Luisa is thinking of learning how to drive the car so that you both can go out while I'm working.

Regarding your business, you and my brother have mentioned that you can put it in my name and have us take it over. I appreciate the offer, but the more I think about it, the more I think you should sell the restaurant and eliminate that headache. When we move back, I might do what I'm doing here and drive trucks. I enjoy it, and it allows me to travel and see different places. Think about it. We can always help you with it for a while if you'd like to keep it, but if I'm being honest, I have no interest in running a restaurant and being tied to a business that has to be open every day on schedule.

We love you very much and look forward to your response.

Your son,

Salvador

IN ARGENTINA, RETIREMENT, or social security benefits, sometimes take months or years to process. My mother explained that she couldn't visit until she started receiving her benefits. She was afraid to leave the country and delay the payments further.

She explained that owning the restaurant gave her something to do and occupied her mind and body. She wasn't ready to sell it, and if I didn't want what she and my father had worked so hard to grow, she'd hold on to it a little longer by herself.

"I feel like she's upset that I don't want the business," I said to Luisa over our morning coffee.

"Do you think she really needs help? Maybe we should leave her alone to work as she has been."

"Theo says it's too much for her. I thought encouraging her to sell the restaurant would solve the problem, and we wouldn't have to make the trip back. But if she insists on keeping the business, I guess we'd better return."

"If Theo thinks it's too much for her, why can't he help?"

Theo is busy building his legal career. He stops by to make sure she's okay, but he's not there daily. Plus, he's been there alone for the last ten years. I understand that it's my turn."

"So . . . what should we do?"

"I think we do as we discussed. You go with the kids, and I'll meet you there in a few months. We'll work the business while I look for alternatives and investigate the trucking business there. Then I'll convince her to sell it."

Luisa gave a slight nod, but her eyes had a faraway look.

"What are you thinking?"

She shook her head. "Nothing important."

"Tell me."

"It's just . . . to uproot our whole life just to investigate . . . what if it doesn't work out?"

I scooted my chair closer to hers and put an arm around her shoulder. "We'll make it work. Just like we do here, right?"

She offered a small smile. "Right."

"And we'll take care of *Mamá*."

Finally, I saw more interest. "I think it will be good for her to have you home again and to participate in her grandkids' lives."

I shrugged and nodded. *Mamá* wanted me home, Theo wanted me home, and I always wanted to return to my country. If it had to be now, then so be it. Life had gotten comfortable in America, but I didn't have the enthusiasm I'd had in the past. Maybe starting again in Argentina was exactly what I needed.

I FELT LIKE I'D SWALLOWED an egg that lodged in my throat when I had to watch my family board the plane a month later. I hugged Julia super tight and told her I'd miss her.

"I'll miss you too, *Papi*."

"I'll be there soon, okay?"

I tried to hug my little guy too, but he complained that I hugged him too tight and tried to wiggle away. "Hey," I said.

"Give *Papi* a kiss."

He gave me a peck. I put him down and rubbed his little curly red head.

Then I hugged and kissed Luisa.

"I'll write you and call you. *Mamá* doesn't have a phone, but my brother does."

"My sister's neighbor does too."

"Okay, well . . . I love you. I'll wrap things up here soon. I want to get a little more money. I'll try to ship some of our stuff before I leave."

"The pictures, ship those."

"Okay, you'd better go."

She took Julia by the hand and carried Alejandro down the gangway.

My shoulders drooped as I walked away, and I felt like crying. Would it be easier to do it this way? Right now, it didn't feel like I had chosen the best route. I got home and opened a can of soup.

The next day, I went to work. I got a load for Pennsylvania, and I was glad. The more time I spent on the road, the less I'd be at home alone. Things were different now that we had the kids. The house always seemed full and busy and happy. I never liked being alone, but it wouldn't be for long, so I had to deal with it for a little while. I used to cook for myself. Now Luisa did all that, and I barely even remembered how to cook.

The first month dragged on. I called my brother, and he told me Luisa and the kids got there fine. He'd picked them up in Buenos Aires and drove them to Rosario, where they got settled with *Mamá*. He was delighted to meet the kids, especially Alejandro, since he'd never met him. And, of course, Julia was now a little girl, not a baby as he'd remembered, so it was like he was meeting her for the first time too.

He told me not to worry, that he'd check in on them and *Mamá* every week, but that I should resolve whatever I needed to resolve and head back soon. Times were changing, and he didn't like *Mamá* being at the restaurant alone. If I chose not to run it, he hoped that between the two of us, we could convince her to sell it.

FIVE MONTHS LATER, in October of 1974, Luisa and my brother had purchased a condo with the money we'd saved the last couple of years. It sat empty for now while Luisa lived with my mom in the apartment behind the restaurant. She and the kids were in my old childhood bedroom. The kids liked being in Argentina with all their aunts, uncles, and cousins.

Luisa wrote that Julia attended school and that learning to read and write in Spanish was only slightly challenging for her. Alejandro rode a tricycle my brother bought him up and down the sidewalk in front of the pizzeria until one in the morning while she helped my mother run the restaurant.

When I spoke to Luisa on the phone, she sounded annoyed and worried. "I sometimes think . . ."

"What?"

"I don't know. Your mother said the other day that this restaurant couldn't provide for two families."

"Two families? What the hell does that mean? What two families?"

"I guess she meant that it doesn't make enough for the four of us and her."

"She hasn't said that to me. Is she having second thoughts about me taking over the restaurant?"

"I don't know, but she didn't like that I had to use profits from the restaurant to pay for Julia's school uniforms and books. But where else is the money going to come from? I work there and don't get paid a wage. And you don't send us any money.

"And I was upset the other night because Alex played by himself outside, and when I took a break to put him to bed, she acted like I was abandoning her. She told me that if I was too busy to help, I should go to sleep, and she'd take care of the restaurant alone like she always had before I got there."

I laughed because my mother could be sarcastic.

"It's not funny. I spent all day and night working while my son was outside alone on a tricycle. It's summer, and the customers were sitting outside too, but she thought it was unreasonable that I put him to bed?"

"I'm sorry." I didn't know what else to say.

"I picked Alex up, and we both went to bed. She apologized in the morning."

"It's hard for her. You know, honestly, she's been doing this alone for so many years. Maybe she resents that we're coming back to take over. My brother thinks it's a good idea, but maybe it's not. I don't know what she wants."

"I don't know either, but I do like being back in Argentina. How much longer are you going to take? Maybe if you were here, it would be different. You're her son, and she loves you."

"She loves you too."

"She doesn't know me. I went from being your girlfriend, who she only knew from a distance to your wife that she didn't know at all, to a woman who lives with her."

"Okay. I'll see what I can do."

"Just come. Whatever money you have is fine. When are you going to ship our things?"

"Ah . . . well, our stuff is gone."

"What do you mean?"

"I placed everything in the basement and moved in with Mateo since I'm going to leave soon, but we've had a lot of rain, and the basement flooded. Everything was ruined."

"Salvador! My pictures of the kids?"

"I'm sorry." It seemed like I said that a lot lately.

"I can't believe you. How could you be so irresponsible?"

"Do you think I knew it would flood? Shit, give me a break."

She grew silent.

"Look, I'd better go. This call is going to cost a fortune."

We said our goodbyes, and I sighed. I sat on the couch in Mateo's apartment, thinking about my mother, and wondered what she'd meant or if Luisa had misunderstood. *Mamá* was an independent woman. She'd had to be with *Papá's* illness. She'd taken care of him and the restaurant without anyone's help. Maybe giving up control and sharing her space even with Luisa was hard for her.

"How is she?" Mateo asked, startling me and pulling me out of my contemplative state.

"Tired of being there without me, I think. My mom is getting on her nerves."

"Yeah, mother-in-laws, you know."

I smiled. I told him about the restaurant not making enough money. "Not that I care about that. I don't want to work at the pizzeria anyway. I'll probably drive trucks like I do here. Or should I bring Luisa and the kids back and forget the whole thing?"

"You know how our country is. People barely survive. I wouldn't even think about going back."

"You wouldn't?"

"No way. In fact," he grinned and rubbed his hands together. "I think we're finally going to move to California."

I shook my head. "Yeah, sure. You've been saying that for years."

"Well, this time, I'm serious. Camila agreed, and I'm thinking that we're going to pack up and make the drive out next month."

California. Sounded great.

"It's the Golden State, land of opportunity. Sunshine. Beaches. You could come too."

"Can you imagine what Luisa would say?"

"Send her the plane tickets to Los Angeles instead of New York. It can be a new start for all of us."

"I don't know."

"Forget Argentina, *Loco*. Just move on. You're not Argentine anymore; you're not going to fit in."

I frowned. What the hell was he talking about? I'd be Argentine until the day I died. "I love my country, and I miss it."

"So, miss it. But don't move there and doom your family to poverty."

I thought about it that night as I drove to Philadelphia. I had to admit that Mateo made some excellent points. I could always drive to California with them, check things out, and fly to Argentina from there if I didn't like it or didn't find a good job. What did I have to lose?

I thought about my mother and the restaurant, and I felt a nagging uncertainty and guilt for even thinking about not returning home.

But running that damned restaurant and me taking over the business was my brother's idea, and my father's before him. My mother had run that pizzeria without either of them for years. And maybe having me come back to *help* had always been a tactic to get me back home. My mother had agreed with whatever my father said, and now she did the same with my brother, but deep down, I knew I'd only get in the way.

What did I know about running a restaurant? She'd be fine and probably happier alone. I could visit her often. Maybe she'd like to visit us in California if we moved there.

A familiar thrill of anticipation of the unknown, of adventure that I hadn't felt in a long time, began to grow in my gut. I started to feel alive again. Maybe the future I'd been fighting for wasn't in New York, but it was in America on the opposite side of the country. And in that moment, on a dark highway to Philadelphia, I made a momentous decision. I was going to California!

American Dream

"I have spent my life judging the distance between American reality and the American dream." — Bruce Springsteen, musician

CHAPTER TWENTY-NINE

In December of 1974, I traded my heavy jackets and long sleeves for light short sleeve button-up shirts. I used the money I'd been saving to move to Argentina and what I made selling my truck and rented a studio apartment in West Covina, where Mateo also rented a home a few miles away. The apartment had a living room and bedroom in the same room, a tiny kitchen and miniscule bathroom. This was after we all spent a couple of weeks in a hotel trying to orient ourselves. The only things I brought with me were the clothes I could fit in the trunk of my car.

Mateo's sister from Argentina contacted him the first week we were in California and told him she wanted to leave Argentina. She planned to live with him for a while until she could afford her own place. Mateo apologized and said he wouldn't have room for me too, which was fine. I didn't even consider sharing a house with him. The last few months living in their apartment in New York, and driving cross country with Camila, even if she drove in a different car, was torture enough for me. I needed my own apartment anyway if Luisa and the kids would join me soon.

Before I could begin to look for work, I developed a crazy toothache, so I contacted an Argentine association for a recommendation. Doctor Perez saw me and said I had an infection. He put me on antibiotics and told me to return in ten days which I did.

"You have some decay and a cracked tooth, which allowed bacteria to get in. You might need a root canal, but I'll see how deep the decay is," he said when I returned after I finished the antibiotics.

"I just moved to California," I explained. "I'm trying to find a job and get established. Do you have a payment plan?"

"We'll work something out."

He managed to save the tooth, fill it, and save me some money.

"What kind of work do you do?" he asked me.

"Anything."

He laughed. "You might want to be more specific."

"I've painted office buildings, cooked at a top Spanish restaurant, and driven trucks in New York. But I'd like to do something new. Maybe have my own business."

"Go back to the Argentine Association. They're good at connecting Argentines to help each other out."

"I will. And thank you for this."

"I recommend you come see me more often if you stay in the area. You want to get regular dental care."

I hadn't seen a dentist since I moved to America. "I will."

THE FOLLOWING WEEK, I went to a "meet and greet" in Burbank that the Argentine Association hosted once a quarter. The city of Burbank, like all California cities, was made up of quiet communities of family homes and dotted with shopping centers. Unlike the boroughs of New York, everything out here was spread out over long distances, and you ended up having to drive miles to get anywhere. It took me almost an hour to get to Burbank from West Covina.

Once I arrived, I checked in and placed the little visitor's tag on my shirt. Many businesses attending this event seemed to be pushing their products or services rather than looking for employees. I strolled around the tables that encircled the room and introduced myself to business owners.

On a back patio, Argentine Association volunteers prepared an *asado;* inside, other volunteers offered glasses of wine. Food was included with the $5 ticket I paid to get in. Business owners were probably subsidizing most of the costs.

"Are you looking for an insurance agent?" a woman behind one of the tables asked.

I smiled and paused at her table. "Eventually," I said. "I just moved from New York and had an agent there."

"What will you be doing in California?" she asked.

I shook my head and gazed at her, feeling overwhelmed. "I don't have the slightest idea."

She laughed.

"I don't even know what I'm doing *here*. I really just need a job. Are you hiring?"

"An agent?"

"I'll do anything. I'll walk your dog. Wash your car. What can I do for you?"

She continued to smile. "You're funny."

"Am I? I'm serious."

"Well, I wish you luck. What's your name?"

I pointed to the name tag on my shirt. "Salvador. People call me Sal."

"Sal, I don't have a dog, but if I ever get one, I'll give you a call."

I shook her hand and took one of her cards. "When I'm ready for a new agent, I'll give *you* a call."

I strolled around the other tables, and finally, having shaken dozens of hands and introduced myself to everyone in the room, I got a plate of food and a glass of wine and sat at one of the round tables in the center of the room. The food was good. It appeared the most I'd get out of this place would be a good meal. And maybe the inspiration to do what these people were doing. They had their own businesses. Plumbers, doctors, dentists, insurance agents. I looked up at the woman insurance agent and caught her eye. She was watching me. I held up my wine glass and she smiled.

Then she got up and made her way to my table. I stood and pulled out a chair for her.

"Giving up?" she asked.

"I need a good meal before I go sleep in my car."

She laughed. "I hope you're kidding."

"Kind of. I rented a home, but I'd better get a job soon, or I *will* be sleeping in my car."

She leaned forward, placing her chin on the back of her hand. "Why don't you become an insurance agent?"

I cut into a piece of exquisitely prepared rib meat, just like the beef we had back home in Argentina, and savored it as I thought about her question. Then, I took a drink of wine. "My dad was an insurance agent in Argentina for a while. And he was a journalist."

"What does he do now?"

"He died."

"I'm sorry."

I shook my head. "It's part of life, right? How difficult is it to become an agent?"

"Not difficult. You have to study for the state exam. Pass. Get hired by an agency. They give you a starting salary, usually until you build your client base."

"I shook my head. That will take forever."

"Not forever, but a while. Building a business takes time."

I wiped my lips and smiled at her. She was nice and pretty, but she had no idea how quickly I would run out of money if I didn't find a job fast. "Thanks, but I think I'm going to pump gas or something. I saw a sign at a gas station by my house that they're hiring."

I stood, leaned down, and kissed her cheek, not Argentine style, just one cheek. Then I winked and left.

An insurance agent, me? Right.

BUT THE NEXT MORNING, I found myself thinking that if I wanted to be more successful, I needed to create a different life in California. Odd jobs and working for others were for people who wanted to stay poor. I had to have my own business and take control of my future. As I lay in bed, smoking a cigarette, I picked up the woman's card. Victoria Colombo. Her face smiled back at me. She had a respectable job that probably paid well. I could have that too.

On impulse, I put out my cigarette, took a shower, and dressed in a nice pair of slacks and a button-up shirt. No tie. This was California, after all. I grabbed my car keys and drove to her office on the third floor of a three-story office building in Glendale. Her name hung on the office door, along with a couple of other people's names.

When I walked in, I saw her immediately behind one of the desks, speaking animatedly on the phone. I held my hand up to wave. The big open office accommodated three agents, with no dividers separating their desks. A receptionist, who sat up front, asked me if she could help me.

"I'm here to see Mrs. Colombo."

The receptionist nodded. "Please take a seat."

In a few moments, she hung up her call, stood, and invited me to sit at one of the chairs in front of her desk. "Hi, ah, I'm sorry, I don't remember your name."

"I'm hurt," I said with a smile, holding a hand to my heart. "Salvador."

"Sal, that's right. How can I help you?"

"I came to take you to lunch."

She narrowed her eyes. "Excuse me?"

"Successful insurance agents take lunch breaks, don't they?"

"Are you flirting with me?"

Immediately, I shook my head and realized how I sounded. "Oh, I'm sorry. No, not at all. I want to find out more about becoming an agent as you suggested, and I know your time is valuable, so I thought —"

She held a hand up. "Relax." She smiled. "I'm kidding. And I'd love to take a lunch break." She reached for her purse and told the receptionist she was going out to lunch.

"There's a coffeeshop not too far from here. It's not Argentine food, but it's not bad. Is that okay?" she asked.

"Yes, any place."

"Should I drive?"

"If you'd like. Or I can."

Victoria pointed to a royal blue Lincoln Continental in the parking lot. "I'll drive. My car's right here."

When we got inside, she turned to gaze at me. "Salvador, are you alone?"

"What do you mean?"

"Do you have a family?"

"They're all in Argentina."

She nodded. "I don't mind helping another Argentine. Especially a cute young one, but—"

"No, really, I didn't mean to give you the impression that—"

She placed a hand on my cheek, and I stopped talking, frozen with a little bit of fear and a lot of curiosity. What was she doing?

"Do you genuinely want to become an insurance agent?"

I nodded. "I think I need to have a career. I've been in this country for ten years, and I have so many dreams built up inside me. It feels like I'm going to explode sometimes with the desire and need to do something important." I stopped. "To become someone important." I eased back, away from her hand. Why was I telling this stranger this? "I just don't know how to do it."

I looked away from her intense stare.

Her hand had slipped from my face to my chest, but she reached up again and touched my chin to make me face her. "I'll show you. If you're serious and put in the effort, I'll help you."

"I'm absolutely serious. I'll do whatever you say."

Victoria pulled back and started the car, then she smiled, the intense moment slipping away. She drove to the restaurant, and I ordered a sandwich and a coke; she ordered a salad.

"So, tell me about yourself."

"What do you want to know?"

"Everything."

I widened my eyes and looked up. "I'm a hard worker. I'm ambitious. I *do* like dogs."

She laughed.

"You know I'm Argentine and that my dad died. My mom is still in Argentina."

"Education."

"I dropped out of college when I came here."

"Why?"

I shrugged. "I didn't feel I needed the degree and wanted to come here to work to earn money."

"Are you intelligent?"

I grinned, looking cocky, I'm sure. "Extremely."

Victoria ate some of her salad. "And modest like most Argentine men."

"Look, I can pass that test if that's what you're asking."

"Good. Then the first thing you need to do is study."

"That's not a problem."

"There's a school you should attend."

I shook my head. "I don't have money for that. I'll learn on my own."

"Mm," she said, not looking happy about that plan.

"So, tell me about you?" I decided to steer her away from me and my personal business.

"You don't need to know anything about me."

Now I wanted to. "You're intelligent. You don't like dogs." I smiled. "You're good at what you do."

"How do you know I'm good?"

"You're a woman who owns a luxury car and an office in Glendale. You dress amazingly in fancy clothes. You smell like you're wearing expensive perfume. You *look* successful."

"Then you've just learned another lesson, Sal. If you want to be a successful salesperson, and that's what you are as an insurance agent, then you need to look the part. Buy nice clothes, a suit or two. Cut your hair."

I touched my shoulder-length hair that was the style. I no longer had my old suit that I'd gotten married in. "I will when I get money."

"Don't wait. Get a credit card if you need to."

I'd never thought of applying for a credit card. Who would give a guy without a job a credit card? "So, am I wrong? You're not successful? All this is fake?" I waved at her perfect hair and clothes. "Or do you have a wealthy husband?"

"I *am* successful, and I'm divorced, so I earn my own money."

I nodded and ate my sandwich. She didn't touch the rest of her salad.

"Do you miss Argentina?" I asked her.

"Yes. We all do, right?"

"Yes," I said. Argentina lived in my soul. "I dream of returning one day, but it's not as easy to find work there, so when I do, I want to have enough money saved that I don't have to worry about working when I'm there."

"Is that why you came here? To become wealthy?"

"I used to think so. I thought it was easier."

"Yes," Victoria smiled. "Argentines think that in America, money grows on trees."

It was a cliché, but yes, they did think money came easy. And in many ways, it did. I lit a cigarette and leaned back to watch her play with the lettuce in her salad bowl. "But I think maybe the real reason I left everything I knew was for the adventure of it all. To try to make it on my own. To prove to myself that I could."

"Mm," Victoria said, putting her fork down and giving up on her salad.

"But now I care more about doing what I need to do to really make some money. I still want to do something that matters, but I realize I can't do anything important without money."

"Well then, you will probably do very well in the insurance business."

I finished my cigarette and put it out in the ashtray. "Thank you."

"For what?"

"Helping a guy you don't even know."

"Don't make me sorry. You seem like a nice person. Are you?"

I thought about that for a second. "I can be." I guess I was about to become whatever I needed to be successful, just like I told her.

We rode back to her office in silence, and I walked her to the office building door. "Thanks," I said again and leaned forward to kiss her cheek, but she angled her face, and I accidentally kissed her lips. I was about to apologize, but she caressed my face. "I'll get you the material so you can start studying for the exam. Call me in a day or two."

I nodded as she turned around and left. My heart started to beat fast, and again I was afraid. I should never call her again. I wasn't sure what was going on or what she *thought* was happening. But I sensed two things. The first was that she could help me achieve my dreams quickly. And the second . . . that she could get me into trouble if I wasn't careful.

CHAPTER THIRTY

I deas with potential, those that inspire me, will quickly consume all my attention, especially if they hold the promise to change my future. I found it hard to think of anything but starting my insurance business, and it was difficult to wait a couple of days to call Victoria. I wanted to get started immediately. So, I waited a whole day after our lunch and called her on the second day to see if she had the study material.

"I'll bring it to you," she said, "Give me your address." Victoria was different from other women I'd met. She took control, obviously used to telling others what to do, which felt odd when she issued commands. Maybe because all the women I'd met in New York were either my friends' girlfriends or office girls in trucking companies more used to taking orders than giving them. Victoria ran her own business and didn't have to listen to anyone else.

About an hour later, she knocked on my door. "Wow, you really have just moved in," she said as she walked into my place.

I had a few boxes with clothes, shoes, and other odds and ends I had brought with me, and they were scattered in my small living room still—no furniture except for a plastic patio chair. "Please, sit here. Can I get you some water or wine?"

She laughed. "I saw that this apartment building has a pool with chairs and tables. Maybe we should go sit out there."

"Okay, that's where I got the chair anyway."

She shook her head. "*Pibe*, you need a lot of help."

"*Pibe*?" She just called me a kid.

"No offense."

She was a little older than me, but not by much, possibly ten years. Maybe she was in her early 40s. "Well, *Piba*, that's the nicest way someone has told me I'm immature."

She waved away my comment. "Honestly, I didn't mean it that way. Shall we go outside?"

We sat in the sunshine under the umbrella while she explained the insurance business and handed me some manuals and pamphlets. "When you're ready, you can make the appointment to take the course to prepare for the exam."

"I told you, I don't need a course. I'll study on my own."

She shook her head.

"I will."

"Salvador, look at me." She frowned. "Take this seriously. It's challenging. Even with a course, you'll have to study for a few weeks and make sure you understand all the rules."

"I told you I'm smart and wasn't kidding or exaggerating. I'll study on my own, and I'll be ready in a week. I need money. I want to start this business quickly."

She placed a hand over mine. "Start reading and see how you feel. Maybe I can help you out with the cost of the course, and you can pay me back when you get established."

"Really? You'd do that?"

"Hey, Salvador," I heard Mateo's voice behind me. His gaze landed on Victoria's hand covering mine, and then he looked her over more thoroughly, from her head to her perfectly coordinated business suit and pumps.

I moved my hand away. "Mateo. What are you doing here?"

"I was in the neighborhood. Hello," he said to Victoria.

"Victoria, this is my best friend, Mateo. He's also an Argentine from New York."

She held out her hand, and he shook it.

"Just a minute," I said to her and waved for Mateo to follow me. We walked around to the other side of the pool.

"Who's that?" he asked.

"A business associate."

"Business? What business?"

"I'm going to open an insurance agency. She's going to help me."

He glanced at her as she watched us. "Why is she going to help you?" Mateo asked.

"Why all the questions?"

"Because you looked awfully friendly with her."

He was getting on my nerves. "Look, I'll come to see you in a few days. I need to get established and see what happens with this idea. You haven't had to work since your insurance settlement, but some of us are trying to earn an honest living."

For the first time, he looked angry. A frown replaced his easygoing, awe-shucks personality, and he pointed at my face. "Honest? Is that what you are? Do you really want to go there?"

I clenched my jaw, not responding for a few seconds. Then I smiled and patted his shoulder. "Come on, *Flaco*. There's nothing to worry about, okay?"

"I hope not." He walked away and waved at Victoria as he headed out.

"A problem?" she asked.

"We drove out here from New York together. We've been friends practically from the day I moved to this country."

"He didn't look pleased with you."

I shrugged. "Just guy stuff. *Canallas*, you know how they are."

She laughed. "Oh, so you're a Newell's Old Boys fan."

"Is there any other team worth cheering for?"

She stood. "I've got to get back to work. Look over the material and let me know what you think. I'll find out when and where the next course will be held. And buy you a ticket?"

I should say no. I didn't want to owe Victoria money or anything else. I thought of Mateo's words. *Honest? Is that what you are?* But I shoved aside his hypocritical judgment. I didn't want to think about what he thought, or anyone else thought for that matter. I had to do what was best for me. "If that's what you think is best," I said to Victoria.

"Okay then," she said. "Let's do this."

ALTHOUGH THIS CALIFORNIA weekend in January promised to be warm and perfect for laying by the pool with a cold beer, I spread my books and handwritten notes on my carpet along with a cup of coffee. I opened the book on property and casualty principles and settled on the floor with my back resting on the wall to absorb the information.

I was sure I could learn everything by myself, but when Victoria called with the course registration information, I allowed her to enroll me. She came over the following week to see how I liked the course and to test me, and help me study, and her questions were helpful. I took notes. She was right about needing more than one week, but it wasn't that difficult.

After about four hours, I put aside the paperwork and listened to her business stories as we sat together on the carpet.

Then she stretched. "You really need some furniture. My butt hurts."

"I know, and I'm hungry. Let's go get some food."

"I'm starving, too," she said. "Where do you want to go?"

"Wherever you want."

"There's a nice place by the beach." She stood. "Have you been to any of the beaches?"

"Not really. I haven't had much time."

"Well, you're missing out."

We strolled to her car. As she drove, I reached across and eased her hair back.

She angled her head, giving me a quick glance. "What are you doing?"

"What are *you* doing? With me?"

"I don't understand your question."

"You must have other friends. Men who want to take you out. What are you doing with me? You know what I'm asking."

"I'm not with you. I'm just helping you get your business established."

I eased back. "Right."

"I guess I saw some of myself in you. Except when I came to America, I was married to my jerk of an ex-husband. So, when I got divorced, I had to make it on my own. It was hard."

"Why was he a jerk?"

She shrugged. "Domineering. Verbally abusive. Didn't want kids. When I accidentally got pregnant, he made me abort it. Our marriage was essentially over after that."

We got to the beach and parked. Victoria immediately slipped out of the car, then held her hand for me to take. I gazed at her face, trying to read her intentions, then took her hand.

We walked along the sand, neither one of us speaking. Finally, I stopped and faced her. The waves were methodical, and the breeze blew slightly. I didn't know what she wanted from me, but she wanted something. I reached behind her neck and pulled her lips toward mine. She didn't resist as I kissed her deeply. She seemed lonely, maybe a little unsure of herself, at least with men.

"You're beautiful," I said. "Your ex-husband was an idiot."

She leaned in and kissed me this time.

Afterward, I said, "But I'm not the guy for you."

"What if I want you anyway?"

I pulled away and cussed. I thought of Luisa for the first time since I started seeing Victoria. I didn't care about Victoria. I really just wanted her help. But if she had other ideas, I should just end it now. Not that I'd always been entirely sexually faithful during our marriage, but I'd been emotionally faithful. This felt different. I shook my head. "You deserve better."

"I can help you. I know you don't have money right now. I'm going to pay for your license. Help you start your agency."

"All out of the kindness of your soul, huh?"

She touched my shoulder. "Am I wrong to think you're as interested in me as I am in you?"

Interested? I hadn't had sex in months. Yeah, I was interested. But not the way she meant. "You're not wrong."

She sighed, relieved. "I like you. You're full of passion. And I'm . . ." she lowered her gaze.

"You're lonely." And maybe a little desperate. And she was willing to trade her money and time for attention from a man she barely knew.

"I work a lot. I haven't had a real relationship since my divorce. I didn't realize how lonely I've been. Maybe it's time I worked a little less and remembered what it was like to have fun."

I thought of my father this time, what he'd say, the disappointment he'd surely feel and express. But he was no longer alive, and it had been three years since he'd been here to offer advice. I couldn't hear his words anymore. I didn't care. I wasn't that same boy anymore who could be influenced by a disapproving parental tone and the need to please him. I had to do what was best for me. I wanted Victoria. I wanted anything she wanted to give me, and I didn't give a shit if anyone else approved.

I took her hand. "Let's go eat. I'll show you how to enjoy life to the fullest."

"YOU NEED A SUIT," SHE said as we entered a men's clothing shop in Los Angeles. She spoke to the store clerk and instructed him to find me a well-fitted suit.

"We can measure you, sir, and have one tailored for you."

"No, you can make adjustments as needed from the suits you have here, can't you?"

"Of course."

"Well, let's do that." The expense of a tailored suit was ridiculous, and I didn't want Victoria to spend that kind of money.

I was measured and prodded. Victoria chose shirts and ties for me. Then she paid the bill, and we left to have dinner. She also insisted that I get a haircut. During dinner, she brushed back my short hair.

I nuzzled her neck. "Thank you for the clothes. You didn't have to do that."

"I wanted to. You looked so handsome."

"I did look pretty good, didn't I?"

She smiled. "We have to get you set up as an agent in my office now that you've passed the state exam. As soon as you officially get your license, of course."

"I don't want to be an agent in your office."

"What do you mean?"

"I'm going to start my own agency."

She drew back. "Well, sure, but you need to start slower. You'll work for me."

"No, I won't."

"Working on your own wasn't the plan," she said.

"Plan? What plan?"

"I thought you understood that I was helping you so you'd be an agent for my agency."

"No, Victoria. You helped me because you were attracted to me and wanted me, let's be honest. You've got me. But I'm not working for you."

"I paid for your state exam and everything else because I want you working with me."

I placed a hand on her lips. "Stop. Eat your food."

"Salvador, getting enough clients to start your agency takes forever. In my office, I can feed you clients."

I placed my hand on her leg, moving it up. "Feed me something else. Eat your food so we can go to my apartment. I want to take all your clothes off."

"You're not listening to me."

"No, I'm not, so shut up already."

She was about to say something else, so I kissed her. "I want you," I whispered.

Kissing me back, she stopped arguing. She would continue to badger me about working in her office, no doubt, but I had no intention of giving in. I wanted to start my own agency and control my business.

At my apartment, where she also insisted on buying furniture even though I told her I couldn't pay her back, she made herself at home. We had divided the studio apartment visibly in half. On one side of the room, she'd placed my double bed with a couple of nightstands, on the other side, a floor lamp, a couch, a coffee table, and a recliner. Somehow, she made it all fit and look good. She went to my bathroom.

"Take your clothes off and get in bed," I called.

In the kitchen, I poured myself a glass of water and looked through my pile of mail: a few bills and a letter from Luisa, who was not happy that I'd moved to California.

Victoria came back out of the bathroom in her panties and bra and sat on my bed, opening my nightstand drawer. "I should keep some fresh underwear at your place."

"Mm," I said as I looked at the due date for my utility bills. Shit, they were going to turn my electricity off if I didn't pay it next week.

"You're married? And you have kids?" Victoria asked. She stood behind me and tossed a different letter that I'd received from my brother last week on the counter in front of me. She'd pulled it out of my drawer.

I drew in a breath and looked at a very angry Victoria. "We're separated. She's in Argentina."

"You're married!"

I moved away from the kitchen counter and approached her.

"Don't touch me," she snapped.

"Calm down. We're separated. She's in Argentina," I said.

"You lying bastard. I read your brother's letter."

I reached for her, but she yanked her arm away. I had gotten to know Victoria well in the last few weeks, and she just needed to be controlled and seduced. So, I wrapped my arms around her, pinning her arms to her side while I kissed her neck, and kept repeating. "I want you. I need you. Calm down."

"Let me go."

"No, you don't want that. Victoria, stop," I raised my voice. She kept fighting me. I kissed her. She didn't kiss me back. "I love you," I said finally, though I didn't. I loved Luisa. I always had, but I didn't want to lose Victoria right now.

She stopped struggling. "Let me go," she said.

I did. And stood back.

She stared at me and cupped my face with both hands. "What did you say?"

"I said I love you. Come to bed with me."

"What are we going to do about your wife?"

I picked Victoria up and carried her to bed. "You let me worry about that. And you worry about keeping me happy. Because I am happy with you. You know that?"

She kissed me. "I don't want to lose you," she whispered with a frown and tears glistening in her eyes.

"Then don't."

WHEN VICTORIA LEFT the next morning, I read Luisa's letter dated March 25, 1975. Things were bad in Argentina. The damned Peronistas didn't do enough damage to the country the first time they were in power. Now, Peron's bitch wife Isabel had become the Vice-President and then President of the nation when Peron died. The country was in turmoil since everyone who disagreed with the Peronistas was labeled a subversive. Protests in the streets were common, especially after people started "disappearing." Luisa said there were bomb threats in Julia's school almost every week; she'd had to pick her up and bring her home. Julia also ended up getting hepatitis and was under the doctor's supervision.

My mother's restaurant had been shot up in a drive-by, and the neighborhood increasingly had become more dangerous.

I sighed and ran a hand through my short hair. Damn it. I needed to bring my family back. Things were coming together here, but I hadn't even started working yet. But I knew that I would not move back to Argentina with all the upheaval going on there. The U.S. had its issues too, but nothing as dangerous and violent as what was happening in Argentina. The war in Vietnam, at least, was officially over, and the soldiers were returning home.

I sat down to write Luisa and told her that as soon as Julia's doctor cleared her medically, I wanted Luisa to let me know so that I could send them all tickets to fly to California.

Victoria paid all my expenses right now, so I hadn't spent much of my money. I could start my agency soon and start working. All I had to do was find clients, and I would. I made a few Argentine friends at the Argentine Club, so maybe I could start convincing some of them to let me be their agent.

Mateo wasn't talking to me, unfortunately. His sister had opened a deli in West Covina, and I went to see it with Victoria. This time, Mateo pulled me aside angrily. "We love Luisa, and if you're being unfaithful to her, you're not welcome here. And we're no longer friends."

I laughed. "It's not like that. This is . . . temporary."

"You make me sick," he said. "Just leave."

"Seriously? Come on."

"I'm very serious. And you think Camila won't tell Luisa what you've been up to when she sees her?"

"Don't tell her then. What happened to guys sticking together, of having each other's back?"

"Having your back? Yeah, I'm here for you if you need food or help finding a job, or if someone is trying to screw you. But if you're the asshole hurting your wife and kids, then to hell with you."

I bought a couple of sandwiches and Victoria, and I left. If that was the way he wanted to play this, then fine. I didn't need him anymore. Did he think this was any different from the scams we had participated in together in New York? It was all a game. And I was tired of losing. This time, I was in control, and whoever wasn't with me, whoever didn't support me, could stand aside. I had no use for them.

CHAPTER THIRTY-ONE

Julia's doctor cleared her for travel. Luisa's letter made it clear that I needed to return to Argentina or send plane tickets for them to return to the U.S. And I agreed, of course. We'd been apart too long. I missed them all, and my kids were growing up without me.

"I'm going to bring you back," I said to Luisa. "From everything you've said, it doesn't seem wise for me to return to Argentina now."

"I wish I could disagree," she said. "But every day it's worse. The *militares* have destroyed our beautiful country and created nothing but poverty."

"Maybe it will change in the future," I said, hoping that would be true. "But for now, you'll like California. This state is truly paradise. But give me a month or two to get a larger apartment and start working. I got my insurance license finally, so I should start making money soon."

"No more than two months, Salvador."

"I know. Don't worry."

I spoke to my mother for a few minutes, but her words were drenched with regret and pain. "I thought this time you would truly come home."

"I wanted to, *Mamá*. But I'm still searching for that elusive thing, that key, that mythical door I'm supposed to pass through to become the man I'm supposed to be. Maybe here in California, I'll find it, and then I'll be able to come home."

"*Querido mio*, I have this fear in my heart that tells me that if you didn't come home this time, you never will. This was your final opportunity to return."

Tears filled my eyes, and I gripped the handset of my phone tightly. I had that fear too. But I also had a fear of returning to Argentina a nobody, worse than a nobody, a failure with no job prospects in a country that was failing. "*Mamá*," I said. "You know me better than that. I make my own opportunities. Right now, it has to be here, but one day soon, it will be there."

"I hope it's before I'm gone," she said. "I'm not getting any younger."

"Oh, come on. You're as healthy as a horse."

She laughed. I told her I loved her and hung up, feeling guilty. But what could I do? I had to live my life my way.

IN APRIL, I INTERVIEWED with Security Life of Denver, a smaller Life and Health Insurance provider with an office in Hollywood, and applied to be an agent. I had zero clients and would be establishing a new agency, so they were skeptical. But since I was newly licensed to sell life insurance and eager to get started, they gave me an opportunity. Victoria said that if I didn't work with her or start my agency, my best bet was to be an internal agent, and she was right. I sold five life insurance policies in my first month because I hustled and started calling every Argentine I'd met in California.

At the end of the month, Victoria and I celebrated. We lay in bed drinking champagne after a hot roll between the sheets. I glanced at her after, trying to think of a way to tell her that Luisa and the kids were coming back. Would she understand?

"What?" she asked.

I looked away. "Nothing."

She stretched closer and rested one arm around my waist, placing her head on my shoulder. "Tell me what you're thinking."

I couldn't. But what came out was, "I was thinking about my daughter."

"Tell me about her."

"She's cute and smart, and she loves stories. She always wants us to tell her a story."

"What kind of stories?"

I chuckled. "Any kind."

"Tell me a story," she said.

I groaned and stretched to get my cigarettes. I lit one and blew smoke above our heads, watching it swirl. "Hmm, let me see."

Victoria smiled and waited.

"Do you know the legend of *el Carau*?"

"No, what is it?"

"*El Carau* is a bird, but he wasn't always a bird."

"Interesting, what was he?"

"Well," I sat up straighter, and she eased back. "He was a young man who had a sick mother, and she sent him to get her some medicine. On his way to the neighboring village, he heard an accordion playing. Did you know I played the accordion as a young boy?"

She smiled. "I didn't know that. You must have been cute."

I grinned. "I was a serious musician and played the best tangos when I wasn't too lazy to practice. Anyway, the boy was intrigued by the cheerful music, so he followed the enticing sound and found a bunch of people dancing out in the countryside. He saw a pretty girl and couldn't help himself; he asked her to dance.

"He completely forgot about the medicine for his mother as he danced and enjoyed himself until a guy came up to him and tapped him on the shoulder to tell him that he was very sorry, but his mother had died."

"Oh no," Victoria said. "That's terrible."

"It was, but the bastard said it didn't matter, that he would grieve later because he was having too much fun. He kept dancing with the girl all night. In the morning, he asked the girl if he could go home with her. Do you know what she said?"

"She said no."

"That's right. She said she'd never take home someone who had no love for his mother. He was shocked and heartbroken, so he went home crying. God saw his pathetic sobbing, and to punish him for his cruelty toward his mother, he turned the boy into a large bird full of black mourning feathers. And ever since then, the bird cries at dusk and through the night. This was to serve as a warning to all young men to respect their mothers." I put the cigarette out in the ashtray on my nightstand. "And that is the legend of *el Carau.*"

Victoria pulled herself up and sat beside me. She kissed my temple. "Why are legends always so dark?"

I stared ahead at the blank wall of this tiny apartment that lacked personality or warmth. "Because humans are dark. We're all selfish bastards." Tears clouded my vision.

Victoria turned my face, caressing my cheek, and gazed into my eyes, frowning. "We don't have to be."

"But we are. You know what I got out of that story when I was a kid? That the boy was selfish and dumb and impulsive, but that God is cold, unforgiving, and vindictive. So, which is worse?"

"It's a folktale, Salvador."

"Right." I pushed away from her and stood. "You should go tonight. I have some work to do."

"Go ahead and do it. I don't mind."

"Really, you should go."

"Okay," she said, an edge to her voice. Victoria didn't like to be told what to do. Too bad.

She got dressed while I made coffee in my kitchenette. She stood beside me. "I had a good night."

"Me too," I said.

"I love you," she said.

I scoffed. "Even if I've broken my mother's heart?"

"Even then. I would still go home with you."

I gazed at her. And that was why I couldn't really love her back. Luisa would never say something like that. She wasn't a fool. "Yeah, good night, Victoria."

THE FOLLOWING MONTH, I made enough money to buy the airline tickets for Luisa and the kids and wrote to tell her I'd be sending the tickets.

The week before they were due to arrive, I swallowed my pride and knocked on Mateo's door. Camila opened it, took one look at me, and closed the door.

"Damn it." I knocked again, banging harder.

"Get the hell out," she said as she opened the door again.

"I want to talk to Mateo."

"You are the lowest of the low, nothing but a miserable insect. My husband doesn't want to have anything to do with you anymore."

I rubbed my forehead. "Come on, Camila. Give me a break. Luisa's flying out next week. I need Mateo's help. Go get him."

Mateo patted her shoulder and jerked his head to tell her to move aside. Then he stepped out on the porch.

"I know what you're thinking. I know you're judging me, but I love Luisa. You know that."

"It's your business. I'm not involved. We're no longer friends."

"Yes, we are. You're my *best friend*, Mateo. We're brothers. I don't want to live in California without your friendship."

He looked uncomfortable as he rocked back and forth on his legs. I knew he didn't want to lose our friendship.

"It's been the four of us for so long," I pushed. "You're there for me, and I'm there for you, remember?"

He looked kind of choked up. "Luisa and the kids will be back?"

"Yeah, and I want to move to a new place. Start fresh. Will you help me?"

"You son of a bitch," Mateo said with a frown. He stared at me. "What do you want me to do?"

"I need help moving. There isn't enough room for three more people in my apartment."

"What about the woman? Is that over?"

"Yeah," I said with a shrug. "Of course." Though it wasn't.

MATEO KNEW A GUY WHO knew a guy who had a truck. He agreed to help me move all my stuff to a small, converted apartment in El Monte—a small house behind a larger home.

We made three trips back and forth and carried all my stuff to the new place. Once we were all finished, we sat outside on a low wall and had a beer.

"I'm working with my sister at her Argentine deli. It's going well for her. Mostly it's a lunch joint, a deli with a few products people can buy, but I think it could grow into something good."

"I'm glad it's going well. Maybe I can sell her worker's compensation insurance if she ends up hiring people."

He laughed. "Maybe. I also got a job for the city parks coaching soccer. It doesn't pay much, but I get to be outside, on the ground, instead of hanging from buildings. I help kids, and it's a lot of fun. Camila is going to a dental hygienist school."

I enjoyed catching up with him after so many weeks of not seeing each other and him not talking to me. "It's weird living so far away from each other, isn't it? In New York, we were always in the same building or at least in the same neighborhood."

Mateo put his beer down, not drinking much of it. "I like it here, though. It's always sunny. Life is slower." He grinned. "I like it a lot."

I looked at my little place. Hopefully, we wouldn't have to stay here long. Once I started making real money, I'd be able to move to a nicer place, maybe a house like Mateo's.

I performed a few clerical jobs for Victoria, and she way overpaid me. I bought food and gas with that money, but in the last couple of weeks, I told Victoria I was too busy to see her. And I didn't tell her I was moving. It was better just to disappear and end things like that.

I finished my beer and stood. "Well, I'd better go get things straightened up in there. Luisa won't be happy to see it looking like a tornado hit the house."

"Hey," Mateo said. "I hope things work out for you two."

"Of course. Why wouldn't it?"

He shook his head. "I don't know, man."

"Thanks again for helping me move."

He nodded. "When Luisa gets settled, let's get together." He turned to go. "Oh, by the way, Camila is pregnant."

"Wow! Congratulations," I said, knowing he was probably happy. "Your first kid is always exciting."

"First biological kid. I love Niki with all my heart, but this is definitely exciting. I'll see the new baby from the moment it's born."

"We'll get together and celebrate then, *Flaco*. Take care."

I went into the tiny house and looked around. I pulled out a cigarette and sighed. I was tired of moving all the time. Someday soon, I was going to get a permanent home.

ON JULY 9th, ironically, Argentine Independence Day, I finally got my family back. I couldn't believe how big the kids had gotten. I picked up little Alex and held him up over my head. He looked kind of unsure, the little rascal. "You've gotten big and strong," I said to him. Then I looked down at Julia. "And you look like a young lady." She looked at me shyly. I hadn't seen them in fourteen months, which I imagine is a long time for kids.

I kissed and hugged Luisa. "It's so good to see you."

"It's good to see you too. It's been crazy. Our country is not headed in a good direction."

"Mm, well, same old story on repeat."

I drove them home, and Luisa and I chatted about my mom, the neighborhood, my brother and his two boys, and other family members. Everyone sent their love.

"It's small," I said as we walked into the house. "But it's temporary."

She gave me a look that seemed to say *it's always temporary*. Or maybe it was my own guilty conscience saying that. "It's nice being in a house instead of an apartment like in New York."

"This is your room, Julia," I said. "It's nice and big, isn't it?" It wasn't really. I found two twin beds at a secondhand store.

"There are no toys," Julia said.

I sat on her bed. "Come here."

She eyed me but didn't move from beside her mother. Luisa pushed her forward. "Go sit next to your father. What's wrong with you?" So, she did.

"What kind of toys do you like?"

"I have some dolls in my suitcase. Alex likes cars and tricycles."

"They have very nice toy stores here. Maybe we'll go visit one and get you guys some toys. What do you say, *Gordita*?"

She nodded but her eyes filled with tears.

"What's wrong?"

"I miss Grandma and Argentina."

"You just got here. You'll love it in California. And we'll bring Grandma to visit us soon."

"Really?"

"Sure, why not?"

The kids stayed in their room, opening their suitcases, and getting their things out. Luisa and I went to the kitchen to have a cup of coffee. "Are you hungry?"

"I'm mostly tired. So, why California now? You were doing so well driving your truck in New York. What are we doing here?"

"Like I told you, I decided to try it out when Mateo and Camila came out, and I think it's going to work out." I poured coffee into our cups.

"I waited and waited for you."

"You said yourself that it's not a good time to return." I took a seat across from her and added some sugar to the coffee.

"It might have been different if you had been there."

"Sure, with idiots bombing schools and protests out in the streets every day, it would have been different. Luisa, give this place a chance. The energy is so different from New York and the east coast."

"You cut your hair."

I ran my fingers through my short hair. "As an insurance agent, I needed to look less like a hippy and more professional. You don't like it?"

"I kind of liked your hippy look." She shook her head. "Well, on second thought, this clean look is probably better."

It was good to have Luisa back. I'd missed her more than I realized. I reached across and held her hand. "When you married me, you knew it was going to be an adventure."

"I don't think I knew what I was doing."

"What is that supposed to mean?"

"Just that we need more stability."

"We'll have that here."

"I hope so."

We went to bed early, and it felt strange to sleep with my wife again after so much time, but it was right. Everything felt right again.

In the morning, I took the family out to eat breakfast. We went to a Mexican restaurant.

I ordered eggs and chorizo for me and some scrambled eggs with tortillas for the kids. Luisa ordered a tostada. When she got her food, she stared aghast at her plate. "What is this?"

"It's a tostada with beans and cheese. Isn't that what you ordered?"

She looked horrified. "I just wanted some toasted bread. You know, a tostada. With butter. Maybe some dulce de leche."

I laughed. "Okay, I'll let the waitress know. You're going to have to get used to the Spanish here. It's a little different. And so is the food."

She pushed the food away and looked out the window. "I love all the palm trees."

"What's that *Mami*?" Julia asked.

"Those tall trees. Those are *palmeritas*."

Julia had a little notebook, and she wrote down the word and started drawing the tree. Alex ate chips happy as could be. Every once in a while, he'd call his sister and make her give him something: water, a crayon, her attention.

"Your mother was in tears when we left. At first, as you know, it was difficult to learn to live together. I'm sure we got on her nerves. But after so much time . . . she was hoping you'd join us, and we'd stay."

"We will someday. Maybe soon. I think I'm finally going to make money here. Real money, not the nonsense I made in New York. And when we're ready, we now have a paid apartment in Rosario, so it will be easier to move."

"I just hope things improve there. The military has taken over the government. Your brother really wants your mom to sell the restaurant. It's dangerous for her to be there alone. Maybe if you tell her to sell, she'll listen to you."

For now, all I cared about was working and building my business. I had four people to feed, and I couldn't worry about what was happening in Argentina. I agreed that my mother should sell the restaurant, but I'd told her that before. She'd have to make that decision when she was ready. We had to stop telling her what to do. Or maybe I was being a *Carau*, again.

CHAPTER THIRTY-TWO

The following week, I met with a representative of Security Life of Denver. He congratulated me on the clients I had already gotten. I would receive training on building my agency. For now, I was a captive agent, but they agreed to pay me a salary for a short time until I built my own agency as Victoria had said.

But it didn't matter. Like an excited young boy, I continued to let everyone I knew that I sold Life and Health insurance. And I made a couple of new sales each week while having fun. This was a new game, and I was learning to play it well.

Luisa had been back a month when I got home one night to find her talking to Victoria. How the hell had she found me?

"What are you doing here?" I asked her, putting my briefcase down on the floor by the front door.

"Well, look at you," she said. "Don't you look professional?"

I glanced at Luisa, who stared at me like she wanted to murder me. I did look professional, wearing one of the suits Victoria bought me.

"I think you'd better leave," I said to Victoria, hoping she wouldn't make a scene.

"You were separated? Really? That's what you told me?"

I opened the front door. "Get out."

"Get out? You're just going to throw me out like trash?" Her face reddened and contorted into something ugly and menacing. "You bastard."

I felt my own face heat, and I knew it matched the rash of red in hers. Victoria had to know deep inside that our relationship was temporary. She just didn't want to see it.

"You used me. The clothes you're wearing, the furniture your wife is using, even the insurance license you have to make money, I paid for it all. Does she know that?" She turned to Luisa, who stood there like a statue. "I paid for everything. I took care of him while he got on his feet and while you were in Argentina."

Luisa raised an eyebrow. "That does seem very smart. To pay for a man."

"I love him." She turned to me and moved forward, placing a hand on my shoulder. "I love you, Sal."

I pushed her hand off me. "Get out, Victoria. Don't make this worse."

"I'm not going to give up on you." She turned back to Luisa. "I love him, and I know he loves me too. He just feels he has an obligation to you and your kids."

"What the fuck are you talking about, you crazy bitch," I said.

Luisa looked at me, no tears in her eyes. "I'm not going to fight for a man. If you want him, take him. He's worthless."

"Okay, that's enough!" I yelled. "Get the hell out of my house. I'm not going to say it again. I don't love you. I never did. You were just a desperate old woman who wanted some attention from a guy ten years younger than you. You got what you wanted. You got to dress me, play with me, and indulge your fantasies. I did too. Now, we're done."

Julia came running out when she heard the screaming. "*Mami*," she said, holding on to Luisa's leg.

Victoria turned her attention to Julia, tears pooling in her eyes. "This is your daughter, the one who likes stories?" She wiped under her eyes. "She looks like you."

I looked at the ceiling, counting to ten to keep from losing my temper more than I already had.

"Hopefully, some man won't do to her someday what you did to me."

That was it. I grabbed her upper arm, gripped hard, and shoved her out of the door. "Don't come back."

"Don't do this, Sal. We have something special."

"Stop humiliating yourself. It was a sleazy arrangement, and now it's over."

"You used me, you cold son of a bitch." Tears ran down her face.

"And you enjoyed every minute of it." I slammed the door shut and locked it. I want to say that I felt some guilt, some shame, but I was just angry that she had been stupid enough to come to my house and confront my wife.

"Go to your room, Julia," I said when I turned around.

"But *Mami* —"

"Goddammit, get the hell out of this room. Now!"

She backed up, looking at me with fear, then turned and ran into the bedroom.

"Luisa."

"Don't. Don't say a word. I don't want to hear it. I won't believe anything you have to say anyway."

"I'm sorry. I don't know what else to say."

"You're sorry? While I was working my butt off helping your mother run her restaurant, trying to take care of two kids by myself, dealing with bomb threats and crazy Peronistas shooting up the streets, you were here sleeping with another woman, and you're telling me you're sorry?" Luisa had a scary way of saying all that without raising her voice, which sent chills up my spine.

"It wasn't like that. I just needed her help."

"What are you talking about?"

"She told you. She helped me study for my insurance test, helped me pay for the state exam, and clothes, even food. I needed her. All she wanted was a little company in return."

Luisa's mouth dropped open. "You are a despicable man. Wait, I can't even call you a man. You're nothing but a . . . forget it. I'm not going to stoop to your level. You used that woman; she's right. Don't you have any shame?"

My jaw hurt from tightening it and keeping from screaming. Luisa didn't get it. The only thing I did wrong was sleep with Victoria, I admit that. The rest I didn't ask for. Victoria tried to buy my love, and it didn't work out for her. It never was going to work out. "She meant nothing to me," I said and moved closer to Luisa. "I love *you*."

With a huff of disgust, Luisa turned away.

I reached for her arm, but she yanked it back and raised her other hand. I thought she was going to slap me, but instead, Luisa stared into my eyes. "I used to love you. I adored you. You were brilliant and exciting. Everything you said and did made my heart sing. Even when I started to see the signs that you weren't who I thought you were, I told myself that it wasn't true. That you had some bad luck and were trying to do good because you were a good man. But now I see exactly who you are. You killed that innocent love I had for you. It's dead. Now, let me go."

I did, shocked and hurt by her words. I wanted to hit her, and hold her, and cry all at once. Instead, I left. I went out. Victoria was long gone, thank God. Fuck her for coming to my house. I didn't even know how she found me. She couldn't have left well enough alone. We'd had a good time. Why hadn't that been enough for her? Like I'd leave my wife and kids for a woman like her. She was crazy.

I had nowhere to go. So, I drove around for a while, thinking of what to do to make Luisa forgive me. The only thing I could think of was to work, make money, and show her that I'd made a good decision. For some reason, Victoria had been placed on my path; all I did was accept the gift I was given.

When I got back home, Luisa lay in bed. The kids were asleep. I lay in bed beside her and hesitantly touched her back. She moved away from me.

"I'm going to go back to Argentina with the kids."

"Don't be ridiculous," I said. "You're not going anywhere."

"I don't want to live with you."

I punched my pillow. "Too damn bad. You're my wife, and you're not going anywhere unless I tell you that you're going. Forget the whole thing, and let's move on with our lives."

Luisa didn't respond.

She barely talked to me for months. She was polite, but things had changed. As far as sex, she didn't deny me, but there was no passion there either. It was a physical exercise that left me empty.

One day I came home, and she and the kids were gone. "Luisa," I called, fear suddenly clogging my throat. On the refrigerator, a magnet held a note from Camila. *The kids are with me. Luisa is in the hospital.* She left the name and number of the hospital.

What the hell?

I rushed to the hospital only to be told visiting hours were over and that my wife was in recovery. I could see her in the morning when they planned to release her.

"What happened? Why is she here?"

"She had a hysterectomy."

"Why? And how did she get that done without my approval?"

"I don't know, sir. You can speak to the doctor in the morning."

I went to Mateo's place.

"Hi, Asshole," Camila said.

"Shut the hell up, Camila. I'm in no mood for your shit."

"You are nothing but a rodent."

I slammed the back of my fist on her door. "I want my kids."

"Come in."

"Hey," Mateo came forward. "Calm down. Come have a glass of wine. The kids are playing in Niki's room."

I stalked into his sunken living room, wanting to get my kids and leave.

"Come on, sit down for a few minutes."

"Why the hell would she have a hysterectomy?"

"She had ovarian pain, and the doctor found growths that weren't dangerous, but since she has no intention of ever having another child with you," Camila said. "She told them she wanted the procedure done."

Mateo must have seen the fury on my face. "Camila, you're not helping. Leave us alone."

She shrugged and left. Mateo gazed at me. "You fucked up, *Loco*. You don't want to see it, but it's true."

"Maybe."

"Luisa is amazing. You're lucky to have her. How could you betray her like you did?"

I lowered my head and rubbed my forehead. "I don't know. I was trying to do the right thing for all of us. I didn't think she'd ever find out."

"Even if she hadn't, what you did wasn't okay. The truth always comes out. Look, she's angry and hurt. Just let time heal this mistake. Don't be upset about the surgery. I think it's good that she had it anyway if she had growths. You have two beautiful kids. Be happy with what you have and take care of it."

I considered this, meeting his kind eyes. "You're right, *hermano*."

Mateo gave me a lazy smile and his glass of wine.

"She was gone a long time, you know. A man can't be alone for so long."

"Don't tell her that. Just be kind. Be good. It will go away."

I hoped so. But Luisa said something had died between us, and that's exactly how it felt deep in my soul. And I wasn't sure I could revive it.

CHAPTER THIRTY-THREE

The next day, Luisa was discharged from the hospital. I helped her get into bed. "Are you going to be okay while I'm at work today?" I asked her.

I could tell she still had pain or discomfort, but she nodded. "I'll be fine."

We hadn't gotten Julia enrolled in school yet, so thankfully, she would be home. "Help your mother today, okay?"

"I will, *Papi*."

I spent the day visiting a doctor's office building and explaining the products I had to offer his employees. Many support staff and employees seemed interested in life insurance and took my card. Hopefully, some of them would become clients.

When I got home, I made a quick spaghetti dinner. Luisa said she wasn't hungry, so I fed the kids. I washed the dishes and went to the bedroom, drying my hands. "Did you eat earlier?"

"I had a yogurt. I'm not hungry."

She'd always been thin and not a heavy eater. "Well, you should eat more than yogurt."

"It hurts to go to the bathroom. I'd rather not yet."

That made sense. "I sat on the bed beside her."

"Why didn't you tell me you were going to do this?"

"Because it doesn't really affect you."

That irritated me. "Really? You not being able to have more kids doesn't affect me?"

"You don't want more kids."

"How the hell do you know? Did you ask me?"

"Fine, *I* don't want any more kids. I did, but not anymore."

I ran a hand through my hair. "This was a permanent decision. You can't change your mind. It wasn't a choice to make because you're angry with me."

"The doctor recommended it. Not everything is about you. And I don't want to talk about this anymore. It's done."

I stood and threw the dish towel across the room. "Well, I do want to talk about it!" I shouted. "This was a fucked-up thing to do. Camila said you didn't have to have a hysterectomy. You *chose* it."

"Yes, because the last thing I want is to get pregnant and have another child with you and be stuck in this marriage any longer than I have to be."

"Well, that's just great, Luisa. How long are you going to keep this up, huh? You *want* our marriage to be over? Is that what you want?"

"It *is* over."

"Maybe it is. Maybe I'll fly you back to Argentina, and you can live there alone and see how happy you are without us."

"You're crazy if you think I'd leave my kids with you." Luisa started to cry.

"They're my kids too."

"Yes, you really thought about your kids while sleeping with another woman."

Julia ran into the room and onto the bed beside Luisa. "Stop it, stop it, stop it," she said. "Leave my *mami* alone."

"Julia, go to bed."

"No, *Mami* is hurt. *You* leave her alone. You're making her cry, and she's hurt."

"I'm not going to tell you again. Go to bed. Your *mami* is fine."

"I'm not leaving her."

Goddammit. I reached for Julia's arm, and she started to scream like I was killing her.

"Salvador, what are you doing?" Luisa said.

I grabbed Julia by the arm and pulled her away from the bed. She dropped all her weight, and I had to drag her crying and screaming out of the room. I placed her on her bed. "Go to sleep."

"You're fighting, and you're mean, and you're going to hurt my *mami*," she cried. "I can't sleep."

A lump grew in my throat. I had already hurt her *mami*. "We're done fighting. Go to sleep."

Luisa glared at me from the bed. "I hope you're proud of yourself."

I sighed and went around to my side of the bed. "Luisa, can't we work this out?" I asked, close to tears. My little girl looked at me like I was a monster. My wife hated me. "I'm not proud of myself at all."

"I don't know how to forgive you," she said quietly and closed her eyes.

What was happening to us? "I hope you can someday."

MY PROMISE NOT TO MOVE often became another promise I couldn't keep. We started 1975 by moving to South Gate, a crime-ridden dump of a city, then to a decent house in Lynwood two months later, which ended up being another place with gang members, pedophiles, and just all-around high crime. The house had a block wall surrounding it but sat behind a liquor store where guys made drug deals out in the open. Occasionally, they got arrested, but a week or two later, they were back. And the landlord told us that the old man across the street molested kids, so I should keep my kids away from him. What the fuck!

The next-door neighbor was a Vietnam Vet and he wasn't all there mentally, she told me, but he actually seemed nice when I met him and we spoke. He volunteered to teach the kids karate. Alex was kind of small, but I allowed Julia to train with him. She might as well learn to defend herself. I liked the guy. He had two young boys and a lovely wife. We became neighborly and chatted over our chain link fence in the front yard whenever we saw each other.

The neighborhood was rough, even for the kids. Julia came home crying one day because she'd gotten attacked by a Doberman. "He grabbed my arm, so I had to pull out of my sweater that Grandma knitted for me and run."

I checked her arm, and she seemed fine. Only a few scratches were visible on her skin.

"Grandma sent it from Argentina," she said, her lower lip trembling.

"That's okay. I'm sorry about the sweater, but I'm glad he didn't hurt you. Weren't there other kids walking to school that could help you?"

"There were, but they laughed and told the dog to *sic* me."

"Fucking degenerates in this neighborhood," I said. I didn't want to move again, but I'd probably have to do so soon. I just didn't have the time to think about moving.

The good thing was that my insurance business had really taken off. I worked all day selling insurance and studied in the evenings to expand the insurance products I could sell. After a few months, I passed the exams to get my Auto, and Casualty and Property licenses and started working for Jefferson National Insurance Company. I became a district agent.

"I'm going to open my own office in Los Angeles with another agent," I told Luisa. "We'll need someone to run the office while we're out in the field. Would you like to do that?" I knew how much she liked to work, and I was doing everything I could to keep her happy and put the past behind us. She seemed to be trying also, for the kids' sake, I was sure. Even though she could, she didn't bring up Victoria ever again.

"What would I have to do?"

"Paperwork, process the applications when we sell a new policy. Answer the phone. Schedule appointments if people call. Just office stuff."

"What about the kids?"

"Julia is in school all day, and she walks home. She can pick Alex up from the pre-school, and they can wait for us to get home."

Julia was only in second grade, almost third, but she was responsible, and I didn't fear her staying home alone. We told her never to open the door to strangers or the man across the street. And if something scared her, she could run next door to get the veteran to help her.

Luisa immediately agreed, and we found a small office in La Cienega, only a 30-minute drive from the house. We spent a weekend getting the office ready with three desks, a couple of filing cabinets, and installed phone service, nothing fancy.

Every morning, we drove to work together, which was great because it gave us a chance to talk without the kids interrupting.

"You need to learn to drive," I told her as we made our way north on the 405 freeway.

"I really miss New York. There are no tall buildings. Los Angeles is a joke. Transportation is a worse joke."

"Which is why you need to learn to drive."

"I have you. You can drive me wherever I need to go. I'm always with you anyway."

I didn't push her, but eventually, she'd see how helpful it would be to have her driver's license.

"By the way, I don't want Julia taking karate lessons from that neighbor anymore," Luisa said.

"Why not?"

"I was over there the other day to pick her up, and he made a pass at me."

"What!"

"He offered me an alcoholic drink. I said no, but he gave me a coke anyway, and then he tried to kiss me."

"That son of a bitch. I'm going to kill him when we get home."

"A guy who was trained by the military to fight? A black belt in karate? He'll *kill* you."

"You want me to do nothing?"

"I took care of it."

"How?"

"I slapped him and told him he should be ashamed of himself. His wife is so nice. He backed off right way. I handled it."

The truth was that the guy could kill me without even trying. "Still, I should say something."

"Just let it go. I only told you because I'm going to tell Julia not to go over there anymore. I wanted you to know why."

I frowned, fuming inside the rest of the drive to work. I wanted to go over there and knock the permanent smirk off that bald-headed bastard.

I OFFICIALLY JOINED the Argentine Club in Burbank and met many guys who were super well off. Like the group I used to meet with in New York, these were Argentines with influence who had achieved success in their fields.

But unlike the New Yorkers, the California immigrants were warmer, and more willing to help and guide me. I felt like I'd known them all my life. And I was lucky. Since I was a young boy in high school, I was blessed with a unique magnetism to attract others. That sounds conceited, but no, I'm not saying I was the most charismatic guy in the room. But then and now, I didn't have trouble making friends. I'd walk into a classroom, and friends would instantly call me over, demanding my attention. And the more attention I received from them, the more energy I felt. Nothing had changed except that the popular kids now had the power to help me.

One, a doctor who owned a few clinics in Los Angeles, liked me from day one and sought me out as a drinking buddy, a Bridge or Rummy partner when we played cards, an ear to listen to his stories.

"Salvador," he said to me one day when we were at the club playing cards, and I was complaining about living in Lynwood. "You need to buy a home. Stop renting in these terrible neighborhoods. Look for something better. If you start living in better places and expecting more, you'll get more. That's how life works."

I thought of my father and the advice he used to give me and suddenly missed him. "You're right," I said.

"Of course, I'm right. You need to start investing, and property investments are always good."

That night, I talked to Luisa about the idea of owning property here in America. We'd always rented because our stay was always going to be temporary. But it no longer felt that way.

"Buy a house with what money?"

"We don't need a huge down payment. I'm making good money, you know I am. And you wanted more stability. This will give us that. We'll have our own home. What do you say? You want to go look at some houses?"

She shrugged. "Sure, if you think we can afford it."

So, we went house hunting, and it was fun. The kids thought it was a huge adventure, and Luisa and I enjoyed dreaming of what we'd do with each house we looked at. Finally, we settled on a little home in the Valley. It had three bedrooms and a nice backyard with huge trees. The kitchen was a little small, but perfect for us. The best part about the property was the location in a safe family neighborhood with good schools.

"I say we put an offer on this one," I said to Luisa. "It's not as grand as some of the others we looked at in Glendale and Burbank, but we can afford it. What do you think?"

She seemed excited. "I think it would be great for the kids to have a permanent home in a safe neighborhood."

"Then let's do it! I want us to have a stable home and be happy again like when we first lived in New York."

Her smile faded. "We were young then. Nothing will ever be like that again. And what about our condo in Rosario?"

"Maybe it will become a retirement home. We're here now."

We put the offer in and waited anxiously to hear back from the realtor.

In the morning, we got a call that the sellers had accepted our offer. Luisa was vacuuming the carpet in the living room. I yanked the plug out of the wall and picked her up, twirling her around.

First, she jumped, startled that the vacuum had stopped, then she laughed. "What are you doing? Put me down?"

"We got the house." I put her down and kissed her. That night we opened a bottle of champagne and stayed up talking and dreaming of our new life in The Valley.

It took us about 45 days to close, but when the day came and we got the house keys, when we pulled our moving truck up the driveway, I felt a surreal emotion that clogged my throat.

I unlocked the house and picked Luisa up to carry her over the threshold. She laughed, and the kids watched us with questions in their eyes.

"Will you carry me next?" Alex asked.

"No, *Loco*, you carry your wife, not your children. It's a tradition. *You* get to walk in like a man."

He shrugged and ran inside. Julia followed. "My band teacher said I need to put jewels on my saxophone."

She'd joined her school band, and we were treated to the loud squawks of her saxophone every night when she practiced. "Jewels? Why?"

"Because we moved to a rich neighborhood."

Yeah, compared to Lynwood, this was paradise. "He was kidding, Julia. It's just a nice house, and it's ours. And that's what's important."

She nodded.

"When your *Papi* first came to this country, he dreamed of this," I said, tears clouding my vision. I wanted to have a family and a place to call my own. "That's going to be your room." I pointed to a room that had its own bathroom. She'd soon be a young lady and want her own bathroom. She walked away to look at her empty room.

The old days of struggling in New York seemed finally to be behind us. I had a growing business, and now we would have our own home. The American Dream was real, and finally in September of 1975, twelve years after arriving in this country, we were finally living it.

CHAPTER THIRTY-FOUR

I received a call from my district manager at Jefferson National, who wanted to talk to me in person, so I drove to his office in Burbank, where he handed me a printout of my clients' insurance claims.

"Your claim rate is 15% on your auto insurance policies. Do you see any patterns?"

I sat across from him and studied the report, seeing the names of my clients. Frowning, I looked at my manager. "Not really. I mean, they are all obviously my clients."

"They *were* your clients. For about a month, then they had an accident, collected money for car repairs or injuries, then dropped the insurance."

"Yeah," I said, not happy with what he was telling me. "I see that."

"Look, I'm not going to beat around the bush. The pattern is that they are all Argentine."

My frown deepened, and I drew a breath. "Most of my clients are Argentine. *I'm* Argentine."

"Well, Argentines are notorious for filing false claims. I'm not saying you're profiting from this, but . . . I don't want you to write any more policies to Argentines."

I stood, a hot flash of anger overtaking my ability to think for a second. "Profiting? You think I had something to do with what you *think* these people did?"

"Sal, I'm just telling you to find other clients. Something fishy is going on. We're investigating these policyholders."

"And me too? You're investigating me for being a good salesman?"

"Your name was kicked down to me, and I am not asking if you were involved, I'm telling you a high percentage of the policies you sell are filing claims. Much higher than normal, and immediately after they become insured."

"Well, Argentines are my market." I tossed the sheets of paper on his desk.

"Not anymore if you want to keep working here."

"Yeah, well, fuck you and fuck this agency." I stormed out of his office.

I went back to my office, cussing up a storm when I got there.

Luisa sat back and listened to my tirade. "You quit?"

"They're not going to tell me who my clients can be."

"Ah . . . but is it true? Is 15% high? And did you know about this?"

I pinned her with a look that I'm sure looked murderous because she flinched. "Are you asking me if I was involved in defrauding the insurance agency I work for?"

She drew in a breath. "Were you?"

"I can't fucking believe this?" I shouted and turned away from her, looking out a small window in the office at cars driving by and people going about their normal lives. "Have you looked at our bank account? Does it look like I've taken money or had a payoff?"

"You do gamble a lot, and—"

"Shut up, Luisa before I get really angry." I walked back to my desk. "Even my own wife can't stand beside me. Shit!"

"I've done nothing but stand beside you. You can't blame the agency for being upset and not wanting you to insure more Argentines. It's your clients who made you look bad. It's them you should be angry with."

I dropped onto my chair, deflated. "I am. Those sons of bitches."

"Now what?"

"Now, I apply to a new agency and take my good clients with me." I lit a cigarette, not happy with this setback right when I decided to buy a home.

"Please do what they said and stay away from Argentines," Luisa said.

"You should be ashamed to say that," I said, disgusted with her attitude. "You want me to discriminate against my countrymen? Eighty percent of my client base are Argentines. A few might have done something wrong, that doesn't make them all bad."

She looked away, and started packing her briefcase. "Illegal," she said. "Not wrong."

I watched her, rubbing my clean-shaven chin, thinking that she's never understood business and what it takes to get ahead. Maybe if I hadn't listened to her in New York and followed Edmundo's lead, I would have done better there. Illegal was a relative term, wasn't it? I finished my cigarette.

She zipped her bag closed and gazed at me.

"Don't ever let these people group us into a box," I said, annoyed at her. I always searched out Argentines, and she never did. I joined the Argentine Clubs, found Argentine friends and clients. And she always had a problem with them.

She stood. "These people?"

"Don't forget who we are. That asshole was trying to tell me that all Argentines are crooks. Like there aren't American crooks. Fuck him. I'll find a new agency to work for."

"I want to go. Are you ready?"

"No, I'm not. And when are you going to learn to drive?"

She stared at me. Her face showed no emotion. "This weekend. Teach me to drive this weekend."

WE PUT THE KIDS IN the back seat of the Plymouth on Saturday morning. As I drove, I explained to Luisa what I was doing. I explained the laws of the road, then pulled over, and we switched seats; I took the passenger seat, and she the driver's.

I showed her how to adjust the mirrors, and she took forever to get them just right. Too damned precise and methodical. "You'll pull out into traffic when it's safe, but it does have to be today."

"Okay," she looked at her side mirror and over her shoulder.

"What are you doing? You think you're ready to pull out?"

"I'm getting ready."

"No, you're not ready. Where is your blinker? Do you think other drivers are going to magically know that you're about to merge into their lane?"

"Stop the sarcasm, okay?"

"Well, then listen and do what I'm telling you to do."

She put the blinker on, waited until no cars were coming and pulled out slowly.

"Give it more gas." Did this woman not realize that crawling down the road was more dangerous than actually moving forward?

She went a little faster. I showed her how to change lanes. We drove, made right turns, left turns, drove faster, stopped. Most of the time, she did well, but she was way too nervous. Comfort would come with practice, I hoped. That night, we went home, and I had three glasses of wine and went to sleep on the couch, glad that the day was over.

On Sunday, we went out again.

"Just let me drive without you talking the whole time. You make me nervous."

"*I* make *you* nervous?"

She drove a little better, still too cautious, but she seemed more confident than the day before.

"All right, we're going to pull over, and you're going to park," I said as we approached an intersection.

"Before or after?"

"Just keep going?"

"Past the streetlight?"

"Yes, just drive. Why are you asking me such a stupid question? Damn it, you took long. Now the light is changing to yellow."

"Keep going or stop?"

She got frazzled, and it didn't appear that she was going to stop. A pedestrian was waiting to cross. "Stop, stop, stop!" I shouted.

She slammed on the breaks. The kids in the back seat screamed. Luisa turned the wheel, and we hit the curb and the streetlight. Thankfully, the pedestrian jumped out of the way. "Goddammit!" I jumped out of the car to see the damage. The curb slowed us down a lot though I'd probably have to take the car in for an alignment. The fender was a little dented.

I opened the driver's side door. Luisa was calming the kids down. "Get out," I said.

She stepped out, and I backed the car off the sidewalk.

"You're not going to leave Mommy, are you?" Julia asked

"*Mami*," Alex screamed for Luisa.

"Of course, I'm not going to leave her. Sit back and stop asking ridiculous questions."

I pulled to the side of the curb and stopped. Luisa got inside.

"You're always yelling. I didn't know what you wanted me to do." She shook and gripped her hands together.

"Just be quiet. I told you exactly what to do. You didn't listen."

"You weren't clear."

"What does the yellow light mean, Luisa?"

She didn't answer.

"Stop the fucking car, that's right. You only cross the intersection if the light is green. If you hadn't taken so long to do what I told you to do, you would have crossed and pulled over. But when the light turns yellow, it's too late, you stop. Was that clear this time?"

"From now on, I'm going to practice on my own."

I didn't respond. Hopefully, she wouldn't kill herself or others.

WHEN I SHARED WHAT happened with the insurance agency with my friends at the Argentine Club, they were just as incensed as I was. "Oh, so none of us can be trusted, huh?" my doctor friend said.

"Apparently not."

"I have a good friend, my insurance agent, as a matter of fact. He works for Farmers Insurance. They're a well-known company with a good reputation."

"Yes, of course, I'm familiar with them."

"I'll tell my friend to contact you to help you apply and transfer your business to the new company. I'm not sure what you signed or if you can take your clients with you, but Farmers will be able to guide you."

"I might have to start fresh, but Jefferson National can't tell clients not to leave if they want to."

He patted me on my shoulder. "It will all work out. You were right to stand up for yourself and for Argentines."

It felt good to be among people who understood me. We drank whiskey and laughed. Just about every one of the guys said they had friends, good referrals to get me started at the new agency. They had my back, reminding me that when it came down to it, I could only count on other Argentines.

I'd join Farmers and build an even more extensive clientele. Nothing was going to stop me.

CHAPTER THIRTY-FIVE

We saw Mateo and Camila a lot less now, mainly because we lived in different cities but also because we were all so busy. Still, we tried to get together every other weekend or at least once a month.

Six months after we moved into our house, we had a barbeque at our place to finally celebrate being homeowners. It took us some time to get it decorated and furnished.

Luisa didn't want to bring any of the old furniture Victoria had purchased. Even though we'd kept it through our rentals, she didn't want to bring it to our home. Luisa didn't say this was the reason. She just said we deserved to have new furniture. I wasn't going to argue with that logic.

We bought nice modern couches and a large TV. A contemporary bedroom set for us. The kids kept their furniture, but we did take them to ToysRUs and let them choose a bunch of toys to fill up their rooms.

Alex bought a Big Wheel that he loved to ride up and down the sidewalk on our block. Julia bought girl things, among them, another doll. She had so many that she didn't really play with anymore, but we bought both kids everything they chose.

Once Luisa got the house looking like she wanted, we decided to have the official get-together. Camila had given birth to a little girl, and she and Mateo spent most of the time talking about the baby, which was fair since all I talked about was the house.

"I built a nice, Argentine-style brick barbeque grill," I bragged, showing Mateo my handiwork.

We sat outside on the back patio, grilling ribs, chorizo, and other organ meats that I bought at an Argentine market in Los Angeles.

"I sure don't miss New York," Mateo said, stretching his legs out, holding the back of his head with his interlaced fingers under the hot fall sun.

"I do," Luisa said. "Though I'm getting used to it here a little."

"It's different," Camila agreed, "but California is more laid back, relaxing, and people are nicer."

I shook my head. "People are fake. They smile to your face and stab you in the back."

"Why did you stay and buy a house then?" Camila asked.

"I have a career here, and you can't beat the weather. Plus, we'd never be able to afford our own home in New York."

"You're right there," Mateo agreed. "We have a pool. Our house is amazing. All we had in New York were damp, run-down apartments. I'll never go back." Mateo and Camila bought the house they were renting in West Covina.

"Well, here we are, for better or worse," I said, toasting with our glass of wine. "To us."

THE KIDS WERE HAPPY in the new house. No wild street kids, no dangerous neighbors, a big backyard to play in, and a dog Julia had wanted since she'd been a little kid in New York.

Luisa drove them to school, and sometimes the neighbor next door took them with her kids, and they walked home in the afternoon. Julia looked after her brother until we got home in the evening.

I moved into a new office just a couple of miles away from our new home. Farmers Insurance happily took me in, and I worked hard to reestablish a client list. This time, I *was* more careful. I interviewed all my clients. I didn't sign just anyone, Argentine or not.

When Alex was in first grade, he came home with a note from his school that he was in trouble, and one of us had to talk to the teacher.

"What did you do?" I asked him.

He frowned and looked at me defiantly. "I didn't do nothing."

"The teacher says you're in trouble for doing nothing?"

"I was just doing my job."

I waited to hear more, raising my eyebrow and waving at him to continue.

"I'm the safety monitor, and no one is supposed to be in the halls after the bell rings, and this kid wouldn't show me his hall pass."

"Okay, so what happened?"

"I told him to show me his pass, and he wouldn't. Then he tried to run past me."

"Yeah," I said, knowing it was about to get bad.

"So, I told him to stop. I warned him. But he just kept trying to get around me and run away. So, I had to stop him."

"Alex, what did you do?"

"Nothing. I just took his shoes and threw them over the fence so that he couldn't run away."

I tried to control the twitching of my lips. "You threw his shoes over the fence?"

"Yeah."

I looked at Luisa, then I couldn't control myself; I burst out laughing. "You threw his shoes to keep him from running away?" I laughed even harder.

Luisa frowned. "It's not funny."

"It's kind of funny," I disagreed.

"Then he started crying like a baby, and a teacher came out, and she said I was in trouble. I tried to explain that I was doing my job, but she still sent me to the office." Alex frowned, his bottom lip trembling.

"Your job was not to throw another boy's shoes over the fence," Luisa said.

"But he wouldn't stop," Alex whined.

"He wouldn't stop," I repeated. "He stopped him." I continued to chuckle.

"You're not helping," Luisa said.

"That idiot teacher sends us a note complaining about his behavior, and it's about *this*? Give me a break."

"Salvador."

"Okay, okay." I cleared my throat. "Alex, you can't take shoes or clothes off other kids and then toss them away."

"But —"

"No, buts *Loco*. Listen to me. He didn't follow the rules, but you didn't either. What were you supposed to do?"

"I was supposed to write a warning ticket, but he ran away and wouldn't take the ticket!" He was starting to get angry. His face grew red, and he was about to cry.

"Hey," I tapped his shoulder. "It's okay. Don't get angry. You're not in trouble. Next time if something like that happens again, tell a teacher and let the kid go. It's not your job to chase him and especially to put your hands on him."

"Then he'll get away with it. That's not fair."

Boy, my little red head was tough. "Sometimes, life is not fair. But you can't do something wrong because someone else does something wrong, understand?"

"Yeah, but the teacher said I can't be hall monitor anymore, and I don't care. I don't want that stupid job anyway."

I stared at him and nodded. "I'm with you. Let someone else do that stupid job. Like maybe the teacher herself." I kissed his forehead and told him to go play.

"That's your idea of punishing him?"

"Punishing him for what?"

"For fighting. For taking another boy's shoes. You thought that was funny?"

I leaned back on the couch and put my feet on the coffee table. Then I lit a cigarette, trying to ignore her, but she kept waiting for an answer. "Yeah, I thought it was hilarious. Fuck that teacher. Couldn't she have handled that better? She couldn't have explained to him the right way to manage the situation and how to be a good monitor and leader. He's six years old. What does he know? They're supposed to teach him, not punish him. Instead, he got in trouble and lost his 'job'? I'm going to that school tomorrow to tell that teacher to keep my kid in his classroom and to hire an adult *hall monitor*. They're supposed to be educating him, not using him for free labor anyway."

Luisa shook her head.

I chuckled again. "Pretty genius. Take his shoes, then he can't run. Worked didn't it? My son is a genius. That's what I'm going to tell that teacher."

Luisa sighed. "There's no use talking to you. I'm going to go make dinner."

"Good," I muttered. "Make dinner."

LUISA STUDIED AND GOT her life insurance license in early 1977. As my business grew, it helped that she was not only my office manager but was also able to sell insurance. I shared my office with another agent, an outgoing American woman that Luisa liked, which worked out because Luisa looked forward to being in the office. This year turned out to be prosperous, and we were mostly happy, though I still detected an undercurrent of resentment from Luisa. She seemed detached. Or maybe it was just me.

I got more involved with the Argentine Club because, at least with them, I felt appreciated, and we went every Sunday for a barbeque during the day. The ladies chatted and hung out together while the men played cards or watched a soccer game. Then at night, we ate the perfectly prepared *asado* and danced tangos into the night. I loved getting on the dance floor with Luisa because when we performed the passionate dances, we still felt like the old us. Luisa loved to dance, and I knew this was what she enjoyed most about going to the club.

The kids entertained themselves. The club transformed one room into a kid's room with toys, a ping pong table, a foosball table, and other games to entertain them. I didn't see them for hours.

Most of my new friends were members of the club. Many of my clients also came from Argentine Club regulars. And they recommended their friends to me too.

So, I was angry when Luisa, on the drive home from the club one night, said she didn't want us to go anymore. "What are you talking about?" I asked.

"I just don't want to be here every single week."

"But I'm one of the main volunteers, and it's fun."

"It's not fun for me. Those women do nothing but gossip. I'm tired of listening to them."

"You can't get along with anyone. You're never happy about anything. Whenever I'm enjoying something, you have to spoil it."

"Maybe we can come once a month. I just don't want to be here every Sunday. I'm tired. We work all week, then on the weekend, we're here, and I still have to clean the house and cook."

"You sit in the office all week. What's so hard about that?"

She sighed.

"Julia," I said, looking at her through the rearview mirror. "You like coming to the club, don't you?"

She nodded. "It's kind of fun."

"Alex, do you like coming to the club."

"Yeah," he shouted.

"See, the kids like it. I like it. You're the only one who wants to spoil things."

"I'll tell you what," Luisa said. "Next week, the three of you go and leave me at home."

"Fine, we will."

When we got home, I threw the car keys across the room. They hit the wall and dropped on the floor, and I went to our bedroom.

"Well, that was scary," Alex said. "I didn't think he was going to do *that*."

I heard Luisa shoosh him, and she told the kids to go to bed. She stayed up doing something. It sounded like sweeping and moping the floor. She was insane. I fell asleep before she came to bed.

FOR CHRISTMAS, I BOUGHT Luisa her own Cadillac. She drove the old Plymouth, and I had a new Caddy. So, I bought her a Cadillac of her own; though it wasn't new, she'd have a luxury vehicle instead of the old car she'd learned to drive in. And I liked how the house looked with two Cadillacs parked in the front yard.

The kids were super excited after they'd opened all their Christmas presents, and I made Luisa close her eyes, held her hand, and led her outside to see the car.

"You bought me a car?" she said when she opened her eyes and saw the light blue Cadillac.

She looked surprised. Not necessarily happy. "I already have a car."

"Not a Cadillac. And this one is newer than yours."

"Don't you like it, *Mami*?" Julia asked.

"I do. I'm very . . . surprised."

"You're supposed to be," Alex said. "It's a present."

She smiled. "Thank you. Wow."

I pulled her close and kissed her. "You're welcome."

The insurance business called for me to work long hours and constantly search for new clients, but it paid well. Not having to worry about money as I had in New York made me feel more secure and willing to be more extravagant with my purchases. I was sure that Luisa thought buying another car was a waste of money when she already had one, but we had to keep progressing.

One of my doctor friends invited us to his house in Beverly Hills on New Year's Eve to ring in 1978. As we walked in, he had a monumental ice sculpture of an angel at the entrance. The kids oohed and awed.

"Don't touch anything," Luisa warned.

But when we got inside, other people's kids ran all around the spacious living room, and no one seemed bothered by it. We dressed well, of course, since it was a party, but we were the least well-dressed and the poorest people present. The doctors and business owners who went to the Argentine Club were all in better social positions than I was, but it didn't bother me. They seemed to appreciate me for who I was.

I'd never been to a party like this one with catered food, a bar, a band, and dancing that lasted past midnight. He must have invited three or four hundred people who roamed inside the house and mingled around the pool in the backyard.

On the way home, we drove almost in silence. "Did you have a good time?" I asked Luisa.

"I did. What a beautiful house."

"Mm, yes, amazing."

We pulled into the driveway of our humble home after three in the morning. I carried Julia to bed, and Luisa took Alex, who was lighter.

"*Papi,*" Julia said as I set her on the bed.

"Good night," I said.

"Those people were rich."

"I know."

"Now I know why you said this is just a regular house, and my saxophone shouldn't have gems. We're not rich at all."

I sat on her bed. "Julia, let me tell you something. Money is not that important."

"Of course, it is. Don't you want to be that rich?"

It wasn't that long ago that I arrived in New York with those exact dreams. I'd be rich overnight, go back to Argentina, build my house, get married, and live happily and peacefully. But when I really thought about it, it wasn't becoming rich that mattered. And I didn't want my daughter to believe that was important either. "No, I've never cared much about money or even the things I can buy with money." And that was the truth, I realized. I cared about succeeding, making a difference, and proving to myself and others that I could achieve any goal I set my mind to.

She rubbed her eyes. "Why?"

"Sometimes, people worry so much about having a lot of money that they forget that life is short and that it's more important to enjoy it. You understand that?"

She nodded.

"That man who owns that house works many, many hours, and he has a college degree that I don't have. I'll never be in his position, but that doesn't bother me. I'm not really impressed by people's jobs or degrees. I'd rather be a simple man and spend time with my friends and kids, and enjoy my life."

She gazed at me, no longer looking sleepy. She was going to enter junior high soon and was becoming a young lady, and I knew she paid more attention to things now than she did when she was younger.

"But Papi, you work long hours too. And you like having your own house and nice cars."

"And those things are nice because they make life easier for us. In Argentina, you remember all the crazy things that were happening and how difficult it was to live there?"

"Not really. A little bit."

"In America, it's easier to live free, and anyone can get a job, work hard, and take care of his family. We have liberty and democracy and opportunity, and that's beautiful. That's what has always been important to me and why I choose to be here. But the more things you have, the less free you are sometimes."

She nodded.

"I never want to give up my freedom for money." I patted her leg, knowing I'd given up a lot more than that with some of the choices I'd made. I'd given up pieces of my soul, and I was almost helpless to change now. Call it stubbornness, call it ego. I wasn't sure. But I didn't want her to do the same as me. "Anyhow, I don't like my wealthy friends because they have money, but because they are nice people, and they're fun to be with."

She sat up and hugged me. I hugged her back tightly. I would never be as good a father as mine was to me, but hopefully, I had a few words of wisdom to share with my kids occasionally.

CHAPTER THIRTY-SIX

I wanted so badly to travel to Argentina to see the 1978 World Cup games, but I just couldn't afford the plane ticket or the price of a game. Yes, I was making good money, but I also had a mortgage, office rent, and other bills now, plus it cost money to run my business. So, instead, I watched most of the games at the Argentine Club with the guys on a large screen.

I also bought a new piece of technology called a VHS machine. With this gadget, I could record games that played on the television and watch them again and again. It was expensive because it had only been on the market for a year, but I bought one anyway. As the games progressed and Argentina made it to the World Cup Finals, I spent hours the entire month of June with my tapes rewatching the games and cheering for our team.

Luisa didn't go to the club anymore, not even to watch Argentina play in the World Cup. She stayed home with the kids and watched the games from home.

But when Argentina won, I hurried home to celebrate with the family. The kids had made me an Argentine flag out of an old white sheet. As I pulled into the driveway, the flag hung and waved on the porch. Tears filled my eyes, and I picked them both up and kissed them as soon as I walked inside.

On days like this, I really missed my country and wished I could return.

MATEO CALLED ME AT work and asked if I could meet him for coffee. I had one appointment with a client in the morning, so I agreed to meet him after. "Let's have lunch," I said.

He had to drive an hour from the Valley to West Covina, but he said he'd come to me. We met at Sizzler, close to my office.

"Hey, *Flaco*, what's going on?" I asked after we were seated and waiting for our steaks. "You sounded upset, and you look like shit."

"I feel like shit," he said. "I don't even know how to tell you this."

I frowned. Was he sick? All of a sudden, my light, happy feeling was replaced by something scary and oppressive. "Tell me what?"

"Camila and I." He burst into tears. Tears!

"What the hell, Mateo." I looked around the restaurant, but no one was looking at us. "Tell me what's wrong before I have a heart attack."

"We're getting divorced. She cheated on me."

My mouth opened to say something, but I was too stunned. Finally, I said, "That bitch."

But he cried harder and shook his head. "I love her. I told her I'd forgive her."

I bit my lower lip, furious at her and at him for being so weak. "Come on, Mateo. Have some self-respect. You forgive her? You should kick her ass to the curb."

He got a hold of himself and shook his head. "I told her we could get counseling, that I'd change, that I'd do whatever she wanted, but she said she wants a divorce. She loves this other guy."

I cursed and wanted to tell him he was better off without her, but he obviously didn't believe that. "What can I do?"

"Can I stay with you for a few days until I find a new place?"

"Seriously? You're leaving? Why don't you throw her out since she wants to be with someone else?"

"Come on, Sal. I have the girls to think about, and they need their mother."

"You're too nice. That's your problem."

"That's what you think, but we fight all the time, and I can be a real ass. Plus, things in the bedroom have been bad for a long time."

"I don't want to know that shit."

They brought our food, but neither one of us was hungry now. "You need help getting your things out of the house?"

"I have a bag of clothes for now. I don't need anything else."

"Okay, well, you can sleep in Alex's room. He can move to Julia's bedroom for a little while."

"I'll sleep on the couch. It'll just be for a few days until I rent a place and get my head on straight."

We left our steaks and baked potato on our plates and headed to our cars. I patted his back. "I'm sorry, *hermano*. You don't deserve this."

He got into his car, a broken man, and my heart ached for him.

AFTER MY LUNCH WITH Mateo, it was late afternoon, but I had work to do in the office. When I got there, Luisa wasn't there, so I called home but got a busy signal. Damn it, Julia was probably on the phone again.

As soon as Julia started junior high, she started to change. After a year at that school, she never spoke Spanish anymore. We spoke to her in Spanish, and she answered in English.

I finally told her one night to speak Spanish, and she stormed into her bedroom and slammed the door. I followed her.

"Dad! Privacy," she said.

"You don't have privacy. This is my house. And another thing that you'd better remember, when you walk out of this house, you're in America, but when you walk back in, you're in Argentina, and you'll speak Spanish and respect our culture."

She glared at me. "That's lame."

I didn't even know what that meant. "Say it in Spanish."

"What?"

"What you just said, say it in Spanish."

"I don't know how. And this isn't Argentina, get real."

I took three steps into her room, and she flinched and scooted back on her bed, her back against the wall. "Okay, okay," she said. "But if you cared so much about me knowing Spanish and knowing about the Argentine culture, then maybe you should have raised me there."

I felt like I'd been slapped by my own daughter. I drew in a breath, unable to respond, but she was right. My kids were becoming Americanized, and it was my fault for staying here so long.

"You just earned yourself an essay. I want a ten-page essay on Argentina."

"What?" Her voice started to break as if she was going to cry. "I have homework."

"You have one week. Go to the library and check out books on Argentina. You learn about *your* country; it's not just mine. No going out, no seeing friends until it's done." I left her in her room fuming, but I didn't care.

The only thing that mattered to her lately was her friends. And every time I called home, I got a busy signal because she was on the phone talking to the same kids she'd just seen at school. And today, when I called looking for Luisa, again I couldn't get through.

Irritated, I called the operator and asked to make an emergency break through to interrupt the call.

The operator connected me, and immediately I started yelling at Julia.

"I'm sorry," she said. "I haven't been on that long."

"Every damned time I call, you're on the phone talking nonsense with your friends."

"I had important things to talk about."

"You just got back from school! Look, never mind. Is your mother home? She's not in the office."

"No, she's not here either."

"Okay, your uncle Mateo is coming to stay with us for a few days. Tell your mom if she comes home. He's going to sleep on the couch."

"Okay," she said. "Is Niki coming with him?"

"No. And stay off the phone."

About a half hour later, Luisa walked into the office.

"Where the hell have you been?" I barked.

"Ah, the bank. The post office. The gas station. Why?"

I ran a hand through my hair. "Mateo and Camila are getting a divorce."

Her mouth dropped open.

"Did you know she was cheating on him?"

"What?"

"You heard me."

"How would I know that? They're going to divorce over that? They can't work things out?"

"She's in love with the other guy and wants a divorce."

Luisa put her purse on her desk and sat down. "I can't believe it. I'm stunned. I'll call her." She reached for the phone.

"No. Don't talk to that bitch ever again."

"She's my friend."

"She was."

Luisa shook her head, and tears filled her eyes. "You know, no wonder you have hated each other for so long. You're exactly alike."

"What the hell is that supposed to mean?"

She grabbed her purse. "I'm going home."

"Luisa, wait."

"I'll see you at home."

"Hey," I shouted, and she paused at the door. "Mateo will be staying with us for a few days."

She nodded. "Okay."

Mateo found a place of his own within a week. They started divorce proceedings, put their house on the market, and hired lawyers to fight for custody of his child. It got ugly, and for a while, I didn't see much of him.

MEANWHILE, OUR FAMILY had settled into a comfortable routine. The kids went to school and did their own things with their friends. Luisa and I went to work. Life was almost boring. Every so often, to fulfill my need for excitement, I'd take the whole family to Las Vegas. I'd rent a hotel room, give Julia a key and some money to eat at the buffets, and tell her to watch her brother while Luisa and I gambled or went to a show. These weekends away provided some entertainment and broke up the monotony of life.

There were also brief moments when my teenager was still my little girl, and I enjoyed being a father. Sometimes, we'd go to an arcade by my office and play video games. We both loved dogs and going on day hikes. We both wanted to bring the dog on these trips and voted Luisa down, who hated dogs, even though she insisted she didn't hate them. She said she was okay with them if they stayed outside and out of the house.

We both loved to read and discuss deep subjects, and on rare occasions, we'd stay up late at night, long after everyone was asleep, and talk about life, like my theories about why I doubted God's existence, which I know confused her.

Even though she was definitely an American girl, and worse, a Californian, she was still interested in Argentina. She enjoyed going to the Argentine Club. She loved her grandmother and wanted to talk to her on the phone all the time. She loved our food.

And Alex was at a perfect age to pal around with me. I bought him a drum set, and he drove us insane with it, banging his little heart out, but I loved it. He was all boy, always climbing trees, throwing darts, chasing our Pitbull around, or taking toys apart and putting them back together again. He'd graduated from his Big Wheel to a bike and eventually to a skateboard. He came home filthy every day. He joined a T-ball team. Both kids liked baseball; Julia played softball. I would have preferred that she play soccer, but American kids rarely played soccer, and it was difficult to find teams for them to join.

One day, we got on our bikes and rode to the arcade. I gave the kids ten dollars each while I played a wild game of space pinball. Once they blew through their money, we walked the bikes to my office so I could check the answering machine.

On the way home, I told them we'd race our bikes to see who could get home first. Whoever came in last had to rub the other two's feet, I told them.

"That's disgusting," they cried, but they started pedaling fast to get ahead.

I zoomed past them, but for some reason, after a couple of blocks, the brakes on my bike failed. I rode full speed down Woodman Avenue and was about to cross a busy intersection. The kids behind me were yelling for me to stop, and I hoped to hell that *they* would stop because I would have to go for it and cross the busy street. I entered the intersection with cars zooming past me and around me, honking and yelling out of their windows.

As I reached the other side of the road without dying, I rode over a patch of grass that slowed me down. I jumped off, my heart thumping in my chest and my breath coming in gusts. The kids had stopped at the red light, so they were a couple of minutes behind me.

"Are you crazy?" Julia said when they pulled up beside me.

"You could have been killed," Alex said, though he was kind of laughing. "Man, those cars just missed you, and you were moving around them like a maze."

"My brakes," I said. "They wouldn't work." I checked them out, squeezed the handles, and nothing happened. "This piece of shit." I'd bought the Schwinn bike at a yard sale for Julia, and she wouldn't ride it because she said it was an old lady bike because it had large fenders and a fat seat. So, I kept it for myself.

"Oh, my God." Julia shook her head. "You scared us to death."

"Well, I'll have to ride it home the way it is."

"No, you should walk, Dad," Julia said.

"No way, it's too far. I'll be fine. Let's go."

We rode back home at a slower pace, and the kids couldn't wait to tell Luisa the story of my near-death experience. It had become a funny tale by then. We all had a good laugh around the dinner table, and I was happy for the day I'd spent with my kids.

In short, life was good as I ended the decade of the 70s. I had promised myself that it would be my decade, and it had been. And yet, I was dissatisfied, bored, and unsure that my life had any purpose. Was life really about working to pay your bills, watching your kids grow up and slowly leave you, and eventually growing old?

American Ambition

A man does what he must - in spite of personal consequences, in spite of obstacles and dangers and pressures - and that is the basis of all human morality. — John F. Kennedy

CHAPTER THIRTY-SEVEN

During the summer of 1980, Mateo introduced me to a couple of his Salvadorian and Mexican friends, parents of kids he coached on the soccer field.

One guy, Paco, had a trucking business, so we had a lot in common.

"I kind of miss being a truck driver," I told him as we shared a beer in Mateo's backyard.

"I'm making a killing. I bring home about five thousand a month."

"Really?" I did well selling insurance, but it was a constant hustle to get new clients, to convince people they needed insurance. A lot of talking, a lot of networking with the right people, a lot of being stuck indoors. "That's not bad."

"Well, if you ever want to get back into it, let me know. I'm thinking of buying a new truck and hiring drivers."

"Yeah, thanks. I have an insurance business now." And if I did want to get back into trucking, with my experience, I wouldn't drive someone else's truck. I'd get my own. Be my own boss.

That night at dinner, I told Luisa about my conversation with Paco. "Can you believe he makes that much money?"

"No," she said, placing a plate of mashed potatoes on the table beside the *milanesas*. "I can't. He might make that, but what does he spend on truck payments and insurance? And gas! With the gas shortage, price increases, and long gas lines, he must spend a fortune. And what about the tickets police rain down on truck drivers, and all the other expenses that come with owning a truck?"

I shrugged. "Well, sure, he has expenses. He didn't say the five thousand was pure profit. Still, that's pretty good."

"It's a horrible business. You were always gone. Always dirty."

"It paid our bills."

"So does the insurance business, and we live a much more civilized life."

"I'm just sharing my day and what we talked about. Why is this suddenly an attack on my previous work?"

"It's not an attack. I just don't want these guys filling your head with dreams of how easy it is to make money with trucks. It's not true. We know from experience."

"Can I go now?" Julia asked.

"Not until everyone is finished eating," I said.

"Why do we have to sit here and listen to you two argue?"

"Because that's what families do. And we're having a discussion, not an argument."

She rolled her eyes and sat there, holding her head as if it weighed a ton. I asked Alex about his day, and at least he had positive things to say tonight.

"I got all my homework done during class and went to play catch with Jeff. I think we're going to win our baseball game this time."

Not with his coach, but I nodded. "Keep practicing, and you'll do great," I said.

"Yep," he agreed and reached for a hunk of bread.

"Well, I think it might be a good idea to buy a truck and try it out," I said to Luisa.

"What about your insurance business?" She pushed her plate away, mostly uneaten.

"It practically runs itself now."

"You mean I run it." Luisa had always been meek and agreeable, but she'd gotten stronger, and I didn't dislike this more assertive, confident version of my wife.

"Sure, you run it. Exactly. You can do almost everything I do at the office now. I can drive a truck a few times a week, and you can handle the office. We can always use the extra money."

"Does it matter what I think? You're going to do what you want anyway."

Sure, because I was always the one with the ideas and creativity and a sense of adventure. And she was always the one to find every obstacle and point it out.

I FINALLY CONVINCED *Mamá* to visit us. She arrived during the summer of 1981, and I was so overcome with emotion from seeing my mother again after so many years I couldn't even speak. I pulled her tight against my body when she walked off the airplane and hugged her like I had when I was a little boy.

After I let her go, *Mamá* cried as she kissed the kids and told them how much they'd grown.

Alex gave up his room, or at least his bed, for his grandmother and slept in our room. He spoke non-stop, explaining to her what the items in his room were, bragging about his baseball trophies.

"They're amazing! You must be a good player to have so many trophies."

"No, everyone gets one," he said with a shrug.

Mamá couldn't believe how much Julia had grown. She had been a nine-year-old little girl when she left Argentina, and now she was a teenager who wore jeans and rock-n-roll shirts every day, permed her hair into wild curls, and spoke Spanish poorly. But to her grandmother, she was still a little girl, the little princess as my father used to call her.

"California looks like paradise," she said as she finally settled at the kitchen table to enjoy a cup of tea and some cake Luisa bought at the Argentine store.

"You can't beat the weather," I told her. "You finally sold the business. How do you feel about that, *Mamá*?"

"It was hard to let it go," she admitted, "but it was time. A busy restaurant was a lot for me to take care of myself. You and Theo were right. Thank you for allowing me to stay in your condo, by the way. It's yours whenever you decide to come back."

"*Mamá*, it's been sitting there empty for years now. I'm glad you're there."

"Without the obligation of the restaurant, I went to see my sister in Mendoza and relaxed a little, and now here I am with you and Luisa, and my adorable grandchildren." She pinched Alex's cheek, and he smiled shyly, even though he wasn't typically shy. "I'm a happy grandmother."

Having *Mamá* at home with us didn't change our routine. The kids still had to go to school. We still had to work. But we did take some time off to travel with her during the summer. We took her to Lake Tahoe, Las Vegas, and of course, all over Southern California, especially the theme parks.

She planned to stay only for two or three months but at the end of the summer, she extended her stay after we begged her not to return so soon and to spend Christmas with us.

In the meantime, Luisa continued to care for the insurance agency while I drove the truck I purchased, doing local runs. Paco had been right. After a year of driving my one truck, it was bringing in way more than the insurance agency.

"I'm going to buy a second truck and hire a driver," I announced one day.

Luisa didn't respond. She didn't have to. It didn't matter what she thought anymore. She had no vision. So, I bought the second truck.

Three months later, I bought a third and a fourth.

"Salvadorito," *Mamá* said, "don't you think you're growing too fast?"

"There's more business than my current trucks can handle, *Mamá.*"

But I spent more and more time dealing with the problems the trucks had. Blown tires and other mechanical issues were daily concerns. And as Luisa had correctly pointed out, the drivers accumulated tickets because the highway patrol loved to harass truck drivers. These problems were not as much fun as driving a truck myself.

I spent most weekdays putting out fires or fixing trucks in my front yard. "Son of a fucking bitch," I cussed from the inside of the truck engine.

This was the greeting Julia got daily as she walked past me on her way to the house as she returned from school. "Hi Dad."

I grunted, wanting to say something but too frustrated to even look up from the engine.

After I took a shower and we had dinner, I was ready to collapse into bed every night.

"Salvador, we need to take your mother somewhere this weekend. You're spending all your time working."

"Of course, I'm working. I have bills to pay."

"And the insurance agency is failing. You're never there anymore."

"If it's failing, it's because you're not doing your job. I left it in your hands."

"Are you kidding me? I'm not the agent, you are. You're not bringing in new business. And all I can sell are life insurance policies. I'm dealing with existing clients, the kids, your mom. And Julia is graduating from junior high school in a few months. Did you know that?"

"Sure."

"Why don't we take your mom and the kids to Disneyland this weekend? Your mom is leaving after Julia's graduation, so we should make the most of the next couple of months."

"Not this weekend. Maybe after the graduation."

Luisa nodded and rolled over to go to sleep.

THOUGH I WAS OFTEN frustrated, things were not all bad. For one, the trucking business made a ridiculous amount of money. At the end of 1981, I had made about $100,000 dollars, and for the first quarter of '82, I was on track to make about the same. As Luisa had said, though, I had expenses that easily took half, and I wasn't much of a bookkeeper. *Mamá* and Luisa told me to hire an accountant to determine my costs. "Soon," I said. "Maybe next year."

But in April 1982, Argentina decided to claim their rights to the Malvina Islands off their southern coast. The British called them the Falkland Islands. The two nations both had claims on them since the early 1800s. When Argentina declared its independence from Spain in 1816, they also proclaimed sovereignty over the Islands that were only 300 miles off the coast of Argentina. The British claimed they had been there before the Spanish, and in 1841 they easily kicked out the few Argentine officials and installed a lieutenant governor and British civilians to occupy the Island. After over 100 years of occupation, the islanders were all British subjects.

In 1964, when I left Argentina, the UN had decided to try to resolve this issue and arrive at a peaceful solution. But apparently, after so many years of discussions that led nowhere, the military government of Argentina decided to forcibly occupy the island.

With my country at war, I told my mother to postpone her travels home a little longer.

"But I've been here almost a year already."

"Staying a little longer won't matter then. I'll talk to Theo to get you an additional extension. Considering there's a war, I'm sure they'll grant it."

I sat late into the night, watching the one-sided news.

Mamá sat with me. She rubbed my back. "Go to sleep, Salvadorito. You need to rest."

"Our boys are not trained for war. I worry about what the British will do."

"There's nothing we can do. Just pray."

"Yeah, like that will do any good."

By May, the war had heated up. The British started their aerial attacks on Port Stanley. And they sunk the Argentine Navy Cruiser General Belgrano. Two days later, the Argentines sank the HMS Sheffield. Then the U.S., which promised to stay neutral, shifted its support behind Margaret Thatcher and the British.

I felt helpless and angry. The bastard Reagan was supposed to stand by his Latin-American neighbors, but he turned his back on us. Other nations at the UN condemned Britain for its continued colonialism and imperialism.

TV news and talk show hosts who were ignorant and didn't know the history or understand what they were saying filled the airwaves with nonsense. The talk show host Phil Donahue had a segment about the war, and I decided to call in to share my opinion and give them the facts.

"What do you want to say?" the screener asked.

"I want to tell the truth, the Argentine side."

"What exactly is that?"

"That the British have held that island illegally for years. The island is in Argentine waters, and the British are the invaders, not the Argentines. And the Americans are violating their own Monroe Doctrine."

"You can't say that."

"What do you mean I can't say that? I'm living in a free country, aren't I? That's what I think and believe. Why can't I say it?"

But they refused to allow me to give my opinion. I slammed the receiver into the phone cradle.

"What's wrong?" my mother asked.

"Don't worry, *Mamá*," Luisa told her. "He's fine."

"They just want to make us look bad," I screamed, infuriated with the lying news stations and the American government. "They don't care about the truth. Fuck them!"

I bought a special radio to hear international stations to get news directly from Argentina. The signal wasn't perfect, and I didn't know if I could trust the information coming out of Argentina either. Of course, they claimed they were winning, while we heard the opposite.

"You hear that, Julia?" I said as she walked past to her bedroom. "Don't ever trust what any government is telling you."

"Ah, huh," she said and kept going. The days when she was interested in anything important had ended. Mostly, she avoided us and hid in her room.

It was difficult to think of anything but the war, but I had to continue working and driving my trucks, so I went into the yard to get my loads for the day.

Inside the small trailer where the dispatcher handed out the paperwork, he spoke with his assistant, pointing to the small TV he had in there, to the news reporting on the war. "I hope the Brits kill every one of those stupid Mexicans. They're all a bunch of uncivilized peasants," he said as I walked into the trailer.

My blood pressure instantly surged as his words struck me and pierced my heart, adding another deep wound to the many I hadn't even known I'd collected through the years as I worked to fit in, to become an American. But I never would; to them, I'd always be a foreigner, an uncivilized peasant that deserved to be killed for having the gall to stand up to the British and take back what was ours.

He must have seen the look on my face when he noticed me standing there. He glanced at the dispatcher, then back at me. "Hey, Sal," he said. "You're from one of those countries, aren't you? I didn't mean—"

My fist connected with his jaw before I had a chance to think about what I was doing, sending him backward, falling on his ass, the back of his head bouncing on the floor.

"What the fuck," the other guy said, bending down to help my dispatcher stand and get his balance.

"You fucking piece of shit," my dispatcher said, rubbing the back of his head, recovering from the strike.

"Kill every one of *my* countrymen? They're Argentines, you ignorant hick, not Mexicans. You're too stupid to even know the difference, and *we're* uncivilized?"

"Get you're shit and get out. You're finished here. You're lucky I don't call the cops and have you arrested for assault."

I swung again and landed the second punch on his nose, and kicked the other in the stomach before I left.

Unable to see straight, I didn't bother with my trucks. Instead, I got into my car and stepped on the gas, sending gravel and dirt flying in all directions. I slammed my hand on the steering wheel. Every kid in Argentina could take a blank world map and correctly add in the names of each country; they could tell you where every U.S. state was located; they learned world history and literature. American kids were taught nothing. Most couldn't even name the states in their own country, much less pinpoint where Argentina was.

I remember Julia saying once that New Mexico was in Mexico. When I asked her why she thought that, she said that her teacher had told her so. I had to make her pull out a map and find it. I thought maybe she had misunderstood, that her teacher had said that it used to be part of Mexico. New Mexico became a state in 1912; it had been a U.S. territory since 1852 as part of the Gadson Purchase. I had to give her a history lesson. *Me*, a stupid peasant.

So why was I surprised that these idiots, uneducated men in the trucking business, didn't know anything about Argentina? As I drove home, my vision blurred. Maybe it wasn't that I was surprised, just angry and frustrated that men who were my intellectual inferiors were my bosses and had all the power while I had none.

I went home to call my drivers and tell them that they wouldn't work today.

"I have to go get my trucks. I'm going to have to change companies. They fired me today, and I don't want to work for those racist jerks anyway," I explained to my drivers.

While I washed my cut and bruised knuckles, I shared with Luisa and *Mamá* what had happened.

"That's terrible," *Mamá* said. "How could those men be so insensitive?"

Luisa didn't say anything, but I could tell by the look on her face that she was shocked by what had happened.

Two of my most loyal drivers came over that night to take me to get my trucks. Frank would drive one, and I would drive the other. Gerardo gave us a ride. I decided to go at night because the day dispatcher wouldn't be there.

We drove into the yard, and I directed Gerardo to the trucks. As we approached the first one, five guys came out of hiding behind other trucks and under trailers wielding baseball bats. One swung at my head, and thankfully, I ducked, then ran under a trailer.

Frank was hit in the back, but he turned around, gripped the bat, and pushed the guy down. He ran and hurried to climb into one of my trucks. I tried to make my way back, but three men chased after me.

"Right there. Get him! Don't let him get away," they yelled at each other, probably planning to beat me to a pulp and leave me bleeding in the yard.

Gerardo revved his car and drove toward me. "Get in," he yelled from the window.

But I wasn't going to leave my truck. I ran for it, but a couple of guys caught me. I felt one blow to my left side and another to my back. I covered my head. They kept hitting me with bats and kicking me. But Gerardo drove the car toward us like he was going to run over them, flashing his high beams. Finally, they all took off running.

I struggled to get up.

"Shit, are you okay?"

"I don't think anything is broken," I said, although my ribs ached. Holding my side, I limped to my truck. "I'm okay," I said, though I hurt everywhere.

It hurt to climb up, but I got inside the truck, started it, and left the yard. Frank followed. Thankfully, they hadn't damaged my trucks. They were too stupid to think of that. It was just me they wanted to punish.

When I got home, I took a long shower, and Luisa held icepacks to my side and back.

"I can't believe they did this. What criminals."

"Payback for the punches I threw. Good riddance. I'm done with them."

"We should call the police."

I laughed. "Luisa, the police won't help me. I threw the first punch, and besides, they'd just deny it. They'd say they had nothing to do with those men being there."

"So, what are you going to do now?"

"The only thing I can do is hope to find more work before next month's truck payments, insurance payments, mortgage payments, and the other million bills we have." I lay back in bed and stared at the ceiling. "And when the Argentines win this war, I'm going to sell everything and go back home. Fuck this country."

CHAPTER THIRTY-EIGHT

The following week, I contacted five brokers and even a couple of freight carriers to get work for my trucks, but everyone turned me down. They were all blackballing me. A couple of freight carriers flat out told me that they'd heard I was trouble, and they didn't want to deal with a hothead like me. Others just told me they didn't have any work for me.

"But I know you have work. You're advertising for owner operators to apply."

"As I said, we don't have any work for you."

I was falling behind on my truck payments. Everyday those trucks sat, I lost money. So, I decided to sell a couple of my trucks. I had two that were paid off.

I finally found one company that gave me work for one truck, so I started driving again.

"You should come back to the insurance agency," Luisa said. But that wasn't going well either. "I got a job at a clothing store called Judy's in the meantime," she told me.

"What do you mean? What about the office? What about handling the paperwork for the trucks?"

"There isn't anything for me to do at the office. We have no new business. I sit there all day, doing nothing and we need money."

"So, you went behind my back and got a job?"

"It wasn't behind your back. Why are you acting this way? I'll still help with the trucking paperwork."

"Yes, you will, and you need to be in the office too. Our current clients might call and then what? Tell the clothing company you changed your mind."

"I didn't change my mind, and I'm not going to do that."

I slammed my hand on the kitchen table and she jumped. "I don't need one more person in my life whose working against me. We're either in this together or we're not. You choose."

But the following week, she went to work at Judy's sorting clothing or whatever she was doing. I refused to talk to her. If she wanted to go against my wishes, she'd do it alone. She worked and came home to make dinner for the kids and *Mamá*. I ate out.

She asked about the financial paperwork for the truck, and if I needed her to deposit any checks, but I ignored her. I did it all myself. But I wouldn't be able to keep this up. If she kept working at that stupid store, I'd just have to overload her with work.

Luisa brought clothes home for Julia who loved all the girly fashion which made me even angrier. She was undermining my role as the head of this household.

Around my driving schedule, I went to the insurance office. On my answering machine, I had multiple calls from my district manager. He accused me of abandoning my clients. I should sell my business and close my agency if I wasn't going to work, he recommended. Many of my clients had already left me. My wealthy doctors didn't like that I'd started driving trucks. They thought the work was beneath me, and they wanted a full-time insurance agent. The hell with them too. They didn't own me. I wasn't their puppet.

As I sat at my desk, I ran a hand through my hair and held my forehead. Everything was falling apart, and I didn't know what to save.

The phone rang. I didn't want to, but I picked it up. Mateo said, "I can't believe you really answered your phone."

"Hey *Flaco*, how have you been?" He'd followed the whole disaster with Argentina too. The war ended in a humiliating defeat in June, riots broke out in the streets of Buenos Aires and Rosario and culminated in the ousting of the military regime.

"I'm wondering if you want to go have a drink. Camila is getting married to the jerk she cheated on me with, and I could use a night out."

He still wasn't over her. He'd fought for custody of their daughter and lost. She'd received partial custody. Now, he'd have to watch another man raise his daughter. What a kick in the balls. "Yeah, I'll meet you."

We met at a little Argentine grill in Los Angeles that had a bar section. Something else I didn't like about California was that they didn't have just bars, it was always some kind of grill. In New York, you could go to just a bar.

We ordered our drinks and sat in silence. "I just turned 40," I said. "I can't believe that."

"Happy birthday."

"Yeah. Look at us. We should have pockets full of money and be living in Argentina."

"Thank God we're not in Argentina." Mateo shook his head.

"The only good thing to come out of the war, according to my brother, is that they are finally going to hold elections and have a civilian government. No more military dictatorships," I told him.

"I'm dating a couple of hot women," Mateo said, changing the subject. I got the feeling he didn't care much about what happened in Argentina.

"Yeah? Good for you."

He shrugged. "I'd rather have what you have."

"I'm not sure *what* I have, except for a lot of debt and two failing businesses." I told him about the confrontation with my boss and all the backlash that followed.

"Maybe you should have controlled your temper."

"Naw, guys like that need someone who will stand up to them and tell them they're garbage. They're bullies used to pushing immigrants like us around." I drank my whiskey and waved at the bartender to bring me another.

"But he still has his job, and you don't."

"I don't need that job. I don't need anything."

Mateo drank his beer. "Aren't you supposed to be cheering me up?"

"I can't be sad for you. Let her get married. Have fun with your girlfriends. You're free."

"I don't want to be free, *Viejo*. I want my old house, to come home to my girls. I love being a father."

I understood how he felt, but what could I say? "You're a good father. You'll always be a good father. Camila always seemed only partially into you, Mateo. I'm sorry, but she never was all in. Just move on."

WE WERE ALL CHOKED up to have to put *Mamá* on a plane after having her in our home for eleven months. The kids had gotten used to her living with us. Despite all the turmoil and war in Argentina, the year spent being together and acting like tourists, we'd treasure forever.

"What was your favorite place to visit, *Abuela*?" Alex asked, "Say Universal Studios."

"You can't tell her what to say," Julia said. "Why bother asking then?"

My mom was close to tears the whole time we were at LAX. "I loved everything. Especially being with you, my little redhead *querido*," she said, kissing his cheeks.

Alex didn't even pull away. "When are you going to come back, *Abuela*?"

"I don't know. I've been here a long time. Maybe you can come see me next."

"Sure," he said as if a trip to Argentina were the easiest and most natural thing in the world.

I sat beside my mother. "Look *Mamá*, if things don't improve over there, you can move here permanently with us."

"Oh, no. Rosario is my home for better or worse. But if you ever get tired of struggling here, you can always come home."

"I know."

"I see how difficult it is for you here. At least in Argentina you have family, *Hijo*."

"I'll keep that in mind, *Mamá*."

When the flight attendant called for passengers to board, we all cried and hugged her. My lungs couldn't seem to draw in enough air. The silence in the car as I drove home echoed the empty feeling inside me. Luisa patted my thigh as we drove home. It was just the two of us again, like when we started out in New York. Not exactly since we had the kids but still, the two of us were alone, fighting to keep what we had and survive.

MY LUCK HAD CHANGED, and it didn't appear that I was going to get any breaks. My two trucks got spotty work. I managed to keep Frank as my second driver, and I drove the other truck. When I was away, I called home and Luisa sounded relieved and agitated at the same time.

"What's wrong now?" I asked.

"All the bills I paid from our checking account, the house, the truck payments, utility bills, everything bounced. I went to the bank to see what happened and they told me that the IRS took all our money."

I let out a string of curses. I was at a pay phone at a truck stop. No one seemed to notice or care. The IRS had sent me a couple of notices for missing tax documents the last four years. But I didn't have money to pay them; they didn't need my measly few thousand dollars. So, I figured they could wait until I got back on my feet. What benefit did I get from all the money they took every year anyway? But now it seemed they screwed me when I could least afford to pay those back taxes.

"Damn it. I worked like an animal to get the money to pay everything on time."

"What do I do?"

"I guess I'll try to send double payments next month and try to get more work for the trucks."

"You're already working around the clock."

"Well, I'll work harder," I said.

"If only you hadn't made me quit my job at Judy's. At least I'd have some money."

"You were making peanuts. I need you at the office." I promised my district manager I'd revive my business and serve my clients better. Luisa would call them all, see them, and do whatever she needed to do while I drove the trucks.

When I got home, I called an Argentine lawyer from the club. "What can I do about the IRS?"

"Just be glad they didn't arrest you for not filing your taxes. There's nothing you can do."

"They can just go into my bank account like thieves and steal my money?"

"They see it as collecting what you owe."

"Why the hell do I owe them anything? What kind of system is this? This damned country is always screwing the little guy."

"Salvador, what can I tell you? In Argentina, they take your taxes before you get your paycheck. Here, you have to file. It's the way it is. I would contact an accountant and get squared away on the missing years, see what you owe."

"Are they going to keep taking my money?"

"If you still owe, and if you don't file the previous returns, yes."

"Shit!"

I went home. Luisa was at the office, and the kids were in school. I stood in my living room alone, looking at the things I'd worked so hard to buy and maintain. Now what? Was I supposed to keep working just to have the government take every penny I made?"

Overcome with a sudden rage at the unfairness and the reality that no one cared about my struggle or the struggle of the average person, I opened my sliding glass door and started throwing my furniture out of the door onto the patio. I kicked it, picked it up over my head, and hurled it outside. "Son of a fucking bitch!" I shouted at the top of my lungs. Stuff. Just a bunch of stuff that meant nothing. I hated this life. I hated this house and my work and—

The front door opened, and Julia, returning home from high school, took one look at the living room, at me as if I were a maniac, and her jaw dropped. Without saying a word, she stepped around the mess, slipped into her bedroom, and closed the door behind her.

I dropped my head back and closed my stinging eyes. My temples throbbed. I was going to have a stroke if I didn't calm down.

Grabbing my keys, I left. I wasn't sure where I was going. I just had to get out. I got on the freeway and drove until I reached the coast, out by Long Beach. I parked the car and walked out to the sand, just walked like a zombie, and dropped down before I reached the shore. I hugged my knees and stared at the waves as they pulled out and returned with a crash, again and again.

What a metaphor for my life. I tried, and I tried, and each time I crashed. I didn't want to do it anymore. The American Dream was a farce. It didn't exist. I lay back in the sand, drained, defeated.

I watched the clouds above me move slowly and transform. They were free, blowing wherever the wind took them. Something I wasn't. I was stuck, trapped, and unhappy. The clouds began to form shapes. One looked like a feather, another a bird in flight with its wings outstretched, another a heart, a dinosaur. And oddly, I remembered that dream I had in Argentina as a young man before I decided to move to America. I sat upright. What was it? Something about dreams—ambitions and desires—being like clouds. They only seemed real before fading away and revealing themselves as illusions. My dream had been about the utter foolishness of believing and yearning to become something special. I didn't understand it then, but now it was so clear. Holy shit?

I didn't believe in premonitions, but maybe I should have paid attention and stayed put in Argentina.

"It's not too late," I said to myself. "I can go back."

I looked up at the clouds that looked like nothing but clouds now.

It was time to return to Argentina and get the hell out of this country that drew people in, promising riches and success, only to drain their souls and toss them out to die an empty shell. Not me. I was finished.

CHAPTER THIRTY-NINE

Luisa and I sat at Denny's coffee shop close to the office where we used to go at least once a week when we were getting the insurance agency going. In those days, we spent hours together strategizing about how to get more clients. Today, we had to discuss how we would dismantle everything we'd built.

"You want to sell everything?" Luisa asked, surprised or skeptical, I couldn't tell.

"Except for our clothes or what we can take on an airplane."

"Julia isn't going to want to leave before she graduates from high school."

"Frankly, I don't care what she wants. If her family moves, she's moving. It will be better for her in Argentina anyway. She has an attitude that I don't like these days." At least while her grandmother had been here, she'd spoken Spanish because she'd had no choice. And her language skills had improved a lot.

Luisa looked sad. Didn't she want to return to Argentina anymore?

"We're behind on the house payment. We're going to lose it anyway if we don't sell it. We should try to get something out of it."

"I thought we'd grow old here, and the kids would always have a place to return to."

"They'll have that in Argentina."

"Well." She squared her shoulders. "When do we tell them, and when do we leave?"

"This is the way we should do it," I said. "We send the kids first to stay with *Mamá*. If we don't have to worry about them, we can sell the house and the furniture, the trucks, cars, everything. We keep working the insurance business to save money, and then we take all our profits and go home to our condo in Rosario."

"Where your mother lives?"

"We'll all live together for a while. Then I'll get *Mamá* another smaller apartment. She doesn't need three bedrooms."

Luisa frowned. "I don't know about sending the kids first. Without us? To a foreign country?"

I laughed. "To *our* country."

"It's not their country, Salvador. Everything will be different for them. They won't know anyone."

"Our family is there. Aunts, uncles, cousins, their grandmother. It's more than *we* had when we moved here. They'll be fine."

"All people they don't know."

"It's the best way. And it'll only be for a few months. It shouldn't take long to sell the house." I wasn't dismissing her concerns, but I had to be the strong one here. She'd see that without the kids to take care of, we'd have clearer heads and take care of business faster.

"YOU'RE GOING TO DO what?" Julia shouted. "Sell our house? Move where? Are you guys crazy? They just had a war over there."

"Things have changed. They have a Democratic government now."

"I can't believe this. You want me to leave my school, my friends, everything."

"Julia," I said. "Your school and friends are not everything. There are more important things."

"What about our dog?"

"We'll find him a good home."

"Oh my God," she said. "I'm going to throw up." She ran into her bedroom, slamming the door behind her. Then we heard the door from her bedroom to the backyard patio open. She ran out the side gate.

"Julia!" Luisa yelled, hurrying to chase after our daughter.

But I held Luisa's arm.

"Let me go after her."

"Give her some space. She'll be back." In so many ways, Julia was like me, and the worst thing someone could do when I was upset was try to talk to me. She needed time to think.

"You're going to let her leave?"

"She'll probably go to her friend's house to tell her how horrible we are. Or to a pay phone and talk for an hour like she does."

Alex sat on the couch, petting the dog's head, having observed the whole encounter without a word.

"What do you think, *Colorado*?"

He shrugged, and his eyes filled with tears. "Can we take, Lobo?"

"I wish we could, but they don't let dogs travel in airplanes. They put them in cages with the luggage, and he'd probably die."

"I'll miss him. He's my buddy."

"Me too. But we'll find him a home where he'll be happy. You'll get to live with your *Abuela*, meet your cousins, and go to soccer games. You're going to love Argentina."

He nodded. "I know where Julia will go. Do you want to follow her in the car?"

"No, let's give her some time. We'll go get her if she doesn't come home in a few hours."

Luisa and I waited until Julia returned a few hours later when it was dark. Luisa had paced frantically, asking me every few seconds when we were going to go find her.

"I should ground you," I said as she walked in. "Don't ever leave without telling us where you're going again."

She didn't appear to have much fight in her; her eyes were red, her face splotchy. She gazed at me. "I love you," she said. "But I'll never forgive you for this." She looked at Luisa. "You either."

And she disappeared into her room.

WE DIDN'T HAVE LONG before the mortgage company would foreclose on our house. So, the following month, in February of 1983, we took the kids to LAX, which was more heartbreaking than I imagined. Possibly what made it worse were Julia's friends, who all showed up at the airport to say goodbye. Suddenly, I began to question if my decision was wise after all.

"I'll come back," she promised them. "As soon as I turn eighteen when I'm an adult, I'll be back." They hugged each other and cried as if someone were dying.

I shook my head at the drama. Teenagers. I wanted to tell her she wasn't coming back. No way would I let my daughter live here alone. But, of course, I was immediately struck with my own hypocrisy. Hadn't I done that to my parents? And I went to a foreign country. As much as I hated to admit it, this was her country. My only hope was that she would like it there so much that she'd forget about her friends here and choose to live in Argentina with the rest of us.

I gave both of my kids a long hug. "We'll see you soon," I said.

Luisa cried and clung to them, but finally, they had to board and take that long trip to my birth country, where they would get to know our culture and our family, something I'd deprived them of for too long.

All the teenage kids stood there, wiping their eyes. Luisa didn't seem to notice them. For a second. I couldn't drag my gaze away from her; I'd never seen her look so devastated. "Why don't I buy everyone some breakfast?" I suggested.

The kids, all good kids that I'd known for years, looked at me, at each other, and nodded. They'd had sleepovers at our house. I knew their parents. I liked the girls and was even fond of their boyfriends. And they loved my daughter. The girls put their arms around Luisa, and we all watched the plane take off before we left.

PUTTING THE HOUSE UP for sale and selling our things at a yard sale were like little pinpricks in both our hearts. As each item sold or we gave it away, it was like watching pieces of our life disappear. All the moments we shared with our kids in this house, all our dreams vanishing as if they were pages of a calendar that a gust of wind blew away.

The worst was getting rid of Lobo. But while driving the truck, I'd met a guy in Bakersfield with a big farm. One day, I put Lobo in the car, and Luisa and I drove there.

"Hey Sal, where's your big truck?" the farmer asked.

"I'm not driving it anymore. In fact, I'm moving back to Argentina."

He nodded. "You talked about that a lot. Finally decided to make the move, huh?"

Lobo barked in the car. "I'm hoping you have room on your farm for our four-legged family member."

"Is he a pit bull?"

"Part pit bull, but he's a family dog. He can get a little wild, and he's bitten a couple of people, to be honest. This is why I thought he'd be happy out here where you have land, and there aren't many people."

"Let me see him."

We took Lobo out, and he wagged his tail and licked the guy's hand. He bounced around acting like a puppy.

"I guess I can take another dog," he agreed.

Even though Luisa didn't like dogs, this was her children's pet, so she hugged him. With a lump in my throat, I patted Lobo's head and Luisa's back. We both cried as we drove away. Lobo jumped and ran beside his new owner, oblivious that we were leaving him behind.

Knowing that our kids were waiting for us kept us moving forward, willing to sell everything and move as quickly as possible. The kids had arrived safely. My brother picked them up in Buenos Aires and drove them to their grandmother's home, our condo, where we should have been living years ago.

It took two months to sell the house and go through escrow, so we temporarily moved into the insurance office. Thankfully, the other agent who shared the office with me had moved to her a larger office about a year earlier.

Since I had to close my agency, Luisa and I were hired to work as internal agents for another agent. Our job was to visit factories and warehouses and explain the benefits to the new Hispanic employees in hopes that they would buy more life insurance. Luisa was a superstar. She convinced more people to extend their insurance coverage than I did.

At night, we sat in that little office where we were not supposed to live, and Luisa cried.

"What's wrong?" I asked her, though, of course, I knew.

"I miss the kids. Here we are, living in an office a couple of miles from our house, our kids thousands of miles away. How did we get here, Salvador?"

When we sold the house, we made very little money, and what we did make, we had to finish paying off the IRS. I was disgusted with the whole thing. But at least now, we could put some money in the bank. "We're saving money. If we work a little longer, we'll be able to leave soon."

Luisa's depression grew as the weeks went by. It didn't help that Julia was miserable in Argentina, and every time we spoke to her on the phone, she told us how unhappy she was and how much she missed us and her home.

It took a while to get the kids enrolled in school. The documents from the American schools had to be legalized and accepted in Argentina, but after four months, they started school, which helped to occupy their minds and gave them something to focus on. Hopefully, they'd make friends and begin to adapt.

After a long week of working, I didn't think I could stand another weekend of moping around the tiny office.

"Come on," I told Luisa. "Pack an overnight bag."

"Why?"

"Just do it."

I drove to Ensenada, Mexico, where we spent the weekend walking on the beach, eating lobster, drinking margaritas, and trying to enjoy ourselves and remember what it was like years earlier when it was just the two of us. I missed those days.

We sat overlooking the ocean, enjoying a drink. Luisa had a fruity piña cola and I had a beer. "It's beautiful, isn't it?"

"It is," she agreed.

"I kind of wish I'd decided to move to Mexico instead of California."

She made a scoffing sound.

"At least we would have been with other Latinos." We watched the sunset over the water.

"Well, we did what we did. If you'd asked me, I would have stayed in New York."

"You always did like it better there."

"I got used to California, especially the weather, but it felt like the countryside to me and lacked the excitement of New York."

"I'm glad we got to see both coasts and even a few states in the middle of the country. It hasn't been all bad, has it?"

"Of course not."

I wanted to apologize for losing everything. Some of it had been my fault; I'd blown so many opportunities. But mostly, I'd been screwed over by others so many times. An apology felt insincere, and besides, what was the point? We would move on to a new stage in our lives and make the best of it. Life was about forward progress, and it never helped to look back. What was over, was over.

Moving back to Argentina had always been the plan, part of our destiny. As I sipped my beer, I wondered how difficult it would be to find work in Argentina. My next step should probably be to find out.

CHAPTER FORTY

The next week, when we got paid, I contacted an Argentine travel agent in Los Angeles and bought myself a ticket to Argentina. When I got back to the office, I told Luisa that I would check on the kids and see about my job prospects.

"You bought one ticket? To *visit* the kids?"

"You're not the only one who misses them. They seem to be doing well, but I thought it would be a good idea to see how they're really doing. To take *Mamá* some money."

"Salvador, I'm going to kill you. I've just had it."

"What? I thought you'd be happy that I decided to check on them. You're always crying and worrying about them. Plus, I need to make sure I can find work."

"Don't you think it's a little late to think about *if* you'll find work? You'll just have to."

"Of course, but what if I don't, what if we get there and I can't make a living there? I need to go reassure myself that we'll all be okay."

"Why aren't we just moving? What are we doing here?"

"Saving money."

"We're spending money! Spending money on the rent for this office. Spending money on food and restaurants. Spending money on a stupid weekend in Mexico."

"I was trying to get your mind off the kids."

"My mind is never off the kids. They're growing up without us."

"They're not growing up without us. It's only been six months."

"You're insane, you know that? We were supposed to join them in a couple of months."

"It took longer than that to sell the house."

"And now you're going to visit *by yourself*?"

"I'm going to go check things out. See the apartment. See the situation over there. It's smart to do that before we move." I'd be gone only for a couple of weeks.

"I don't give a damn what the situation is. We sold the house and everything in it. Our kids are there. We're moving no matter what the situation is."

I grabbed my pack of cigarettes and went to stand outside and smoke. Then I walked to the arcade to play pinball. She was never happy.

THE KIDS WERE THRILLED to see me and looked happy. Both of them spoke flawless Spanish and had picked up the Argentine accent, which made me proud. They were even doing well in school and had lots of friends.

Julia studied on an old desk that my parents must have purchased in the 1930s and wrote her school essays on an equally old Royal typewriter.

"Oh my God," I said to her. "My dad used to write me letters using this typewriter."

"I love it. It's an antique."

"It sure is." I ran my fingers over the top of the glass keys, thinking about the hours my father spent bent over this machine, first as a journalist, then writing to his son, offering loving advice. I lowered one of the keys, feeling the resistance and remembering how he'd tell me how tired it made him to write me as his disease advanced. Typing on this machine must have been quite the exercise. But he did it, week after week.

I sighed and noticed Julia watching me. "You need more light in this room. How do you even see?"

"I get by," she said.

I sat on her futon. "What do you think of your country?"

"It's great. I wish there were burger joints, but the Argentine food is great."

I laughed. "Hamburgers are definitely an American thing. But it's a different, more relaxed life here, isn't it?"

"Yeah, people are laid back. Things I used to think were important, like not leaving the house without make-up, I don't worry about anymore. People here are nice, and the kids love their parents. We go dancing with my friends or hang out and drink beer with their family. Do you know there's no drinking age here?"

I smiled and touched her face. "Do you like beer?"

"Not at all."

Again, I laughed. "So, you still think you want to go back?"

She nodded. "When I graduate, I want an airline ticket back to be my graduation present."

"I don't know, Julia."

"I'm working really hard. I'm probably going to fail every class. I don't even know how to write and read in Spanish, but I study, and my friends are helping me. If I do it, all I ask is that you send me back to the U.S."

"You'll break your mother's heart."

She looked down at her feet. "That's not fair."

No, it wasn't, but it was all I could use. "I'm sure I broke my mother's heart when I left."

She met my gaze. "I'm glad I'm getting to know Argentina and my family. They're all awesome. But my future isn't here, Dad."

"Sometimes," I said. "I feel like we're a family without a country. We don't belong anywhere."

"I know where I belong," she said.

I envied that statement more than she'd ever know.

I CALLED SOME OF MY old high school friends, and we went downtown for a few drinks. The streets of Rosario weren't as flashy as those in Buenos Aires, but restaurants were full of cheerful customers, and people flocked to walk the pedestrian streets and window shop. The bars played modern music now, much of it borrowed from American artists, all Madonna and Boy George. When I left, it was all tangos and Folklorico.

"Are you coming back for good?" Gustavo asked as we took a seat and ordered drinks.

"That's the plan. What kind of work do you think I'll find?"

"Well, this isn't the United States. Work is difficult to get, especially at your age, but you're smart. Your brother is a lawyer with connections, so I'm sure you'll find something."

"Yeah," I said, not as confident. My old friends here had worked at their careers for the last twenty years. They were established, settled, and almost bored with their lives, but they didn't have to worry about finding work.

"Honestly, I don't know why you'd even consider coming back. You must have a great life in the U.S."

I gazed at him and thought for a fraction of a second about telling him the truth, but why ruin his illusion of life in America? "It's a different world, for sure. I had a huge house with a massive backyard with fruit trees, two Cadillacs, and I ran two businesses. Finding work is easy, and anyone can have their own business."

Gustavo shook his head. "I'm telling you, if I were you, I'd stay there."

"The whole war and the Americans taking Britain's side really soured me on living there. You're always an outsider in America."

Gustavo sipped his whiskey and waved away my comment with the same hand. "Of course, the Americans took Britain's side. What did you expect? They're different threads on the same fabric. Who cares? Our loss had nothing to do with America's involvement. The military here botched up the war like they did with everything they touched. Good riddance. I'm glad they're gone. If it took losing a war to get rid of them, then we'll swallow that defeat."

We stayed a little longer catching up, flirted with some women, bought them drinks, and pretended we were in high school. Afterward, we went back to Gustavo's place with the ladies. I didn't want to wake the kids or *Mamá* up, so I spent the night at his house.

The following day before the kids woke up, I had coffee with *Mamá*. "I think this condo might be a little small for us. What do you think?"

"I'll move out, and then you'll have three bedrooms."

"I didn't mean that. But even if you moved out, the kitchen is small. It might be smart for me to look for something else."

"Well, that's up to you, but this is your condo."

I called a real estate agent and spent the afternoon looking at houses and condos, and I found an old home that I liked though it appeared to be in some disrepair. In Argentina, it was common to have a home in the front, right off of the sidewalk, and one in the back. This one was in the back, but the house was located downtown in the best part of the city, just a few blocks from famous Pellegrini Street. I could buy it and slowly fix it up. We could live with *Mamá* while we remodeled the home.

I didn't have time to waste since I had to return to California soon, so I called my brother to draw up the contract. I wrote a check to close the sale. We had enough saved from the work we'd done selling insurance, and investing in a new home was an excellent way to spend the money. Luisa would be excited.

In a week, the home was mine. Thankfully, closing on a property in Argentina didn't take months if you had cash. I took the kids to see it. They were excited, too, until we walked down the long hallway to the back and stepped onto the backyard porch.

"Dad," Julia said. "This place is a dump. The walls are falling apart, and some parts of this house are missing complete walls. There's no kitchen or at least no appliances. Does it even have electricity and gas?"

"Of course, it has those things." Though I didn't honestly know.

"You checked? It's all working?"

"No, but it's a house downtown, which is hard to get. I'm not worried about utilities right now. We'll probably need to upgrade the wires and plumbing. It's a fixer-upper, but we'll do it a little at a time. Don't you see it?"

The expression on her face said she didn't see it, and she doubted I'd ever get it in livable condition.

"I see the possibilities," Alex said. "If you don't get it fixed, we can always play soccer up here. If I kick the ball hard enough against that wall, it will probably come tumbling down." He laughed.

But they weren't the only ones with doubts. My brother and his family came to have Sunday dinner with us, and as I was telling my mother about the place, my brother kept shaking his head and laughing.

"Come on, it's not that bad," I said.

"I tried to talk him out of it," Theo said to my mother and held his hands up as if to have it on record that this wasn't his idea. "You saw it?" he asked Julia.

She nodded, looking somewhat uncomfortable. "It has . . . potential."

"See?" I slapped my brother's arm. "Potential. I like that."

My brother kept shaking his head and eating my mother's gnoc-chis.

EVEN THOUGH THE KIDS were disappointed to see me go and didn't understand why I had to return, I went back to California a happy man. I'd made an investment.

"You're going to love this house," I told Luisa. "It's downtown, close to everything."

"That's great," she said. "But tell me how the kids are doing."

"They're fine. Now, we're not going to be able to live there right away, okay? We have to remodel it, but the owners practically gave it away. We'll live with *Mamá* until we get it exactly like we want it."

"Okay. Do the kids like their school? Are they happy?"

"It's like they've lived there all their lives. They're doing fabulous. Don't worry about them anymore."

"So, when do we move?"

"Well, I spent all the money we had on the house. So, we'll work another month or two to get our airline tickets and some money to live on until I can find a job, then we'll head back."

Three months later, Luisa decided she was finished. "I haven't seen my kids in nine months."

"Why don't you go visit them?"

"Salvador, we're either moving there, or we're not. So, I'm going, and I'm not coming back. This isn't a visit. I worked fifteen-hour days this week, and I'm taking the money I made and buying a ticket."

"Okay," I said. "Then you go, and I'll finish up here and join you soon."

She frowned and opened her mouth to speak, but instead of saying anything, she just stared at me. "You're not going to come? You really want me to go alone."

"I don't want you to go *now* at all, but if you need to see the kids, then go. I understand. I missed them too, and you're right; it's been nine months. But we can't return with zero money. I wish you'd come back and work a little longer."

"Salvador, I don't understand or know what you want anymore. Go or stay. But I'm leaving to be with my kids and look for a job there."

I watched her get ready for bed. "You know, Julia said she's coming back when she graduates."

"I know. She wrote me a letter telling me you promised to buy her a ticket to California when she graduates." She puffed up her pillow and lay down. "She just doesn't realize that you never keep your promises."

I sat there for a long time, not angry, not sad, not anything really. I couldn't seem to connect with my wife anymore. And my kids? Maybe I'd lost them too.

ONCE LUISA LEFT, I didn't know what to do. I kept working at the insurance agency. After about a month, I went to see our boss wondering if he had other opportunities for me.

"I did this kind of work for my wife, but I'm not good at being an employee. I need to be my own man, have my own business."

"Are you saying you don't want to work anymore?"

"I'm thinking we could make some good money together some other way."

He smiled. "Well, I like to make money. What ideas do you have, Sal?"

"I have some Argentine friends who made a lot of money staging accidents years ago."

He sat up straighter as if he was really interested.

"They know more about it than I do. Back when I started with insurance, I didn't understand what they were doing. In fact, I got in trouble with my regional manager."

"I can imagine."

"Right. But I've learned a lot since then, and I know what they did wrong and why they and I were flagged."

"What are you suggesting?"

His tone changed, and I paused. "I'm . . . I always tried to keep things on the up and up, you know, be honest and do things the right way. But that never got me anywhere, and—"

"Salvador, you'd better stop before you say something you'll regret."

"Okay."

"I think you'd better leave."

I saw on his face that he didn't want to hear my idea, not really. He only pretended to be interested. "We can keep working the same way we've been if that's what you want."

"I don't have any more work for you, Salvador."

"You mean—"

"You know what I mean. I'll have my secretary issue your last check."

I stood, disappointed because this could have been an opportunity to make quick money. But I nodded and left. I didn't want to keep working for him anyway.

American Family

"All happy families are alike; each unhappy family is unhappy in its own way." – Leo Tolstoy

CHAPTER FORTY-ONE

G reg took me to a tire shop in Wilmington, not far from where he lived in Long Beach. His friend worked regrooving tires. Basically, he took old tires, added new treads, and then resold them. I didn't know much about this type of business, except that I'd purchased used retreaded tires for my trucks in the past, and they saved me a lot of money.

I watched the guys work and make the tires look almost brand new.

"See, we can open a shop and make a killing," Greg said.

The problem was that Greg spent most of his time drunk or high. I met him as soon as I left the Valley. I packed my bags and left the office. Without the insurance job, I wouldn't need the office and couldn't pay the rent anyway, and I was already two months behind.

I drove to Long Beach, where I'd had my epiphany about returning to Argentina. I parked the car and slept in it. I spent the day walking on the beach, thinking about how to earn enough money to get to Argentina.

I met Greg there on the beach. He was a famous surfer. I thought he was kidding when he told me that because he had been passed out, sleeping on the beach, just another homeless bum. But he was hungry, so I shared a half sandwich with him and a bottle of water. We sat on the low wall that separated the parking lot from the sand. And he showed me pictures from his wallet of when he was younger, healthier, and a good-looking blond boy with a huge smile. He had been an all-star USA surfing champion.

"I participated in all kinds of surfing championships in Huntington Beach."

I handed him back his pictures as he kept telling me stories. I told him I was sleeping in my car.

"Shit, I'm renting a motel room down the street. You can stay with me."

If I wanted to, I could stay with Mateo, but I didn't want to stay with anyone. "If you have a motel room, why are you sleeping on the beach?"

"I got drunk and fell asleep," he said. "Come on. You can at least take a shower."

Yeah right, so he can rob me blind. But I didn't have much, so I agreed. I gave him a ride to his motel. I took a shower, and we hung around talking. I found out that he'd been married, had children, developed a cocaine addiction, and was still struggling with drug issues.

Sad. And I thought *I* had problems.

I left the motel, thanked him, and wished him well.

I don't know why some people touch something inside you, but he did. This handsome American guy, with beach blond hair and blue eyes, had been on top of the world in his younger years, and seeing what he'd become tore at my heart. Here I thought it was just us immigrants who were trampled on and that we had no hope of tasting the American dream, but he was a white American who had failed too, who was struggling but was a good-hearted man.

So, the next time I saw him on the beach, I called him over, and we developed a friendship.

Now here I was a month later, with him suggesting we start a business together. "I'll tell you what, Greg. Let's do it, but with the first money we make, you check into a rehab facility and get clean."

"Awe, come on, Sal. I don't need to do that."

"That's the deal. If I'm going to go into business with you, you need to get clean."

This tall guy with broad shoulders rocked back and forth like a little boy. "Sure, okay."

He took me to a place where trucking companies threw away old tires, and we picked a few of them up. His friend let us use his retread equipment and showed me how to create new grooves safely and test the tire to ensure it was stable.

Then we loaded the tires into my car, took them to truck yards, and sold them. I couldn't believe how easy it was. We walked away with a couple of thousand dollars. "Shit," I said to Greg. "That was amazing for two days' work."

"I told you, Buddy." He patted my back.

"Listen, Greg. Let's buy our own equipment. Your friend isn't going to allow us to keep using his business. Then, afterward, we'll pay for your rehab, okay?"

"No problem, but I'm going to need a little of that money for food and, you know, stuff."

I gave him two hundred dollars and paid another week of rent at his motel so I could stay with him, and with the rest, we bought a retread machine. Eventually, we'd have to rent a shop.

"I get social security benefits and money from the VA. I'm a veteran too."

"Really?"

"Yeah, so don't worry too much about sharing the money. I do blow most of it on drugs, so sometimes I need enough to get through the month."

"We're going to get your problem fixed."

He nodded.

We worked in the Golden Sand motel parking lot, using an extension cord from the motel room to work on the next tires, but the manager saw us and told us we couldn't do that.

"Druggies can shoot up in the parking lot, but I can't retread a tire?"

"You're stealing our electricity. And you can't run a business here."

I tried to tell him that I wasn't running a business, but it wasn't worth arguing. I found a little shop in Long Beach and rented it.

It felt good to make money again. After a month and a half of selling tires, I checked Greg into rehab. In the meantime, I kept working by myself. I called Luisa to see how they were doing.

"Where have you been?"

"It's a long story. I lost the insurance job and—"

"What? How? Things were going so well when I left."

"The guy was a jerk. Maybe he didn't like that you were gone and we weren't working together. I think he was attracted to you."

"*What*? Are you crazy? He's happily married, and his only interest in me was the money I made for his business."

"Yeah, either way. He didn't want to work with me anymore."

"I've been worried about you. So has your mother. What are you doing now?"

"I'm fine. In fact, I found a new way to make money selling retread tires."

"What's that?"

"Fixing old tires and reselling them. It's just going to take a little while to save up the money to move."

"That's not good. Your mom handed me all the utility bills now that I live here. Can you send some money?"

"I'll try."

"I've started looking for a job here, but no one wants to hire an older woman," Luisa said. Then she told me that the kids were doing well and that she was happy to be with them. We didn't talk long because international calls were expensive.

GREG GOT OUT OF REHAB after 30 days. They recommended that he stay longer, but he would only commit to 30 days. When he got out, he looked good, though, much healthier.

"Hey, nice pickup," he said.

"Yeah, I sold the car and bought a pickup instead. It's easier to carry tires. I'm staying at a different motel," I told him, "To keep you out of that old environment, you know?"

"Good idea," he said.

Greg and I worked hard all day, and in the evening, we hung out with other truck drivers, had a few beers, and sometimes Greg invited girls over to party with and unwind. It wasn't the best atmosphere, but I didn't care. My only interest was in working the business and making money.

When I got up one morning to go to work, Greg said he didn't feel well, so he stayed home. When I got home, I found him in the room with a couple of girls snorting coke. "Ah, shit, Greg."

"Sal, it's okay. Don't worry about it. Come and join us."

"Are you crazy?"

"Come on. Live a little."

"I don't want to end up like you. No offense."

"You won't. You're too smart."

I sat down, exhausted, and decided, what the hell. I was curious. As soon as I tried it, I was filled with a crazy headrush and a feeling of explosive energy, like I could go back to work and retread a dozen tires tonight. In fact, that was a good idea. "Let's go, Greg."

"Where?"

"Let's go get some tires and work on them tonight. Then tomorrow, we can sell them and not have to work all day."

"Now? Are you crazy? Sit down and have a good time." He pointed at the girls.

I threw the girls out. I wasn't interested in that. "Come on, come on."

We picked up discarded tires, took them back to our shop, and worked for hours while I thought about how much we'd make if we did this every day for a month.

"How many days do you think we could stay up using that stuff?"

"Longest I've ever stayed awake was three days, but it wasn't good, Sal. It takes a toll on your body."

I imagined it would. As the drug wore off, I wasn't quite so confident about what we could accomplish. When we got back to the room, I felt exhausted and depressed, and I ended up sleeping all day.

We had dinner together that night. "You've got to go back to rehab, Greg. We can't do that again."

"No way."

"Then our partnership is over."

"But I love working with you, Sal. You're my only friend."

"Then go to rehab. You should have stayed longer the last time."

"Listen," he said. "Let's go hang out at the beach. I miss being on the beach listening to the surf. All you want to do is work."

I shook my head and left him at the restaurant, calling me to come back. I worked on my own that day, selling enough tires to pay for a couple of airline tickets to Argentina, and I only needed one. Screw Greg.

When I returned to the room, he said he'd go to rehab. The following day, I took the money I'd made, paid for his rehab again, and left him there.

Two months later, when I spoke with Luisa, she informed me that Julia had graduated from high school and was ready to return to the U.S.

"But I'm leaving here soon. What the hell is she going to do in California alone?"

"She's going to get a job and go to college," she said. "She might as well go back while you're still there. You can help her get set up before you return to Argentina."

"I don't have a place for her to live. I'm in a motel living with a couple of guys. And I don't have the money to buy her a ticket."

"I asked your brother to buy her a ticket. I gave him money when I first arrived in Argentina because he needed to pay some gambling debts. So, he owed me."

"Shit." What was I going to do now? "Okay, okay. I'll figure things out."

A WEEK BEFORE JULIA landed in LAX, I rented a studio apartment in Long Beach. Greg and a truck driver who stayed with us sometimes helped to move my things into the apartment. I picked Julia up at the airport and then drove past the motel to get the last of my things.

"I didn't know your daughter was so beautiful," Greg said.

I introduced them, and Greg pulled out his surfing picture like he always did when he met someone new to boast about his previous life as a surfing star. My heartstrings tugged a little each time he did that; it was as if he was proving to others that he hadn't always been the man he was today.

"That's amazing," she said. "Have you taught my dad to surf?"

Greg laughed. "No, he has no balance."

I didn't want Greg to befriend my daughter. "Once I get her settled, I'll come pick you up for work." I waved goodbye, and we drove off.

"He's an interesting guy. Where did you meet him?"

"Long story." I glanced at her quickly as I drove the ten miles to the apartment. "Well, now you're here where you wanted to be. I only have a tiny apartment. Sorry."

"That's okay. I don't need much."

"What are you going to do here, Julia? I work a lot of hours. I can't be responsible for you."

"I'm going to enroll in a community college. You don't have to take care of me. I'm grown now. You do your thing, and I'll do mine."

Right. "And where will you get money to go to college?"

"I guess I'll get a job."

"You can work with me. I'll pay for your classes."

"Okay." She seemed overjoyed to be here. Excited, ready to take on the world. She reminded me of me when I first got to this country. But she was more centered than I'd been. And this wasn't a foreign country for her as it had been for me. Plus, she had help; she had me.

I smiled. I'd missed her, and in a way, I was happy to have her here too.

WE GOT HER ENROLLED in college, and I showed her how to keep track of my books for the business. I told her to order business cards so that I could pass them out to the truck drivers. She agreed to do it all.

Greg and I arranged for him to meet me at the shop, but he only showed up sometimes. He stayed clean for about two weeks after he got out of rehab, then he went back to blowing all his money on drugs. He seemed to come to work only when he ran out of money.

One night, I picked Julia up at school and took her with me to collect tires since I couldn't rely on Greg.

"Where are we?"

"I'm going to get those tires on the other side of the fence."

We got there after ten at night, and since the yard had no lighting, it was extremely dark. She looked around nervously. "Are you allowed to do that? No one is here?"

"They don't mind; they let me take tires all the time."

"Then why don't we come back when they're open in the morning?"

"Just sit here and drive away as soon as I tell you."

I jumped over the fence and pushed the tires through an opening. I had to be quiet because they did have dogs. Once I got the tires on the other side of the fence, I loaded them quickly on the back of the pickup.

Then I got in and told her to drive. "Now, hurry up. Let's go."

"Shit, Dad. I don't like this. Are you sure you're allowed to take these?"

"Yes, yes, now go." Technically, no one had given me the tires. If the owners caught me, they *could* call the police. But they wouldn't miss the tires. I was doing them a favor.

She frowned as she drove away. We dropped the tires off at my shop so I could inspect them in the morning.

When we returned to the apartment, I took a shower, and she sat down to do homework. "I don't think those tires were trash, Dad."

I lay down on the couch to go to sleep. "Sure, they were. And one man's trash is another man's treasure," I said. "Remember that."

"Aren't you supposed to pay for the used tires anyway, not just take them?"

"Are you doing your homework or telling me how to run my business?"

She frowned. "I just don't want you to get into trouble."

I closed my eyes. Like I was afraid of trouble. It followed me around like a lost puppy. Julia was still working when I drifted to sleep without any of her worries to disturb me.

CHAPTER FORTY-TWO

In truth, Julia was no bother. She'd changed so much from when she'd left to move to Argentina. She was a young lady now with none of the teenage attitudes she'd had before. She came to the shop with me in the morning and took orders on the phone when truckers called. First thing in the morning, she helped me pass out business cards and flyers to the truckers, who happily accepted the cards from a cute girl, much more than they would if I'd offered the advertisements to them. Sometimes, when I came back from delivering tires, I found truckers in the shop talking to her.

"What are you doing?" I asked her.

"What do you mean?"

"Talking to those guys, *I mean*."

"What am I supposed to do? They come to buy a tire or ask you to retread their old tires, then they stay and talk. Am I supposed to ignore them? Plus, it's not like I really have work to do here. Most of the time, I'm doing homework. So, I talk to them."

"Just be careful. You can't trust those guys."

"All right, but I don't know what you want me to do or tell them."

"Tell them your dad will call them and that they can go."

"I'll try that. By the way, Greg came by and took two tires."

"Son of a bitch." That druggie was never going to get better.

"He wasn't supposed to?" she asked.

"No, he's going to sell them to pay for his drug habit.

"Hmm, he did seem kind of weird."

Most of the time, our days went smoothly. During the evenings, I let Julia take the truck to attend her college classes, and I watched TV alone or had a drink with the apartment manager right across from our unit. I could hear when Julia got back. One night, I lost track of time, and Julia was back when I walked in.

"Where were you?" she asked.

"Just having a drink with Ellen across the way."

"Why?"

"To unwind, be friendly. There's nothing else for me to do."

She stared at me. "You know, Mom and Alex are still waiting for you to move to Argentina."

"I know that. You think I don't?"

"I just don't see you making any plans to move."

"It's complicated. Just do your homework, and don't worry about what I'm doing."

But a week later, I got a call from Luisa, who wanted to know what was going on.

"Just working, you know the norm."

"Why did I get a letter from my daughter telling me to return to California if I want to save my marriage?"

"*What?*"

"Sal, I don't even want to know. I'm coming back."

"What the fuck! You're all coming back? I'm going to be moving there soon."

"I'm so tired of your garbage. You can't even imagine how tired I am! We've been waiting and waiting. The kids lived here without us for months. Then all three of us waited for you for months. I'm here still waiting. And you're still in California."

I was seeing red. I wanted to hang up on her, but I drew a breath. "You know how difficult it is to get the money to go."

"You always have money for everything except to actually return to the place you say you want to live."

I didn't need this crap. "I don't have the money to send you a ticket," I said, hoping that would shut her up.

"Of course, you don't. I'm buying my own ticket."

"But I bought a house for us to live in Rosario. We can have a wonderful life there."

She laughed. "The kids showed me the house you bought. You must be kidding. That thing needs to be bulldozed down."

Now, I did hang up on her. Whatever. She and Julia could stay here. I'd move back and live with my son.

When Julia returned from school that night, I wanted to kill her. "What the hell did you write your mother? Now, she says she wants to come back."

Only momentarily stunned, Julia stopped and put her school bags down. "Good, it's super hard for her to support us in Argentina. She works long hours at a high school and barely makes any money."

"Everyone works hard. I work hard!" I shouted. "You should have minded your own damned business. If I wanted my wife to come live with me here, I'd have called her myself."

Her face flushed, and she seemed to want to respond, but she turned around and went to the bathroom. When she came back out, she announced she was going out.

"Out where?"

"I have a date with Francisco."

"The truck driver?" He was a good-looking young Mexican guy, one of the ones who kept hanging around the shop talking to her, but he was older than Julia, and he never asked me if he could take my daughter out. "I don't think so," I said.

"I don't need your permission. I can date whomever I want. *I'm* not married," she said and quietly closed the door as she walked out.

Infuriated, I grabbed her schoolbooks and tossed them across the room. She was ruining everything.

WHEN LUISA ARRIVED by the end of 1984, she immediately demanded that any money I made would go to buy Alex a ticket so that we could all be together again.

To be honest, she didn't have to do much convincing. As soon as I saw Luisa, my heart melted, and the crazy disconnected, anxious feeling I always got when she was gone disappeared. I'd missed her so much, even though she yelled at me.

When she saw the shop, she refused to let Julia return. She pulled me aside. "There are drug needles in here."

"Oh that," I said. "It's probably, Greg, my partner. He's harmless."

Luisa frowned. "I think there's something seriously wrong with you. Did you bring your daughter here? Have you seen some of the men working in these nearby yards?"

Luisa also took one look at Francisco and told Julia she couldn't date him.

"We're just friends, Mom," Julia said.

"Make friends with men who are not truck drivers." And the relationship ended just like that.

Luisa scolded me and complained about everything, but still, I felt happy to be with her. I always felt more settled and motivated to be a better man when she was around. We left that little studio apartment before Luisa arrived and moved into a larger place.

By the time Alex came a month later, we had settled in a one-bedroom apartment. The kids got the room, and Luisa and I slept in the living room. The apartment, still too small for the four of us, was the best I could do on such short notice.

Julia got a job at a fast-food restaurant which made me mad. "You need to focus on your education," I told her. "You can keep helping me with my business, even if your mother doesn't want you to go to the shop anymore. There are other things you can do."

"Dad, I need real money. You don't pay me. You never have money to pay me."

"I pay for your classes and put gas in the pickup. I feed you."

"I need actual money. I need work experience. I need a bank account and my own car."

"This family needs to learn to stick together more. You need to learn that you're either with me or against me. Right now, you're showing me that you're against me."

Julia flinched. I didn't realize I was yelling. But she quietly changed into her work uniform, got on a bike she'd bought, and went to work.

"I don't think it's safe for her to be on that bike. She doesn't get off work until midnight," Luisa said.

"She'll be fine. If she wants to be an adult and do whatever she wants, let her figure out how to get to work and back."

"But all she wants to do is work and go to school. What do you mean *do whatever she wants*?"

"Let her figure it out."

Luisa listened to me for about a week, then she took the truck and went to pick Julia up from work, which again, pissed me off.

BETWEEN LUISA AND GREG, the little shop started to grow. Luisa gave Greg orders, and he listened to her. If he came to work high or drunk, she sent him home.

Alex started high school, and Julia did her own thing. She met another boy, an American boy this time who was her age and spent most of her time either at school, at work, or with the kid. She came home to sleep, and that was it.

We made enough money to move to a house out in San Bernardino. So, I moved my shop out there. Julia refused to move with us.

"Where do you think you're going to live?" I asked her.

"I'm going to move in with my boyfriend."

"The hell you are. Is he going to marry you?"

"Marry? Are you kidding? I don't want to get married."

"Then you're not moving in together."

"You don't understand. You're moving to San Bernardino, and his mom is moving to Tennessee. So, we're going to get a place together to stay in Long Beach where we're both working and going to school."

"Only whores move in with men they're not married to."

"Salvador!" Luisa said.

"Whatever, Mom, don't worry about it. He's one to talk."

"What's that supposed to mean?" I asked.

"You know what I mean. And look at where we're living. A woman got stabbed outside our window a few weeks ago. Does that even bother you? It could have been Mom; it could have been me. We live in the worst part of town. You tell us we're moving to Argentina and sell everything that mattered to us, even our dog, then you never moved. You didn't even try."

"I did try!"

"I'm done. I'm done with all of it. If you want to go to San Bernadino, do it, but I'm not going." She looked at Luisa, then got her purse. "Sorry, Mom." And she left.

Luisa didn't look sad or upset. She seemed proud to see Julia walk out of that door. I lit a cigarette and gazed out the window, wondering when exactly I'd lost control of this family.

ABOUT THE TIME LUISA went back to Argentina and I moved to Long Beach, Mateo decided to move back to Argentina too.

"What do I have here anymore except painful memories?" he'd said. "Maybe it's time for me to return."

"But you love California." I'd been surprised.

"Yeah, but my mom is getting old and not doing well. My sister's deli is doing amazing here. It makes more sense for me to return and take care of her. And besides, you'll be there soon, right?"

He didn't have to worry about taking his kids or a wife. He just up and moved. I wish it had been that easy for me.

But he visited often because of his girls. So, Luisa and I went to see him at his sister's deli. Alex had a band event in school. He played the clarinet in a marching band, so he didn't come with us.

"You both look good," Mateo said.

"How's life in Argentina?" I asked.

"Really good. I met a nice woman, and we're going to get married."

"Congratulations!"

Camila had divorced the man she left Mateo for; now, she and Mateo were friends and got along well. Luisa and Camila had re-established their friendship years ago, but it wasn't the same for any of us.

"I'm still planning on leaving, but for now, I guess we're all back," I told him.

"Well," Mateo said. "The important thing is that you're all together." He put his hand on both of ours. "Fight for what you have," he said.

"How are your girls?" Luisa asked.

"Wonderful. Niki had a great time visiting me in Argentina. She and Julia hung out a lot and went to Bariloche to ski. I'm sure glad the girls have maintained their friendship."

"Me too," Luisa said.

"I have some money and gifts for my mother," I said to Mateo. "Do you think you can take them to her when you go back?

"Sure, as long as they fit in my suitcase."

"I appreciate it."

"Oh!" He pulled a picture out of a duffle bag from behind the counter. "Look what I have." He handed it to Luisa. It was the picture of the four of us at his and Camila's wedding.

Luisa ran a finger over the top. "How I miss those days in New York."

"Me too," Mateo said. "But I've started a new life, and keeping all my pictures of Camila isn't wise or healthy. I thought you two might like this one."

She placed a hand over Mateo's. "Thank you."

On the drive home, Luisa quietly gazed out the window, maybe thinking the same thing I was. It was hard to remember the days when we'd been such good friends, dancing to tangos in their apartment or walking down the streets of New York City at night, the city lights encircling us as we laughed and had drinks at a bar or coffee at a Cuban cafe. These days, we didn't have much in common anymore. Maybe that happened with all friendships. People drifted apart, changed, and all that was left were memories of times that used to matter.

THE TIRE RETREADING business kept slowly growing, but it didn't provide enough to support a whole family. In the summer of 1985, my brother's son came to visit from Argentina, and I thought maybe I'd show him the business, and he'd stay to work for me. I tried to help him get a driver's license. I sent Greg with him to the DMV to make sure the kid asked for the proper forms to take his test.

But as my nephew took the written test, Greg tried to explain how to fill out the form.

"Sir," he was told by a DMV worker. "You can't talk to him while he's taking the test."

"It's okay. He's from Argentina and doesn't speak or read fluent English."

"Then he can take the test in Spanish, but you can't talk to him."

"I'm just trying to explain a few things to him. I'm not going to give him the answers."

The DMV officer grabbed Greg's arm, and Greg reacted, striking his shoulder and pushing him away.

My nephew told us the story, thinking the experience was hilarious. "He just kept yelling, 'I'm a Vietnam Vet. I'm a Vietnam Vet' as they threw us out of the DMV."

But come to find out, he didn't need a driver's license to drive in California since California recognized foreign driver's licenses.

Luisa did not laugh. "I'm sorry that happened, *Querido.*"

"No worries. Honestly, *Tio*, I don't need to drive. I'm not going to stay here long. I just want to visit and see Hollywood. I can play my guitar and find a band to hook up with."

But I wished the kid would stay. I liked having family from Argentina visit.

"That Greg guy is pretty crazy, though, *Tio.*" He laughed. "He sat there on the curb and smoked a joint, talking about how unfair this country was to immigrants. Cracked me up."

That night, Luisa wouldn't shut up about Greg. "I don't want to see that man ever again. Aren't you ashamed that your nephew had to put up with that drug addict?"

"Greg is a good man. He just has a problem."

"I don't care anymore. I don't want that man around our son or our family."

"I'm going to convince him to go back to rehab. Longer this time. We'll pay for it. It's the least I can do if you don't want me to see him anymore." So, I paid for Greg to go to rehab for six months, and I told him not to contact me anymore once he got out. And sadly, I never heard from Greg again.

Because the relationship with Luisa kept getting worse, I left the tire retreading business and decided to return to insurance. She liked when I had my own agency. But there was no making her happy. She complained if I spent money on clothes, shoes, business cards, anything.

"You have to spend money to make money," I told her. "And I'm sick and tired of you bitching and complaining all the time. Maybe the best thing for us to do is to get a divorce. Is that what you want?"

She didn't get angry. She didn't seem to have any emotion at all. "You know," she said. "That's the best idea you've ever had." She turned away and went into the bedroom.

I stood there alone for a few minutes. Alex was in school. My nephew had left for Hollywood to rent a hotel room and become a rock and roll star. Julia didn't live here. Then a terrible, crazy anxiety shot through my body. I didn't know why I'd said what I'd said. I ran into the bedroom, where she was packing a suitcase.

"What are you doing?"

"Leaving."

"Come on," I said, a nervous laugh escaping my lungs. "I didn't mean that. Please, Luisa."

"I can't handle this anymore. I can't deal with your craziness."

"But this is us. Always an adventure, right? Seeing where life takes us?"

"This hasn't been an adventure; it's been a nightmare and has gone from bad to horrific."

I ran a hand through my hair. "I know, I know. This isn't the way it was supposed to be. But we can't give up. We still have Alex to raise. You can't just leave."

Those, I guess, were the magic words. Alex. She didn't want to hurt Alex. I saw it in her eyes, a resignation, a reprieve. "I'll fix everything, I promise. I'll call Julia, and have a family discussion, and everything will be better."

"I honestly don't know how you can at this point."

"Trust me."

CHAPTER FORTY-THREE

Julia was still living with that loser kid in Long Beach. They drove to our home over the weekend, and I sat them and Alex down.

"So," I started. "I've made a lot of mistakes." No one contradicted me, and I didn't expect them to. "Life has been difficult. It's not easy to raise a family, make money, or be perfect. And when you were all in Argentina, I should have gone. I kept waiting to get enough money. To take something back with me. To not go back a poor loser, you know what I mean?"

The kids nodded. Good, so far, they were with me.

"Anyway, this is what we're going to do. Within the next few months, I'm going to work day and night, five jobs if I have to. I'll save enough money to buy four tickets for all of us. We're all going to fly to Argentina, together this time, and start our life there like we'd planned."

Luisa looked at me, stunned. Julia's boyfriend raised his eyebrows and looked at Julia, who shook her head. Alex looked angry.

"Ah, Dad," Julia spoke first. "I'm not going back to Argentina. We've talked about this. I'm working and going to college in Long Beach. I can't go with you guys."

"I'm not going back either," Alex said. "Been there. Done that."

"You're not an adult. You have no choice."

"He can stay with me," Julia said.

"I'll stay with my girlfriend," Alex concluded, and I recognized the attitude, the same one Julia had when she was in high school.

"Wait a minute," Luisa interrupted them both. "That's what you wanted to talk to your kids about? That was the big fix? No one is going to follow you back to Argentina. I'm not going either."

I stood, picked up my rolling office chair, and threw it across the room. Julia's boyfriend stood and put an arm out as if to shield her. I wanted to punch the skinny-ass punk.

Instead, I drew a deep breath and ignored all their surprised stares. "Well, then, you've all made your choices clear. You're either for me or against me, and now I know where you stand."

Alex got up and went to his bedroom.

I turned on the TV and took his spot on the couch. If that's the way they wanted to play it, then I guess we were all stuck here. They didn't realize that everything I did was for them. I'd have to rebuild my insurance agency and try to make it work. Whether they realized it or not, they needed me. I couldn't go to Argentina by myself and leave them here to fend for themselves.

THE DAY LUISA LEFT me, I became violently ill. We had an actual fight. Shouting. Pushing each other. We became ugly people we'd never been with each other. And when she left, I ran to the bathroom and threw up. I wanted to turn back the clock to an earlier time in our lives.

I remembered how much I wanted her to join me in America as I built a life for us and achieved my dreams. I remembered when Julia was born and how happy we were, and when we had baby Alex, we thought life couldn't get more perfect to have a boy and a girl and live in the greatest country in the world.

I wanted all of that back but didn't know how to get it. I tried to be tough with my family, and it backfired. Maybe if I had made more money, if I had a fancy position or a job they respected, they would all be here today beside me. Everyone wants to be around rich, successful people. It's easy to abandon a guy who's hard on his luck. And that's what they had all done after everything I'd sacrificed for them.

I had to find Luisa, so I called the only person I thought Luisa would turn to. I called Camila.

"I'm looking for Luisa. She left me."

"What did you do now?" she asked.

"We had a fight. Please, tell me if she's there."

"Salvador, if she's finally had the intelligence and guts to leave you, I would never tell you where she was, even if I knew. But she's not here."

I hung up and called Julia who was at work. "Your mother left me," I said, tears making my voice break.

"Where did she go?"

"I thought maybe she was with you or that she'd called you."

"No, she didn't. I'm at work, but I'll drive out as soon as I can. Okay?"

"Today?"

"Yes."

Julia drove the two hours from Long Beach to San Bernardino alone. She'd broken up with the loser boyfriend. For that I was grateful at least. "Where is she?" she asked.

"I don't know. I really thought she would have called you."

"She hasn't yet, but I'm sure she will. Where would she go?"

"I called your aunt, Camila, but she said your mom's not there. I don't really believe her."

"What happened?"

"We had a fight, said mean things to each other, pushed each other, and she just left."

"You pushed Mom?"

"She pushed me too."

Julia narrowed her eyes and shook her head.

"I know. It's no excuse. I shouldn't have done that."

"Well, Dad. I don't know what to say. Where's Alex?" She didn't sound sympathetic, only annoyed.

"He came home from school. I told him your mother left me and that we were going to get a divorce. He grabbed his skateboard and left. Probably to his girlfriend's house."

"Maybe you shouldn't have said you were getting a divorce. Is that what you think will happen?"

I didn't think Luisa would forgive me this time or take any responsibility for her part in the destruction of this marriage. "She's gone. I don't think she'll be back. But maybe I can convince her if we figure out where she went."

Unfortunately, Luisa didn't come back, and I didn't find her. She filed for divorce. She'd stayed with Camila for a while, just like I thought she would, then she moved out on her own. Alex stayed with his girlfriend until Luisa got settled and then went to live with her. I told him to come home, but he refused.

A couple of guys I'd met at the trucking yards moved in to help me pay the rent on the house. My new friends were Mexican, and it felt good to be with Latinos who understood what it was like to be an immigrant in this country, to struggle daily just to survive. They also knew how to have a good time, and I needed to be distracted. We had fun weekend parties, ate crazy hot peppers and chased the sting with tequila. Since my family didn't want to rebuild a life together anymore, I decided to live the life of a single man and enjoy myself for a change. I also gave up on the idea of returning to the insurance business. I was only doing that for Luisa.

Trucks had always been the best way for me to make money. Enough time had gone by from when I had the trucking business that I could probably work for a company or two as an independent contractor. I could buy a truck, just one truck, and start driving again. Go where the spirit led me. I just had to figure out how to do it. The problem was that I didn't have enough money to buy a truck yet.

Julia stopped coming to see me when the guys moved in.

"You can come," I told her when she was here. "Most of the time, they're not home. They're driving their trucks."

"Yeah," she said. "Okay." But she didn't. So, I drove to Long Beach to see her and took her out for breakfast.

She had started dating a new guy, another American who seemed a lot older than her. I didn't like him, so I told her to come alone.

"Is your work going well?" I asked her. She was working in human resources for a wheel manufacturing company and producing their company newsletter.

"It's okay. It's helping me get through college."

"Maybe you'd like to invest in a truck. I'm going to buy a new truck. If you want to pay part of the down payment, I can give you the money back with interest once I start working."

"Dad, I would, but honestly, I barely have enough money to pay my bills and tuition. I moved in with Kevin to save on rent."

"Of course, of course," I said. "I'm thinking of going to visit Argentina for a while."

"That's a good idea. Maybe you should stay and try to find a job there. It's what you've wanted to do for so long. It might be good for you, and you might be happier."

I nodded.

"I have a couple hundred dollars that I can give you toward your ticket if that would help."

I wasn't sure what I saw in her eyes. Pity? "No," I said. "I'm fine.

And I did have enough money to pay for my ticket. I packed my clothes and left everything else in the house to my friends. I told them I was moving out and took my name off the rental agreement. They gave me a few bucks for the furniture and kitchen appliances.

Luisa didn't take anything with her when she left. She sent Julia to get her clothes, but that's all she took.

As I was packing my bags, I couldn't find my documents. I couldn't even find my passport. Goddammit. They took it!

I called Julia at work.

"Where's my passport?"

"Dad? Hold on a sec."

She put me on hold, then came back in a few seconds. "What's going on, Dad? I'm at work."

"I know you're at work. I called you there, didn't I?"

"I'm not supposed to take personal calls. I can call you after I get out of work or when I get out of classes tonight."

"All I want to know is what you did with my passport."

"Your passport? I didn't do anything with it."

"You packed your mother's things, and you took my passport."

"I did? I don't think so. All I took were her clothes. But I'll call her. I'll tell her to check her things, okay?"

"She's not going to tell you the truth. She'll hold on to it to keep me trapped in this country."

There was a momentary pause. "Ah, why would she do that?"

"And you're in on it. You probably took my passport on purpose. You're all always trying to hurt me, keep me from achieving my dreams." If they had all stayed in Argentina where I sent them, we'd be there together, living happily. If they'd just stuck by me and supported me, but no, they wanted me to fail.

"I don't know what you're talking about. I'm the one who suggested you should go to Argentina, remember? I have to return to work," she mumbled. "I'll call Mom and see if she has your passport."

"Call her now. I'll call you back in fifteen minutes."

"No, don't—"

I hung up and went to search the bedroom again. Damn them to hell. Maybe they hid it here in the room. I tore everything apart, pulled out every drawer and turned them upside down. I emptied boxes. I even pulled the dresser out and looked behind it and underneath it to see if they'd taped the passport to the back. But I didn't find it. I called Julia back.

"Dad, I told you. I'm at work. I'll call Mom later. Don't call me back here."

"I'm going to keep calling until you guys give me back my passport."

But she stopped taking my calls. So, I got in my car and drove to Long Beach to her work. When I got there, I told the receptionist to call Julia.

Julia entered the lobby looking completely stunned to see me.

"Did you call your mother?"

She gasped and touched my upper arm. "Are you okay? You seriously drove all the way out here to ask me about your stupid passport?"

I jerked my arm away from her touch, and I pointed at her face. "You and your mother are conspiring against me. You stole my passport!"

"You are totally crazy. And lower your voice. You're going to get me fired."

"Good! I don't know why you're wasting your time working here making peanuts."

"Oh my God." She pushed her hair away from her face. "For the last time. I don't think I took your passport unless it was tucked between Mom's clothes. If I did, it was an accident, and I will call her when—"

"Call her now!"

"She's at work. Everyone is working. It's the middle of the day." Then she huffed and looked at the receptionist, an apologetic glance. "Can I borrow your phone?"

The young girl who looked to be about Julia's age nodded. "Of course. Just be quick, okay? I've called security."

"Oh no, you didn't have to do that. He's my dad. I'll be quick. I'm sorry." She dialed Luisa's number and held out the receiver so that I could hear it ring. It rang and rang. Luisa didn't even have an answering machine. "Happy?" Julia asked.

I wasn't. I was furious. "Just please give me back my passport. It's all I ask."

Two security guards came out, and I was getting ready to punch them if they touched me.

"It's okay," Julia said. "Mario," she said to one. "It's cool, really. This is my Dad. Dad, this is my friend, Mario."

Mario held out his hand. "Nice to meet you, sir. I think it's best if you finish this discussion at home," he said. "You know how it is. People get a little nervous when someone comes around yelling."

Mario was Cuban. I could tell. There were a lot of Cubans in New York, not as many in California.

I nodded. "I'll leave." To Julia, I said, "Call your mother and find my passport. I want it back."

But neither one of them found the passport. I had to reapply for one, and in the meantime, I was unable to travel to Argentina.

I did buy a used truck though, and I started driving long distances. I called Julia when I came to town every few months. She was polite but made it clear that she didn't want to talk to me—the hell with her.

On one of my trips home, almost a year after Luisa left me, I had to appear in court to finalize the divorce.

"I don't want anything from him," Luisa told the judge when he asked if she wanted child support.

"You're entitled to child support. Your son is still in high school and will need help. This is for your son, not for you. Are you sure?"

"I'm sure. He can give his son money if he chooses. Otherwise, I'll take care of him myself."

And just like that, what we'd had for twenty years was over. I'd wasted all that time trying to build something real and solid. If only we were given a glimpse into the future. If we chose path A, this would happen. If we chose path B, that would happen. If I hadn't written Luisa that letter and told her to come to America to marry me, I could have had a different life. And so would she. She wouldn't be here with that smug look on her face. She'd be living in Argentina in poverty. She should be grateful for all I'd given her and instead, she'd left me.

But as I watched Luisa leave the courtroom with Alex and Camila who had come with them, my anger faded and was replaced with something different. They walked away from me so easily. My heart ached as if all the losses I'd ever had had been piled one on top of the other because I knew this was a happy day for her, a day of freedom. But not for me. Given the choice, I would have done it all again, with her. I loved her still.

CHAPTER FORTY-FOUR

I'm not a man who can be alone for long. Maybe this has been a defect in my character all along, one that has contributed to much of the pain in my life. Maybe this was why I decided to remarry a kind Mexican woman who took great care of me. I wasn't planning to get remarried, but her oldest son lived in the same apartment complex where I lived in El Monte, and we started hanging out on the weekends.

Linda visited often and made delicious meals for all her kids. One thing led to another, and we started talking about life and our grown kids, and how being alone was depressing. I probably had too much tequila when I told her that we should get married and keep each other company. We weren't young. We'd done the "in-love" thing, so it wasn't about that. Her husband had died, and she'd been alone for ten years. We both wanted someone to come home to at night.

"Okay," she said.

"Okay what?"

"I'll marry you."

My head was swimming, but I yelled out to the house full of her family members. "We're getting married!"

And everyone cheered—everyone except her oldest son. After the dinner party was over, he followed me to my apartment and asked me if I was serious about marrying his mother.

"Why not?" I said.

"Because if you hurt my mom, I'll beat the shit out of you and leave you bleeding in the gutter."

By then I was almost sober. "Stay out of this. Your mom deserves to have a life that includes more than cooking for you."

He lifted his chin. "I know that."

"Good, then let her be happy and do something for herself. I'm a fun guy, right? Let her have some fun."

He didn't respond, but he didn't stand in our way. So, a month after meeting her, we were married. It was the summer of 1987, and I'd been divorced a full year by then.

A man may lose the love of his life, but he can't lose his children. That consoled me a little until I realized that I had zero relationship with either of my kids, and it was time to fix that. I told Linda that I wanted Alex to move back in with me and learn to be a man, something that wasn't going to happen if his mother continued to raise him. Since, we had an extra room in the apartment, he could live with us. Linda agreed.

The next morning, I drove to Luisa and Alex's apartment. "I want to talk to my son," I said to Luisa.

"Come in." She knocked on Alex's bedroom door. "Alejandro, your father is here to see you."

Alex stood taller each time I saw him. When he walked out, I noticed he was as tall as me. "Hey," he said.

"I can leave you alone," Luisa said. "If you want. I'll go to my bedroom for a little while."

"No, stay," I said. "I need you to hear this too."

Alex shrugged and crossed his arms.

"I'll get you some water," she said and went into the kitchen, coming back with a glass of water for me that she set on the table.

"Here's the thing, Alex. Now that I'm happily remarried and have a good home, I want you to move in with me. This isn't a healthy environment for you."

Alex leaned on the wall. "What isn't a healthy environment?"

"Living here, in this neighborhood with your mother. You'll move in with me, and you'll be better off. I'll pick your friends, and you'll do the right things to grow into a real man."

He laughed. "A real man like you?"

"A boy needs his father."

Alex shook his head. "You're unreal. You come in here telling me I'm living in a bad environment with my mother who works day and night to provide for me. You tell me *you're* going to pick *my* friends. I've seen your friends. *I* should pick *your* friends." He pushed away from the wall. "Do me a favor, leave and don't come back. I don't have a father anymore, so don't waste your time pretending to be one."

"Don't you talk to me like that."

"I'm going out," Alex said to Luisa. He stormed into his bedroom and returned a second later, stuffing his wallet into the back pocket of his jeans, his car keys in his hands.

"Alex, wait," I said.

"Just leave us alone. Haven't you done enough damage?"

He left, without slamming the door, something I probably would have done.

Luisa stood by her small kitchen table, an awkward silence hung in the air. Then she said, "Well, you said what you came here to say. Now, I agree with Alex, leave and don't come back."

"He's my son. You can't keep me from seeing him."

"I wouldn't dream of it. I'm not like you. I won't turn my kids against their father. You've done that all on your own."

"You did this. You left and ruined everything."

"Please! You come in here telling him you're going to pick his friends? You don't even know how to talk to your son. How about telling him you miss him? How about telling him you want to help him to achieve his goals? Do you even know what he wants or who he is?"

I didn't. Not anymore, maybe not ever.

"He was a little boy when we sent them to Argentina, and when he came back, he wanted so desperately to have a relationship with you. Did you even notice that, or were you too busy putting a stranger through rehab and doing who knows what with that tire business?"

"I was trying to create a home for us."

"Oh Salvador," Luisa said. "We only had one home once, for a short time in the Valley. And you couldn't hold on to that. If you'd just stayed in the insurance business, if you'd just for once stuck with what was working." She shook her head. "I don't want to go over all this again. Please, just leave."

A lump grew in my throat. "I was doing fine with my trucking business until the war. The stupid war messed everything up." My words came out strained.

"It's always something else, Salvador. It's never your fault." She opened her front door. "I'm sorry, I know you tried. All I can tell you now is that you need to learn to talk to your children. It's not too late. Don't lose them too. Alex is hurt. You hurt him; we both hurt him. Give him time and don't give up on him."

I didn't go home right away. I didn't really have a home. Not the one I wanted. I thought of dropping in to see Julia who had bought a house nearby with Kevin, now her fiancé. But I just couldn't deal with more rejection. So, I left.

OVER THE NEXT TWO YEARS, I tried to rebuild my relationship with both kids. Alex was busy taking classes at the community college, seeing his girlfriend, and working. He never had time to meet me for lunch or to see me. I stopped in to see Julia whenever I drove through. Sometimes it was late, and I kept going, but only once did I ring her doorbell at one a.m.

She and Kevin opened the door, blinking away sleep. Didn't young people stay up later?

"Do you know what time it is?" Kevin asked.

"I do. I'd hoped you'd still be awake."

"No, we're sleeping. We have to be up at three a.m. to deliver newspapers," he said, sounding annoyed.

"Newspapers? Why are you doing that?"

"To make money. Because we both have three jobs to save for our wedding."

"Come in, Dad," Julia said.

"I thought maybe I could take a shower," I said.

Kevin cursed. "Seriously?"

"That's okay, don't worry about it. I'll be home soon."

"Let me give you a cup of coffee, Dad. Then maybe you can come over for dinner some weekend when you're not driving."

"Sure, Linda and I would be happy to come for dinner."

I took a few gulps of hot coffee but didn't finish it. They both looked like they were struggling to stay awake. It probably wasn't smart to drop in at that hour, but hell, if I wanted to see my daughter, her future husband had better get used to the idea that I'd see her whenever I wanted. I stood and kissed her goodbye, promising to see her again soon.

A couple of months later, we were officially invited to dinner. Julia barbequed Argentine style ribs, and I gave her tips. "This is how you set the charcoal in a nice pyramid. Then spread it out when they're almost all white." I showed her how to set the meat on the grill.

She listened and watched me. "Thanks, Dad. I remember the grill we had in the Valley. We ate barbeque every Sunday, and I thought the American kids were lucky because they didn't have to eat beef every day like us."

I laughed. "You didn't realize how lucky you were."

"No," she said, a pensive look on her face. "I really didn't."

"I didn't either," I said.

Then she backed up. "Will you finish grilling the beef? I'm going to set the table."

"Sure."

During dinner, Linda and I shared our idea of opening a clothing factory. Linda made these cool pants and sold them to friends. "They only cost me about three dollars to make and I sell them for $12," Linda shared with Julia.

Julia gazed at her, a questioning look on her face. She'd never warmed to Linda. "And you think you're going to get enough people to buy these pants that you can open a whole factory?"

"Over time," I said. "Every time Linda makes them, she sells out."

"They look like cheap pajama bottoms. No offense. I just don't see people rushing to buy these things."

"It might cost me less once I get a commercial sewing machine and buy the cloth in bulk," Linda explained.

"Whatever," Julia said. "Hopefully, you'll be successful."

"Don't mind her," I said to Linda, patting her back. "Julia was born a little adult."

Julia frowned. "What is that supposed to mean?"

"Never mind."

"No, I want to hear it."

"Look at you. Almost a college graduate, working at a government school."

"A *government* school? I'm a tutor. I'll be a teacher soon."

"There you go. You'll have your guaranteed job, with guaranteed income. You bought a house. You'll be married soon. Everything is the way it's supposed to be. A perfect adult."

"You say that like it's a bad thing."

"Society brainwashes you into thinking you want and need all those things. You think you're doing fine but you'll never be free."

Her frown deepened. "I am free."

"If you say so."

She raised an eyebrow and shook her head, clearly not able to grasp what I was telling her. Soon, she'd be a slave to her job, her house, her husband, and she won't even realize how trapped she is.

She stopped eating, pouting instead. I thought of what Luisa said about getting along with the kids and learning to talk to them. "I'm glad things are working out for you and that you're getting married to this fine young man."

Kevin hadn't participated in the discussion, but he didn't seem any happier than Julia about our conversation.

"When is the big day?"

"I've told you. We're three months away."

"Tell me what I can do for you."

"We figured paying for the wedding is out," Kevin, the smart ass, said.

"There's something you can do," Julia responded. "If you really want to do something for me, I only want one thing."

"Anything," I said.

"I want *Abuela* to be at my wedding. Will you buy her a ticket to California and convince her to come?"

That request hit me right below my heart, a place that made it difficult to breathe. Julia wanted *Mamá* to come to her wedding. She was my sweet little girl, after all. Tears filled my eyes. I didn't want my mother to see the mess I'd made of my life, but . . . "I'll call her tomorrow and tell her that I'm sending her a ticket."

"You promise?"

"Yes."

"Really promise? You're not just saying that, are you? Because I don't want to get my hopes up, if you're not going to do it. Just tell me if you can't do it."

"I told you, I'll buy her a ticket. I'll fly there and pick her up if I have to. She'll be at your wedding."

Julia stood and wrapped her arms around my shoulders. "Thank you, *Papi*."

This was the first time she'd used the Spanish term in years. I hated when she called me Dad. I hugged her tight against me, feeling a deep warmth fill my heart.

JULIA'S SUMMER WEDDING in 1990 took place outside in the foothills of the beautiful San Bernardino mountains instead of a church. For that I was glad. As much as Luisa tried to make Julia grow up a Catholic and forced her to go to Sunday school and take her first communion, Julia seemed to reject that corrupt cult. But she and Kevin said they chose to get married outdoors because in nature they felt closer to God, very hippy-like. Whatever the reason, I was grateful I didn't have to step foot in a Catholic church.

I proudly walked Julia down the aisle to the gazebo at the end of the flowery path. Alex, one of the groomsmen, looked so handsome and grown up in his black tuxedo and red bowtie. He even shook my hand and gave me a hug when I arrived with *Mamá*.

Both Julia and Alex were thrilled to see their grandmother. She broke the ice between us as soon as she arrived a week before Julia's wedding. We went to restaurants together and the kids laughed and acted like we were a normal happy family.

The day of the wedding, *Mamá* couldn't stop touching her grandkids. "I missed them so much. Look how much they've grown," she said to me. "When you first sent them to me, it was difficult to have children in my life again, especially when the weeks turned into months. I had a hard time adjusting. But then they left . . . that was even harder, to lose them."

"I know, *Mamá*. But look at how beautiful they are now," I said, as we watched the photographer pose the wedding party. "Julia is an amazing young lady, and my boy is becoming a good man."

"And you don't get to be a part of it, Salvadorito. It hurts me so much."

"It's different but they're grown now. Even if I was still married to Luisa, it would be a different relationship with them. You know how it is when your children become adults."

"I do know, *Querido Mio*. You live with your heart permanently stuck in your throat as they build a life for themselves that doesn't include you."

I kissed my mother. I wanted to say I was sorry, but that was the way of the world with parents and children.

Julia chose not to include dancing at the reception, so we didn't get the typical father/daughter dance. But we took pictures together and the videographer interviewed me. I got to say how proud I was to see my baby get married. After the ceremony, they had a delicious dinner, followed by the cutting of the cake. Then before I knew it, it was over. A limo came to take them away. They were off to honeymoon in Paris like in the movies or the fairytales.

I stood beside Luisa, throwing birdseed wrapped in little bags. Kevin's mom forgot to open the bag and threw it at his head. It was a great shot, and I have to say, I loved it.

"Ouch," he said, and everyone laughed. Then they ran and jumped into the limo.

"Remember when the Llonch couple threw rice at us?" I asked Luisa.

"Julia didn't want to throw rice because it's bad for the birds. She wanted to be environmentally friendly. Kids these days. They think of everything."

I smiled. "I'm sorry we didn't get a real wedding or a honeymoon like they're having."

Luisa looked at me. "We had a great wedding and honeymoon in the most amazing city in the world."

I was too choked up to say anything. I just nodded, then stepped away.

The guests—her friends from high school and work—Camila and Niki, who was Julia's maid of honor, all started to leave now that the bride and groom were gone.

"Alex, when do you want to see your grandmother again?" I asked him before he left.

He hugged his grandmother. "Anytime, *Abuela*. I work a lot. They're going to make me the general manager at the department store. But you tell me when, and I'll ask them to adjust my schedule. It's not every day that the most beautiful grandmother in the world is here to visit."

"And it's not every day that the most handsome grandson in America is here to hug," she said.

"I'm the only grandson you have in America."

She laughed and so did I.

"I'll call you with my schedule, okay?" Alex said to me.

"Okay, *Hijo*."

CHAPTER FORTY-FIVE

Mamá made no secret of disliking Linda, even though Linda was kind to her. She even asked if she could stay with Luisa a few days when Alex came to dinner. "I only have one daughter-in-law in America, and that's the mother of my grandchildren," *Mamá* said.

"Shh," I said. Linda was in the kitchen, cleaning up after making a delicious beef stew with potatoes and carrots and onions the way we eat it in Argentina.

"I didn't say anything wrong. It's true. You have a new wife, and that's fine. I hope she makes you happy, but I will always love Luisa, and I want to spend time with her, and more time with Alex."

"I understand."

So, *Mamá* went home with Alex for a few of days which was fine since I had to work anyway, and I knew she didn't want to stay in our little apartment alone with Linda.

Once I returned from a three-day drive to Washington state and back, I went to Luisa's apartment to get *Mamá*. Linda stayed behind, but we planned to take *Mamá* somewhere nice over the weekend. Maybe we'd go to the Santa Monica Pier and then go eat some fish.

I rang Luisa's doorbell and she answered. "Oh hi, come in," she said. "Alex took your mother to get ice cream. They'll be back soon."

"Okay. Do you have any coffee."

"I can make some."

From her kitchen table, I watched her prepare a pot of coffee. "Did *Mamá* enjoy staying with you?"

"We had a nice time catching up. I miss talking to her on the phone or getting letters from her like we used to. I should call her. I don't know why I haven't." She leaned on the counter and shrugged. "I suppose I didn't know how she'd feel about our divorce. If she'd hate me."

"You'll always be her daughter-in-law. That's what she told me."

Luisa nodded, a soft smile on her lips. "Yes, she told me that too. And I'm so glad because I love your mother. We spent a lot of time together over the years when I went to stay with her waiting for you to join us."

Of course, Luisa loved my mother. And *Mamá* loved her. Luisa was Argentine and that mattered to my mother. And she was her grandchildren's mother, probably the most important fact.

I stood and walked to the counter, where she poured coffee into a mug and handed it to me. "Thank you."

"You're welcome."

Then I placed the cup on the counter, took Luisa's arm, and leaned in to kiss her.

But she jerked back when she realized my intention. "What in the world are you doing?"

"Luisa, I still love you."

"Oh my God." She sounded exasperated and angry.

"I do. Just like my mother does, that's never going to change. Let's go away for a weekend to Vegas like we used to. Let's talk about everything that went wrong and fix it."

"You're married!"

"That doesn't matter. I don't love her; don't you know that?"

She shook her head as if trying to erase my words, maybe even me. "I don't believe this. You'll never change. Get out of my apartment, Salvador."

"Luisa, this is wrong. It's always been you and me together. I miss you. I miss what we had."

"Get out!" she shouted. "I can't stand to look at you. You can't be faithful to anyone. I feel sorry for Linda."

The mixture of pain and sorrow and anger swirled around in my chest. "You're all I've ever wanted, but you've never understood that. You never understood me."

"No, I never have understood you, you're right. I can't understand a man who cheated on me every time he had the opportunity, who destroyed every home we ever had, who abandoned his children, who . . . never mind, just leave. You talk about love, and you don't know the meaning of the word."

I stared at her and realized I didn't know her anymore. Where was that young girl who had danced her way into my heart? Maybe that was the problem, we stopped dancing. We became two out of sync lovers, uncoordinated and disconnected. "Tell Alex to bring *Mamá* to my car. I'm parked on the street." I left her apartment determined to put space between us. I didn't want to see her ever again. Every time I did, it reminded me of everything that was wrong in my life, everything that I'd lost. The kids could come to see me if they wanted, but I wouldn't be back.

Alex showed up a few minutes later. "Hey, do you want to come in and have some ice cream?"

"No, your mother threw me out."

He narrowed his gaze. "What did you do?"

"Why do you think I did anything? I was nice to her. I told her I still loved her, and she threw me out."

Alex's face grew flushed, and his jaw hardened. "Well, that explains it. Just leave her alone. She doesn't need any more mental abuse from you. I'll bring Abuela." He took a couple of steps away, then returned and bent to look at me in the car. "What happened to you? When did you become so clueless? Was I just too young to see that you've always been like this?"

"Alex, you don't know what you're talking about. You don't know what it's like to work so damned hard, and to . . . fail. And to make mistakes you can't take back."

He blinked rapidly and wiped his eyes.

I gazed at him. "I hope you never have to know what that's like."

His face hardened again. "I'll never be like you, don't worry." Then he left.

I leaned my head back, tired and feeling old even though I was only in my fifties. A few minutes later, Alex returned with *Mamá*, gave her a big hug, and opened the car passenger door for her.

"I'll see you again before I go back to Argentina, right?"

"Yes, of course. Julia said we'd have a barbecue at her house when she comes back from her honeymoon."

She kissed both of Alex's cheeks through the rolled down car window.

"Later," he said to me, and strolled back to the apartment.

ONCE *Mamá* left, I didn't call the kids again, and they didn't call me. Maybe we all needed space from each other.

Julia did come see me for Christmas about six months after her wedding. I invited her to our apartment, and she and Kevin came for dinner, but being together felt awkward.

"What's wrong?" I asked her.

"Nothing, I'm just tired. With you and Mom being divorced and Kevin's parents being divorced, we have four parents to visit. It's kind of exhausting, that's all."

"Maybe you shouldn't always do what you're supposed to do, and try doing what you want to do," I suggested.

"Meaning what?"

"If you don't want to go to four different houses, then don't."

She rolled her eyes.

I filled her wine glass. "You can't live your life to please others."

"Dad, you say these things and all it does is infuriate me. Honestly, just don't give me advice."

"It's the only thing I have to give you," I said, remembering how much I valued the advice my father gave me while he was able.

"I know what you're trying to say, but pleasing others is a good thing. Being good to others and thinking of how they feel and what is good for them and being responsible is what we're supposed to do as caring human beings."

"There we go with *supposed to* again. You're not *supposed* to do anything. If you don't learn that, you'll never be truly happy."

"You missed my birth. You missed Alex's birth. You missed my high school and college graduation. You missed so many important events. Don't you think you were supposed to be there for these once-in-a-lifetime events? If they didn't matter to you, you could have been there for Mom or for us. Some things you do because you're supposed to."

"No one appreciates that," I told her. "You think they do, don't you? But you'll learn. People are nice to you when they want something from you, and when you're no longer any use to them, they'll drop you. Even your own family."

She shook her head. "You make no sense."

Kevin put his arm around the back of her chair, a protective move. Part of me wanted to punch him and another part wanted to pat him on the back. "We've got to be at your mom's place soon."

Linda interrupted. "Let's have some dessert before you go, and let's not talk about upsetting things."

I shrugged. "It's not upsetting." I'd had a little too much to drink, but I knew what I was talking about. "One day, Julia. You'll understand that you owe it to yourself to figure out what makes you happy and to work to get that. The hell with what everyone else wants."

"Is that what you did? Are you happy?" she asked, obviously angry.

Linda was standing there; I couldn't say much. "I wanted the American dream. I believed in it with all my heart." I took a drink of wine, savored it, and gazed at my angry daughter. "I didn't really know how to get it. I chased it and tried to cheat to get it. I didn't understand some of the rules, like the IRS, I should have understood that, and anyway, I made too many mistakes."

She looked at Kevin and sighed.

"I've loved and hated this country. But yes, I'm happy. When I look at you and at Alex, I . . ." I held my wine glass up. "You both are the American dream."

"Dad, I have to go," she said. "I'm sorry."

"I just want you to be happy," I said. "I want you to follow your dreams."

"I am." She kissed my cheek. "I can do both. Follow my dreams and be considerate and responsible for others."

"Me too, I can do both."

She smiled. "You work on that. Put others first. You did that at my wedding by bringing *Abuela*. She was incredibly happy and so was I. Didn't that feel good?"

I caressed her head. "Yes. That did feel great." She thought that was altruistic? I wanted to see my mother too.

At the front door, Linda and I waved, watching her leave with her husband, escaping. She just visited me because she felt she had to. I stepped back into my apartment, slamming the door shut. "Give me some whiskey," I said to Linda. I'd rather none of my kids visit me than have them feel obligated to stop by for a few minutes and lecture me.

Linda handed me the glass of whiskey, and I sat back on my couch to drink alone as she cleaned off the table. She turned on the radio to play Christmas music as she worked. I thought I'd feel less alone by remarrying, but somehow, I felt more alone than ever. I wondered if she felt the same.

CHAPTER FORTY-SIX

Moving on was difficult. But the facts were that my kids were grown and on their own. Luisa hated me, and that relationship was over and beyond repair. My new family was not bad. Linda had her own grown kids, and I enjoyed hanging out with them on the weekends or when I wasn't driving.

They came over and weren't judgmental, unlike my kids, whom I didn't see for months at a time. I was okay with that; I was starting to accept my new life.

It had been six years since Julia's wedding. She was still a teacher but told me she was writing a novel the last time I called her.

"Remember when I used to write stories when I was going to college in Long Beach?" she asked.

"Was that what you were doing? What are you writing?"

She laughed. "Romances."

"Ugh, love stories? You might as well be writing fantasy."

"I like the idea of people falling in love and living happily ever after."

She was writing lies, but so be it. "You always have loved stories, even as a little girl. I think you got it from your grandfather. He was a journalist, you know?"

"Of course, I know. Maybe using his typewriter in Argentina caused some of his talent to rub off on me."

She should be so lucky. *Papá* was a gifted writer. "Well, keep following your dreams, Julia. You never know."

I talked to Alex about as often as I did Julia. He'd mellowed out a lot. He was a hard-working young man who had become a supervisor at a shipping company. He lived with a group of friends and always had a new girlfriend, a real stud like his father.

We met for breakfast or lunch when I passed through San Bernardino. "Maybe you can go with me on one of my trips," I said to him.

"Maybe you're dreaming."

"I just think it would be fun to spend some time together. Do guy things."

"Guy things like driving a truck across the country?"

"It wouldn't be so bad, would it?"

"I work, Dad. I can't leave for days."

"How did you and your sister let yourselves get trapped into jobs where you're working for someone else?"

"We like to have food and pay our bills."

"I've always had food," I said.

He reached across and slapped my belly. "Too much food. Maybe what we should do together is go workout. I'll show you how to lift weights so you can get in shape."

"Sure," I said, even though he was probably kidding.

Still, it was nice to see him sometimes, and to be honest, I was proud of him. He would do so much better in life than I ever had.

Maybe it was a good thing that neither of my kids listened to me much and had steady jobs.

Last year, I went to see *Mamá* in Argentina. She was getting very old. I didn't know how many more years she'd be alive.

"I think I'm finally going to move back, *Mamá*."

I don't think she believed me. I didn't blame her. But this time, I meant it and felt in my soul that I would return. I was just going

through the motions in America. I was no longer striving for anything; I no longer had big dreams and goals to achieve. I didn't care
about returning home a huge success. I just wanted to come home.

"Your life is in America, *Hijo*. It always has been."

"I'm going to divorce, Linda. I don't really know why I married
her except that I was lonely, and she was nice to me. But I met a
woman here years ago when I came to visit the kids. We've kept in
touch, writing letters to each other, and I think I want to move back
and see if something happens with her."

"What about the kids?"

"They don't need me. And maybe they can come and visit me
here."

"Well, like always. If you decide to move back, you have a place
here with me. I would love to end my life knowing my son finally returned home."

I kissed the top of her head. One way or another, I'd make sure
she had her wish.

While in Argentina, I met with Mateo. He was happily living in
Rosario with his new wife and baby girl.

"I can't believe you had another kid at your age."

"Well, my wife is a lot younger than me."

"Lucky man. That's what I need to do." We stared at each other.
"Naw," I said, "I don't need any more kids." And we both laughed.

We talked, we reminisced, but our lives back in New York were a
lifetime ago, and these days we had little in common, just a love for
each other. I promised him I'd be back, and he, like my mother, just
nodded. "I'll believe that when I see it."

It seemed like we were always beginning again. Weren't those
Kennedy's words? *Let us begin*? But they snuffed out the poor guy
and his dream before he could get started. Maybe he should have said
instead: Let us endure.

SOMETIMES LINDA TRAVELED with me when I had long, out-of-state hauls. The drives were peaceful; there was something about driving long distances that I loved. Seeing the country, being outdoors without anyone telling me what to do, and maneuvering a giant machine across multiple highways all made me feel free and in control.

Linda was going to join me on my trip to Missouri, but her daughter was having a birthday party for her children and wanted Linda to be there.

"That's fine," I said. I liked being alone anyhow. I hadn't talked to Linda about getting divorced, but I would soon enough.

She packed me a cooler with food and another with drinks, and I headed out. July tended to be hot, but otherwise, the drive to Missouri was nice, and I made it in two days. They reloaded my flatbed trailer with heavy machinery to bring back to California.

Once they loaded it by late afternoon, I decided to have dinner and wait until the sun went down. I got back on the road at about ten which was perfect; it would be better to drive at night and avoid some of the heat. I got on US 61 to head out.

The equipment was heavy, so I drove slowly up an incline. Even though the speed limit was 60 mph, I couldn't get over 30 mph. I yawned, a little tired, but I could probably make it to Tulsa before I had to stop to sleep.

I thought of when I was teaching Julia to drive. Unlike her mother, she had no fear. So, after spending some time on the city streets, having her make turns properly by checking her mirrors and looking over her shoulder when changing lanes, I was satisfied with how she was handling herself, and I told her to get on the freeway onramp.

"What?" she said, glancing quickly at me.

"Keep your eyes on the road and as soon as the light turns green, move to the right lane and merge onto the 5 freeway."

"Okay, but shouldn't I practice more on the streets first?"

"No, driving is driving. Freeway driving is just a little faster. You might as well learn."

So, she did as I instructed and merged onto the freeway, stepping on that gas pedal. "This is great," she said.

"Check your speed. You have a speed limit to observe, right?"

"What a stupid law."

She liked going fast and had no problems driving on the freeway. She liked speed. I never cared to go fast.

Now, no matter how much gas I gave the truck, it struggled to make it up the hill. Finally, as I crested the top, the truck started going a little faster.

But immediately when I reached the top, I saw a car stalled in my lane. There was no way I could stop a truck this heavy, so I quickly checked, and I was clear to merge into oncoming traffic to pass the stalled car. No one was coming my way. It was the only way to avoid hitting the car.

As I turned the wheel to change lanes, a woman in the stalled car opened her driver-side door and ran out into the lane I had merged into.

"Shit, shit, shit," I yelled. I had a split second to change course and not kill this idiot woman. So, I quickly turned the wheel to the right again, knowing that now I was definitely going to hit her car, but better her car than her.

As I connected with the car, my truck started to skid. The flatbed was just too heavy. I turned the wheel to the left, thinking I could get control, then to the right, but it was impossible. I slammed my foot on the break, pumping, trying futilely to stop what I saw happening. The truck thundered toward a guard railing. At a speed that now seemed much faster than 30 mph, I hit the guard railing and braced myself because I was headed down a steep embankment. The truck became airborne and seemed to float for a second before rolling down the hill. The semi didn't stop until I hit a cluster of maple trees at the bottom. I felt crushing pain as gravity flung me forward, and the steering wheel pierced my chest. My ribs snapped right before I blacked out.

I don't know how long I lay there, bleeding and barely able to breathe. I couldn't move, but I thought I heard sirens. Someone was coming to help me. They knew I was down here. The excruciating pain made it impossible to move. My legs, my ribs, my head. Everything hurt. This was a bad accident. Though I wanted to, I couldn't move. I couldn't get out of this truck.

I remembered when I was a little boy, probably not more than three. I used to run down to the community swimming pool. I swam like a fish, and one of the older boys showed me how to dive from the highest Olympic diving board.

One day, I jumped and flew down like a bird. Momentarily free, I enjoyed the feeling of falling. But I hit the water so hard that it felt like my head had slammed against a concrete slab. I blacked out, and the next thing I knew, I was lying beside the pool with *Mamá* bent over me.

"This little boy comes here every week and throws himself off that diving board," a woman told my mother. "You should see him. He's amazing."

"He could have killed himself," *Mamá* said. "How could you let him do that?"

After that, I was no longer allowed to go to the pool alone. My head and neck had hurt so much that I didn't argue. It had been a bad accident. But this one was worse. I was cold and could no longer feel any pain.

I fought to stay awake. But as minutes passed, I felt my energy fading, and my grasp on what just happened was fading too. Did the woman make it? Did I save her? Please let me have saved her.

I thought of Julia's comment that Christmas when she was first married about doing something altruistic, and I smiled or tried to smile. I wasn't sure if my facial muscles were working. But she was right. It felt great to do something noble for someone else. I wanted to tell her that I'd saved that driver's life. And I would as soon as I got back home. But now, I just couldn't . . . keep . . . my eyes . . . open.

CHAPTER FORTY-SEVEN

Julia

I unlocked my front door, home from teaching a class full of fourth graders, exhausted and ready to eat dinner and go to sleep. As always, my dachshund and basset hound crowded me at the door, barking and whimpering, so I took a moment to pet them. Then I climbed the stairs to the bonus room, hit the answering machine, and sat on my black leather couch, closing my eyes to listen to the messages while I thought of possibly ordering pizza. I didn't feel like cooking.

But the first message was from my uncle in Argentina. "We heard that your father passed away," he said. "We're all devastated. Please call me when you get the chance."

I sat upright. "What?" I played the message again, trying to make sense of my uncle's words which were in Spanish, of course. Passed away? My father? How was that even possible? My father seemed invincible, a man who would exist forever, a shadow, a weight from my past that I'd never entirely dislodge and didn't really want to. How did a man miles away know that my father had passed away? And how had this happened?

I picked up the phone and called my mom. Immediately, I knew from her guarded tone that something terrible truly had happened. He must be hurt but certainly not dead.

"I don't know how to tell you this," she started. "I think I should come over."

"Uncle Theo left a message on my answering machine. I think I already know. How did it happen?"

"All I know is that it was an accident. Salvador was driving his truck, of course."

"Oh. Okay."

"I'm coming over."

"No, don't. Go tell Alex. He needs to know, and he's going to need you."

I hung up and went downstairs, but I only made it halfway down before I had to stop. I sat on the steps with the dogs beside me, licking my face and whining. They were hungry.

When Kevin got home, I was still there. My mind blank, a numbness having taken over my heart because I felt nothing.

"What's wrong?" he said, his smile fading as he dropped his briefcase and started up the stairs.

"My dad died last night. And I can't cry."

Kevin climbed up beside me, pulled me into his arms, and held me. "You're in shock," he said.

"We should have let him take a shower."

"What, honey?"

"That time, when he came to our house in the middle of the night, he wanted to shower. We should have let him take a shower. I'm a terrible daughter."

"No." He kissed my forehead, helped me up, then drove me to my mother's house, where my mom and brother were. We all hugged and grieved the loss of the most difficult man in our lives. One we all loved despite how much he'd hurt each one of us.

NO ONE FELT THE LOSS more than my grandmother. When Linda spoke of burial services, I shook my head. "My father will be cremated, and my brother and I will take him back to Argentina."

"That's not your decision to make. He was my husband."

"Linda, forgive me, but I don't give a shit. He's my father, and all he ever wanted was to return to his country, and that's what's going to happen."

But she didn't honestly care. She collected his life insurance money that he had through his trucking company. In the end, that's all she was interested in. She allowed us to do what we wanted with Dad's body.

I paid for his services, for everything, and my brother and I flew to Argentina.

We hugged my grandmother tightly as she cried. I still hadn't shed a tear. The three of us stood in her living room as we had years earlier when we were just kids and had been shipped to this foreign country to live with her.

Everything had been odd and frightening back then. Now, it felt like coming home.

"You have something for me," she said.

Out of my carry-on suitcase, I pulled out the box of ashes, what was left of the son she'd sent to America as a young boy. My heart ached for her, but I handed her the box. She took it, hugged it to her breast, and turned away, walking down the hall to her bedroom without another word.

"*Abuela*," I said, but my uncle grabbed my arm.

"Let's leave her alone for a little while," he said, and I gazed at him, the man who looked so much like my father that he could be his twin. I wanted to hold onto him and pretend that Dad hadn't really died. But he had. This was real.

———— ❧ ————

WE STAYED IN ARGENTINA for a couple of weeks. I visited family. Saw old friends. I walked along the Parana River, then sat on the steps of the Argentine flag monument that overlooks the river. This was my father's country, one that he loved with all his heart. For so long, I didn't get it—why he left and why he never came back, no matter how many times he said he would. But I've come to realize that it doesn't matter how much you want something if you don't have the courage to go after it.

I met Alex at a coffee shop downtown. Tomorrow, we'd fly home. "Do you ever wish Dad had returned when he sent us here and said he would? That we had all stayed to live here?"

Alex nodded. He'd been the one who cried the hardest during the funeral. "I loved it here. I had friends, and we had our cousins, aunts, uncles; I had soccer." A corner of his lip went up into a half smile. "I could have lived happily in Rosario the rest of my life."

"It was never the same when we went back," I said.

"No," Alex agreed. "Well, now he's here, in his precious Argentina. I hope he rests in peace."

Tears filled my eyes. "You know," I said, watching a little child drop tiny bookmarks on the restaurant tables, hoping to get a few cents. "I wonder if he . . ."

"If he what?" Alex asked.

"If he ever really loved us."

The little boy handed me a bookmark. I looked at it and gasped. It said, "If I were a cat and had nine lives, I'd live them all with you."

The server chased the little kid away.

"Wait," I said. "I wanted to give the boy some money."

"No, don't encourage them," the server said as if that child were a stray dog begging for food.

The little kid ran down the cobblestone pedestrian street and disappeared among a crowd of people.

"Look," I said to Alex. "Look at what this says."

Alex's brows came together. "Yeah, so?"

"I asked if dad ever really loved us, and then this bookmark fell into my hand."

Alex smiled sadly, maybe with a little pity in his warm brown eyes. "It didn't actually fall into your hands, but hey, it could be a sign, huh?"

Maybe I wanted to believe Dad cared about us, maybe not as much as he cared about himself or about Argentina or about the American Dream, but that he loved us just a little.

Alex stood and held out his hand. "Let's go home."

I nodded. Dad had given me Argentina. I loved being here; it would always live in my heart. And I'd always be grateful for the time I got to spend here. But he'd given us our life in the United States too. As he said, a country that he loved and that he hated. Still, it was ours now, thanks to him.

I took my little bookmark and love for my father and flew home with Alex to my country to vigorously pursue my version of the American Dream.

The End

Change is the law of life.
And those who look only to the past or present
are certain to miss the future.
John F. Kennedy

DEAR READER:

If you enjoyed *Let Us Begin*, please take a few moments to review this novel in all the places where books are sold, including reader sites such as Goodreads[1] and Bookbub.

Reviews help authors, and they are also useful to other readers looking for great books.

Thank you!

---

1.   https://www.goodreads.com/book/show/123258760-let-us-begin

Don't miss out!

Visit the website below and you can sign up to receive emails whenever Julia Amante publishes a new book. There's no charge and no obligation.

https://books2read.com/r/B-A-IARP-YZFGC

BOOKS 2 READ

Connecting independent readers to independent writers.

Also by Julia Amante

That Was Then
This Is Now
Let Us Begin

Watch for more at https://www.juliaamante.com.

About the Author

Women's Fiction author of *This is Now, That Was Then, Say You'll Be Mine*, and *Evenings at the Argentine Club,* Julia Amante writes emotionally rich stories about family, love, and the passion of chasing and achieving one's goals.

Julia began her writing career in 2000 writing Latina romance under the pseudonym, Lara Rios when Kensington Publishing released a new line of Latino romance books. These books reflected the flavor and rhythm of Latino communities in the U.S. and delivered richly textured commercial fiction about a population that had been mostly ignored by publishers at the time. Julia sold four romances to this publisher before moving on to write longer Chick Lit novels for Berkley Publishing by 2006. Her book *Becoming Latina in 10 Easy Steps* was optioned by Disney's ABC Family to become a future TV series.

In 2009, Lara Rios became Julia Amante when she changed her writing style to reach a new audience. Amante wanted to expand her writing to include not only romantic relationships, but the more complex bonds women have with parents, children, and friends. These novels continued to feature Latino characters and the cultural flavor of Hispanic life in America, but they also dealt with universal issues that appealed to women of all cultures.

Julia learned to value her roots and to be proud of her Latina heritage, as well as to be grateful for the life her parents built in the U.S. The beauty of America is that both cultures could be interwoven together, and Julia illustrates this in her novels. To her, being Latina is not separate from being American; her immigrant story is part of the great history of this country.

Julia's other passion is education. She received her B.A. at the University of California, Riverside, and her M.F.A in Fiction from California State University, San Bernardino. She currently teaches writing at Crafton Hills College and California State University, San Bernardino.

Read more at https://www.juliaamante.com.

Made in United States
Orlando, FL
01 October 2023

37477350R00222